ADIRONDACK
DETECTIVE
GOES
WEST

JOHN H. BRIANT

Chalet Publishing
P.O. Box 1154
Old Forge, New York

ADIRONDACK DETECTIVE GOES WEST

Library of Congress Catalog Control Number 99-96188

ISBN 0-9648327-5-5

VOLUME IV

Graphics and book design
by
John D. Mahaffy

Printed in the United States of America

Chalet Publishing
P.O. Box 1154
Old Forge, New York 13420-1154

Dedication

To my wife, Margaret,
who inspired me and kept the oil lamp lit.

and

To all the Adirondack people who reside
in these precious mountains within the Blue Line.
And, to all the people who love and visit this special
place on earth known as the Adirondack Park.

Best Wishes,

John H. Briant

ACKNOWLEDGEMENT

I wish to extend thanks to John D. Mahaffy for his outstanding artistic ability and tremendous talent. He has been there since the beginning of my literary journey with the ADIRONDACK DETECTIVE SERIES, featuring JASON BLACK.

Thank you, Lydia L. Maltzan, for your computer skills and professionalism.

To my wife, Margaret, thank you for your understanding, insight and honest opinion, and keeping the lamp flickering.

To my many fans and readers, I thank you for making it all possible.

FOREWORD

Jason Black, Private Detective, working cases in his beloved Adirondack Mountains of Northern New York State is summoned to Arizona to render aid to his former U.S. Marine Corp buddy, Jack Flynn, a private detective from Phoenix, Arizona.

Black is accompanied by his lovely wife, Patty, and soon they experience a lifestyle much different than that of their Adirondack Mountains in Northern New York. They soon learn that the so called Wild West is alive and well.

The twists and turns of the Arizona investigation is fraught with danger as Jason seeks to find a clue to the mysterious disappearance of a photo-journalism-student whose father owns a large horse ranch.

Will the probative private detective be successful? The answer to the question is somewhere between the covers of this mystery.

Other books by the Author
One Cop's Story: A Life Remembered 1995
Adirondack Detective 2000
Adirondack Detective Returns 2002
Adirondack Detective III 2004

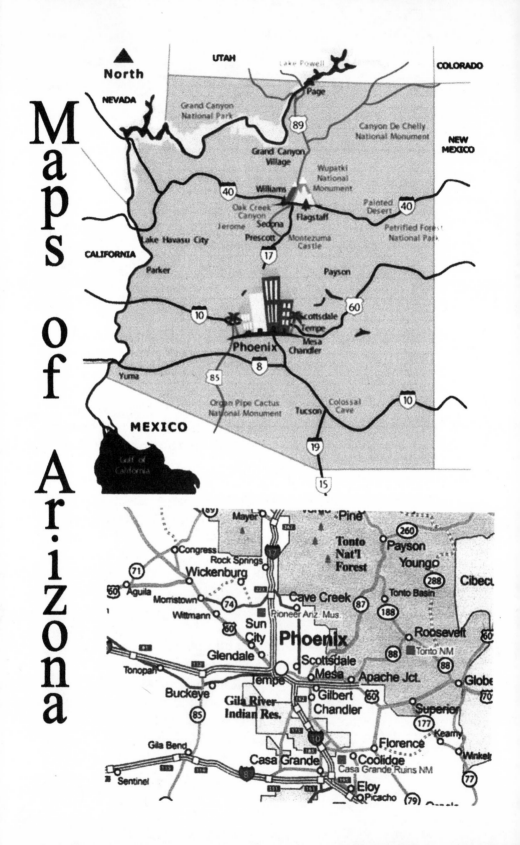

CHAPTER ONE

Here we are, thirty-seven thousand feet above Mother Earth, winging our way toward Phoenix, Arizona. Patty is curled up in her seat next to me sound asleep with her long blond hair flowing against my right shoulder. She's wearing very little make-up. A flight attendant has just stopped by to take a drink order. I settled for a glass of cola. I didn't feel that I should wake Patty in her deep sleep. I'm taking this time to reflect on the events preceding our flight. A fast moving set of circumstances occurred to bring us to this present location.

We had just returned from the doctor's office, where it had been established that Patty is indeed pregnant. Her doctor had found her in excellent health after a thorough physical and had assured us that Patty should have a normal pregnancy. Needless to say we were overjoyed with the news. Patty went back to the diner for the busy lunch hour while I drove back to our log home nestled in the Adirondacks. As I entered our home, the telephone was ringing. I hurried into my office and answered it before it activated the answering machine. The sobbing voice on the other end blurted out,

"Jason, Jason! We need you, we need you! Jack has been shot!" Through the repetitive sobs I recognized Ruby Wolkowski's voice immediately.

"Ruby, calm down, calm down. Try to get control of yourself and tell me what happened." I used my firm but caring

1

voice, trying to hide my own concern. My knees buckled under me and I grabbed the chair to steady myself.

"Jason, Jack was driving to Tucson on I-10 when he came upon a shootout between two coyote-smuggling gangs. Shots were being fired in all directions, and one of the bullets went through Jack's windshield and struck him in the left shoulder." In her broken voice, she continued. "According to the police on the scene, Jack must have managed to pull off on the shoulder behind a semi-trailer outfit."

"What! When did this happen?" I asked, feeling my own blood pressure rising at this news about my good friend.

"This morning at about 9:00 a.m. I was contacted by an Arizona highway patrolman, who knows Jack well. Jack is now in the Maryvale Medical Center in Phoenix and is being operated on as we speak. I'm going to the hospital as soon as I finish talking with you," she went on, trying to control her trembling voice.

"Ruby, I'm upset! Do you know what Jack's condition is?" I could hear my heart pounding. Private Investigator Jack Flynn and I were like brothers and now his life could possibly be in jeopardy.

"His condition is serious. That's all I can tell you right now, but the highway patrolman told me that he called out, 'Jason Black.' That's why I'm calling, Jason. Jack needs you. Will you come out and help us?" Her voice continued to choke up and her breathing was rapid.

"Yes, Patty and I will fly out as soon as we can make arrangements," I assured her.

Before I hung up, I tried to comfort Ruby and soothe her emotional state, telling her that she had to be strong. I mentioned that Patty and I were expecting our first child, but I felt strongly that she would be accompanying me on the trip. I then called Patty at John's Diner. I didn't want to alarm her over the phone with the news of Jack being in a Phoenix hospital. I just told her to come home as soon as possible. Then I placed a call to Wilt Chambers and luckily found him at his home in Boonville. I told Wilt that Patty and I had to fly to

Arizona because my close friend Jack Flynn was in the hospital. I didn't go into detail about the shooting.

Wilt asked, "What can I do to help, Jason?" He sounded worried.

"Would you mind taking Ruben for a while? I don't exactly know how long we'll be gone, therefore, I would rather place him with you instead of Lynne's kennel."

"Don't you worry about anything. I'll check your place every day and take Ruben to Boonville with me. He'll be good company for me. You know, I get along fine with that big fella."

"Patty and I will appreciate it, Wilt. One other thing, could you drive us to the Syracuse airport to catch a flight?"

"When you folks are ready to go, give me a call. It'll only take me about forty-five minutes to get to your house. Have you checked with the airport yet, Jason?"

"I'll call them as soon as we hang up."

"Jason, I'll be here at the house all afternoon." Wilt sounded eager to help.

When I hung up I called the airport to check on a flight. The first one available was the next day at 4:00 p.m. on American Airlines, Flight 227. The reservation clerk advised me to be at the airport an hour prior to flight time, indicating the tickets would be ready for pickup at the counter upon my arrival there.

I called Wilt back and asked him to be at our place at 12:00 noon the next day. He indicated that he'd be there. Good old dependable Wilt. He could always be relied upon.

"Jason, don't worry about anything. I'll take care of everything while you are away."

"We appreciate that very much, Wilt." I told Wilt that I would see him tomorrow and we hung up.

Patty pulled into the yard shortly after I hung up the telephone. She came rushing into the house.

"What's the matter, Jason? You were so vague on the phone. Is something wrong?" she asked, wrinkling her forehead.

I told Patty to sit down and relax. I tried to be composed not wanting to alarm her in her condition, I informed her that Jack Flynn had been hurt and was being treated for a gunshot wound at a Phoenix hospital. Patty's face dropped as she began to cry. I reached over to her, put my arms around her, and held her close.

"Everything will be alright, Patty. Please don't cry." She knew how much I thought of Jack. I quickly went into details of our airline reservations, my call to Wilt, our arrangement for the ride to the airport, and his care of Ruben. I told her I realized that this trip would interfere with all our Christmas plans, but if it was alright with her, we would celebrate upon our return. She nodded her head in agreement.

I put the teakettle on and made us each a cup of green tea. After we drank our tea, Patty and I packed our bags quickly, knowing that if we had forgotten anything, we could always buy it in Phoenix.

Patty called Lila at John's Diner and explained the dilemma we were facing. Lila understood and told Patty not to worry. Lila loved Patty more like a sister than an employee and had always appreciated Patty's loyalty to her and the diner. She told Patty to take as much time off as she needed to accompany me to Arizona and assured her that her job would be waiting for her when we returned. I had told Patty many times how fortunate we were to live in Old Forge, where people care about each other and come to the aid of their neighbors in any given situation. We had no idea when we would be returning to the Adirondacks. We both understood our priority was to render assistance to my former-Marine friend. I knew deep down in my heart that he would do the same for me. I knew, too, that I'd have to take extra special care of Patty, especially during this time. She was early into her pregnancy, still feeling strong, albeit a bit sleepy and queasy. We were overjoyed with the prospect of having a child. We didn't care if it was a boy or a girl; we would both love him or her with all our hearts. I know I could have left Patty at home, but not knowing how long I would have to be gone, I thought it best that she accompany me to Arizona.

I continue to gather my thoughts now, looking over at Patty as she still sleeps. I knew she was tired, and also knew that she really doesn't like to fly. My mind races back to our hurried departure. Hopefully I checked out the house closely. I try not to worry, as I know that Wilt will be on top of things. On the way to the airport, we stopped at the post office and completed a mail-forwarding slip to me care of Flynn's Investigations, Inc., with the 99th Avenue address, in Phoenix.

CHAPTER TWO

The stopover in Pittsburgh was of short duration. It would be dark when we landed at Sky Harbor. I knew that Ruby would be waiting for us. She was a loyal employee of Jack's and knew the operation of Flynn's Investigations very well. She would be able to answer all my questions. During the stopover at Pittsburgh, I hastily called Wayne Beyea, my private investigator friend at Plattsburgh, and informed him of Jack's hospitalization.

I asked Wayne if he would mind filling in for my private investigation office at Old Forge in the event an important case that needed immediate attention should develop during my absence. I told him that I was having all my calls forwarded to Flynn's Investigative Agency in Phoenix and that I would call him if anything should develop. I'm fortunate to have a close friendship with Wayne. He immediately indicated that he would be happy to accommodate any new cases I might receive. I told him that I would arrange for the funding of any eventual investigation, although I already knew he understood that he would be paid for any investigative work performed.

In about an hour, we boarded the plane bound for Phoenix. After the instructions from the flight attendant, we settled in to enjoy the last leg of our journey. Soon, the flight attendant stopped by our seats and asked us if we would like something to drink. We both ordered colas. The attendant further advised us that dinner would be served shortly and chicken was the one and only entrée. She returned shortly with two cans of cold cola, one caffeine-free for Patty. She handed me two plastic glasses and I reached over and gave Patty her drink.

"Jason, I'm so thirsty, honey." She looked at me with a sleepy smile and took the glass from my hand.

"Sweetheart, how are you feeling?" I asked with concern. I was still getting used to the idea that she was a newly expectant mother-to-be.

"I feel fine, darling." Then her face clouded. "I know that you are concerned about Jack. I'll pray for him, Jason." Tears were welling up in her eyes, and I was sure they were from more than the weepiness of early pregnancy.

"We'll both pray for him, Patty. He's like a brother to me and I know that if it was me lying in the hospital with a gunshot wound he'd be there."

"I know that he would be," she replied and then asked, "Where will we be staying, honey? Did Ruby mention it?"

"We'll have to wait and see. Knowing Ruby as I do and how efficient she is, I would bet that she'll have the answer to your question when we see her."

Dinner on the flight was very good and the portions were ample for me, however Patty picked at hers because of a touchy stomach, especially flying. The attendant took good care of us, clearly an asset to the airline. I told Patty that someday she would probably meet an executive and she'd be swept off her feet. She seemed like a wonderful young lady with her whole life ahead of her. She had already confided in us that her first love was to become a schoolteacher, and that she loved children. For now, though, she would represent her airline in a professional manner as an attendant on Flight 227. Patty and I were so pleased to meet her. It restored our faith in the concept of public service.

We had gone through a security check at Syracuse and hopefully it had been all worth it to know that our flight to Phoenix would be safe and secure. My wife and I would rather take our chances in an automobile, but in this case it was necessary to reach our destination as soon as possible. The phrase, *semper fi*, is deeply ingrained in the hearts and souls of former US Marines. I will never forget some of the tight spots that Jack and I had endured during our service days. Of course, we were much younger and full of vim and rigor. There were two other people who remembered the Flynn and Black combination, our two master sergeants Elmer Kessler of Delano, California, and Richard Crandall of Bellingham, Washington. I'm certain—and Jack would agree—both sergeants aged a little when he and I were assigned to their barracks. It wasn't because Jack and I were troublemakers. No, we were the opposite. Our gear was always spit and polish, and our sleeping areas and foot lockers were always squared away. We were good marines. If anything, it was the jokes that Jack told around the barracks, keeping everybody in stitches as the two sergeants tried to sleep. But the jokes poured out of Jack like oil out of a new well. Still, when we were discharged, the two master sergeants bid us farewell and threw a party that would go down in history as one of the best parties ever held at Camp Pendleton.

As we flew toward Phoenix and Jack, Patty's excitement grew, and she asked me many questions about Arizona. I was able to give her some of the historical facts of certain areas in the state. I told her that in the summer months the temperatures soar to well over a hundred degrees and that air conditioning is a must in the Phoenix region. To find a cooler area in the summer, one would have to travel north to the Flagstaff area, which is seven thousand feet above sea level. I described in detail the many planting seasons, and the variety of crops that are harvested several times each year. Suddenly the flight attendant announced "please fasten your seat belts." The captain spoke on the intercom, advising that we'd be landing at Sky Harbor in fifteen minutes. Christmas being ten days away, he wished everyone a happy holiday season. The wind currents were strong as the big plane descended. Patty looked over at me with true anxiety and asked, "Will we be alright, honey?"

"We'll be fine, sweetheart." As we felt strong air currents

against the outside of the plane, I reached for her hand to give her comfort and assurance that the landing would be safe.

When the plane touched down, we could hear the wheels running on the tarmac. The pilot had made a perfect landing. Patty and I felt a sense of relief to be back on the ground, even though we were almost three thousand miles from home. Now we could concentrate our attention on our friend, Jack Flynn. I took our carry-ons from the overhead compartment. While deplaning, we thanked the captain and the attendants for the safe flight to Sky Harbor. We followed the other passengers as they rushed toward the escalators to the baggage pickup area where we had two large suitcases to recover. Patty held onto my hand as we descended to the lower floor. It took a few minutes to retrieve our luggage. I checked the tags closely, as several of the suitcases looked exactly alike. My thoughts turned to Jack lying in the hospital with a gunshot wound; as a friend rather than a family member, I wondered how soon before I would be allowed to see him.

With our luggage in hand, we headed toward the lobby. We had just passed the security checkpoint when I heard a familiar voice.

"Jason! Jason Black! Over here!" It was Ruby Wolkowski. She came running toward us wearing a warm smile. I set the suitcases down. Her smile immediately turned to tears as I embraced her.

"It's so good to see you, Ruby. How's Jack doing?" I asked.

"He's holding his own, Jason. The operation was a success. They removed the bullet, which luckily didn't strike any major organs, and according to the surgeon, he's going to be fine." Ruby looked tired and her face was drawn from the worry over Jack.

I introduced Patty to Ruby and they embraced. Patty then began to tear up. Patty is a compassionate person. When she had met Jack at our wedding, they had formed an instant friendship. I'd been sure that she would feel the same way toward Ruby, Jack's loyal secretary and associate. We proceeded to Ruby's car, a large four-door sedan. She popped the trunk open and I lifted the luggage into it.

As we entered the car, Ruby turned towards us. "Jason, you and Patty are staying at my place for tonight. Tomorrow I'll take you to Jack's forty-foot Prevost. It's parked at a lovely resort, with excellent amenities, located in the southwest valley between Goodyear and Buckeye."

"Are you serious, Ruby?" I asked. "I had no idea that Jack even owned a motor coach."

"Yes, I am. He purchased it just a few weeks ago. It isn't brand-new, but close to it. After Jack was taken to the hospital he asked me to contact you right away. He told me that you and Patty would be welcome to stay in the coach."

"Have you seen it, Ruby?" I asked.

"Oh, yes. I went with Jack when he picked it up and drove it to the RV resort. I know that you and Patty will enjoy it. It's almost as large as a good-size apartment. And another thing, Jason, it will offer you and Patty good security. Some of the apartment-complexes are plagued with prowlers, and if Patty has to stay alone, the coach will offer her the best possible safety."

"I see what you mean. It sounds like a reasonable solution to our temporary housing dilemma." I knew it was just like Jack to make these arrangements even while suffering from a gunshot wound.

"We'll get you settled in the morning, and tomorrow in the early afternoon we'll go to the Maryvale Medical Center to visit Jack. He told me to be sure to get you both settled first and then to come to visit him."

"Ruby, I understand that some of the RV parks or resorts are questionable." I was curious.

"This resort is a good one, as most of them are. Jack has done some work for the owners and he feels they are top shelf all the way."

I knew that it had to be a good park if Jack approved. "And are you managing the office while Jack is on sick leave?" Flynn's Investigation Agency was getting bigger in scope.

"No, I'm performing my secretarial duties as always. Jack had me bring in one of his operatives, William Reidy, a retired police lieutenant, who has been with us for about three years. They call him Bill. He is an excellent operative and has outstanding management skills. I'm certain you will meet him soon. He knows about you and how close you and Jack are. Jason, when Jack was shot he was heading to Tucson to interview a father of a twenty-one-year-old woman who's been missing for over two months. The police department there has exhausted all their leads. Consequently the family is very upset and ended up contacting Flynn's Investigations. They have been apprised of Jack's hospitalization and are patiently awaiting someone to interview them. Jack doesn't want anyone doing the interview except you."

"I'm certain there are other investigators that could perform the interview. Why me?" I was puzzled because I knew Jack must have several experienced men.

"Yes, we have some excellent operatives, but Jack insisted that I contact you. I know Jack has a lot of confidence in your methods, Jason. When you're ready I will give you the case folder that is already prepared. Also, you will have one of our cars at your disposal. I hope you can drive a stick shift."

"No problem. I can drive anything."

"The car has already been delivered to the resort and is parked by the coach. I'll give you the keys when we get to my place. We'll have our breakfast in the morning and then we'll go to see Jack. By the way, Jason, before I left for Sky Harbor to meet you and Patty, I called the hospital and they told me Jack was sleeping. They have him sedated quite heavily."

"Ruby, is there anything I can do?" Patty asked sincerely. She had been quiet during our conversation.

"Patty, no, not at this time. If I do need any help, I'll certainly remember your offer. Jason told me of your good news. Just take care of yourself," she cautioned.

"I certainly will," Patty acknowledged.

Ruby lived in a tract home site located on Glendale Avenue about three miles from Flynn's Investigations office. She informed me that the shoe store and the leather products shop had closed and the operator had moved back to Modesto, California to be near his family. That store had been next to Jack's office. Instead of advertising for another tenant, Jack decided to expand his office space. The other thirteen tenants in the L-shaped refurbished shopping center seemed to be prospering. Ruby, Jack, and Captain Silverstein had been somewhat apprehensive when they had purchased the run-down shopping plaza, but with good planning and careful management skills, they had brought the complex back to life, and the rent checks kept coming in. Their retirement fund kept building. I had previously shared with Patty the story of this trio who had put their heads together to make this busy place successful.

By the time we pulled into Ruby's driveway, she and Patty had already made plans for a future lunch and shopping trip together. Ruby's modest home, constructed of cement blocks and painted with white stucco, had an attached two-car garage. Ruby turned off the engine. "We're here, folks. Patty and I'll go inside unless you need help with the luggage."

"I'll take care of it, Ruby," I replied. I thought of Jack lying in the Maryvale Medical Center. I knew him to be resilient and prayed that he would return to good health in a short period of time. There isn't a tougher man than Jack Flynn, one cocky Irishman, who could take on any two men in a fair fight. But he also had another side that could be as gentle as a lamb. He was a unique individual. I knew we would be brothers till death. Patty and I would gratefully see him the next day.

I made two trips from Ruby's car to the house. The two pieces of luggage were heavy. It seemed Patty must have put my exercise dumbbells in one of them. Ruby held the door open and I entered through the hallway. I noticed several paintings of desert scenes with cactus plant life, one with a large saguaro reaching out towards the cloudless blue sky. They appeared to be done in oils.

"Ruby, these are beautiful. Did you paint them?" I asked, admiring them closely.

Patty and I were novices when it came to painting landscapes, but were always interested in art.

"Thank you. No, Jason, I didn't do these. A friend of mine has an art studio and had these left over from an art sale. I purchased them from her. I love them. I would never part with them."

"They go well with your interior decorating, Ruby," Patty agreed.

"I bet you two are hungry. Before I left for the airport I made up some salads and prepared a small platter of cold cuts. And I hope you like pink lemonade." Ruby placed her jacket in the closet and put on an apron.

"You didn't have to fuss for us, Ruby," I told her. "We could have grabbed a bite someplace."

"It was no bother, Jason," she replied. "I thought you might be tired after the flight."

Before we sat down to dinner, Patty and I freshened up. Ruby had the dining room table set with tableware and napkins. On the table was a platter of assorted cold cuts, along with shrimp salad, potato salad, a dish of assorted pickles, Kaiser rolls, a container of mustard, and a small dish of mayonnaise. The bright orange tablecloth accented by two tall brown candles in cut-glass holders caught my eye.

"Everything's ready, but before we start eating, I'll phone the hospital to see how Jack is doing."

Ruby placed the call and was told that Jack was doing fine and that he was asleep. When she cradled the receiver, I noticed tears had come to her eyes, but she quickly replaced them with a smile. As we seated ourselves around the table, she asked me to say the blessing. I added a prayer for Jack's speedy recovery from his gunshot wound. I wanted to ask Ruby for any other details regarding the shooting, but decided I would question her later.

The light lunch was tasty. I was surprised at how hungry I was. I admonished Ruby for all her efforts, but she quickly informed me that she had purchased almost everything from her local supermarket, which boasted a great deli. I advised her that she certainly should give us the name and the directions. They just got two new customers.

As we finished our meal, Ruby left the table and surprised us when she returned with a Key lime pie. She cut generous portions and served each of us. The pie, of course, teased my taste buds. Patty told Ruby that she had never tasted such a delicious Key lime pie before in her life. I agreed with her.

Ruby told us that Jack had assisted her in acquiring her new home. I could tell how proud she was to have a place of her own. According to her, Jack had accompanied her when she went looking for her furniture. The house was tastefully furnished. I told Ruby that we did not wish to inconvenience her any more than we already had, and we would go to a motel for the evening, but she insisted that we were her guests.

We spent the rest of the evening chatting in the living room. Ruby checked with the hospital again and was told that Jack was resting comfortably but was still sleeping. She advised the nurse that she would visit Jack the next afternoon with two friends. We talked well past midnight and then retired to our rooms. The guest room was furnished with a queen-sized bed, a lovely dresser, and two chairs, all in cherry wood. To complement the attractive pieces of furniture was a shiny hardwood floor. We could almost see the images of our faces in it when looking down. The bedroom had an adjoining bath, which offered complete privacy.

Patty and I were anxious to visit Jack in the hospital. He evidently had happened to be in the wrong place at the wrong time, but who would expect to be driving along on I-10, a major interstate, and come upon a gun battle between two rival coyote gangs in broad daylight? It was a miracle that Jack hadn't been killed. He was very fortunate to have received only one wound, to the top of his left shoulder. According to Ruby, the police investigation uncovered that one gang suspected the other of infringing on their operation of smuggling illegal aliens across the border. Thus the gun battle ensued.

We said our evening prayers, thanked the Lord for our safe flight, and asked for Jack's return to a speedy recovery. We wondered if Ruben, some 2500 miles away, was on his best behavior for Wilt. We knew that Wilt would take good care of the big K-9.

Patty and I were both exhausted from the excitement of the flight to Arizona. I kissed her goodnight and we fell off to sleep in each other's arms. I certainly hoped that Patty wasn't pushing herself too much.

CHAPTER THREE

It was about 8:00 when we woke up. Patty rubbed her eyes and I had a rare sneezing spell.

"Are you alright, honey?" Patty asked.

"Ah-choo! I-I'm okay. Must be allergic to the Arizona air," I replied, reaching for a tissue.

"I smell the aroma of bacon, honey," Patty said. "Ruby must be cooking."

"I'm hungry. How about you?"

"I am," she replied.

Patty went into the bathroom first. In a few minutes she came out fully dressed in grey slacks with a pink top. She looked beautiful with her blond hair flowing down to her shoulders. I took a quick shower, shaved, and dressed. After combing my hair I went into the kitchen and breakfast nook area, where Patty was assisting Ruby at the toaster.

"Good morning, Jason. Did you sleep well?" Ruby asked.

"Slept like a baby, Ruby. That's a comfortable mattress on that bed," I replied.

"Only the best for you and Patty, Jason." She winked at Patty. The gals seemed to be getting along famously. Patty liked Ruby a lot. Ruby mentioned that she had called the hospital, but had been unable to speak with Jack, as he was being bathed. She indicated that she had left word with the nurse that we'd be arriving at the hospital around 1:30 p.m.

After breakfast I helped Ruby and Patty with the kitchen and then assisted Patty with our luggage. Ruby gave me the keys to Jack's Prevost and keys to the automobile that was already parked with the coach at the resort. When the luggage was repacked I took it out and placed it into the trunk of Ruby's Chevrolet. Ruby checked all the doors, locked the house, and set the burglar alarm. I was aware of the high crime rate in Maricopa County and was pleased to see Ruby was cognizant of it. Jack had mentioned to me many times about the number of cases that the detectives are assigned. Shootings are prevalent and occur every day. With a population of almost three million, it was no wonder that the crime rate was placing such a strain on the justice system. Every category of crime took place in the area and it was well known that it was the crossroads for drug activity and meth labs. Law enforcement and special details were always seeking out the violators, but when one group was apprehended, another group would spring up in another location.

I jumped into the back seat and had Patty sit up front with Ruby. Ruby informed us that she had to stop by the office before we headed to Goodyear, the location of the resort, but she would only be a few minutes.

Traffic on 99th Avenue was heavy in the morning. Comprised of four lanes, it ran north and south and most of the traffic flowed toward I-10, the main interstate from the east coast through Arizona and on into California. Semi-trailer trucks and cars, along with every type of motor vehicle imaginable, were constantly in motion heading east and west.

We pulled into the busy shopping plaza, which was a hub of activity. A big smile crossed Ruby's face as she pulled into the parking space, which had a small sign designating the name "Wolkowski" in front of the entrance to the office. Ruby went on to tell us that Jack's organization was growing and that they now had a staff of ten operatives statewide, all with a background in police investigations. She told us about William Reidy, who was the oldest of the staff. Bill had been a police lieutenant with an eastern city located in New York State. He had been moved from the Tucson office to manage the Phoenix office while Jack was hospitalized.

I had had no idea that Jack had increased his staff to that number. However, it was understandable with the population growth in the region. Several of his men headed up private security in some of the Phoenix businesses, and each had the authority to hire part time people if it became necessary to do so. At least the temperatures were tolerable at this time of year. In fact, we would be able to enjoy some more comfortable temperatures from the range of seventy during the day to forty and fifty degrees during the night times. Quite a difference from the temperatures they would be experiencing in the Central Adirondacks at this time of the year.

Ruby was a good driver. She pointed out various places of interest as we motored south on 99th Avenue toward I-10. The new housing tracts were predominant on both sides of the highway. Some were free-standing homes and others appeared to be apartment complexes. Some of them would be occupied on a full time basis; however, others would be closed up in late spring and then reopened when the snowbirds from the northern states would come to enjoy the winter months in the Phoenix region. We entered the westbound ramp for I-10 and headed west toward Buckeye.

Our conversation turned to Jack. We were hopeful that he wasn't in any great deal of discomfort, and I expressed my desire to see him.

"Jason, I have made arrangements for Jack after his discharge from the hospital. His health insurance policy allows for some home nursing care," she said with concern.

"Hopefully Jack will heal completely and return to good health. Bullet wounds are bad, especially if they strike a vital area of the body. I'm pleased that he will have the nursing service available when he's released."

Ruby continued to point out places of interest. She told us that the vast housing tracts had taken over the cotton fields. I knew that the Goodyear Tire Company had started the cotton crops years ago. The cotton was used in the production of tires in the early days of the company. Patty and I both noticed there were many fields of flowers and row upon row of vegetables, such as spinach, cabbage, asparagus, and then more flowers. The fields were flat and they went on as far as the human eye could see. We observed some of the large cotton harvesters and saw the compacted cotton that looked like railroad box cars lined up along the edge of the highway. Many of the farm workers appeared to be of Mexican heritage.

Ruby filled us in on some of the details of the resort where we would be staying. Privately owned, it was located between Goodyear and Buckeye off Van Buren Road. This park was very unusual, as one of the previous owners had planted several hundred fruit trees, with one tree on each RV lot, adding to the attractiveness. Each site also had a cement pad, which was definitely a convenience during the infrequent rainy spells.

"Ruby, I'm looking forward to seeing Jack this afternoon. Patty and I said a special prayer last night for his speedy and complete recovery."

"Don't worry, Jason. Jack is resilient. He's tough. You know how you Marines are. He'll be fine."

I looked at Ruby as she slightly turned toward Patty, who was sitting next to her on the passenger side of the car. I noticed the tears sliding down her cheek. "He'll be okay," I replied, attempting to give Ruby some encouragement.

Both the westbound and eastbound lanes on I-10 were congested, but traffic appeared to be completely stopped in the eastbound lane as an accident was being investigated by the Arizona Highway Patrol. The traffic was backed up as far as the eye could see. We were fortunate to be in the westbound lane.

Although traffic was heavy westbound, we were able to proceed with little difficulty, in spite of the rubberneckers that slowed traffic in order to get a peek at the accident. When we reached exit 124, Ruby took the Cotton Lane ramp. A few minutes later we pulled into the entrance of the Roadrunner Resort. The American flag flew overhead while several banners on shorter poles moved back and forth as the wind bucked against their fabric. Ruby pulled into a parking space and applied the emergency brake.

"I'll be right back. I've got to check in with the office. The security gate is just ahead and I'll need a code to enter. It won't take a minute."

"No problem, Ruby. Take your time." I looked over at Patty, who was checking out the area through the passenger-side window.

"Those plants are beautiful, Jason. I've never seen plant life like that before. We didn't have anything like that in Kentucky, and we don't at home either."

I looked out at the plants. "Honey, I don't think they would grow in our colder climate. We have such a short growing season," I said in agreement.

"The landscaper or gardener certainly knows his or her business. It makes for a picturesque scene, Jason." I could tell she was genuinely impressed.

"I agree, sweetheart." I shared Patty's love of plants and flowers.

Ruby returned shortly and got into the car, and we headed toward the security gate. "I think you and Patty will enjoy it here, Jason. It is very secure, and out here in the Wild West you want to live in a safe place." She sounded very serious. "In some of the more affluent areas where the wealthy people reside, such as Paradise Valley, most live in gated communities, or have their own security personnel or guard dogs. There are seven or eight prisons in the region, and many of the inmates, when discharged, don't return to their homes. They stay around Phoenix, especially in the wintertime, and some repeat their offenses." We listened intently to Ruby's comments, for she had lived in the area for a long time.

Ruby rolled the window down and punched in a security code. The large gate arm lifted, permitting us to pass by into the main resort. I observed the different types of fifth-wheelers, camping-trailers, and motor homes, many forty feet in length. Some of those coaches must have cost well into the six figures.

They sure were impressive.

Ruby's large Chevrolet sedan crept along at five miles per hour in accordance with the speed-limit signs posted throughout the resort. There were numerous speed bumps along the resort roads to aid in the enforcement of the limit. While driving to our site, Ruby pointed out the amenities the resort had to offer: the clubhouse, the swimming pool, the shuffleboard court, and the dog run. Several large restrooms were strategically situated throughout the resort for the campers' convenience. She advised us not to worry about getting familiar with the grounds, because she would furnish us with a map of the layout. Jack had selected this park because of the excellent location and the overall appearance. The resort was a convenient distance from the office, and security seemed to be adequate.

While Ruby gave us our tour, I reflected back to the events that had brought us here. Jack from his hospital bed had wanted me here in Arizona to work on this very sensitive case. Jack's client had been informed that Jack had been shot and was in the hospital, but Ruby had assured him that an investigator would be in touch with him as soon as possible. Jack had been en route to Casa Grande to interview the client when he had been shot as the two human-smuggling gangs, known as coyotes, traded bullets between Phoenix and Casa Grande. According to Ruby, Jack hadn't been wearing his bulletproof vest. If the bullet had been four inches to the right, it would have struck his heart. I tried to glean more information from Ruby about the client, but she said she would prefer to have Jack explain the case.

Ruby pulled her car into a parking place next to a white Camaro which was parked next to a large Prevost motor home.

"Wow! Ruby, does Jack own this beautiful coach?" It must have cost a fortune. I estimated it to be at **least** forty feet in length.

"This is it. We hope you'll like staying here while you're in the Phoenix area."

"It's a sharp-looking unit," Patty chimed in. "It is huge."

"Let's go inside. I had a professional cleaner go through it and you should find everything to your liking." Ruby produced her key and opened the door. The three of us climbed in. "Do you think you can drive this, Jason?" Ruby asked, jokingly.

"Yes, I can drive this big baby. Why do you ask, Ruby?" I was inquisitive.

"Just in case, if you have to. You never know where the case you're going to be working on may take you. With this, Patty can accompany you and you don't have to worry about hotel or motel rooms. This is equipped to tow the white Camaro."

I couldn't help but wonder what Ruby knew that I didn't. I guessed I had better wait and see.

"You know, Jason, that Jack has always wanted you to move out here to Arizona and join his organization. He doesn't think you'll ever consent to the move, but remember, he thinks a great deal of you. Above all, he loves you like the brother that he never had." I knew in my heart that he did consider me as a brother, but I also realized that in the hot summer months I would be unable to survive those hot, extreme temperatures that soared into the hundreds. And I would not leave my mountains.

"Yeah, I know, Ruby, I know." I looked at Patty, and she gave me a girlish smile.

The interior of the coach was beautiful. It definitely had all the whistles and bells. The color scheme was mauve with an accent of a gray overtone. The one word that would describe this apartment on wheels is **magnificent**. It must have cost Jack big bucks.

I told Ruby that I would bring the luggage into the coach, and she threw me the keys to her car. While I went outside to the car for the bags, Ruby continued to give Patty a tour of the coach, teaching her the operation of some of the gadgets that she would be using.

I had always heard that campers were a friendly group, and I quickly found a reason to agree. As I was bent over removing the bags, I heard someone approach me from behind.

"Can I give you a hand with those, fella?" He was a good-natured chap. I turned toward him and said, "Thank you, sir, I've got it, but thank you for offering." We introduced ourselves and chatted a few minutes. He smiled and walked on. In a few minutes I had all the luggage plus our two carry-on bags placed into the coach. Ruby and Patty had just finished up their tour of our temporary Arizona home. This would be a new lifestyle for Patty and me. We checked the coach again and found everything secure. Several people walked by and smiled. The maroon coach seemed to catch the eye of the residents of the resort. I told Patty, "I bet they think that we're loaded with money." She laughed.

Ruby and Patty climbed into the sedan. I told Ruby that I just wanted to check the Camaro. I unlocked and opened the driver's side door. Right away, I observed the telephone, a CB, and shifting lever on the floor. The vehicle appeared to be in good condition. It had been serviced just a day or two before our arrival. I put the key in the ignition and turned it over. It started immediately. I let it idle for a minute or two, then turned it off. I got out and locked the car door. The girls were waiting for me. As I walked toward Ruby's car, I noticed that we had a lemon tree loaded with fruit on our lot. I could almost taste the lemonade that we would soon be making. I climbed into the car. Patty was taking in all the sights. People were milling around the resort. Groups were out for a walk while others were washing and waxing their coaches. The shuffleboard court was busy, and people with beach towels draped over their shoulders were headed toward the pool area. Several waved at us as we made our way through the resort. Ruby kept the speed to the designated five miles per hour. We were soon out of the restricted area and heading toward I-10.

The traffic was light as Ruby took the center lane just east of 115th Avenue and continued east. She took the exit ramp at 51st Avenue and headed north toward the Maryvale Medical Center. While Ruby handled the sedan like a professional driver, Patty and I talked about the different things we had observed at the resort and how the Prevost motor coach would serve us well as a temporary home for the time it would take Jack to return to normal health. Ruby pulled into a parking space and turned off the engine.

We exited the car and went into the hospital. We followed Ruby to the elevator, where she pushed the button to the seventh floor. The hospital halls appeared to be immaculate, and the floors were highly waxed. When we arrived at Jack's room, Ruby entered first. Jack was sitting up in bed with a couple of pillows supporting his back. His big smile told us that he was glad to see us. There was a half a glass of fruit juice sitting on a tray next to his bed.

"Jason Black and Patty, how in the hell are you two love birds?" Jack appeared pale, but joyous to see us. Ruby smiled as Patty went over to Jack and kissed him on the forehead. I went over and clasped his hand, which was moist, possibly from a slight temperature.

"Are you in pain, buddy?" I asked Jack.

"I'm on pain medicine, but I think I'm improving. Hope so, anyway."

I was so happy to see him.

We talked about the shooting incident. He repeated what I knew, that he had been headed to Casa Grande to interview a person regarding his missing twenty one-year-old daughter. Then he solemnly advised me that indeed this was the case he was going to assign me.

"I will have Ruby make up a file folder with all the information, Jason. The police and other officials have exhausted all their leads, and the father has engaged my agency to look into the matter. I haven't very much information to go on, but this is the reason I had Ruby contact you. I know your ability to ferret out information that would give you a lead to pursue. I need your help on this one, buddy. The temperatures now are somewhat more comfortable than in the summer. I knew you wouldn't mind helping me under the circumstances." He sounded excited. Jack knew that Jason was methodical in his thinking and the execution of his ideas on all his investigative cases.

"Yes, that's why we're here. I'll do my best, Jack, but as in any other case, I can't promise you a successful conclusion."

"Jason, I understand. I'll take care of all your expenses and pay you well for your expertise. You can take Patty with you. In fact, you may have to travel with the Prevost. Have you had any experience driving a motor coach and towing a vehicle?" he asked.

"Yes, I have had experience with that type of vehicle. That won't be a problem." I was actually looking forward to working on this challenging case.

Ruby and Patty, so Jack and I could conduct our business, drifted out of the room and went down to the cafeteria for some coffee and conversation. I stayed with Jack.

Jack filled me in on the father and told me that the family was well off financially. He informed me that the man's wife had been killed in an automobile accident near Douglas, Arizona about a year before. The daughter, in her third year of college at the time, took the tragedy hard and started to imbibe in alcohol a little too much, but it would appear that she straightened herself out and became a dedicated student. Jack didn't supply me with any names, but indicated that everything he had would be in the folder.

Internally, I was very upset and felt sorry for my friend. I thought of how he had been such an asset to the Phoenix Police when he was with the department. His former colleagues are still telling tales about the Irish detective who had a significant impact on crime in Maricopa County. They have always said that Jack was tough, but fair, and over the years he earned the respect of the citizens, the cops, and even some of the bad guys and gals.

"Jack, if you're too tired, tell me and I'll leave when the girls return."

"No, I don't want you to leave yet." Jack's face fell. "Tell me, Jason, how have you and Patty been? I think of you both often. You know how much I wish that you'd come out and join me on the agency full-time. I know you won't, though. You've always stood by your decisions, and I respect you for that."

I smiled. "We've discussed that many times, Jack. By the way, I have some great news for you. Patty is expecting and has been pregnant for about two months," I said rather shyly. My friend looked intently at me.

He grinned and said, "Congratulations, poppa. I'm happy for you. You'll make a great dad."

"Her doctor indicated that she is in excellent health and the pregnancy should be normal. We're excited and looking forward to the baby. When we get back home, we'll start to acquire a few more things for the baby's room."

Jack asked if we had picked out any names yet. He said he would like to be considered to be an honorary uncle to the baby or possibly the godfather. I told him that he certainly would be on the short list of prospective godfather, but definitely the honorary uncle. Just then Ruby and Patty returned.

"How was the coffee, ladies?" I asked.

"Great, guys. We thought it would be good to leave you two alone to have some time together," Ruby answered.

"Patty! Congratulations! Jason just told me the great news. I'm happy for you both."

"Thank you, Jack." Patty went over and gave Jack a kiss on his forehead.

"Ruby, make up that folder for Jason in the morning. By the way Christmas, is next week. I would like to treat the three of you to a Christmas dinner at the Biltmore Hotel in downtown Phoenix. I won't be able to be there, but this would be my present to the three of you."

"He means what he says," Ruby added. "I've heard they have a really great buffet."

"You don't have to do that, Jack. You're too kind." I knew this Irish former cop, now a private detective, was tender underneath that hard crust. That's the way Jack is. Always trying to do something for people. "Patty and I thank you from the bottom of our hearts but, we'd rather have dinner with you, Jack. You shouldn't be alone on Christmas," I said, firmly.

"Oh, no. I won't hear of that. Believe me, the hospital food is okay, but definitely not on Christmas. I'll get by." Then he immediately changed the subject. "Oh, don't worry about an Arizona private eye license. You're working on mine as a private consultant. You will be added to my employees insurance policy tomorrow. Be at the office in the morning, and Ruby will have you sign some papers tomorrow." He paused for a moment and sighed. "I'll be glad when I get out of the hospital. Jason, you'll meet Bill Reidy tomorrow. He is managing the agency while I'm in here."

"Jack, I want you to get some rest and not worry about the business. Ruby and Mr. Reidy will take good care of your day to day operations at the office. That's an order, marine; do you hear me?" I said firmly.

"Yes, sir, I understand. I hope the criminal justice system deals with the human smuggling dilemma. It's getting way out of control. " His face appeared drawn.

We could see that Jack was tiring. Each of us gave him an embrace and told him that we'd see him soon. We ended our visit and left the hospital.

Ruby felt relieved to know that we'd be in Arizona for a while. She drove us back to the resort. We asked her if she'd like to come in and visit for a while.

"Jason, I think I'll be on my way. If there is anything that you and Patty need, just give me a call. I'm going to stop by the office to catch up on some things. I'll see you there tomorrow. I'll prepare the folder that Jack was talking about. All the information will be in it that you'll need to begin your investigation. Hope you will find the motor coach comfortable. Do you see what I meant about it being like a small apartment?" Ruby got out of the car with us and gave us each an embrace. "I'm so glad, Jason, that you and Patty were able to come to Arizona to help us out."

"We're glad to be here. You know how we feel about Jack. He didn't deserve to be shot." I could tell that Ruby loved Jack as a sister would a brother.

"I'll see you both tomorrow. You should have everything in the coach that you'll need, except groceries. I would have shopped for you, but I thought it best to leave the shopping up to you folks."

"We'll be fine, Ruby. Be careful on the highway. I haven't seen this much traffic in a long time. I noticed that some of the drivers change lanes without looking."

"They certainly keep us on our toes. You have to be careful, Jason."

We watched Ruby drive out of the resort. This was going to be a new lifestyle for us. We unlocked the door and went inside. It didn't take long for us to familiarize ourselves with the workings of the motor coach. While Patty prepared a grocery list, I checked out our temporary home very closely. The refrigerator was working and the ice cubes were already frozen. I theorized that Ruby or one of Jack's other employees had come out to the resort and turned everything on, anticipating our arrival. I could see already that for a short-term residence, this was an ideal concept. It was about 5:15 p.m. when we locked up the coach and went to the supermarket that had recently opened up in the area. It was located approximately three miles away, in a large shopping plaza with several other shops and services available. We went into the store. I pushed the shopping cart, while Patty methodically selected groceries that we needed. It was a delight to view the variations of the fresh vegetables available to us because of their many growing seasons in the area. We knew that we'd be eating out frequently, as the restaurants in the region were abundant. However, there would be times that Patty and I would take turns preparing the cuisine we enjoyed. Ruby had already informed us that chicken is popular in the region, whether it be lime chicken, orange chicken, sweet and sour chicken, or fried chicken. While we were shopping, Patty suggested that we have grilled hamburgers for a light supper. We picked up sugar for our lemonade.

With our shopping completed, we left the store with our groceries, all placed in plastic bags. I opened the trunk of the Camaro and placed the purchases in the compartment. Patty climbed behind the steering wheel after stating, "I'll drive, honey!" I knew she needed to acclimate herself to the highways of Arizona, so I climbed into the passenger side. The ride back to the resort was made exciting when three dirt bikes, operated by three teenagers, darted out onto Van Buren Road directly in front of us. Luckily the road had a wide shoulder and Patty was able to pull sharply to the right in order to avoid striking the last rider. She laid on the horn, but they quickly disappeared through a housing tract at a high rate of speed. "Whew! That was close, Jason," she blurted.

"You're not kidding. Too close for comfort!" My wife had certainly just showed me that she could handle a car, even in Arizona traffic. I hoped this excitement would not affect her negatively in her present condition.

We finally reached the resort. With the identification pass hanging from the inside rearview mirror, the security person on the gate waved us through. The resort was a busy place. As we navigated through it, the beautiful sunset caught our eye. It was humbling to both of us. I told Patty that we'd have to purchase some good sunglasses to protect our eyes. She agreed as she pulled into our space and turned the ignition off. We both exited the car and I unlocked the coach. I told Patty to go inside and that I would bring in the groceries. I went to the trunk and opened it. The gallon of fat-free milk had tipped over, but was intact. I brought some of the groceries to the door of the coach. Patty took them from me while I returned for the remaining two bags. When I closed the trunk the next door neighbor waved at me just before he opened the door to his fifth-wheel trailer. I waved back and continued on into the coach. I remarked to Patty that we had a friendly neighbor. Patty and I decided that we would not divulge anything about the investigative work that I would be pursuing. There would be times that we'd be away and other times we might have to take the coach and tow the car out of the park. We both agreed that we'd be friendly and enjoy our new lifestyle whenever we could, while remaining circumspect about why we were in Arizona.

While Patty was preparing a light supper of grilled

hamburger patties, a salad, and vegetables, I sat down in the living room in a leather chair. It was very comfortable. There was a large television set mounted just below the ceiling of the coach. The room was plentifully large and, one could say, quite plush.

Patty had picked up the *Arizona Republic*, the Phoenix newspaper, and now I thumbed through the pages. Coming from a law-enforcement background it was natural for me to focus on articles involving the world of police and the violence that is present in our society. "Man Found Dead on Sidewalk," "Three Mexicans Found Slain along Route 101," "Mother Kills her Baby," "Bookkeeper Embezzles Funds." The headlines went on and on. Plenty of crime in an area that had grown to almost three million: along with unbridled growth comes an undesirable element that fosters criminal activity.

Patty's supper was delicious. She had made a fresh spinach salad with slivered carrots, mushrooms, and red onions. She had sprinkled it with a small amount of sugar, tossed it lightly with our favorite Italian dressing, and topped it off with crumbly blue cheese. She had broiled two large ground-sirloin patties and served them on two grilled hamburger rolls. Iced lemonade made with our fresh lemons worked well as our drink. We sat and enjoyed our first cuisine in the Prevost coach. During our meal we listened to FM music. From our window we viewed the last rays of the sun as it disappeared. Patty looked at me. "Honey, we've got to be sure to take some pictures of these beautiful sunsets." Her eyes opened with amazement as she viewed the red sky spreading across the skyline; almost comparable to the gorgeous sunsets in the Adirondacks when the sun sets over the lakes.

"We will, dear," I replied, remembering regretfully that in our hasty departure we had left our good camera at home. We'd remedy that by purchasing a single-use camera at the local drug store.

After the delightful meal I assisted Patty with the dishes. The coach definitely did have all the whistles and bells. I could only imagine the intricate plans that had gone into the creation of this magnificent home on wheels. Jack certainly had selected a beautiful model. It seemed to have its own personality. After tidying up the coach, Patty and I decided to take a walk around the resort. Before we started out, I placed my briefcase in the trunk of the Camaro so I would be ready for my meeting with Ruby in the morning. I made sure I locked the car.

The resort was rectangular in shape with a capacity of about three hundred units. The office was situated in the front near the entrance and exits. It was surrounded by a six-foot wall almost completely around the perimeter of the property. There was a clubhouse with kitchen facilities attached. The basement area of the clubhouse had an exercise room with treadmills, stationary bicycles, and weight machines. The shuffleboard court was located in the center of the resort. The entirety appeared to be well managed. From what Ruby had told us, Jack had done investigative work for the owners in the past and had become an acquaintance of the owner, James Patterson.

Patty and I walked around the park twice and then climbed the stairs to the upper deck of the administrative building. From benches on the upper level one could view much of the surroundings. We looked out onto a land area that was flat and level. New housing tracts were rapidly replacing the prolific cotton fields that had once been prevalent. Around us had been predominantly an agricultural region with very few services in the immediate area; now, however, in order to serve the fast growing communities, new restaurants and stores were being developed to meet the needs of the newcomers. Behind the resort was a large irrigation canal under the control of the Roosevelt Irrigation District that services the needs of the local farmers.

As we completed our walk and prepared to enter the coach for the evening, our next-door neighbor approached to introduce himself. He identified himself as Art Panighetti from the Syracuse, New York region.

"It is a pleasure to meet you, Art. This is my wife, Patty." I was surprised to have someone from New York State as my neighbor in Arizona. "By the way, we're upstate fellow New Yorkers here on a junket getting away from the winter."

"It is nice to meet you, Patty." Art extended his hand and shook my hand, then Patty's.

"My wife's name is Marilyn. She has gone to bed early or I would introduce her to you folks." Art appeared to be in his fifties and stood about six feet in height. He was wearing an orange golf shirt and beige slacks. "If I can be of any help to you during your stay, feel free to call on me."

Patty excused herself and went inside the coach while Art and I continued our conversation. We discussed various people whom we both knew who resided in the Syracuse area. I was amazed to learn that he, too, had once been a member of the New York State Troopers. But he had stayed only for six years and thus it was understandable we had never met. He was amazed to hear that I was a retired member of Troops B and D. It was evident that we had a lot in common. We both at one time had been members of Troop D, but were assigned to state police stations in other areas of the troop.

"Art, it's certainly nice to meet you. We'll probably be seeing each other around the resort. My wife and I will be in and out. We'll catch you later." I didn't want to go into detail with Art about my purpose of being in Arizona even though it probably wouldn't have been a problem considering Art's background in law enforcement, I still opted to keep my work confidential at this time.

"Nice to meet you, Jason. Maybe we can get together for a cookout or something," he said as he departed.

"Have a good evening. We'll get together soon. Good night."

I went into the coach and found Patty already in her nightgown, reading the paper.

"Patty, how are you feeling, precious? Are you tired?"

"Jason, yes, I'm a little fatigued. I was going to press your slacks for tomorrow, but they're in good shape. I have everything you need for tomorrow laid out on the end of the dresser."

"Thank you. Sweetheart, you're precious. I want you to get a good night's sleep." I leaned over and gave her a peck on the cheek.

"Flattery will get you everywhere, Jason," she teased.

"Why, what do you have in mind, my sweet?" I looked over at her and her smile was very inviting. I gave her another kiss on the forehead, this one more lingering. She responded by getting out of the chair and we embraced. We retired to the living room area of the coach and listened to several musical CD's. It was very relaxing as we sat together on the leather davenport.

"Well, how do you like Jack's coach, Patty?"

"I love it. Wish we could afford one, honey."

"Maybe someday, honey. Right now we have a lot on our plate. You're expecting our child. That's the most important thing right now, and we're here, a long way from home, to assist Jack."

"I know. I know what you mean. Well, I can dream, can't I?" She giggled.

Before I got ready for bed, I called Wayne Beyea in Plattsburgh. He indicated that he had not received any cases to speak of, except a couple of stale dated checks from Mountain Bank. I told him to place them in a file and hold them for me or call and leave a message on the answering machine that Jack had made available for me. I wished Wayne and his family a happy holiday season and ended the call. Wayne would take care of any important cases that came up.

I dialed the number for Wilt Chambers. I wanted to check and see how Ruben was doing.

"Hello," Wilt answered.

"Wilt, Jason here. How is everything? Is Ruben behaving himself?" There was a slight pause. I heard a bark in the background.

"Yes, he's a good dog. It's good to hear from you, Jason. I was beginning to worry. How is Patty?" Wilt loved Patty as though she were his daughter.

"She's good, Wilt. How are you and that big K-9 doing?"

"Everything is okay. I will be checking your log home every other day. I checked your propane tank and ordered you more fuel. I think it'll be a good idea to keep the thermostat around fifty-five degrees. The temperatures have been going down below zero overnight."

I chuckled to myself at how lucky we were to be enjoying the warmer climate.

"I should have checked that before we left. Apparently I was in such a rush that it slipped my mind. I was so concerned about Jack that there were several things I forgot to do. It's much warmer here in Arizona, Wilt. The temperatures are quite a bit higher out here."

"You're lucky to be there. You've got a lot on the table right now. How is your buddy Jack doing?" Wilt asked, concerned.

"He's doing well. But I imagine he will have to be in the hospital for a while. There's always that concern about infection."

"Yeah! Infection can take over your whole body, if you're not careful," Wilt replied. We talked for a while about our friends, Dale Rush and Jack Falsey, and the news around Old Forge and Boonville. I wished Wilt a Merry Christmas and a Happy New Year and told him I'd try to call him again before the holidays, though. I told him to pat Ruben on the head for us. He told me to say hello to Patty. I could tell by his voice that he missed us both and we hung up.

I checked to make certain that the entrance door to the coach was locked. I was amazed at the space that the motor home afforded. It certainly did have as much room as a small apartment. I liked it. I went into the bathroom and brushed my teeth.

Patty was already sound asleep when I got into bed. In my health and happiness, I found myself thinking of poor Jack, an innocent, lying in the hospital suffering from a bullet wound. When would this heartbreaking, senseless activity cease in our great land? I couldn't answer the question. It made me wonder about our society in general. I was a mere speck of sand in the wide desert. As a human being who believes in justice, hoping and praying for it, I watched everyday from the sidelines the behavior of some and thought of the fragile balance between good versus evil. My eyes closed....

CHAPTER FOUR

The delicious smells of coffee and bacon permeated the motor coach. I pushed the covers back just as I heard Patty call.

"Jason, breakfast is ready! Would you care for an egg on your pancakes, dear?"

"Yes, I would. Only one, over medium, sweetheart." I was hungry, as usual.

On the way to the dining area, I stopped in the bathroom and splashed some cold water on my face after washing my hands. The mauve hand towel matched the décor. At the table, when I sat down, Patty rushed over with my plate; two hotcakes, one with an egg on top, and two strips of crisp bacon. She set it down in front of me and gave me a kiss on my forehead.

"The hotcakes look wonderful, Patty." I noticed a slice of orange that she had placed by the bacon.

"Thank you for the compliment, my dearest. You just made my day." She beamed.

Patty and I enjoyed our breakfast. I imagined that Jack was probably having breakfast at the hospital with his television turned on to a local news network. He always kept up on current events.

"What time did you get up this morning, Patty? I must have been in a deep sleep, for I didn't hear you get out of bed. By the way, how was your night's sleep?" I asked.

"Just fine, my dear," she replied in answer to my question. Changing the subject, she continued, "I thought that I'd better press your slacks and shirt. Last night, I thought they looked fine, but this morning they seemed to be a little wrinkled. I want you to look sharp when you go to the office to meet with Ruby Wolkowski." She was always thoughtful about my appearance. Patty herself looked beautiful, as usual.

"Honey, thank you, my dear. You're so precious. You know, Patty, Ruby told me that you can join me while I'm conducting my investigations."

"She did!" Patty exclaimed in surprise.

"Yes, seriously, she did. Would you like to join me, honey? I'll only take you along when I know it's safe, so you can see some of the sights. The desert is beautiful, especially when it's in bloom."

"I'd love to, if you don't think I'd interfere with your work."

"Listen, sweetheart, you'd never bother me that way. Of course you can come along, and I'm certain that you'll see some things that you've never laid your eyes on before."

"You mean to tell me that we won't have a repeat of the Draper case up in the Adirondacks, right? We could have been injured or even killed, Jason."

"I know, I know. We were fortunate. If I think there's going to be any problem, I'll leave you here at the resort. Okay with you?" I asked.

"As long as Ruby sanctioned my riding along with you, I'll take my chances. I would love to be with you, dearest. If anything should happen to you out in this desert country, I'd want to be there," she said, setting her jaw.

It was unusual for me, as a private investigator, to be accompanied by my wife or any other person, especially in a company car, but it was sanctioned and I would have the honor of the presence of my wife, Mrs. Black.

In an hour Patty and I were heading east on the busy Arizona I-10 interstate. The Camaro performed well. Apparently Jack had had some special work done on the engine, as I had no problem reaching the 75-mph speed limit posted on the signs along the highway. We continued on to 99th Avenue and took the exit to Jack's office.

This was an ideal time to be in Arizona as the temperatures ranged from 40 degrees in the morning to a daytime high of 70 to 80 degrees compared to the below zero readings in the Adirondacks. But the sun beating down continually necessitated the use of the vehicle's air conditioner. It wasn't long before I reached down to switch it on.

I had planned to call Jack at the hospital before I left the resort, but decided that I'd call him from his office.

"Do you want me to wait in the car, Jason?" Patty asked.

"No, honey. We'll both go in to see Ruby." I got out of the car and went over to the passenger side and opened the door. Patty looked lovely this morning. When I had asked her to join me, she went in to change. She decided to wear a light beige blouse with a matching skirt and a brown light weight jacket. Before I closed the passenger-side door, I grabbed my briefcase and locked the car. We walked toward the office on the flagstone walkway. Patty was just ahead of me. I happened to look down as a small lizard was preparing to cross the sidewalk. Patty had not seen the lizard and I didn't say anything as I did not want to startle her. They are common in this desert country.

When we reached the entrance I opened the door and held it for Patty to enter. The waiting room was empty. Soft music played in the background throughout the office complex. Ruby appeared from an office to greet us.

"Patty and Jason, good morning! Did you have a good night's sleep?" She rushed over and gave us each a hasty hug.

"Yes, we were very comfortable," replied Patty with a warm smile.

"How about you, Jason?"

"Ruby, we both slept like babies. It's a wonderful coach. And it was wonderful of Jack to let us have the use of it." I meant it sincerely.

"I really think it was a good idea. If you had gone into a

rental apartment for the time you're going to be here, you could never be certain about their security. They don't put up with any shenanigans out there at the resort. Believe me, Jack wouldn't park his Prevost just any place. You know how fussy he is, Jason."

"True. By the way, have you talked with him this morning?"

"Yes, he sounded just like his old self. He wants you to call him before you leave today. I was able to assure him I have the file all in order relative to the missing coed from Casa Grande." She turned. "Patty, would you mind if I steal your husband for a few minutes? I have some things to go over with him. We won't be very long. Help yourself to the fresh decaf I've just made. And there are some assorted pastries, if you're interested," she said as she pointed to the table.

"Thank you, Ruby. I believe I will try a cup." Patty walked toward the alcove and the freshly brewed coffee. I followed Ruby into her office. I knew Patty would be comfortable in the waiting room, as there was a rack of the latest national magazines for her to read.

"Jason, it is so good to have you and Patty here. We're sorry to have had to bother you, but you know how much it means to Jack and me."

"More than ever, Ruby, I'm glad you called us. Jack needs me, and I'm here for him. He would do the same for me."

"The case that you'll be working on, as we said, involves a missing coed who attends the University of Arizona at Tucson. She comes from a well-to-do family who has investments in ranches and cattle as well as interests in two bottling firms in Texas, one in Houston and the other in Dallas. The investigation by the local police authority and the feds has been negative so far. They have had some of their best men looking into it. The father, Jerome Huntley, is adamant about the case and feels that the authorities should be doing more. Jack has been in touch with everyone who is involved with the case. Every possible lead has been followed, and as the case stands now, it is at a dead end. Huntley contacted our office and has employed our firm to conduct a separate investigation, hoping that his daughter will be located. To date there have been no ransom demands by anyone. The name of the missing girl is Christine Huntley, age 21, a junior at the university. Here's the file. It contains all the pertinent information. Down deep, Huntley believes law enforcement feels that Christine may have run away on her own. On the date of her disappearance, a background check of Christine was conducted for the two preceding weeks before she vanished. She is the only child. The mother passed away about a year ago in an auto accident. I think that you will have many dead-ends in this investigation. Jack already had been involved in the preliminary investigation and was en route to see Huntley for the fourth time, when he was shot near Casa Grande." Ruby teared up.

"It was unfortunate. There appears to be a great deal of crime in this region of Arizona. Not only do you have the drug trafficking, but there are plenty of border violations. We even hear about it on the radio back east, and how people are found dead in the desert."

"True, it goes on continually." Ruby carefully wiped her eyes with a tissue. "Jason, I have made an appointment for you to interview Mr. Huntley tomorrow. The directions to his ranch are in the folder along with telephone numbers. It's a duplicate of our master file. When I talked with Jack earlier he mentioned that he would like you to call him at the hospital tonight around 7:00 p.m."

"I will call him. I hope he's feeling better."

"He seems to be coming along okay. As you know, gunshot wounds take time to heal. He was just so fortunate that it didn't strike a vital organ." Ruby paused. "If there is anything that you and Patty need, just call me here at the office or at my home any time of the day or night. I wanted to introduce you to Bill Reidy, who is sitting in for Jack, but he had to go to the courthouse. You'll meet him soon. He's from the east. You two should have a lot in common with your law enforcement backgrounds."

"I look forward to meeting him. I'm sure that you have the

telephone number of our coach. Feel free to call whenever you need me."

"Yes, I have it."

She patted me on the shoulder and walked me into the waiting room, where Patty had just placed a magazine in the rack.

"Patty, if there is anything that you need or if you get tired of riding around, you can come to the office and we'll go to lunch, just the two of us," Ruby offered genuinely.

"I will, Ruby. Jason and I want to thank you for the wonderful arrangements that you and Jack have made for us. I sort of dreaded going into a condo. We like the resort and the people we have met are very nice. You must come out some afternoon for a dip in the pool."

"I'll do that when things quiet down in the office. In fact, when Jack gets out of the hospital he would probably enjoy that, too. He could relax by the pool while we have our swim."

Patty and I said our good-byes to Ruby. I was anxious to study the file she had given me. She had placed it in a brown manila envelope. I would wait until we returned to the resort before I opened it. I asked Patty if she would like some lunch. She agreed and we stopped at Bill Johnson's on Litchfield Road, not too far from I-10 on the way back to the resort.

The parking area was massive. There were an assortment of cars and pickup trucks in the half-filled parking lot, with the pickups outnumbering the cars two-to-one. We parked next to a red Trailblazer and exited the car. I placed the brown envelope containing the Huntley case in the trunk and locked the car. Patty took my arm as we walked toward the entrance of the restaurant. As we entered, we were greeted by the hostess. Wearing a blue denim outfit, she sported a cowboy hat and a large six-shooter in a holster hanging from her waist. Patty and I looked at each other and smiled as we realized this must be the dress code, for other cowgirl-attired waitresses carried trays as they scurried back and forth serving their customers.

I turned to Patty. "Wouldn't those outfits be something at

John's diner," I said jokingly. Patty just looked at me and laughed.

"Hello, folks. Would you like a booth or a table?" she asked with a pleasant smile.

"A booth, if possible," I requested.

We followed the hostess through the restaurant to a booth and sat down.

"The waitress will be right with you," she said as she handed us two menus.

Patty and I looked the menus over closely. Both of us enjoy beef barbecue, and we quickly spied it on the menu. The waitress came to take our order. We each asked for the beef brisket sandwich with coleslaw and beans, accompanied by two glasses of pink lemonade. I considered ordering a beer, but as I was driving the company car, I decided against it. The restaurant was decorated in the traditional western motif of Arizona with replicas of rifles, steer horns, covered wagons, and many other memorabilia items hanging from the walls and ceiling. They created the ambience of a bygone era.

The waitress brought our food and placed it before us. The barbecue looked scrumptious, the beans were steaming hot, and the dishes of coleslaw were cold and fresh.

I looked at Patty as she placed her napkin on her lap. I followed suit and we began our feast. It was delicious. The lemonade quenched our desert thirst.

The barbecue, generously covered with the restaurant's own savory sauce, was tender and tasty. We decided to order another barbecue to split. We opted out of ordering dessert, but elected to wait for another time, as we were full. Our appetites were more than satisfied. The waitress was amiable and told us to come back another day and please leave room for dessert.

Before heading to the resort we decided to stop by the hospital to see Jack for a few minutes.

We entered I-10 and headed east. The Camaro performed well. On this portion of the highway the speed limit is sixty-five miles per hour. The needle on the car's speedometer was right on sixty-five. All of a sudden a Chevrolet Corvette flashed by us at a speed I estimated to be about one hundred ten miles per hour. On his tail was an Arizona Highway Patrol car. The cruiser's red lights were flashing and vehicles were pulling over toward the right hand-lane of the three-lane eastbound I-10. Patty looked over at me with incredulity.

"What was that, Jason? Was it a tornado?" Her mouth was agape in amazement.

"Honey, that was a cowboy in a Corvette with a patrol car on his tail," I flashed back, remembering my years on the force.

"Do you think he'll get a big ticket for speeding?" she queried.

The speeder and the highway patrolman proceeded out of sight. We didn't see them again until we exited I-10 at 51st Avenue. The patrolman was writing a citation. As we passed the Corvette, Patty looked over and informed me that the driver's head was slumped down on the steering wheel. We continued to the traffic light, which was green, and turned left toward the hospital. When we arrived at the parking lot, I located a space near the entrance. Patty and I exited the car and locked it and headed toward the door that led to the elevators.

When we arrived at Jack's room I peeked in. He appeared to be reading a magazine.

"Hey, Irish, what's up?" I asked.

He looked over and smiled as we entered his room. "Jason, Patty, it's so good to see you."

Patty rushed over and gave him a kiss on the forehead. I approached the bed and patted him on his good shoulder. Jack looked at me and smiled.

"How are you feeling, buddy?" He appeared a little better than when we had first seen him.

"Much better, much better, Jason. I was certainly fortunate not to have taken a slug in my heart or any of my vital organs. Damned lucky!" he avowed emphatically.

"What caliber was the bullet?" I wanted to know.

"They tell me that it was a .223 caliber with plenty of zip. I'd like to meet the person who fired it." Jack's face flushed for a moment.

"There have been other incidents of human smuggling here in Arizona, according to the papers I've read."

"That's right, and it goes on all the time. The authorities pick up some, but there are many who avoid prosecution. There are so many methods they're using to carry on this type of criminal activity. They've built underground tunnels from Mexico into the United States. They have established routes through many parts of the southwest where illegals cross. Authorities have found so many dying during the hot summer months, the state has even provided water stations to cut the death rates as a humanitarian policy. But as long as there are jobs waiting here to be filled, people will continue the exodus from their countries. And it's not just Mexico. It's Guatemala, the Dominican Republic, Central America—the list goes on and on." His face really became red reliving the ordeal.

As soon as I noticed Jack was getting upset with this discussion, I quickly changed the subject. I did not want his health endangered.

"Jack, Ruby gave me the case file on the Huntley matter. Tonight I'll go through it and familiarize myself with the information."

My friend visibly grew calmer. "It's going to be an interesting one for you to work on. I know if anyone can help locate her, it's you. I've got a great deal of confidence in your abilities, Jason. She may be buried or she may be at the bottom of a gulch or she may be with someone held against her will. There are many numbers of things that could have happened. She may have run away on her own. At the moment it is a mystery. The local authorities and the feds have searched vast areas in the vicinity of Casa Grande. Police informants are on the alert for any possible leads. Parole and probation files have been checked closely as well as inmates who have been recently released from prisons and jails in Arizona. You'll see when you go over the files and reports that a good search for this young lady has been performed. I really didn't have the case very long before the shooting occurred. I wish you good luck. I sincerely appreciate you and Patty for coming to Arizona. I've always been able to count on you, Jason." Tears came to Jack's eyes. I knew that it was his Irish sentimentality that he frequently displayed.

"I'll do the best I can," I assured him.

"If there is anything you need from the office, just call Bill Reidy or Ruby. Have you met Bill yet?" he asked.

"No, he was out of the office when we were there. I look forward to meeting him."

"I hired him about a year ago. He comes from a vast police background and is an additional asset to the agency. He was formerly a lieutenant with the Syracuse police department. You may know of him or some of his associates."

"That's a possibility. I'll look forward to meeting him. By the way, have you had many visitors, Jack?" I inquired.

"Too many, but I was glad to see some of my former associates from the Phoenix Police Department. By the way, Jay Silverstein asked how you were, Jason. The captain has been busy. In fact, some of his detectives have looked into various leads in the city relative to the missing Huntley girl. I advised Jay that you will be snooping around the area and possibly asking for his expertise."

"What was his response to that?" I asked.

"He told me if there is anything he can do to assist you, just give him a call."

"That's great! You never know what might develop. Someone, somewhere must have information that might give us a clue to her disappearance."

While Jack and I conversed, Patty was reading a magazine that one of Jack's friends had dropped off for him. A nurse came into the room with some juice for Jack, and she asked us if we'd like something to drink. We declined and thanked her for the offer.

Jack and I concluded our conversation. Patty went over to the bed and gave Jack another kiss on his forehead. He looked tired, but thanked us for stopping by. He did ask one last question.

"How do you two like my second home on wheels?"

"It is wonderful," Patty replied.

"It's a large one, Jack. Can you handle it alright?" I inquired.

"Yes. So far no problem. You and Patty may have to drive it. Have you ever driven a coach of that size, Jason?" he asked.

"Yeah, I should be able to handle it." I knew that he just wanted that reassurance.

We advised Jack to get plenty of rest, and then left the hospital. The drive to Goodyear didn't take long on I-10. We took the exit at Litchfield Road and stopped by the supermarket to pick up a few items for the freezer. Patty found salmon on sale. She also purchased some shrimp and condiments. Although the coach already contained some food items, it would probably take a few visits to the market before we completed our shopping for all the staples we would require.

This was a different lifestyle than Patty and I had been accustomed to. However, we would adjust. At home our neighbors were a considerable distance from us, so at the resort the close proximity was a bit disconcerting. Any change of routine requires a different strategy.

For Patty's pregnancy, we would contact a doctor in this area to insure there would be no problems, if the need arose. Fortunately Patty felt great, and except for an occasional bout of morning sickness and an occasional queasy stomach, she experienced very little change in her appetite. During her early pregnancy, she tried to keep an active routine.

The checkout lines at the market were busy. With Christmas only a few days away, customers were preparing for the holidays. Patty and I had not been able to do any Christmas shopping, however the area homes were brightly illuminated with colorful bulbs and decorations, just like the homes back east without the snow.

I took the groceries from the shopping cart and placed them on the checkout counter as the cashier scanned the prices. A nametag identified her as Julie. She was pleasant and cheerful and handled her position as cashier in a professional manner. Patty and I thanked her, then rolled the cart out of the store into the parking lot, where many customers with overloaded shopping carts were rushing around. One could tell that the holiday season was upon us. When we reached the car, I opened the trunk and placed purchases in the compartment. Patty pushed the cart back to the return area and I opened the door for her.

The short trip back to the resort took us through an area of new housing developments, mixed among the remaining fields of cotton crops. Clearly this once famous agricultural region was slowly turning into a vibrant community with row on row of houses. We could see large boxcar-size bales of cotton sitting at the ends of some of the cotton fields. Historically, this area that once had served the Goodyear Tire and Rubber Company for the much needed cotton required for making their tires would have to find another location.

Patty and I arrived at the Roadrunner Resort to find three large coaches lined up to register. We stopped at the security gate and entered the code. The long arm of the gate lifted high in the air and we passed under it. With difficulty I adhered to the strictly enforced five-mile-per-hour speed limit. We returned the waves of some of the guests who were strolling along the roadway. I noticed that some of the campers had already decorated their coaches with colorful lights, while others were currently in the process. Patty and I probably wouldn't be doing much decorating, since our home was only temporary.

"Honey," I said to her, "I noticed that they were selling Christmas wreaths at the office. Would you like me to pick one of them up? We could hang it from the door of the coach."

She looked at me and nodded in agreement. "That would be wonderful of you, sweetheart. We should have some sort of decoration displayed."

"It shall be done, my lady. In fact, if I can get some lights I will pick up a couple of strings and hang them on the outside of the coach," I answered.

"Okay, sweetheart, that'll be nice," she said.

"I'll go up to the office a little later and see what they have to offer."

When I brought the groceries into the coach I also brought in the brown manila envelope that Ruby had given me regarding the Huntley missing-person case. While Patty took a few things over to the resort laundry room, I pulled out the file, anxious to see what I had to confront. I sat at the table and methodically went through the paperwork. The file contained copies of the original police reports, as well as a sworn statement from Mr. Huntley, the father of the missing coed, Christine, age 21, from Casa Grande. It appeared that Jack had taken the statement from the father. Reading it I learned that the daughter had left the ranch in a 1989 white Jeep to drive to Casa Grande to do some shopping, telling him she would be returning in time for dinner. She never returned. The father, concerned, finally contacted the authorities around eight, then went to Casa Grande himself to see if he could possibly locate his daughter. He checked the parking lots and restaurants, looking for her car, without results. The statement went on to say that Mr. Huntley had been notified by the police that the Jeep had been located in good condition near the intersection of Route 8 and I-10. I finished reading the statement and turned to the copies of the police reports. They noted that search parties covered the area for days without developing any useful information that would lead to the location of Christine Huntley. The reports reflected that the Jeep was impounded and processed for prints, DNA and other possible evidentiary clues or substances. The results of the examinations were negative.

In addition, the reports provided the names of people who had been interviewed, consisting of students, friends, and neighbors who resided in the area where the Jeep had been located. All the interviews were without results.

Patty returned to the coach from the laundry room and I carefully returned all the material to the envelope. I would look at it again before I conducted my interview with the father, Mr.

Huntley.

"Honey, did you finish the washing?" I asked.

"I've got it all done, both the washing and drying. It's a very nice laundry room. The machines work well and the dryers are hot," she replied.

"That's great. If we have any heavy baskets of laundry, let me lift them for you. I don't want you to lift anything heavy. You have to be careful, honey."

"Don't fret so. I'll be careful, sweetheart." She smiled appreciatively. "You're so thoughtful, Jason."

Since we had a large lunch, we decided that tonight would be the night for some of my favorite delicious buckwheat pancakes. Patty had picked up some maple syrup and sweet butter during our shopping spree. This combination of the two over the golden brown buckwheat pancakes would be a treat. Patty is fond of saying that when she is working at John's Diner, buckwheat pancakes are very popular with the customers.

After our light supper, I helped Patty with the dishes. The coach had a dishwasher, so I just rinsed the plates and placed them in the washer, while Patty put things away.

Patty suggested that we take a walk around the perimeter of the resort. I agreed. We took a couple of light jackets from the closet and went outside. The temperature was about seventy degrees; however, we could feel a slight chill in the air. In Arizona it cools rapidly in the evening. I looked over at Art Panighetti's coach and noticed that his car was gone. Apparently they had gone out for the evening.

We nodded at several couples who were out walking. Patty and I could see that there were advantages to this lifestyle, but it couldn't take the place of our log home in the Adirondacks, which we loved. We both enjoyed the solace that accompanies living in the mountains.

I looked at my watch. Wilt Chambers would be set to check our New York home just about now. We had discussed with Wilt before we left for Arizona that if he found our home burglarized or vandalized he should handle any type of action that was necessary during our absence. Hopefully it wouldn't be necessary to have the police called unless Wilt thought it was important enough to do so.

"Honey, let's take a look at the pool!" She sounded bubbly. "I haven't seen it yet."

"Sure, good idea."

We walked over to the gate, unlocked it, and went inside. Several guests sat around the north side of the pool, while two couples were enjoying the hot tub located on the south side. Everyone waved at us, probably recognizing us as newcomers. It appeared to be a friendly gathering. We stopped and spoke to a couple who were sitting under a colorful umbrella at one of the tables scattered around the pool. He asked if we were enjoying our stay at the resort. I told him that so far we found it to be to our liking. He indicated that this was his fifth winter here. After our brief exchange, Patty and I returned to the coach.

I turned on the television and we watched a relaxing sitcom before getting ready for bed. Patty went to the bathroom first. She came out wearing a pink nightgown. She looked beautiful standing there with her blond hair flowing on her shoulders. I was a fortunate fellow. She was a lovely mother-to-be and of course I was proud to be a new daddy-to-be.

"Jason, I'm going to read for a while. I'll see you in bed, hon." Her voice sounded sleepy.

"I'll be in shortly, dear."

I went into the bathroom and brushed my teeth. The mirror on the medicine chest was revealing. Here I was just past fifty years old, and I was already getting gray hair. I combed my hair. I then went to check the door to make certain it was locked. When I entered the bedroom I noticed that Patty was lying on her back sound asleep. Her blond hair was draped on her pillow. The open book she had been reading was still on the bedspread just below her chest. I reached over, picked up the book, and laid it on the shelf above the bed. I climbed into bed and gave her a kiss on the forehead. She turned over and continued to sleep. I pulled the covers over our shoulders and fell off to sleep.

CHAPTER FIVE

Patty and I were looking down into the Grand Canyon. An eagle circled over us and started toward us. The talons of this gigantic bird of prey were about to swoop down on us. The eagle's eyes were red with rage. I immediately woke with a start. My heart was pounding in my chest. I sat up in bed and Patty woke up, apparently by the movement I made.

"What's wrong, Jason?" she asked, alarmed.

"I had a dream. It felt like a nightmare. We were in danger. An eagle was about to attack us. It seemed so real. Then I woke up. I'm sorry, I didn't mean to disturb you, honey." I felt sheepish for waking her. "I'm sorry I woke you, dear. You need your rest."

"Jason, don't worry. You didn't disturb me. I wonder what on earth caused you to dream of such a thing," she stated, looking puzzled.

"I don't know, dear," I answered, glancing over at the clock. "It's 7:00."

"It's time to get up anyway, my darling. What would you like for breakfast?" she asked, patting me on the shoulder, trying to comfort me.

"Well, I know it won't be eagle eggs."

She laughed in amusement.

While Patty went into the kitchen to start the automatic-drip coffeemaker, I went into the bathroom for a quick shave and shower. I found the lighting in the coach excellent as I drew my razor down under my right sideburn. For some reason the light at home in our bathroom at home did not appear as bright. The shower felt good, especially against my lower spine. An ice-cold rinse brought me to the full state of being awake. I could smell the aroma of the sizzling bacon wafting throughout the coach as I dried off with a large bath towel. I slipped on my robe, went into the bedroom, and I hurriedly dressed.

I heard Patty from the kitchen. "Honey, breakfast is going to be served momentarily."

"Okay, sweetheart," I replied.

While I was tying my shoelaces, I thought about the forthcoming interview I would be conducting with the missing coed's father. I could only imagine—now, more than ever, of course, with my imminent fatherhood—how I would feel if I had had a daughter who had come up missing. It must be heartbreaking.

I proceeded to the breakfast nook, where Patty was placing my three slices of crispy bacon, two fried over-medium eggs, and whole-wheat toast on my plate. She had poured us each a glass of apple juice. I gave Patty a quick kiss on her forehead, a pat on her tummy, and sat down to enjoy my repast. Patty had poached herself one egg and placed it on a slice of unbuttered whole-wheat toast. She did not want to gain too much weight during her pregnancy. Before we started eating, we clinked our juice glasses together.

"Jason, just what would have happened if that eagle had actually reached us?" she asked, half-jokingly.

"We'll never know, darling. Luckily I came to before the eagle actually pounced on us." We both laughed. Then I asked, "How long will it take you to get ready?"

"Am I going with you today?" she asked eagerly.

"Yes, if you'd like to. Ruby said there wouldn't be a problem. Of course, if you'd rather stay here at the resort and browse around, meeting some of the ladies or enjoy the pool, that is up to you." I was hoping she'd rather be with me.

"Honey, I'd love to go with you," she answered. "I just don't want to be in the way."

"It's a done deal. You'll be my honorary partner on this case. You go and get dressed, and I'll do the dishes and tidy up the coach."

Although the coach wasn't as large as our log home, it had plenty of room to move about and did require daily attention for neatness.

While Patty was getting ready I placed a telephone call to Wayne Beyea in Plattsburgh. I was pleased to learn that he had received a request from a Herkimer County attorney to conduct a confidential investigation relative to a marital matter. We discussed some other issues. He assured me that he would consult with me in the event an involved case materialized. We concluded our telephone call with my wishing him good luck in the investigation.

I took my briefcase, which contained my tape recorder and notebooks, from the closet. Flynn Investigations had been seeking permission for me to carry a pistol as an employee of the firm in the capacity of an advisor/investigator, but I hadn't been notified by Ruby as of yet that this arrangement had been approved. I knew she would stay on top of it. I probably wouldn't need a firearm during my stay in Arizona, but I'd rather be equipped to handle any unforeseen incident if the situation should arise. Before we departed I called Jerome Huntley at Casa Grande to confirm our appointment. He sounded distraught over the phone. I assured him that I would be at his ranch within two hours. I asked him if the authorities had developed any new leads. He indicated that to his knowledge there had been no progress. We concluded our conversation.

I checked the motor coach over before leaving, and turned off the radio. Patty and I went out and I locked the door. I seated Patty in the passenger side, jumped behind the steering wheel, and started the Camaro, which responded at the first turn of the ignition switch.

"Honey, do you miss the old Bronco?" Patty asked with a

devilish grin on her face.

"Of course I do, sweetheart, but someday we'll have to say goodbye to it. It has given me such good service for the past few years. You know we won't be able to change vehicles right now with the baby coming soon."

"That's true, honey," she replied. Then she added reassuringly, "Don't worry, we'll get by."

We took I-10 west to Route 85 and then drove south toward Gila Bend. The road was a two-lane macadam highway. Jack had told me it had a bad reputation for fatal vehicle accidents. Sometimes a driver would pass without using caution and strike another car head-on. Jack had mentioned how on several occasions his firm had been called upon to investigate who was negligent in the accidents. Remembering what he had told me, I practiced caution on this hazardous highway. Several oncoming cars pulled in and out in an attempt to pass, but their endeavors were fruitless. This pattern, I was learning, was indicative of many of the Arizona highways. The growth in the area far exceeded the building of new roads that were much needed to keep up with the housing developments springing up in the southwest area of Phoenix. We proceeded on our way toward Route 8. I carefully kept the headlights on. I blamed poor depth perception for many of the accidents Jack had told me about, as well as the inexperience of the drivers.

When we arrived in Gila Bend we pulled into a service station and I gassed up the Camaro and checked the oil. Ruby had given me an agency credit card so I wouldn't have to use my cash or card. After filling up the car we headed toward Casa Grande and my appointment with Jerome Huntley. The directions I had been given led me to a ranch just south of Casa Grande. The entrance to the Huntley ranch was well identified by two large wooden poles with a sign at the top which read "BAR-H-RANCH." The private road was in good shape— though, of course, dusty—as the Camaro made its way toward the ranch house. It was almost a mile from I-10. Patty was looking out her window taking in the view of baled hay stacked in three different buildings that were open on two sides with overhanging roofs on each. Having been originally from Kentucky, Patty was very familiar with horse farms and baled hay. I noticed as she gazed at a corral containing a dozen horses. I could see a slight smile cross her face as she was probably reminiscing. When we neared the house I observed a couple of ranch hands leading two horses to a white horse trailer. The animals were impressive, appearing to be approximately fifteen hands high. Both were black with their coats freshly brushed. I came to a parking area on the east side of the ranch house and pulled into it.

"Patty, I think it best if you wait here in the car while I conduct my interview with Jerome Huntley. I'm guessing you'll be more comfortable staying here."

"No problem, dearest. I brought a book along. I'll read while you talk with Mr. Huntley. It must be difficult for him with his daughter missing." Patty began to tear up. She had always been sentimental, and now since her pregnancy she had difficulty controlling her tears.

"I'm certain you are right. It has to be difficult for him. See you shortly." I leaned over to give her a kiss on the cheek.

I got out of the car, took my briefcase from the trunk, and walked toward the front door of the house. I noted that the building was a combination of stone and brown-stained wood. The grounds consisted of decorative multicolored stone, and the walkway was composed of large slabs of gray slate. When I walked up onto the porch I was greeted by a middle-aged man standing in the open doorway.

"Are you Mr. Black?" he asked.

He appeared tired and drawn, surely from the lack of sleep. He was wearing a blue denim shirt with matching dungarees, and a pair of shiny black western boots. He sported a handlebar mustache that matched his graying hair. His face was handsome and ruddy, and he stood about six feet tall.

"Yes, I'm Jason Black. I represent Flynn Investigations, Mr. Huntley. I believe you've been doing business with Jack Flynn," I said as I reached over to shake his extended hand.

"How is he doing? I heard about the shooting between those two coyote gangs when they exchanged gunfire up on I-10. It was on all the airways. I called his office and talked to Ruby, who confirmed my fears. How's he doing? I hope he's going to be okay. He's such a fine fellow. Come in, Mr. Black, and we'll talk in my office." Huntley stood erect and spoke softly. I followed him into his office. The interior of the ranch house was immaculate, decorated in a southwestern motif. "Have a seat, Mr. Black."

I sat down in a deep leather-covered chair, while Huntley seated himself behind his mahogany desk. As I looked around the room, I noticed a large set of steer horns displayed on the wall and many pictures of horses. On the wall behind his desk was what I assumed to be a large picture of his wife and daughter.

"You certainly have a beautiful place, Mr. Huntley."

"Yes, I'm fortunate in that respect. But since my wife, Ravina, passed away, and now with my daughter missing, I am just about destroyed. The authorities have searched our region high and low. They have followed so many leads, but all have been unsuccessful in locating Christine." His eyes quickly filled with tears. I felt sympathetic towards him, remembering what I had gone through when Patty had disappeared. I somewhat understood what he was experiencing.

"Sir, I've looked at the file closely and it appears that the local police and the other departments involved have exhausted, as you indicated, all their leads thus far."

"Jason—I hope you don't mind if I call you by your first name?"

I nodded my assent.

"I called the Flynn Agency in the hope that, in addition to the official police investigation going on, having an independent investigation conducted might shed some new light on the disappearance of Christine. I don't dispute for one moment that the police are doing their very best on the case, but I want another perspective, possibly to find a clue that the police might have missed. I don't know whether she has been kidnapped or murdered, or just become a runaway. She is a very intelligent young lady, who has been pursuing a degree in journalism at the University of Arizona. As I told the police, Christine doesn't have any enemies that I know of. She's always been popular. She had a few dates off and on, but nothing steady. This ranch is supposed to be hers someday. She loves this place, and her intention has been to obtain her degree and pursue syndicated writing for newspapers, working right from here on the ranch. Believe me, Jason, she's had dreams, hopes, plans. Since Ravina's passing from that auto accident last year, Christine and I became very close, as any father and daughter can be. I love my daughter. We've got to find her. I want to know what happened when she went to town that day."

"Jerome, I certainly can understand your pain and anxiety. I'm anxious to do all I can to help. I read in one of the police reports that she was driving a white Jeep when she went to town. The report indicated that they found no evidence of any DNA, other than hers, or any signs of violence. They found the vehicle parked just off the highway with the keys in the ignition, still operable. It certainly appears to be a mystery. As you know, the search parties found nothing during their searches." I waited sympathetically for his response.

"That's true, but someone must know something." His voice hardened. "That is why I've engaged Flynn Investigations, to see if you folks can possibly come up with information that the police may have overlooked. Jason, in no way am I complaining about the police performance—to the contrary—but like anything else, there is that possibility that some information may have dropped through the cracks and hopefully you might come up with that one clue that could locate my daughter. I'm destroyed over this." His voice began to crack. "Christine and I were planning a trip next year to England to visit castles. And besides pursuing her degree, she has become an important part of this ranch and my horse business." I could see that Huntley was passionately worried about his daughter. Tears continued to slide down his cheeks, though he tried to keep his emotions under control.

"Jerome, did your daughter keep a diary or a journal?" I inquired.

"The police asked that question. Yes, she did keep a journal, and I found it, but it pertained mostly to her studies at the university. The detectives and the feds went through it looking for possible margin notes, maybe names or telephone numbers. There was nothing in the journal. I checked it myself. Very closely."

"If the authorities should return it, I would really like to take a look at it myself. Try to think, not just in the present, but in the past. Could there be anyone that she might have interacted with or any incident that may have occurred that could possibly shed some light on her disappearance? It's very important!" I wanted him to probe deeply his recollections of any past incidents on the ranch or in the community or at the university.

"I've wracked my aging brain, especially during my nights of sleeplessness, to come up with a face, a name, an event or anything else that could bring us any help. No, I honestly can't think of anyone that disliked Christine. She was a vibrant individual. Her outlook was positive in every aspect of her life and her environment. She always showed us love and respect, and we had no problem during her childhood. She is a survivor." Huntley paused, his eyes seeming to turn inward. "One time she was riding a spirited stallion on our east range and a rattlesnake caused the horse to rear up and Christine was thrown off. She had an English saddle on the stallion. There was nothing to hang onto. With a western saddle she could have gripped the horn, but nevertheless, she hit the ground hard and dislocated her right shoulder. The stallion took off, and there she was, all by herself in the vicinity of a rattler. Somehow she was able to roll away down a knoll and get to her feet. I don't know how she managed to walk home, but one of our ranch hands spotted her and ran to her aid." He looked directly at me again. "She has true grit, Jason," he said, adoringly.

"I would say that she has. Do you have a photograph of her

that I could have?" I inquired. "The one in the file is not as clear as I would like?"

Huntley took a photo from his desk drawer and handed it to me.

"I just had a few made up." I looked at the photo. It showed a slim young woman with blond hair and hazel-colored eyes.

The father added, "Jason, Christine is 5' 8" and weighs approximately 120 pounds. You can see she has a ruddy complexion. Some of the students at the university have put posters up for miles around the area and throughout the State of Arizona. Every possible thing is being done. Even my telephone is tapped in the event a call comes in." Huntley handed me one of the posters that bore several telephone numbers. We left it that Huntley would call me directly if he heard of any leads.

"Yes, in a case like this it is a good idea to have your telephone monitored. For the purpose of our investigation, I'll call you on your cell phone, if that is satisfactory with you."

"That's what I want you to do. Here's the number." Huntley gave me his card with his cell number written on it, and I reciprocated.

"Jerome, is there anything else that you would like to discuss with me before I leave?" I asked.

"No, I can't think of anything at the moment. Except, well—there is one place in town that is unique. By that I mean it's a place where the locals gather and discuss the latest gossip over coffee. It's a small restaurant, the Cactus Chuck Wagon, located on North Pinal Avenue. They're noted for their western beef barbecue with pinto beans. The place appeals to all age groups, young and old. If you stop in there for a sandwich, you might be able to pick up some scuttlebutt. Naturally you'll have to sort out the facts from the fiction. The owner, Caleb Johnson, is the cook and operates the place with a couple of waitresses who have been with him for a while. They've all got their thumb on the pulse of the local community."

I wrote the name "Cactus Chuck Wagon" in my notebook. "Jerome, I can't promise you anything, but I'll be the lead investigator for the agency during Jack Flynn's hospitalization. You know how to reach me, so don't hesitate to call me at any time. Any leads I develop I'll pursue to the end. You can rest assured of that."

"Jack Flynn told me that you served in the Marines together. I have a great deal of confidence in you both. In fact, I feel as though I already know you, even though this is the first time we've met."

I guessed that Jack must have told Huntley some of our war stories.

"I'm humbled, Jerome. All I can say is that we'll give it a good run. Take care."

I shook hands with Jerome Huntley. He had a good grip, despite the fact that his eyes were sad and filled with tears. I patted him on the shoulder and left the ranch house. Glancing at my watch I realized I had been with Huntley for about an hour. I walked to the car to join Patty, who was sitting on the passenger side with her head down reading her book. When I reached to open my door, I observed Huntley standing on the front porch. We waved at each other. He probably wondered who I had riding along with me in the Camaro, but I decided not to introduce him to Patty at this time.

It was after one by the time we drove to the North Pinal restaurant. I told Patty that since we were in the area, I would like to stop at the Cactus Chuck Wagon for lunch before our drive back to the resort. The Casa Grande area was new territory for us. The restaurant was located in a residential area with well maintained homes. Most of the landscaping was done in fine stone, with scattered cactus and other desert plant life. The small white stucco Cactus Chuck Wagon restaurant was set back from the highway with a large sign mounted on top of the block building. Several green cactus plants were scattered along the front. Just beyond the cactus was an antique western chuck-wagon, from the long-ago days of cattle drives, when the cowboys or cattle punchers would gather around one at mealtimes while on the trail.

"The sign on top of the restaurant is eye-catching," Patty

said.

"I imagine it does bring in customers. I've never seen a sign quite like it," I agreed.

I parked the Camaro next to a dusty pickup truck which bore registration plates from Mexico. I got out of the car, went around, and opened Patty's door to help her out.

"Are you hungry, honey?" I asked.

"Yes, I could have a sandwich," she replied.

We walked the short way to the entrance. The lower portion of the door was wooden and the upper half was of smoked glass. We walked into the restaurant. A gracious, smiling hostess with two menus tucked under her arm approached us. She greeted us warmly. "Good afternoon. Table for two?" she asked cordially.

"Yes, please. Non-smoking, preferably," I replied.

We followed her to a table and she placed the menus in front of us. I pulled out the chair for Patty and seated her. I then took the seat across from her with my back to the window. From this position I would be able to view the entire dining area. We looked the menu over and decided on the lunch special of the day: brisket of beef barbecue sandwich with coleslaw and barbecued beans. The waitress appeared at our table. Her black hair was pulled back into a tight bun. She appeared to be in her mid-twenties.

"Good afternoon, folks. My name is Maria. What would you like to drink?" she asked.

"We'll each have ice water, please, with lemon," I answered.

"May I take your order now or would you like a few more minutes?"

"I guess we're ready. We'll each have the special," I said, ordering for us both.

Maria wrote our order down on her pad, thanked us, and rushed back toward the kitchen.

I casually looked around the dining area. There were just a few customers at this time of day, as it was past the lunch hour. The place appeared to be very clean, and each table had a small imitation cactus plant in a pot just off-center on the tabletop. Several younger people stood across the room talking with another waitress. I heard laughter, but was unable to understand what they were saying except for the words of a short young man about eighteen years of age hollering out, "cool man, cool!" followed by more laughter. Then they all left. The waitress turned to clean their table.

Patty and I talked about the area, and how much we were enjoying the moderate temperatures, but we agreed it was difficult to comprehend how one would be able to survive the temperatures soaring to 115 degrees from May to September. We both know that taking up permanent residence in Arizona was out of the question. It just got too hot during the summer.

Marie, the waitress, returned to our table with our order. On the tray were our two steaming beef-barbecue sandwiches, accompanied by the pinto beans and coleslaw in two side dishes, with a bottle of barbecue sauce, if needed. She brought extra napkins and refilled our water glasses.

"Honey, the barbecue is delicious," Patty said after her first bite.

"Uh huh," I agreed as I savored the sandwich, grabbing the napkin to wipe excess sauce from my lips.

The coleslaw and the spicy pinto beans blended well with the barbecue. After we finished our late lunch, we both felt stuffed. Maria returned to our table.

"Would you folks care for any dessert? We have an apple-walnut pie that is very popular here at the Chuck Wagon." I glanced at Patty as she stared at me, not giving me an opportunity to answer.

"Thank you, but we'll take a rain check," she replied for both of us. "We're rather stuffed right now."

"I'll get your check. Be right back," Maria said as she turned back to the register.

Maria was a very efficient server, pleasant and friendly. I planned on asking her a few questions upon her return. I had noticed on entering the restaurant a bulletin board near the entrance bearing one of the posters that Mr. Huntley had given me.

Patty excused herself from the table to go to the restroom. The waitress returned with our check. I asked her how long she had been working at the Chuck Wagon and she told me that it had been five years.

"Maria, I noticed as I came in that your bulletin board has a poster about a missing coed. Is she a local person?" I tried to keep my tone as casual as possible.

"Yes, sir, she is. From Casa Grande. She's a regular customer of the Chuck Wagon when she isn't attending classes at the University of Arizona. Her name is Christine Huntley. Her father owns a horse and cattle ranch near the city. She's been missing almost a month. They found her dad's Jeep that she drove to town. Christine just disappeared. They have had big search parties all over the area and many of the students have put up posters. Everyone is very sad about her disappearance. She is a wonderful person." She was obviously sincerely concerned.

"Thank you for telling me about it. That's a sad story. Do you have an extra poster? My wife and I are passing through to the Phoenix area and I'd be happy to keep my eyes open for any sign of her," I continued.

"Are you folks from around here?" she inquired.

"No, we're from New York State and we're visiting Arizona, possibly with the idea of moving to the area. We're staying near Phoenix. We'll be happy to keep our eyes open for the missing girl."

Maria took our check and the money to the cashier. She hurried back with a copy of the poster that contained the information regarding Christine Huntley. Although I had already obtained a poster from Jerome, I wanted to keep my involvement quiet at this time. Patty returned to the table as we were completing our conversation.

We thanked Maria for her wonderful service. I left the money on the table for her gratuity. We bade her farewell as we left the restaurant.

When we reached the Camaro I opened the passenger door

and helped Patty get in. I went around to the driver's side and entered the vehicle.

"Well, honey, how did you like the Chuck Wagon barbecue?" I asked.

"Jason, I loved it, and that tangy coleslaw accompanied by the beans—they were just great!" she answered enthusiastically.

"Patty, before we head back to the Roadrunner Resort I want to drive around the city and look it over. Do you mind?" I felt it was important to familiarize myself with the Casa Grande area. We started our self-guided tour by travelling on E. Florence Blvd, then wove our way throughout the community.

We were pleasantly surprised to observe the missing coed's posters tacked to telephone poles and trees near intersections. A month's time was a long period not to have heard anything at all about her from anyone—an abductor, if there was one, or possibly someone who could have sighted her in some town, city, or village. I know from the reports that area motels and hotels had been contacted and advised of her disappearance, and asked to be on the lookout for her. There were so many possibilities! A trucker, or someone with a camper or motor home or a car could have stopped by her Jeep and abducted her. The silence had to be extremely stressful on Jerome Huntley. He was clearly so deeply troubled during our interview.

I did not stop at the Casa Grande Police Department, as Mr. Huntley preferred that I conduct an investigation without notifying the local department. He wanted my search to be from my own perspective, without interference or preconceived ideas. I would abide by his wishes. My own reason was that such privacy would allow me freedom of movement and the confidentially as an outside observer to collect any important information or facts that might bring the case to a successful conclusion without having to answer any of their questions as to my progress. Anyway, their case appeared to be heading for a dead end, but Jack Flynn is not the type of private detective who would call it quits, and neither am I.

The trip back to the Roadrunner Resort was uneventful. Patty and I talked about the case, and how it brought back our memories of her own abduction a few years back, a frightening, painful ordeal. Patty theorized that if Christine had been abducted and was still alive, she would have attempted to call her father. However, if she were in immediate danger or bound with restraints, such a venture would be difficult. I told Patty that she was on her way to becoming a good detective.

Another possibility we discussed was that Christine could be ill or possibly weakened without proper nutrition. There are so many angles to consider in a case like this. When Patty herself had been abducted by two escaped killers a few years before, and had ended up in a northern New York State hospital in a coma, it was only through a miracle that her Jeep had been found by Jack Falsey in a locked garage. Luckily, Patty had recovered without any permanent damage. To this day, though, she is still extremely skeptical when she is driving and would never again stop to render aid to a stranded motorist unless she knows the individual. Christine, too, could have observed a disabled vehicle and stopped to help, only to be grabbed by a person or persons unknown. Theoretically, abduction could occur in a matter of seconds or minutes with absolutely no witness.

This type of crime can and does occur throughout our country, and surely in the west, with all the open territory, Patty and I speculated it would be more difficult to come up with good, solid leads. We hoped the poster distribution around Arizona and some of the neighboring states could lead to some information. Yet even with the extensive radio and television coverage, nothing had materialized thus far.

When we reached Gila Bend we turned right at the intersection of Route 85 and headed north toward Buckeye and I-10. The traffic was heavy, with cars trying to pass in unsafe areas when they shouldn't have. We almost witnessed a head-on when we were halfway to I-10. Fortunately, we were some distance away and the violator had just enough room to squeeze in.

"Whew! That was close!" Patty said, looking frightened.

"That operator should have his license revoked, if he even has one. That's the second near miss we've seen today, hon." It upset me. Oh, how I wished I could be an Arizona Highway Patrolman for a short time. That bird would be headed to the judge's office. It's just that type of driver on the roads that creates problems for everyone else.

We pulled into the Roadrunner Resort at about 6:00 p.m. We had returned to our temporary Arizona home safe and sound. I pulled the Camaro into a parking space near the main office and Patty got out and went inside to check to see if we had any mail from New York.

While I waited for her, I noticed the resort security person had stopped a car at the main gate. After a short conversation, the operator backed up his vehicle, spinning his tires on the macadam surface and leaving a stench of rubber and marks on the roadway. Not only did the driver put on a show, but he displayed his aggravation with inappropriate hand and arm gestures. The fellow spun the vehicle around backward and almost smashed into the rear of a pickup truck. Still spinning rubber, he shot out of the entrance, almost striking a motor coach coming through it. I heard a siren as a police car shot by the entrance outside the resort, and I hoped that the officer had observed the antics of the crazy driver. For once, the law was ready to pounce on the lawbreaker, I fervently imagined.

It was a while before Patty returned to the car. She explained that there had been a line waiting to pick up their mail.

"Honey, we'll open ours when we get to the coach," I said.

"Good idea," she replied, thumbing through the letters.

I pulled into the space next to the gigantic coach. Both of us got out of the car. Patty carried the mail and I grabbed the briefcase lying on the rear seat. I went first and unlocked the entrance door. There was a hint of dampness inside, so I turned the thermostat up. It took only a few minutes to warm the place. Patty had laid the mail on the table and gone into the bedroom to change her clothes.

I looked at the letters received. Among them were our routine home fuel and telephone bills. To my chagrin, our tax notice showed a rate increase. Every year the tax on our Adirondack property takes a jump. But both Patty and I are determined to pay our taxes as long as we can, for to sell our mountain property would devastate us. There is no place on earth that we would rather live than the south central Adirondack region. It has its own natural beauty, whether it is a gurgling stream or a frost-covered mountain. We will somehow make it affordable, even if it means a little extra hard work on our part to cover the additional expense. That's one of the reasons we had journeyed to Arizona. Not only could I not let Jack Flynn down when Ruby called on us to come to Arizona, but the extra income would come in handy during the slower winter season.

Patty came out of the bedroom and planted a kiss on my cheek. I returned it with one of my own, then rose and embraced her. Our lips came together.

"Jason, not now. Before it gets any later, I'd better get back to business. What would you like for dinner, dear?" she asked, as she turned to look into the refrigerator. "We had better think about dinner before it gets much later. You know how I dislike cleaning up when it's dark."

"Do you have hot dogs and beans?" I loved that combination.

"Franks and beans coming up, my precious. You go ahead and finish checking the mail and I will start dinner. Would you like a green salad?" she asked, not wanting to make the decision.

"I would rather have some of your cabbage salad with a touch of sugar added, if you don't mind, dearest." It went well on hot dogs.

"That's fine. Sweetened cabbage salad it is," she replied.

"Honey, did I ever tell you that when I was in Dewittville, Quebec a few years ago I had my first hot dog with sweetened cabbage salad on top. It was sure tasty. I loved it."

"Jason, no wonder you're so sweet, my darling."

"Come on, babe, quit joking with me." I chuckled.

Patty broke off from our conversation and started to prepare our light supper.

I cleared the table and washed it off with a dishcloth, then took my mail to a comfortable lounge chair in the living room of the coach. The mail that we received, I sorted into two piles. In the morning I would take care of the bills that had to be paid. The balance of it would be checked out more carefully. The forwarding-address form we had changed upon our arrival at the resort seemed to be working fine. We could rest assured that the mail would continue to be sent to our present address until I called the post office at Old Forge to hold all mail until our return.

While Patty was still preparing our meal, I called the hospital and asked for Jack's room. He sounded very good on the telephone. He asked me how the interview had gone with Huntley. I filled him in with all the details and our visit to the Cactus Chuck Wagon Restaurant. He acknowledged that the future of the investigation looked bleak at this juncture. I told him that Huntley preferred that we not contact the authorities, desiring to have our investigation a separate entity. Jack agreed to this condition. I informed him that I would stay in touch with him or his office and keep him apprised of any developments.

"Jason, remember that if you have to take the coach on the road to follow up on any out-of-town leads, feel free to do so. Are you sure you can handle that big rig?" he asked with a chuckle.

"Buddy, I sure hope I can. Rest assured, if I have to use the coach, I'll be careful. I realize it's a big responsibility." I did not want to cause him any additional stress during his convalescence.

"I don't worry about you, Jason. I know you too well. I wish you luck and I wish we could be together, but it looks as though I'll be here in the hospital for a while longer. The doctor says I've picked up some infection in that shoulder wound. The medics are keeping a close watch. As you know, I've been shot before. They've got powerful antibiotics now."

I felt sorry to hear about the infection. He didn't need that. I assured Jack that I would stay in constant touch with Ruby and Bill Reidy. We concluded our conversation, I wished him the very best, and we hung up.

The bathroom in this coach was large. Racks supported two towels that indicated his and hers. I again recognized Ruby's touch. I washed my hands and combed my hair and went to the dining area.

Patty was busy placing the hot dogs on fresh buns. She had prepared plates of diced onions and pickle relish. Mustard was already on the table. Cabbage salad with pineapple was in a small glass dish, next to a small ovenproof bowl full of steaming hot beans. Patty had set a trivet under the hot dish, and at our places mats with napkins, frosted glasses of iced lemonade, and tableware. I had seated Patty and our feast was about to begin, when a knock came at the door. I went to answer it. Our neighbor, Art Panighetti, was standing there.

"Hello, Jason. Are you having supper? I don't want to interrupt, but would you and your wife like to come over later this evening for a while?"

"We were just about to sit down to eat. But yes, we'll come over after dinner. What time would be convenient?" I asked appreciatively.

"Why don't you make it around eight. Would that be okay?"

"That would be fine. We'll see you later then. Thanks for the invitation."

We said our goodbyes and I closed the door and returned to the table. Fortunately everything was still hot. I sat down. Patty had already put pickle relish and diced onions on her hot dog. I was glad there were two more hot dogs on the stove. I fixed my hot dog with plenty of condiments piled on it.

"Darling, I've been waiting to taste a good hot dog. It's delicious," I offered after tasting the first bite.

"I'm glad you like it, honey," Patty replied, patting her mouth with her napkin. "They are delicious," she agreed.

When we finished dinner, I cleared the table as Patty washed the dishes. I walked the trash over to the large metal dumpster located at the east end of the resort, then returned to the coach and read the daily newspaper until Patty had finished cleaning up the kitchen area. Even though the coach was large, there still wasn't a lot of extra space for the two of us in the kitchen, especially when trying to put things away.

The *Arizona Republic* is a good publication. It contains the latest news and activities throughout Maricopa County plus world, state, and regional sections. That evening the op-ed page contained well-written and informative editorials. When I finished scanning the highlights of the day's news, I placed the paper in the wooden magazine rack at the end of the davenport for a more in-depth review later.

We had arrived at the coach too late to catch Ruby at the office, and I assumed that she would be visiting Jack at the hospital later that night. He would bring her up to date on the Huntley interview that I had conducted. I'd be certain to call Ruby in the morning.

At about eight p.m., Patty and I went next door to the Panighettis. Art answered the door and invited us in.

Art introduced us to his wife, Marilyn, who was slender and attractive. Both of them were wearing sport clothes, Marilyn in a beige pant suit with an orange blouse and Art in a decorative cotton short-sleeved shirt with faded, deeply-creased blue denim jeans. We followed Art into the living room of their spacious coach, and engaged in a friendly conversation. Soon it seemed we had known Art and Marilyn for years.

We had so much in common, even beyond that we were all from upstate New York. During our conversation we gleaned that we had visited and enjoyed the same places in Syracuse: the Salt Museum, the local Burnet Park Zoo, the Syracuse Stage, and numerous other places. Art and I talked about Syracuse University football and their excellent basketball program. It was like old home week. While Art and I were having our discussion I noticed Patty and Marilyn deeply engrossed in conversation. The time flew by, and before we realized, it was after 10 p.m.

I carefully avoided going into any details of my ongoing investigation or disclosing the reason for our trip to Arizona being anything other than for pleasure and to avoid the snowstorms that frequent the northeast. I strongly believe in keeping business and friends in a separate category. This was a policy I had employed in my career as a member of the state troopers.

We finished the evening off with hot cups of decaf coffee and slices of coffee cake. Although always cognizant of trying to watch my waistline, I couldn't hurt Marilyn by refusing when she set my piece before me.

We left for our coach at midnight. It had been an enjoyable evening. We promised to reciprocate in the near future.

Patty and I went into our coach and quickly prepared for bed. After a brief goodnight kiss, we soon fell off to sleep.

CHAPTER SIX

We woke up to the ringing of our telephone. I pushed the covers back to get out of bed to answer it. It was our neighbor Marilyn.

"I hope I didn't wake you, but would it be possible to talk with Patty?" she asked apologetically.

"Just a moment. I'll get her for you," I answered surprised.

I told Patty that the call was for her.

"Hello?" Patty said a bit groggily.

After a brief conversation, Patty hung up and informed me that our new friend wanted her to attend the craft group at the resort. Patty had agreed to meet her at the clubhouse at 9:00 a.m. She also had apologized for waking us so early, but she had forgotten to mention it last night.

"Honey, you wouldn't mind if I go to the craft class with Marilyn?"

I knew that she liked crafts. "No, not at all, dearest. You don't have to ask me. I think it will be good for you. Keep in mind that there will be times that I'll have to be working on this case when you would get pretty bored following me around all day. Do you need any supplies for the craft class?" I asked.

"I'll find out today."

"Let me know later and we'll go out to a craft store," I replied.

"You're so sweet, hon. How come I was so fortunate to find you in my lifetime?" she teased.

"Ditto, sweetheart. While you're at the craft class I'll go over to the office to see Ruby and discuss the interview that I held with Mr. Huntley about his missing daughter."

Since Patty had to leave, we each had a quick cup of decaf and a bowl of cold cereal with bananas. While Patty prepared to meet Marilyn, I did up the dishes before I proceeded to get ready to meet Ruby at Flynn's Investigations. Before I left for the office, I called the hospital and talked with Jack for a few minutes. He sounded like his old self and even cracked a couple of jokes. I informed him where I was headed and he asked if everything was okay with the coach, again emphasizing that if I needed anything, I should just tell Ruby and it would be taken care of. I told him that the main thing was for him to get well. I finished the call and prepared to leave.

Patty and I embraced at the door. I set the briefcase down as I held her close to me. The kisses were warm and I told her how much I loved her.

"Be careful driving, Jason," she cautioned.

"I'll be careful, dear. Please don't worry so much. Have fun at the craft class, sweetheart."

I left the coach and entered the Camaro. It started at the first engagement of the ignition switch. But, how I missed my Bronco!

The traffic on I-10 was heavy eastbound. The drivers using this highway were going to work, to home, or to school. With semi-trailer trucks bumper to bumper, this was a true experience of defensive driving compared to the narrow highway system in the Adirondack Park of Northern New York. I had to be on my toes every moment. When I made my exit at 99th Avenue I observed an Arizona Highway Patrolman standing by the passenger side of a vehicle he had apparently just pulled over. I noticed his right hand gripping his pistol, which was still in the holster. He wasn't going to take any chances. As I passed down the ramp, I quickly glanced over and observed a seedy-looking character behind the wheel of an older-model Pontiac. The officer appeared to have everything under control.

I thought of my many hours on patrol, on the highways of my district in New York State. The memories were unforgettable. I had been so fortunate not to have been shot or assaulted during those stops. Civility seemed to prevail in that era. The number of officers today being maimed or killed is unforgivable in a supposedly civilized society. I knew I couldn't do a darn thing about it. People seemed deaf to this issue. It is the families that suffer the pains of their loss.

I continued on to the offices of Flynn Investigations. I located a parking place next to Ruby's car. There were several vehicles parked in the immediate area. I noticed some new landscaping in front of the office, different from our previous visit. Cactus plants prevailed, cleverly arranged on the small stones that covered the area in front of the office. I liked the display of the desert plant life, which would never survive in our part of the country. As I entered the office, Ruby greeted me with a big hello and a warm smile.

"Good morning, Jason. Where's Patty?" she asked quizzically.

"Good morning, Ruby. Patty decided to attend the craft class at the resort this morning."

"Very nice. You must be meeting some of the people at the resort. I know when I was there for a day preparing the interior of the coach I met several of the guests. They were so friendly."

"Yes, they're very friendly. It certainly seems like a nice place. We're very comfortable there, Ruby."

"That's good. If there is anything that you need, just call the office here." She changed the subject. "Tell me, Jason, what you thought of Mr. Huntley?" she asked, tapping her pen on the desk.

"I was impressed with him. He loves his daughter very much and there is no doubt that he's a father in crisis. He has no idea what happened to Christine. She went to Casa Grande in the ranch Jeep and never returned. He did indicate that he is pleased with the investigation that has been conducted by the police officials, but stressed to me that he wanted our investigation involvement a separate entity." I paused. "I just had a feeling by talking with him that something else is going on in his mind. I haven't put my finger on it yet. But whether she took off with someone or whether the person or persons who took her are making it impossible for her to call home, something is definitely amiss, Ruby. I've got a gut feeling about that. Have you heard anything at all from your sources?" I inquired.

"No, I haven't heard a thing. I will confidentially call some of our agency's contacts in law enforcement. I understand Jack would like you to work on this alone and follow any leads that you may develop or leads that we receive here at the office. This will give you more freedom of movement. You don't need any police detectives bird-dogging you, while they're munching on donuts. I know from what Jack tells me that you've made some law enforcement people look good in the past. This investigation appears to be sensitive in nature." She stopped for a moment to gather her thoughts before she continued. "Mr. Huntley is a very well known horse and cattle rancher and a well-respected member of the Casa Grande community. We want to do our job, but at the same time we want to avoid any bad publicity. From the reports that have come across my desk I can see that Christine was close to her father, but also had a streak of independence and possibly had dated some young men whom the father may have never met. We don't know that for certain, but it could be a consideration in this investigation."

I could see that Ruby was on top of this case when it came to the details. "Did you talk with Jack this morning, Ruby?" I inquired.

"Yes, I did, and he mentioned that you called him. He sounded better on the telephone. They are giving him strong medicine to combat the infection. He claims the treatment appears to be doing the job. His shoulder's a little less painful.

He's a tough Irishman. Believe me, Jason, he's a wonderful boss," she said, tearing up.

Again it warmed my heart to see that she was very fond of him.

"He'll be all right, Ruby. It'll just take time." I reached over and patted her shoulder.

She regained her composure. "By the way, Jason, Christmas is rapidly approaching. I've got to make our reservations at the Biltmore, or Jack will be disappointed. What would be a good time for you and Patty?" she asked.

"Ruby, I've been thinking it over. Wouldn't it be better if we postpone our celebration until Jack is able to join us?" I looked over, awaiting her reaction.

"Well, if that's how you feel, we will wait. Jack will understand, although he may not agree." She shrugged her shoulders showing a little annoyance. "Now that we've got that settled, how would you like a cup of coffee or tea?" she asked.

"Do you happen to have any green tea?" I asked with a smile.

"I was waiting for that question, Mr. Private Detective. Jack had me pick up some. He knows you well, Jason. One cup of steaming green tea, coming right up," she acknowledged.

The door from the waiting room opened and a distinguished, slender man in his sixties walked into Ruby's office while she was getting my tea. He smiled as he approached me, extending his hand.

"My name is Bill Reidy. You must be Jason Black, Jack's friend from New York," he said warmly.

"Yes, I am. It's a pleasure to meet you, Bill. I've heard many good things about you." I shook his hand. He had a firm grip.

"I understand you're working on the missing coed case." He had an Irish sparkle in his eyes, which were looking through his steel-rimmed glasses. He had an official air about him.

Ruby returned carrying a tray of coffee and tea in two mugs. "Good morning, Bill. Would you care to join us?"

"Sure. I'll get my coffee, Ruby, and be right back. I want to put my briefcase in my office."

"Would you like some lemon for your tea?" Ruby asked, turning to me.

"Not necessary, thanks. I love it straight," I replied.

Bill Reidy rejoined us in a few minutes. While we drank our coffee and tea, we discussed the Huntley case and the different possibilities that could apply. Bill had retired from the Syracuse PD and during his long professional career had been in charge of missing persons and youth matters. He was well versed in all phases of his former department and possessed a sharp mind sprinkled with his Irish wit. Along with supervising the day-to-day operations of the agency, he was working on a case that involved a forged codicil to a will for an elderly person and looking into a marital case where one of Jack's operatives had been threatened by an irate husband. The husband had been caught in the lens of a camera displaying his uncontrollable rage. Bill didn't go into any details, but it did have a touch of comedy when the unfaithful wife, in order to protect herself, tried to bribe the operative. Bill reminded us that in the world of private detectives, it is the marital cases that can create difficult situations. There are too many highly explosive emotions involved.

"Well, fellows, I'll leave you now as I have to run to the bank to make a deposit. Jason, if there is anything you need, just call me. If any information is developed I'll call you on the cell or at the coach," Ruby said as she headed for the door. "Bill, I'll be back shortly."

"I'll be here," Bill replied.

"See you later, Ruby," I called after her. "I may not be here when you return."

Bill and I talked for a while longer. He asked me if I had an agency credit card and a telephone calling card. I told him I was all set. However, I did mention the fact that I didn't have a firearm, not that I would need it, but just in case, for the wild, Wild West still existed.

Bill said he would check it out and see what he could do to

provide me with one.

He took me through the agency, showing me the record room where all of the cases had been filed since the inception of Flynn's Investigations. With the closing of the establishment next door Jack had picked up several more rooms and had furnished them with office furniture. During the tour I was amazed with this growth. I wondered to myself which office I would have if I had accepted Jack's offer to join his firm on a permanent basis.

"Bill, Jack has certainly enlarged his office space. Now, do you have an office in Tucson?" I was curious.

"No, Jason. I work out of my home at the moment. Jack has been looking at a small building in south Tucson, but I don't know for certain if he is going to acquire it."

"It seems to me that it would be a good place to open an office. Isn't there a lot activity in the area down there?" I asked.

"We have a little bit of everything there," he responded.

I told Bill that it was an honor to meet a retired lieutenant from the well known Syracuse PD. He thanked me and we said goodbye. Ruby, probably tied up at the bank, didn't return before I left the office.

I went to the parking area, entered the Camaro, and warmed it up before I left the lot. The car was in excellent condition and had plenty of power. I pulled onto 99th Avenue and headed toward Glendale Avenue to Luke Air Force Base. I had heard so much about it that I wanted to see it. When I approached the base, I pulled into a filling station and gassed the Camaro.

"Mister, that's some car you've got there." I could tell that this young man liked cars. He asked me if I had ever attended the auto show at the war memorial in Phoenix.

I told him that I really enjoyed driving the Camaro, and that I hoped to attend a car show in the future, as I had heard that the shows were well represented by a huge variety of dealers.

"Thank you, young man. Have a good day." I put the credit card slip in my wallet and left the filling station.

I noticed on my drive that more posters had been tacked on telephone poles regarding the missing coed, Christine Huntley. The students and volunteers had reached out throughout the entire State of Arizona. From Luke Air Force Base I took Glendale Avenue east to 59[th,] made a right-hand turn, and headed down toward Glendale Community College. The campus looked impressive from a distance. I drove through the entrance and toured the grounds. I noticed that they had a truck-driving area and automatically assumed that a semi-truck-driving class was in session because there was a sign on the rear of a trailer designating 'Student Driver.' When I went by, the student was slowly backing the rig between two lines of rubber cones. I imagined that this young man would soon be out on the highway system across the United States hauling various commodities from one point to another. After a few minutes of eyeballing the college, I left the grounds and drove to I-10, going west to the Cotton Lane exit and back to the coach at the Roadrunner Resort. I drove in past the security building, which was not manned and around the clubhouse. A dozen or so bicycles were parked near the entrance door. I could see through the windows that a group of ladies were working diligently on their projects. Patty Black, my wonderful wife, was apparently involved in this world of crafters.

I turned onto our street and proceeded to my parking space beside Jack's large coach.

Upon exiting the Camaro, I noticed that Art and Marilyn, were not at home next door, as their car was gone. Then I remembered that Marilyn was probably at crafts with Patty. I unlocked the coach and went inside. The red light of the answering machine flashed on and off. I immediately went over and hit the button.

"Jason, please call me at the office when you get in. I tried you on your cell phone and it indicated that customer was not available. That's why we issued you the phone, so we could stay in contact. Only kidding, Jason. Call me! Ruby—but you recognize my voice."

I clicked the button and looked at the cell phone in my shirt pocket. Ruby was correct. I had forgotten to turn the phone on.

I dialed Flynn's Investigations immediately to respond to Ruby's message.

"Flynn's Investigations, Ruby speaking." She sounded official. Was I going to be reprimanded for not having my cell phone activated?

"Jason here, what's up?" I waited for Ruby's comment.

"Where in the world have you been, Jason? I've been trying to call you for an hour," she said rather firmly.

"Sorry, Ruby. I plead guilty. I didn't have the cell on."

I heard her chuckle. "I'm fooling with you a little, Jason. Seriously, I received a telephone call from Jerome Huntley. He indicated he was calling from a pay phone knowing his phone was being monitored. He was all excited. Apparently he received a telephone call from a female who didn't or wouldn't give her name to him. All the female said was that Christine had been seen with a Bradley Carter. Then she hung up, according to Huntley." Ruby waited for my reply.

"Do you have any idea who this Bradley Carter is? Have you heard that name before? Did Huntley advise the police department of that information?" I asked excitedly.

"No, he did not. I asked him that question. He made clear that he wanted just you to have the information. Apparently he's not going to notify the police department at this time. I didn't ask him why he wasn't, and all he indicated was to convey the information to you. I contacted the University at Tucson and inquired if they had a student by that name. They checked their records, which reflected that no one by that name was currently enrolled, though a Bradley Carter had been a student at the university a year ago and dropped out. Supposedly he was from Denver, Colorado. They didn't offer any further information, apparently deciding that they had given me enough. That's all I can tell you."

"Thanks, Ruby. I'll call Huntley myself. There is a chance that he could have additional information. I'm sorry that I didn't have the cell turned on. I'm just not familiar with your western ways out here. We do things differently up in the mountains."

"Don't worry, Jason. I was just funning with you. I know how serious you can be." Ruby knew me well.

"By the way, did you talk with Jack today?" I inquired.

"Yes, I called him this morning. He was getting his bath and I heard a lot of laughing in the background. He indicated that he's feeling much better. The infection is beginning to show signs of improvement. He did say that he's getting a lot of visitors from the Phoenix PD and that some members of his old detective squad continue to visit him. Even some of his detractors apparently have stopped by. You know yourself, Jason, when it gets down to the basics, the majority of cops, active or retired, stick together, especially if one of them gets shot or killed."

"Ruby, very true." I paused. "Well, I'll call Huntley. If anything else develops, call me on the cell. I promise I'll have it on," I assured her.

"Thanks, Jason. I'm so happy that you and Patty are here. I hope I can take her shopping some time. By the way, Romeo, when we were together the other day Patty whispered to me that she's expecting."

"Oh, so she told you? Yes, we both are so happy about it." I was surprised, but pleased to learn that Patty had mentioned it to Ruby.

"I'm happy for you both, Jason." Ruby sounded very sincere. But I thought I detected a bit of sadness in her voice, too—not for Patty, but for her own unhappiness from the past over her divorce a few years ago.

We said our goodbyes. I went to my briefcase, retrieved Huntley's telephone number in Casa Grande, and put a call through to him informing him to call me from an unmonitored phone. He called me back in fifteen minutes and identified himself.

"Jerome, our secretary contacted me and gave me the name of Bradley Carter. Tell me, Jerome, did the voice of the female caller sound familiar to you?" I queried.

"After I called your office, I tried to remember if I ever had heard that voice before. She talked in a low tone and her voice was soft and rather muffled. I didn't recognize it. And I didn't detect any dialect or impediment in her speech to make it stand out."

"Jerome, I want you to think. Were there any background sounds during the time that you spoke with this person?" I asked.

"No, no. Well... wait a second. There **was** something. Yes, by gosh, I'm sure of it: there was music playing in the background. Like music from a jukebox. And there were muffled background sounds of other voices. The sounds were faint, and I was unable to make out any words. And now I'm not sure if I even heard that voice before or not. I'll have to think on that. If I can remember, I'll contact you or leave a message on your answering machine." His voice was shaky, erratic.

"I'd appreciate it, Jerome."

My call to Huntley came to a close with us both agreeing that we'd keep in touch. I made a few notes in my notebook, and in one of my entries I advised a revisit to the Cactus Chuck Wagon Restaurant in Casa Grande. I had a gut feeling that there was something more there. Perhaps something at the restaurant could possibly aid in this investigation.

Patty was still at the craft class, so I decided to make some telephone calls to the North Country. There was a two-hour time difference. The first call I placed was to Wilt. I thought he would be at his home in Boonville. I dialed the number, and Wilt answered on the third ring.

"Hello, Wilt here. Can I help you?"

"Wilt, this is Jason. How are you?" It was good to hear that familiar voice.

"Jason, is that you? I'm fine. How are you?" he replied warmly.

"I have a few minutes before Patty comes home from a craft class, so I thought I'd call my old friend and see how everything is going with you and Ruben."

"It's so good to hear from you. It seems that you've been

away a year or two. Ruben misses you both. He whines a lot and looks out the window toward the highway most of the time. Sometimes I take him with me in the pickup when I go out to look at a logging job. I'll tell you one thing, Jason. The other day I had him with me and I had to go into the supermarket to get a pound of coffee. You know the big parking lot by the store. Well, apparently Ruben was lying down in the seat and a fella opened the driver's side door on the Dodge. When I came out of the store I couldn't believe my eyes. Here was the guy lying in the parking lot with his right ankle in Ruben's jaws. Ruben wasn't biting the man, but was securely holding him. I told Ruben to get back in the truck. The door was open and the big dog released the man's ankle and leaped up on the seat. The guy on the ground—maybe a homeless—was whimpering and told me that he was cold and was just going to sit in the truck until he warmed up. I didn't know the guy, so I gave him a fiver and told him to go to the diner for a cup of hot coffee and a piece of pie."

"Was the man from the Adirondacks?" I asked curiously.

"He told me he was from South Carolina and was hitchhiking to Ft. Drum to see his twin brother who may be going overseas. I felt sorry for him." Wilt was always trying to help people.

"That was nice of you, Wilt. How's everything else over in the Old Forge area?" I was concerned about our log home.

"Good, Jason. After I checked your place and found everything in good shape, I stopped by John's Diner for a couple of hotcakes and coffee. It was like old home week. Dale Rush, Jack Falsey, and Charlie Perkins joined me and we had some great conversation. Were your ears burning, Jason?" he asked with a chuckle.

"Wish I could have been there with you fellows." I missed our meetings.

"Dale had his engine on the Stinson lying on the work bench at the marina. He and Jim Jenny are working on it together. You know Jenny is a crackerjack on engines, whether it's an airplane or a snowmobile. Business in Old Forge has been rather slow due to the lack of snow, but we'll eventually have snow and probably more than we want."

"What are you doing for Christmas?" Wilt had donned a Santa Claus suit on many December 25ths.

"I'll be dining with Charlie Perkins and his family. They've got a twenty-five-pound turkey. I can taste it now. Charlie's wife is a fine cook," he added. "What about you?"

"Christmas is just two days away and I haven't even picked up anything for Patty yet."

"You'd better get cracking, Jason."

"I will. It just seems so strange here among the palm trees to think about Christmas. Please say hello to the fellows for me." We chatted for a few minutes longer and said our goodbyes until next time. He informed me that he'd call if anything should arise on the home front.

I then called the hospital to talk with Jack. I was told that he was sleeping and the nurse suggested I call back later. I thanked her and said I would.

Patty returned from the craft class and she happily filled me in on her day with the ladies from the resort. The main project had been making table decorations for the potluck to be held on Christmas.

"Honey, would you like to attend the potluck? Oh, that's right, we're supposed to go to the Biltmore with Ruby. Has she mentioned it to you?" She frowned gently.

"Funny you asked. Just today Ruby wanted to know what time to make the reservations. I hope you're not disappointed, but I told her that I wanted to wait until Jack would be able to join us," I said sheepishly. "I probably should have checked with you first."

"But that's fine with me! I know how you feel about Jack. And I really would prefer to attend the potluck here. I hear there are some really great cooks."

"Sure, sweetheart, we can go if you'd like to. It would give us an opportunity to meet a few more of the residents. What will we be taking?"

"I thought I'd make a broccoli and cheese casserole. The

resort is furnishing the turkeys. How does that sound?" she asked.

"Sounds wonderful. You're making me hungry. I didn't have any lunch. Did you? And speaking of food, what's for dinner?"

"Yes, honey, I did have lunch. One of the girls went to the sub shop and picked up some sandwiches," she answered sheepishly. "I'm sorry. I didn't realize you hadn't eaten. I'll get busy right now with dinner."

Patty asked me to set the table, while she looked into the refrigerator to see what she had taken out of the freezer. "You've got your choice, honey. It's either pork chops or cube steaks," she said, turning around.

"If you have applesauce, I'd like the pork chops, if that's all right with you."

"Pork chops it is." She reached in and removed them. "I also have a box of pork dressing. That will be faster than potatoes. How does that sound?"

"Great!" I shot back.

She quickly prepared our dinner, broiling the chops, fixing the dressing, bringing out some leftover cabbage salad, and spooning out the applesauce. It wasn't too long before we were sitting down to eat the delicious, tender chops broiled just perfectly. I said grace, thanked God for all the blessings He had bestowed on us, and enjoyed the dinner that Patty had so skillfully prepared.

After dinner, Patty and I cleaned the kitchen. When everything was done we took a walk around the resort. The sun had begun to fall and the temperature was cooling. We had definitely decided that we'd only have the wreath that Patty had purchased for decoration and not buy a tree, as there were two or three trees decorated in the clubhouse.

Tonight we would be joining a few of the resort guests to sing some Christmas carols around the resort. When Patty was at crafts, several of the ladies had asked us to join the group.

About 7:00 p.m. we joined twenty some others in front of the administration office and proceeded to sing Christmas carols until 7:30. The night air was cold, but we quickly warmed with hot chocolate and cookies served at the clubhouse by the volunteer group. A good time was had by all.

At about 8:30 we returned to our coach. We watched a Christmas show on the television, I sipped a small glass of red wine, and Patty enjoyed a goblet of sparkling juice. We then retired to the bedroom as the combination of the cold night air and our drinks had made us both sleepy. We rapidly fell into a deep slumber in each other's arms after expressing our love.

CHAPTER SEVEN

I woke up with a start. A vehicle was passing in front of the coach. The heavy rumble of the engine was loud. I looked over to see Patty still in deep sleep. I carefully got out of bed so I wouldn't disturb her. It was 5:45 a.m.—seemingly early, but I guess part of me was still on eastern time. I went into the bathroom and closed the door.

Hot water helped refresh me as I lathered my face. I took my straight razor and slapped it against the leather strap. The blade's edge was sharp as I drew it down my left cheek. My beard was heavy, and no other razor had given me success. When I finished I splashed some aftershave lotion on my face. It felt invigorating. I then quickly took a shower, following my hot rinse with cold water, which left me fully awake and alert. I had been surprised to learn that the water in Arizona was so cold. I put my robe on and went out into the kitchen area. To my surprise, Patty was making the coffee. I went over to her and gave her a quick hug.

"I hope I didn't wake you, hon." I said, feeling sheepish. "What were you planning for breakfast?" I asked.

"Poached eggs on whole wheat toast. Is that all right?"

"That'll be fine, darling. Oh, and Merry Christmas! I almost forgot."

"Merry Christmas, Jason," she replied, cheerfully as she turned to the stove.

The poached eggs were perfect. Patty had added a little warm milk on top of the whole-wheat toast. We both had second cups of decaf. After breakfast we cleaned the kitchen. The Christmas potluck dinner would be held in the clubhouse at one o'clock.

As Patty set about to prepare her broccoli and cheese casserole, I took a bucket of warm sudsy water and went outside to wash the Camaro. I had just finished drying it off when Art came outside. He walked over as I was putting the finishing touches on my wash job.

"Good morning, Jason. Merry Christmas. I see that you're getting it all cleaned up. That's a good-looking Camaro. Is it yours?" he asked quizzically.

"And Merry Christmas to you, Art. No, the car isn't mine. It was loaned to me by a friend." I didn't want to blow my cover at this time and tell him who the car belonged to.

"It's certainly in wonderful condition," Art replied as he admired the car. "By the way, do you ever travel to Syracuse anymore?" Art asked curiously.

"Yes, sometimes I go down to shop. With Patty expecting in a few months, we will be purchasing some things there for the baby's nursery."

During our chat I learned that Art and Marilyn were also going to the Christmas potluck. We made arrangements to sit together. I knew that Art was a retired businessman from the Syracuse area. Now he and his wife were enjoying the fruits of their labor.

It was shortly before one when nearly a hundred residents of the resort sat down for our Christmas potluck. I looked around the room of the clubhouse, enjoying the Christmas decorations. Three artificial Christmas trees were decorated with angels mounted on the top of each. The colored lights were turned on and the illumination brought out the silvery tinsel evenly distributed from the top to the bottom of each tree with candy canes of all sizes and assorted decorations hung on the branches. Various cut-outs of Santa Claus riding in his gift-laden sleigh pulled by reindeer appeared on the walls of the large dining room, and wreaths hung on the doors and windows. As everyone talked gaily, I could feel the Christmas spirit throughout the room. The craft gals had done an outstanding job on the decorations to help the celebration.

The park manager thanked us all for coming, bade us all a Merry Christmas, and asked one of the residents to give the grace before our dinner.

Each table was called separately, and the park residents proceeded to line up before the tables displaying an array of assorted cuisine. Sliced turkey and ham served as the main entrees, with platters of mashed potatoes, bowls of dressing, various dishes of assorted vegetables, and any kind of cranberry combination imaginable. Assorted salads blossomed with fresh lettuce, tomatoes, cucumbers, and radishes, and arrays of pickles—including dill, sweet, and corn relish—placed next to the salads. A separate table had been set up to handle a wide variety of pies, cakes, and Christmas cookies. Patty and I were glad we had brought our larger dinner plates. Soon we were all seated and enjoying the banquet.

The food was delicious, and there was plenty of chatter throughout the room. Patty and Marilyn were engaged in steady conversation. I was so happy Patty had found someone at the resort with whom she had so much in common. Art and I talked about Arizona and all the wonderful places it offered, including the Grand Canyon with the nearby Canyon Village, and Sedona with its breathtaking red rock, just to name a couple. Art vowed that if he were a younger man he would love to reside in the Sedona area if only for the scenic beauty that it provided.

After completing the main course, we each went up to select a dessert. Patty opted for pumpkin pie with whipped cream, and I chose a piece of mincemeat pie with a slice of strong cheese. Art and Marilyn both enjoyed a piece of chocolate fudge cake. Everyone was fully in a festive mood.

The manager of the resort stood up, gave a short speech hoping we all had enjoyed ourselves, and wished all of us a very Merry Christmas. With the exception of the cleanup group, we picked up our dishes and left the clubhouse. Marilyn and Patty walked ahead of Art and me. We talked about how delightful the potluck was and the hard work that it had taken to prepare the numerous dishes that we all savored. The Christmas potluck had been wonderful.

As we went to the coach we thanked the Panighettis for joining us and bid them a joyous rest of the day. Patty and I did up the dishes and put everything away. I had hoped to visit Jack at the hospital, but now it was getting late. I decided to call him instead. Again he was sleeping. I asked the nurse to let Jack know I had called and please to wish him a very Merry Christmas.

I decided to telephone our friends in Boonville and Old Forge. Fortunately I found everyone at home. Charlie Perkins and his family were first on my list to be contacted because I knew Wilt would be there for dinner.

"Hello, Charlie Perkins speaking."

"Jason here. Merry Christmas from sunny Arizona to you and your family, Charlie!"

"The same to you, Jason! How are you and Patty doing out there?"

"Fine, Charlie. Do you have any snow yet?"

"We've got about a foot on the level and a little more up on Tug Hill. There's enough for the snowmobiling folks. I heard a few days ago when it got up to 50 degrees that some kids went out on First Lake north of Old Forge and went through the ice, but thank God no one was hurt. I tell my children all the time to be careful riding those sleds." Charlie loves his family and always worries when he's away on his trips to Vermont.

"Well, Charlie, you folks have a grand day. Did Wilt come to dinner with you? He told me you had asked him." I especially wanted to say Merry Christmas to my good friend.

"Sorry, Jason. He left about an hour ago."

"I'll give him a call at his home later. I've got some other calls to make. We think of you all the time." We said our goodbyes and Charlie told me to say hello to Patty for him.

"Patty, Charlie Perkins sends his regards," I said to Patty

next to me.

"That was thoughtful of him. I hope they're having a nice Christmas," Patty replied, then looked over at me. "Gee, Jason, after that huge dinner, are you going to want to eat tonight?" she asked.

"Yes, they've had a wonderful day. As for us, you're right. We had such a big dinner at the clubhouse. I still feel stuffed, sweetheart. Let's just have a BLT. We should have something so we don't get hungry later." I responded.

"Sounds like a good idea."

"Patty, I know we agreed to wait till we got back home to have our Christmas celebration, but the other day on my way home from Flynn's office, I did stop and picked up a small gift for you. I just couldn't let Christmas go by without doing something," I explained.

Patty turned toward me. "I'm so happy you said that, because I have a gift for you! I just didn't know how to present it, if you had nothing to give me." She went to the bedroom and brought out a beautifully wrapped package, which she presented to me.

I reached into my briefcase and took out a small, gold-wrapped box. Her eyes sparkled as I handed it to her. "Go ahead, hon. Open yours first."

She quickly unwrapped it and opened the box. A smile came across her face as she viewed the silver and turquoise bracelet and slipped it on her wrist. "Jason, I love it! Now open yours."

I hurriedly removed the paper and took the cover off the box which contained a knitted-wool gray and purple scarf, evidently representing the symbolic colors from my years in uniform during my service in the state troopers.

"Now, you see why I've been spending so much time at crafts," she said, beaming proudly.

"Dearest, I love it. You know how much the state troopers always meant to me," I said as I pulled her toward me and gave her a loving embrace.

The balance of the afternoon, we took a stroll around the

resort to walk off our meal, and returned home to take a short nap.

It was about 6:45 when the aroma of the sizzling bacon wafted in from the kitchen area. Although the coach was a large one, anyone in it could anticipate what was going to be on the menu for a meal. I got up from the comfortable lounge chair and went to the kitchen.

"Patty, can I help you with our supper?" I queried.

"Sweetheart, you can set the table." A broad smile came across her face.

I went to the cabinet and took out two napkins, two water glasses, and two place settings. Patty was slicing a large tomato. The lettuce sat in a bowl with some ice cubes on top to give it crispness.

I opened the refrigerator door and to my surprise found a freshly prepared potato salad garnished with a tomato flower as well as boiled eggs that had been sliced thin and placed in a circle around the flower. Paprika sprinkled on it gave it some color. Patty was known for her salads. This particular one offered a mix of salad dressing and mustard in the right proportions.

"Jason, while you're at the refrigerator, please put the salad on the table. Are you any hungrier, honey?"

"I wasn't, dear, but now I am. Thank you for making this delicacy. I love all your salads."

My taste buds began to send a message. "Let's eat."

We both enjoyed the BLT's and potato salad. To my delight Patty had brought out a pitcher of lemonade made with our lemons that I hadn't seen when I had the door open. She was full of surprises.

The evening passed by rapidly. Patty put some music on the CD player. We especially enjoyed listening to *"By the Time I Get To Phoenix."* We both love the song.

It was 10:00 p.m. when I reached up to the light switch and clicked it off. I rolled over, placed my arms around Patty, and brought her close to me. Our passion and love for each other grew stronger as we made love and then fell off to sleep in each other's arms.

CHAPTER EIGHT

Morning came quickly. Patty was already in the kitchen and the aroma of coffee filled my nostrils. I climbed out of bed.

"Are you up, darling?" she asked, apparently hearing me in the bathroom.

"Yes, sweetheart. I'm shaving and then I'm going to take a fast shower."

"Okay, honey. You didn't even hear me when I got up. I took my shower early. We're going to have French toast this morning. Is that okay with you?"

"That sounds good to me. Just two slices. After that Christmas pot luck, I've got to cut down."

We sat down to enjoy our breakfast, quickly cleaned up the kitchen, and Patty turned toward me.

"Okay, sweet. Everything is ship-shape. Now then, if you don't mind, I'm going to the clubhouse with Marilyn to join the crafters again."

"That's fine with me. You ladies must have quite a group involved in that class."

"There are about forty of us and I'm really enjoying the gals."

"It will give you something fun to do, Patty, while I'm involved. Also, remember Ruby wants to take you shopping some afternoon," I reminded her.

"I'll call her tomorrow. Maybe we could all go to see Jack

at the hospital tomorrow evening."

"Good idea! He's on my mind all the time. It isn't fun being in a hospital, and knowing Jack as I do, I'm sure he must be getting more restless as the days go by. We'll take him a new magazine when we go to see him. Not to change the subject, but do you think Ruben misses us?" I sure was missing him.

"You bet he does—especially you, Jason. I bet he's driving Wilt out of his mind. You know how Ruben paces back and forth when we are gone."

"If I have any closure on this case, maybe we'll see him sooner rather than later. Hope so, anyway." I was missing my mountains and my home.

Patty got ready to leave for the clubhouse while I finished dressing. She gave me a kiss on the cheek and left the coach. Marilyn had apparently been waiting for her outside. I could see the two of them talking as they walked toward the clubhouse to meet the other crafters.

I put on a pair of beige slacks with a yellow and brown knit golf shirt. On one of my trips to Flynn's, I had picked up a pair of western-style-boots with a good brand name at a western clothing shop. They were made of brown leather, with pointed toes. They weren't quite broken in, so when I pulled them on I had to give each a pretty good tug. But they felt comfortable on my feet. I finished combing my hair, then splashed on some shaving lotion and a dash of cologne.

I called Ruby at Flynn Investigations to see about any news regarding the Christine Huntley case.

"Good morning, Ruby. Did you have a good Christmas?" I asked.

"Yes, I did, Jason. I spent part of the day with Jack at the hospital. He's looking a lot better, and the infection has lessened, thanks to the antibiotics. They worked well. I tried to call you yesterday afternoon, but I didn't leave a message. I knew if you were there you would have picked it up on the third ring." I could tell by the tone in her voice that Ruby was still worried about Jack. We all were.

"Ruby, I'm going to spend the biggest part of the day in the Casa Grande area. I'll have my cell phone on if you want to contact me. Have there been any new leads since the last time we talked?" I hoped there had been.

"There was a possible sighting on Central Avenue in downtown Phoenix. Captain Jay Silverstein had one of his detectives check it out, but it turned out to be negative. If I should receive any calls concerning the case, I'll let you know immediately. The father must be extremely upset that there are no leads. I feel so sorry for him."

"I'm certain he is," I agreed. "Ruby, getting back to Jack, do you have any idea when he will be released from the hospital?"

"No, I don't. I believe that he will be going to a nursing home for a couple weeks for rehab once he is discharged. He's feeling a lot better, at least. I sure do miss him, Jason." Her voice began to crack.

"I know you do," I said gently. "Well, I'd better get going, Ruby. The traffic is heavy on I-10. I could take Route 85, but that highway is becoming so dangerous. The last time Patty and I were on it we had a near miss."

"You're right. It's like a death trap. Take care, Jason. I'll talk with you later."

I left the coach and locked the door. As I glanced over at Arthur's coach I noticed that they hadn't picked up their newspaper. I picked it up and laid it on their front step.

The Camaro started up right away. I wished that I owned it, especially for the good gas mileage. The other attribute was the maneuverability in heavy traffic; it was the perfect vehicle for tailing the principals of a domestic case. As I headed out of the resort I had to slow down for the speed bumps. There were six of them on the exit roadway. Arthur had explained that they had been added when some of the residents had failed to obey the five-miles-per-hour speed limit inside the resort.

Soon I was on I-10 and headed east. I was able to reach 35th Avenue before the eastbound lanes started to slow down to a creep with people going to work, tourists passing through

Phoenix, and huge semi-trailers traveling bumper to bumper. Fast-growing Maricopa County was outdistancing the planning boards of the highway builders. The main arteries were already becoming antiquated. Millions of vehicles cross I-10 three hundred and sixty-five days a year. I looked down at the speedometer. It read five miles per hour. Thirty-five minutes passed before I was southbound toward Casa Grande. I noticed that northbound traffic was heavy coming in from Tucson and Casa Grande. Some of that same traffic would be headed southbound on I-10 in a few hours.

The Camaro purred like a kitten. Christine Huntley was on my mind. Why did she leave the Jeep at the intersection of Interstates 10 and 8? I mulled over several more questions. Did she stop to help someone? Did she meet Bradley Carter, the dropout from the University of Arizona? Did she just run away? Did someone abduct her? There had to be an answer somewhere. And, the final question: would I be able to bring this case to a successful conclusion?

This area was not my beloved Adirondacks that I knew so well. I felt like I was starting out into a jungle not knowing what or who was on the path around the next corner. My plan for the day was to visit the Cactus Chuck Wagon Restaurant again. I still had that gut feeling that someone there might know something about the disappearance of Christine. The telephone call that Jerome Huntley had received about Bradley Carter from Denver, Colorado only added to the mystery. Who was the person who called Huntley with that information? That question could be key to the case.

I pulled into the parking lot of the restaurant around 11:45. It was a little early for lunch. I parked between two pickup trucks, each towing a horse trailer. I noticed that one of the trailers was empty and the other contained two black horses. I heard one of them snort. They were a matched pair and appeared to be highly spirited. The stench of horse manure tinged the air. I got out of the car and walked toward the restaurant. My new western boots were still stiff. To other people I might have appeared to be a little bowlegged. "Gosh, now they hurt," I said to myself.

A maroon convertible pulled into the parking lot, narrowly missing me. The fellow's radio blasted hard rock music. An earring hung from his left ear. This dude appeared to be into his music and wasn't paying any attention to the pedestrian, me. What I wanted to do, but didn't, was to pull him out of the car and explain to him the proper way to drive into a parking area. I continued on to the restaurant. The wooden door swung in. A hostess was standing behind a podium with a menu in her hand. She was wearing a black cowboy hat. It must have been a little large for her head, because it was down over her eyebrows. She looked up at me with a slight smile.

"Smoking or non-smoking, sir?" she asked cordially.

"Non-smoking, please," I responded.

"Follow me, please."

I fell in behind her. She led me to a booth made of pine with a cushioned seat. Arriving early for lunch gave me a choice of tables. I was satisfied with this one, as it faced the door, giving me a good view of anyone entering the restaurant. I looked over the menu. The specials were the same as on the day when Patty and I had stopped by. My new western boots had become so extremely uncomfortable that, as I sat there trying to decide what to order, I realized I should have brought along another pair of shoes.

In a few minutes the waitress appeared with her pad. "May I take your drink order?" she asked. Then she added, "Didn't I wait on you a few days ago? You were with an attractive blond, I believe."

"Yes. You're Marie, aren't you?" Her name on the tag attached to her uniform reminded me.

"Yes, I am. May I get you a drink, sir?" she repeated with a slight grin on her face.

"I'll have pink lemonade and a pork barbecue sandwich with plenty of barbecue sauce. Oh, and a dish of coleslaw, if you have it." I liked that combination, especially with the coleslaw on top of the barbecue.

"Yes, sir," she said as she wrote the order.

"Please just call me Jason. I'm not used to being addressed as sir."

"Okay, Jason. I'll put your order in."

My instincts still told me that someone here at the restaurant knew something about Christine's disappearance. Time would allow me to learn whether or not my hunch was correct.

Marie returned in a few minutes with my order. The barbecue was steaming hot and the coleslaw was freshly prepared. The ice cubes in the glass of pink lemonade crackled as she set it down before me. "Here you are, Jason. I hope you enjoy your lunch." She brought along extra napkins.

"It looks great. Thank you, Marie." I quickly asked her, "Marie, about your friend, Christine, who is missing. Have you heard anything at all regarding her disappearance?" It was a shot in the dark. I watched her closely for any reaction. She hesitated, and her smiling face changed to an expression of sadness.

"No, Jason, I haven't heard anything, except that she may be with an old acquaintance from the University of Arizona." She pulled out the chair opposite me and sat down. I was surprised, but was glad of this opportunity to probe her further. By her actions, I could see she wanted desperately to talk to someone. My prior experience as an investigator alerted me.

"Marie, I'm a writer and I'm interested in this as a human interest story." I didn't want to tell her I was a private detective. I used this ploy in an attempt to disguise my interest in the case. I knew that I had to be careful about the questions I posed.

"I see. Jason, I'm sort of busy now, but I will be off duty in a couple of hours. I could talk to you then." I was surprised that she was readily willing to talk with me. She added, "I drive the red Chevy pickup out in the parking lot. I'll meet you out there at two."

"Thank you, Marie. I'll be there. I'm driving the white Camaro. I believe I'm parked a couple of spaces from your truck. I have to go to a bookstore in the meantime, but I will meet you at 2:00 p.m. as you suggest. Thanks, Marie." She smiled, but her eyes were troubled.

I finished my barbecue and drank the rest of the lemonade. The luncheon customers had begun entering the Chuck Wagon. It was a unique restaurant, and I surmised that possibly the same crowd had their lunch there routinely. The staff consisted of a counter person and two other waitresses besides Marie.

I took a few minutes to study further the interior of the Chuck Wagon Restaurant with its southwestern motif. Several western-style saddles with saddle horns and stirrups hung in each corner on large wooden pegs. In addition, old-style pots and pans that one could envision being attached to the sides of chuck wagons of yesteryear were hanging from the ceiling, and several antique rifles and pistols rested in glass-enclosed wooden cases. Two brightly colored Indian blankets hung from metal rods, starting near the ceiling and draping toward the floor. A visitor to the restaurant could easily bump into the live cactus plants in three metal containers. I realized that the owner of this privately owned business possessed a flair for interior decorating. This second visit, I continued to have a good feeling about the Chuck Wagon Restaurant. One couldn't help but like the place. Attached to the walls were long thin strips of four-inch boards containing dozens of small wooden pegs for the large hats of the local ranch hands and office workers who frequented the place.

I made mental notes of everything I observed. After I paid my check I stopped at the restroom to wash my hands. The odor of the delicious barbecue sauce—some of the most delicious I had ever tasted—was clinging to my fingers. Mounted on the shelf above the sinks in the restroom was a small mechanical bucking bronco on which sat a cowboy. Every so often the bronco would raise its rear legs and then the front legs. I'd never seen anything like that before, perhaps a bit weird.

When I went outside I could still smell the barbecue aroma in the air. The parking lot was full of pickups and cars. I was surprised to see two Indian ponies tied to a small hitching rail at the end of the lot munching on hay that was mounted on a set of poles directly in front of them. When I got into the car, one of them looked over at me. Both ponies sported brown western-style saddles. I chuckled to myself, started the Camaro, and left the parking lot. I would return at 2:00 p.m. to meet Marie. Finally, a lead—I hoped.

As I drove down North Pila Avenue, many memories flashed in my mind of my days in the troopers and my interaction with the many citizens I encountered on my investigations. It was the waitresses, school crossing guards, teachers, laborers, and other people from all walks of life who had helped me close many of my assigned cases. If it hadn't been for them, some of the cases would still be open without proper closure. Hopefully now, as a private investigator, I would be able to glean some information from Marie, the waitress, which possibly could lead to a clue in solving the mystery of the missing Christine Huntley. My attempt to develop useful information might result in a dead end, but if I didn't make this effort, nothing would be gained.

Jerome Huntley had at the onset of this investigation requested that Flynn's Investigations keep their participation in the case confidential at this juncture. As a private detective assigned to the case I couldn't go against the wishes of the client, but on the other hand I felt that I had to pursue any leads that I had been fortunate enough to develop.

One such case I had worked on in the past had been a large credit-card fraud, in my position as a bank investigator after retiring from the state troopers. My supervisor had slammed a manila folder down on my desk containing a cold case and had said in a gruff voice, "Black, see what you can do with this one." I picked up the folder after he left my office and read the entire contents. It involved fraudulent credit-card purchases totaling more than $10,000 worth of goods and services. The only information the folder revealed was the fact that a waitress at a local fast-food restaurant might be able to shed some light on the case. The supervisor had worked the case previously, but had been unable to locate the waitress.

I can remember that I took the folder, stopped at the restaurant in question during a time when the customer traffic was light, and asked to see the waitress. We sat at a table and talked.

"Why are you questioning me?" she inquired.

I went right to the point and sent out the fishing line, so to speak. I told her point blank, "You're in trouble, young lady." Sternly I continued, "You can either handle the matter in a court of law, or you can handle it with me and the bank I represent. Which way do you prefer?" I kept my voice sharp. Tears began streaming down her cheeks. I loaned her my clean handkerchief and she dabbed her eyes, wiping the tears away.

"Mr. Black, I was with the guy who made some of those purchases in Utica." She fought to control her tears.

That was the break I was looking for. As a result of this interview, I was able to close the case and collect the entire $10,000-plus over a period of time. The bank was interested only in recovering the funds and did not pursue a criminal action. The case involved the son of a prominent dentist and nine of this young man's friends, all respected young businessmen from the area where the fraud had been perpetrated. It was the insidious type of fraud that increases insurance rates and hits unsuspecting people in their wallets.

Now it was years later as I pulled into a gas station and filled the tank on my friend Jack's Camaro. The price of gasoline seemed to be inching up. Backroom board members of the oil industry win, while the poor grunt at the gas pump pays the price. I had planned to stop by the Huntley ranch, but decided against it until I was able to develop some concrete information.

During my initial interview with Huntley everything appeared to be above board. I observed a father genuinely suffering from the disappearance of his daughter. I assumed the relationship between Christine and her father was a congenial one, with a father's love for his daughter. From outward appearances Christine had all the material things that a young woman could ever imagine. The exception, of course, was the loss of her mother a year before. Any loss of a family member is a shock to the dynamics of the family unit. I attempted to put all the pieces together up to this point, but there were still unresolved questions.

It was 1:55 p.m. when I drove into the parking lot of the Cactus Chuck Wagon Restaurant. I pulled in on the far side of Marie's red Chevrolet pickup. I shut the car off and reached over and grabbed my briefcase from the back seat. It was 2:10 p.m. when Marie opened the passenger door of the Camaro and slid in.

"Hello, Marie, thank you for meeting me. Do you feel comfortable talking with me here in the parking lot, or would you prefer another location?" I asked. "By the way, what is your last name?"

"No problem. This is fine. And my last name is Martin. I don't have a great deal of information. Seriously, are you a writer?" she inquired, studying my face.

I knew I had to be up front with Marie and I realized that I had to win her trust.

"Marie, I am a writer. However, I also am a private investigator for Flynn Investigations." I took out my identification card. "We are located on 99th Avenue and we're listed in the yellow pages of the Phoenix telephone directory. This is my ID issued to me by the gentleman who owns the agency, Jack Flynn, a private investigator like myself. I'm telling you this and counting on you to keep this interview confidential. Will you?" I wanted to insure I had her trust.

"Jason, I've been a waitress for a long time. That is my occupation. This job puts me in a position to be close to people, and people talk. If I ever revealed all that I know about happenings and who is associated with this one or that one, I'd be dead. No, Jason, I keep my mouth shut and my ears open. I love working at the Chuck Wagon. The owner is a wonderful man and the cooks and other waitresses are great to work with, and we serve the best barbecue in town. However, as you may have heard or presumed, a lot of chatter goes on inside those four walls."

"I assumed that, Marie. Thanks. Now, what can you tell me about Christine Huntley?" I inquired.

"I am a little older than Christine. I've known her since I was in grade school. She is from a fine family. Her mom passed away about a year ago in that terrible accident. Mr. Huntley, the father, took the death very badly, and Christine was destroyed. It bothered Christine immensely about her mom's passing. She took time off from school. It was a sad time for everybody. Mrs. Huntley was well known and was involved in many civic programs here in Casa Grande. She also volunteered at the hospital and at our local library. She was respected and loved by everyone that knew her," Marie shook her head sadly.

"All I have heard about her has been positive, Marie. Now let's focus on Christine. Does she have a special friend or a boyfriend that you know of?" I asked.

"Christine is very attractive. But she didn't date very much in high school because she went home after school to help with the ranch chores. She did attend the junior prom and the senior prom in high school, I think, and her escorts, I believe, were a couple of local boys. Really, Jason, during that time of her life she more or less helped around the ranch. She loves horses and had several spirited ones that her mom and dad had given her. She loved to ride."

"How about college? Did you ever see her with anyone from the university?"

"I believe that she came into the Chuck Wagon a few times with different college friends. Let me think....Yes, there was one fellow that she came in with several times about a year and a half ago. Now, let's see...." Marie frowned, concentrating. "Yes, I remember now. His name was Carter. Yes, that's it. Bradley Carter. He was from Denver, Colorado. I remember. He was a handsome guy. He told me that he loved to shoot the rapids on a wild river. He seemed like a nice person. Now it's coming back to me. Christine told me later that he became too possessive and that she had broken off from dating him. I think she mentioned that he had left school about a year or so ago.

He took their break-up very hard." She paused. "There is something else that happened, but I can't seem to remember what it was. Something out at the ranch, I believe." I could see her searching her memory for any additional information.

"That's very interesting." I added to my hurried notes. I didn't want to hit her with my next question, but I felt this was the opportunity.

"Marie, this question I'm going to ask is an important one. Before you give me the answer, I want you to think carefully. All I ask is for you to be honest with me. Will you do that for me?"

"Yes, I'll try."

"Marie, did you call the Huntley ranch a few days ago and tell Mr. Huntley that you saw Christine with Bradley Carter?" I noticed tears forming in her eyes. She started to cry. I gave her a tissue to dry her eyes. She didn't respond to my question while she was sobbing. Then she answered.

"Yes, it was me. I know it wasn't right for me to call Mr. Huntley that way, but I know how much he loves Christine. I thought of writing a note, but I figured I could just disguise my voice and make a quick call. That's why I did it. I know it wasn't right for me not to tell him who was calling." Tears appeared again in her eyes. She dropped her chin.

"Thank you for being honest with me, Marie. Can you tell me when you last saw them together?" I inquired.

"It was the day that she came into town with her dad's Jeep. She drove into our parking lot, and when she did Brad Carter got out of a small sports car and went over to the driver's side of the Jeep. I happened to be cleaning the front-door glass and was outside with a full view of the parking lot. I was surprised to see him and I was further amazed when they both came into the Chuck Wagon." She spoke freely now.

I jotted down the information on my pad. "Did you see what type of sports car he got out of?"

"I believe it was a 1986 Mazda RX 7. It looked like my cousin's car, a dark color, maybe a gray."

"Did you happen to see the plate number?" I queried.

"No, I didn't see the number, but probably a Colorado plate. That's where he's from."

"Did you have any conversation with them? Or did you hear any of their conversation?"

"I did wait on them. I noticed that when I approached their table they were talking in low tones. I think they just had coffee. The Chuck Wagon was very busy, so I didn't have a chance to talk with them. As I said, Christine had introduced Bradley to me over a year before. The truth is that at that time they had been seeing each other regularly, maybe on the sly. I don't know if she ever took Bradley out to the ranch. I can't recall exactly, but I think its almost been a year since they broke up. It was then that Christine told me how he had changed."

"What does he look like?" I asked, jotting down the information she had given me.

"He's about 23 years old. I would say he is well over six foot—say six foot three inches in height. He weighs close to two hundred pounds, I'd say. His long hair and eyes are brown. Always kind of hard-looking, I thought. He usually wears denim clothing."

"Do you know if he ever assaulted her?"

"I did observe him twist her arm once. He seemed to have a hot temper, and Christine once told me he was jealous and that was one of the reasons for her break-up with him. Christine is popular and went on to date several fellows. Bradley couldn't stand to see her with another man."

"How do you know this, Marie?" I asked. "I can't understand why you have not gone to the authorities with this information." I searched her face for her reaction.

She coughed and her face flushed. "I wanted to. I didn't want to get involved or cause any trouble for Brad. He was always nice enough to me. What if she went with him willingly? I didn't know what to think!" She caught her breath and went on to answer my question. "But Christine inferred on several occasions how demanding he was becoming. Jason, I used to be invited to the ranch and Christine and I would take long horseback rides together. We were quite close at the time. She is a wonderful girl."

"Is there anything more that you remember on that day they met here? The day she drove her dad's Jeep to town?" I pressed her.

"I really can't think of anything that would help you locate her. I wish I could! Except, well—wait a minute. There **was** something. Bradley did mention the Arizona Biltmore Resort. You know that it's located in Phoenix. I believe it is on Missouri Avenue. I went there to apply for a waitress job at one time."

"Concerning the Biltmore, is there anything else he said? Why would he bring it up?"

"He mentioned it only that once while they were in the restaurant, as far as I know. I **do** know he took her there at least once to play golf. Christine is an avid golfer. And she told me that Bradley had wanted to become a professional one."

I pressed her further. "Do you have any idea why he dropped out of the university?"

"Christine did tell me something about him being found in possession of drugs. I heard afterwards that he left the university and went back to Colorado."

"And you didn't tell the police any of this?" I could not disguise my surprise.

"I was never interviewed by the police," she retorted, trying to justify her position.

"Okay. Sorry." I kept the pressure on. "When they left the Chuck Wagon that day, did you see what direction they each went in?"

"Well, I thought it was odd that when they left she didn't say goodbye to me, but I just figured it was because I was really busy. I saw her drive away by herself, so there was no cause to think there was anything wrong. That's all I know, Jason. Really. You probably already heard that her dad's Jeep was found near the intersection of Route 8 and I-10."

"Yes, I'm aware of that. Now, Marie, if there's anything else that you want to share with me, please tell me."

"Well, it might be important that Bradley is an only child and likes to get his own way. He can be ornery, if he doesn't according to what Christine has told me in the past. He's from a wealthy family and has always gotten what he wanted, according to her. I only met him a few times with Christine, and on those occasions he was always quiet. Maybe he thought I was from the other side of the tracks, so to speak. I didn't know him very well, so I can't really make any type of judgment. I do know, as I said, that he was possessive of Christine. That's all I can tell you."

I nodded my acknowledgement. "I certainly appreciate you meeting me, Marie, and I thank you for the information. At this time I'd appreciate complete confidentiality until I can explore the case further. And will you kindly contact me if you come into possession of additional information pertaining to Christine and Bradley? Here's my business card. I've written my Arizona telephone number on the back," I said.

"I promise I'll call you if I hear anything." Relief showed clearly in her face.

"Thanks again. I certainly appreciate your cooperation."

"It was good to meet you, Jason. I've been so worried. I hope that nothing bad has happened to Christine."

"Let's hope for the best, Marie. I hope not, too."

Marie got out of the Camaro and climbed into her red Chevy pickup. She backed out of the parking space and drove away. I completed my notes, and in a few minutes left the parking lot and headed toward Route 8. I glanced at my watch: late afternoon. I stopped at the intersection of Route 8 and I-10. Traffic was heavy as usual.

Cautiously I pulled off the paved portion of the highway at the intersection and got out of the Camaro. I could see tracks that led to the slight embankment where I believed the Jeep had been found. My cursory examination of the immediate area yielded no results. I did note that some oil had apparently leaked onto the gravel bank. There were other car tracks, but nothing distinguishable. I got back into the car and headed toward Gila Bend. I called Patty to inform her that I was on my way home and not to worry. She indicated that she had just arrived from the clubhouse after a good day working on a craft project with new friends. She announced that salmon was on the menu for dinner, and advised me to be careful driving home.

Route 8 is an east-west highway and continues on to Yuma, AZ, and into California. The traffic was light, so I decided to open up the Camaro for a few miles. I didn't want to flush out an Arizona Highway Patrolman, but nevertheless I didn't think it would hurt to blow out the carburetor.

I was amazed: as I tromped down on the gas pedal, the quick rush forward set me back in the seat. For a moment I thought I was back on the quarter-mile track at Weedsport, New York, with my 1985 Chevrolet sedan. The needle shot up to 85 miles per hour. I took my foot off the pedal and it fell back to 55. I had had no idea that the Camaro could perform so well.

When I reached Gila Bend I hung a right onto Route 85 and headed north to Buckeye and I-10. Traffic remained light on Route 85, for which I was glad, because of the multiple accidents that occur on this two-lane macadam highway.

After finding I-10 heavy with traffic, I was relieved to pull into the resort. I stopped at the office to see if Patty had picked up the mail. She had. I then continued on to the coach and my lovely wife.

When I exited the car I noticed that the Panighettis were out. As I approached our coach, the door opened, and there stood Patty with her long blond hair flowing onto her shoulders. She was wearing a pair of shorts and a blue blouse. Around her waist was tied a flowery apron. I could smell the aroma of the salmon.

Patty put her arms around me when I got inside and kissed me with warm, moist lips.

"I missed you, Jason. I'm so glad you're home. How did your day go, dear?" she asked.

"I spent most of it in Casa Grande, sweetheart. I wished you could have been with me. Did you finish up your craft project?" I asked.

"We still have a way to go. I've been meeting more resort residents. We have people here from all walks of life, Jason. I've met retired teachers, bankers, nurses, and telephone employees. Many of these people are in their late fifties and early sixties. In fact, honey, I've even been approached to join the Red Hats, a social group of ladies who wear purple dresses or shirts and red hats. It's growing all over the country," she said with kindly amusement.

"Yes, I've heard of that group. Are you interested in joining?" I asked, surprised, thinking she would be too young.

"I don't think so. We're not going to be here that long, and I wouldn't be able to attend their planned meetings. Besides, I'm not even **close** to fifty. No, I think I'll just work on craft projects until we leave. That depends, of course, on what happens to your case."

I gave her a hug. "When will supper be ready, sweetheart?" I was famished.

"In about ten minutes, dear," she replied.

"I'll set the table for us," I said.

I proceeded to the bathroom to wash my hands and run a comb through my hair. When I gazed into the mirror, I could see that a visit to a barber was forthcoming. I returned to the kitchen and filled two glasses with ice and water and set them at our places. The mats showed a desert scene of brightly colored flowers and cacti. They were attractive and appropriate for this region. We were ready to eat.

I seated Patty at the table, then served the salmon onto our plates. After making certain that Patty was comfortable, I sat down to enjoy dinner. The salmon was moist and flaky and perfectly complemented by broccoli, carrots, and cauliflower. The coleslaw was cold, and Patty had added a touch of sugar to sweeten it. Being employed at John's Diner, Patty continued to acquire a great deal of knowledge about food preparation and the many recipes that Lila had shared with her. We both benefited from Patty's on-the-job culinary education, as she created for us delightful cuisine.

"Patty, this salmon is delicious. Is it salmon from Oregon?" I inquired.

"I asked the meat department manager when I was at the store, and he told me that it's farm salmon from China."

"From China! Are you kidding?" I couldn't believe it. "No wonder our trade deficit is so large!" I exclaimed.

"That's what he told me, Jason," she replied.

"From China or not, it is delicious!" I chuckled as I took another bite. "By the way, hon, how have you been feeling?"

"Pretty darn good, Jason. Except for an occasional bout with queasiness, I feel great," she assured me.

After dinner and a relaxing conversation, I cleared the table informing Patty that I would clean up the kitchen and wash the dishes.

With that task completed, I called the hospital and asked for Jack Flynn's room. Ruby answered the telephone. She told me that Jack had just dozed off. I brought her up to date on what I had learned in Casa Grande. She was clearly pleased to hear. I told her that I would stop by the office in the morning to discuss the case further, and ask her to please tell Jack that I had called.

After I hung up, I placed a call to Wayne Beyea in Plattsburgh. He answered on the second ring.

"Hello, Wayne. It's Jason calling from sunny Arizona. How are you?"

"We're freezing up here in the North Country, Jason, you lucky stiff." I heard a chuckle in his voice.

"Wayne, do you have anything to tell me?" I wondered if any investigative work had developed.

"I've been meaning to call you, Jason, but I've been too busy. Yes, I do have a couple of matters to discuss with you. Do you have a few minutes?" Wayne sounded businesslike, as usual.

"Go ahead, shoot," I responded.

"A gentleman from the Newton Falls region called me and wanted to speak to you. I told him that I'm standing in for you while you're away. I asked him if there was something I could do to assist him. Well, at first he hemmed and hawed, then finally told me that he believes his wife is not being true to him and that he would like some surveillance done for a few weeks to establish the validity of his concerns. Before I proceeded with his request, I wanted to let you know. He himself attempted to follow her one Saturday evening, but somehow she gave him the slip." Then Wayne paused.

"So he believes that his wife is committing infidelity. How long have they been married?" I queried.

"He told me that they have been happily married for fifteen years. He sounded like a very sincere man on the telephone. At this time I have no idea what his family background is." He paused again to gather his thoughts. "However he did indicate that he's a salesman and is often required to be out of the area for short periods of time."

"Wayne, feel free to proceed with your investigation. Your fees are the same as mine, so there's no problem. I personally do not enjoy working on this type of an investigation, and I know you don't either, but when they come in we do have to take care of them. I'm always careful to make certain that the times of my observations are recorded accurately, for obvious reasons. If it comes to the point that you have to testify in court, the recorded time element is important for the time period is always challenged, but you know that as well as I do."

"I know what you mean, Jason. I don't relish the idea of who is getting in bed with whom, but as we discussed a long time ago, someone has to do this type of work. Yes, I do use a 35mm camera myself. In addition I usually dictate all my notes into a recorder and type them up at a later date. I keep all my tapes for future reference or court, if it's necessary."

"That's a good idea. I usually use a recorder myself," I said.

"I believe that's all I have to discuss on that case. The other matter involves some surveillance at a trucking company. The storage facility is just inside the Blue Line, east of Lowville. The owner of the company has some information relative to two Pennsylvania truck drivers who were fired from their company. These two people have been pilfering freight houses in Pennsylvania and they have broken into a couple in New York State. The police authorities have adopted cases in both states. The owner expressed his desire that we keep our investigation confidential and that to report only to him. How do you feel about his request?"

"His request is legitimate. If you feel that you have the time to handle this matter, feel free to adopt a case on it, Wayne. For my files in Old Forge, I'd appreciate a copy of all of your paperwork."

"You'll have it, Jason. Any idea when you might be returning to the North Country?"

"No idea at this time, but we'll return as soon as we can. My friend, Jack Flynn, is still hospitalized, and when he's ready to leave the hospital, he'll be going to a nursing home for a while for rehab. He's going to be okay. I haven't been able to see him very much, but I'll be glad when he's out and about."

"You two were in the marines together. Am I correct?"

"Yes, we served a hitch in the corps and we both entered law enforcement after our discharge, like you did, Wayne, after your stint in the Navy."

"That's correct. I enjoyed the Navy very much. I did some boxing and became a fleet champion. And, Jason, I enjoyed my next career, too." I could tell from his voice that he was proud to have been a state trooper.

"I know you did. We both know there's no other job like it in the world. Well, is there any other matter that I should hear about?" I inquired.

"No, I believe that covers everything for now. I'll call you if anything else should arise."

"Good luck with the domestic case. Take care and be careful."

"I will, Jason, I will." Wayne's emphasis reassured me he'd be careful on the domestic matter. I was glad, for I know full well the danger in handling some of those cases.

We concluded our telephone conversation and hung up. I

immediately dialed Wilt Chambers. He answered on the third ring. "Hello, Chambers here." I recognized the booming voice of my friend.

"Wilt, I've missed you on Christmas day as you had just left Charlie's. How've you been?" I asked heartily.

"Great! How's Patty?" Wilt's first question was predictable.

"She's fine, Wilt. She's feeling just great. Patty's involved in crafts here at the resort, and meeting interesting people. However, she's homesick for her mountains and John's Diner—and, I'm sure, you," I added.

"Are you keeping busy, Jason?" he queried.

"Yes, I surely am. Say, Wilt, have you driven by the log home to check it out?" I was sure that he had.

"I check it out about three or four times a week. One time last week I pulled in the driveway and spotted some tire tracks that looked freshly made. Well, when I got around the big blue spruce tree that you have planted on the edge of your property, I spotted an SUV. I was driving closer to get a better look at it, when all of a sudden a lady came around from the west side of the house. She was wearing a bright red jacket with a hood. I got out of my big Dodge and asked if could help her? Before she could answer I recognized her. It was Mary Lenhardt, the artist friend of yours. 'You must be Wilt Chambers,' she said. I didn't recognize her at first until she pushed her hood back. I asked her how she was, told her I saw her at Charlie Brown's for lunch occasionally, and she told me how much she enjoyed going there. She was just in the neighborhood and knowing you and Patty were out of town, thought she would check on your property.

"That was thoughtful of her." I was happy to hear my friends were watching out for us.

"And besides Mary, I'm not the only one keeping their eye on your property. Charlie Perkins, Dale Rush, and Jack Falsey have all checked your house at least once while you've been away. Like I said, I check it three or four times each week. Of course, you know we'll all be glad when you get back to the

North Country where you belong."

"We'll be happy to return, but I've got to try to solve the case I'm working on. All I can tell you, Wilt, is that a wealthy rancher's daughter is missing. She's about 21 years old and at this time her disappearance remains a mystery."

"Do you suspect foul play, Jason?" Wilt asked.

"It's too early to say anything about the case, except I don't know. I've got a lead or two that I'm looking at."

"Well, I wish you good luck. I've got to get going. Ruben is right here by the telephone. He's a smart dog, Jason. In fact, he knows I'm talking with you."

"Give Ruben a big hug for us." I noticed Patty looking at me in silent request. "Just a second, Wilt. Patty is going to say a quick hello." I handed her the phone.

"Hi, Wilt. How are you?" Patty asked warmly.

"I'm very good, Patty. Are you taking good care of Jason and yourself?"

"Yes, I am, Wilt. But I miss you! You take care, and thank you so much for looking after Ruben and our place."

"I'm glad to do it. You're part of my family, you know, both you and Jason." Wilt considered us that close.

Patty handed me the telephone. I caught a glimpse of tears forming in her eyes.

I reached for the phone again. "I'm back, Wilt. Listen, you take good care of yourself. If you think that you have to order fuel for our place, go ahead and do it. Just advise the fuel company to send the bill to our Old Forge address, and the post office will forward it out here."

"I'll do that, Jason," he assured me.

"We appreciate all that you do for us."

We talked for a few moments more and said our goodbyes.

"Honey, Wilt sounded good on the phone," Patty commented happily.

"Yes, he did. He continues to be a friend that we can count on, Patty." We both knew we were fortunate to have him in our lives.

"We've got some fine friends, sweetheart," she added.

The remainder of the evening went by rapidly. At about ten we turned the television off and went to bed. We fell off to sleep in each other's arms.

CHAPTER NINE

The aroma of sizzling bacon permeated the coach. When I went into the kitchen area, Patty was turning the slices over on the grill. Three eggs cooked next to the bacon, and four slices of browned bread had just popped up in the toaster. I glanced over at the table. Patty had poured the orange juice. Soon we were savoring the crisp bacon and dunking our toast into the sunny-side eggs. Sweet grape jelly on the wheat toast topped our breakfast off.

"Patty, your breakfast was scrumptious! I loved it."

"Honey, I try to please you. I know one thing: you love to eat. I'm starting to get my appetite back after the first few weeks."

"I'm glad to hear that. Indeed, I do enjoy eating, my precious one, as long as you're the one preparing the delicious cuisine."

I told Patty that I would take care of the dishes and the cleaning of the kitchen. She thanked me and went in to get ready for her craft group that were currently involved in artificial flower decorations. On the way out the door she gave me a hurried kiss. I reciprocated.

After completing my chores in the kitchen I decided that I'd run the vacuum cleaner. Patty had made the bed before she left for the clubhouse.

By 9:30 a.m. I was ready to leave the resort and head to I-

10 and Flynn Investigations.

Traffic was medium. In a few minutes I was northbound on 99th Avenue. When I arrived at the busy shopping center, I pulled into the parking space next to Ruby's car. I got out and opened the rear door. My briefcase had slid off the seat, and a few of my papers had slipped under the passenger side. I retrieved them, placed them back into the briefcase, closed the rear door, and locked the car. As I made my way to the office I observed two painters in front of the pizza shop, working on the wooden trim by the entrance door.

When I entered the office Ruby greeted me with a smile.

"Good morning, Ruby," I said.

"Good morning, Jason. How are you this fine morning?" She was wearing a blue pant suit.

"I'm good. How's Jack doing?" I inquired. I missed my friend.

"I spent the biggest part of the weekend with him. He's becoming more like himself. If he continues to progress well, he'll probably be discharged in a week or two," she said excitedly.

"That's great news, Ruby. I'll be so glad when he returns to his office."

"I agree, Jason. He loves his investigative work. He's getting terribly bored in the hospital. Even the nurses seem to have little effect on the depression that he seems to have. The doctor, though, indicates that the condition is normal under the circumstances."

"I'm sure it is. He'll be okay," I stated.

"Well. I figure he **must** be getting better. He's fidgety. You know how he can get," she said.

"I certainly do, Ruby. Anything new on the Huntley disappearance?"

"There have been some reported sightings in Flagstaff and a couple here in Phoenix. Bill Reidy did some checking and the leads were unfounded. In fact, Bill is in Flagstaff as we speak. I did call Mr. Huntley. He had nothing new to offer except he did receive three hang-up telephone calls two days before. He had no idea who the caller was. On the last one the caller didn't hang up right away, but he could hear music in the background."

I went over all the details with Ruby about my interview with Marie Martin at the restaurant. I advised Ruby that she was a friend of Christine's and that she was more than willing to assist us in our investigation.

"Ruby, regarding the telephone calls that Jerome Huntley received. Do you know whether or not the calls are still being monitored?"

"I think the monitoring of Huntley's telephone has been discontinued for now due to the fact the equipment was needed on another case. Why do you ask?" she queried.

"I just wondered." I made a mental note of this fact, certain that the authorities should have maintained the monitoring process.

With Jack in the hospital and Bill Reidy brought in from Tucson to manage the daily operations of Flynn Investigations, it was still Ruby who has her thumb on all activities. Jack was fortunate to have her on his staff. She had a mind like a steel trap. Besides the office operations, she maintains all the financial business as one of the three landlords of the shopping plaza. The fourteen tenants submit their monthly rent checks directly to Ruby. The checks are deposited into the plaza's business account. Ruby is the contact person for the tenants when it comes to repair work, painting, and the general maintenance of the plaza. She oversees the general operations as well as functioning excellently in the executive secretary position she holds.

While Ruby was handling some incoming phone calls, I spent some time in Jack's new room, which he designates as his personal law library. The room is approximately 20' by 20' and contains two cherry tables, each with four captain chairs. There is a computer, which holds the complete inventory of books, articles, maps, dictionaries, et al. As I saw it for the first time, I considered that it was modeled after a larger library. An element I found especially interesting was that he maintains a newspaper rack with newspapers from every major city in the southwest. The telephones on the tables are red. Jack does a lot of research on each of his cases, and in this fast-moving world a private detective has to keep abreast of changes in civil as well as criminal law.

I was amazed at some of the volumes that appeared on his shelves. I noticed that he had books on Greek and Roman mythologies. I was puzzled when I noticed a small plaque hanging on the wall between two of the large bookcases. The plaque bore the Latin phrase "Festina Lente," which means *make haste slowly.* Knowing Jack as well as I did, and especially being aware of his Type A personality, I chuckled to myself. He was always rushing around; that was his forte. I looked down at the thick wall-to-wall carpet covering the floors. Its dark maroon color blended well with the library room. I imagined that Ruby had had some part in selecting the floor covering. It put the finishing touches on my friend's law library.

When I left the room and went into Ruby's office to say goodbye, she looked up from her desk.

"Well, how did you like our new addition?" She wore a proud smile.

"I love the room, Ruby. Jack is certainly full of surprises. I can tell, though, that you must have had some part in creating it."

She blushed at my remark. "I did have some part in it, but it was basically Jack's idea. Believe me, he's so proud of the room that he interviews his clients there every chance he can. He holds a staff meeting once a month and makes sure that it's in that room. Of course, I have to keep the coffee made as well as furnish fresh baked pastries."

I wondered how she manages to keep track of it all. "I see that it is also air-conditioned."

"That was another project. We now have central air throughout the plaza."

"You really need the air in the summertime." I wiped my forehead just thinking about the 120-degree days in Arizona.

"Jason, we really would like you to join Flynn's Investigations. You would enjoy being out here. I know you love the mountains of New York, but think, you wouldn't have to worry about the snowstorms and icy highways. I know that Patty would also enjoy all that Arizona has to offer. She's such a wonderful gal. You sure lucked out, Jason."

"No way, Ruby. I'd do anything else for Jack, but I'm afraid the answer is no when it comes to moving out here on a permanent basis. That is out of the question. Not only does the excessive heat annoy me, but I'm fearful of what's going to happen when you people run out of suitable water. With the thousands of people moving here each month, having new homes built with large swimming pools, it will soon deplete your water resources. It's out of the question. I want you to know, though, that we love you both like a sister and brother."

"Well, I'll be honest with you. When I talked with Jack early this morning, he told me to bring the subject up again and ask you. Maybe he thought you'd reconsider it because of his being shot. At least, I believe that's how he feels about it."

"Listen, I'm impressed with your effort, and I'm impressed with the proposed salary and the air-conditioned car you've assigned to me, but I can't do it," I said as gently as I could.

"So that's your final answer." She looked at me, unable to hide her sincere disappointment.

"That's it," I reaffirmed as I gave Ruby a brotherly hug and started toward the entrance door to leave. I had opened the door partway when a large, pudgy, bespectacled man in his 50's grabbed the door and pushed his way past me to enter. I could see by his body language that he was an angry person.

I spoke sharply to him. "Please excuse me, brother."

"Go screw yourself," he flashed back.

I could feel my blood pressure rising. I turned around and followed him back inside. By this time he had rushed into Ruby's office, leaving her door ajar. He was screaming at her and I could hear her pleading with him to settle down. The fellow appeared to be so irate he was almost out of control.

It was none of my business, but I felt he was definitely out of order. With rolls of fat draping over the belt that held the clothes on his large frame, he appeared disheveled. He demanded loudly to see Jack Flynn immediately.

Feeling that Ruby could be in danger, I went into the office and confronted the man. "Sir, what can I do for you?" I asked sternly.

Ruby remained silent, apparently shaken from the rude encounter.

The man's eyes were glazed over and his rage continued to increase. "I want to see Flynn, right now!" he shouted.

"I'm sorry, sir, he's not available!" Ruby's voice rose sharply, despite her clear effort to control it.

"I said, now!" he threatened, adding, "Who in the hell does Flynn think he is? Two years ago he took photos of me with a woman. Not my **wife**. He...he's ruined my life! I want to talk with that son of a bitch, now!" He shook his fist at Ruby. I decided to step in further before the situation worsened.

"Maybe I can be of assistance, sir," I offered with icy politeness.

"Who in the hell are you? You're not Flynn!" he snarled sarcastically.

"My name is Black, and I asked you, sir, if I can be of assistance. You seem to have a problem. And, by the way you are not to address Ms. Wolkowski in that manner. Why don't you come into my office and we'll discuss the matter?" Hoping that Ruby would welcome my interference, I decided to use Bill Reidy's office to see if I could settle this guy down before his comments exploded into an uncontrollable diatribe. I couldn't allow this individual to verbally attack Ruby, even though I knew she was capable of handling such a difficult, discontented individual.

I directed the impatient man to walk down the hallway in front of me to the first office on the right. I didn't want him following me in his state of mind. As we proceeded, his heavy body swayed back and forth. He stopped at the entrance of the office.

"Go right ahead and have a seat," I suggested formally. The

chair creaked with strain as the monstrous man succumbed to the force of gravity. I was waiting for the chair to collapse. It didn't. I proceeded with my interview.

"What is your name, sir?" I queried, keeping a close eye on him.

"Wha—what do **you** need my name for? I'm here to see Flynn, the bastard." He appeared to be relaxing a little.

"I'm sorry, sir. Jack Flynn is not available. Now, sir, I ask you again, what is your name? If you have had business with this agency, we will have a record of it." My patience was becoming strained. Suddenly, this individual seemed to snap back to reality and a disconcerted calm came over him. He responded to my question.

"My name is Cyrus Whippleton." He appeared somewhat shaken.

"Now, Mr. Whippleton, what is your purpose in coming here this morning to see Mr. Flynn? Take your time and try to relax a little more."

I looked at Whippleton as he took a deep breath. He seemed to respond to my reasoning and even worked up a slight smile, causing his jowls to twitch.

"You said your name is Black? Well, Mr. Black, about two years ago I became involved in an indiscretion with a woman in my office. I knew it was the wrong thing to do. Unbeknown to me my wife, Jessica, contacted Jack Flynn here at Flynn's Investigations."

I was pleased to see he was settling down. "Yes, go ahead. Continue."

"As I indicated, I knew it was wrong. I loved my wife very much. Well, anyway, this girl at the office kept after me to meet her for dinner, which I did. I didn't think that it would go any further than one dinner and some conversation. It did, however, not every week, but twice a month. One thing led to another and one afternoon when we left the motel, I spotted a car parked near the room we were occupying. The man in the car was holding a camera and it was aimed in our direction. At first I thought it was someone taking a picture of the motel. In about two weeks I realized that the camera was taking a picture of us."

"What happened then?" I asked, knowing full well what was coming next.

"It was so embarrassing. I was served at my place of employment. Jessica was suing me for divorce. I hired an attorney, and as a result a meeting was arranged to discuss our differences. I was able to convince Jessica that I'd never be unfaithful again. I thought everything was going smoothly as we patched everything up. For almost two years we have had a normal relationship—until yesterday. Jessica told me she's leaving me for good. I saw red. My blood pressure shot up, I was seething all night. I couldn't sleep. I blamed it all on Jack Flynn, so I came here," he went on remorsefully. His head dropped to his chest.

"Listen to me carefully, Mr. Whippleton," I began carefully. "Your misbehavior is not the fault of Mr. Flynn. Mr. Flynn didn't tell you to have an illicit relationship with your coworker. He is not responsible for your actions. A private detective or private investigator is called upon to investigate several different categories. Dishonest employees, domestic cases such as yours, missing persons, security checks, background investigations: these are important situations that have to be looked into. Sometimes the cases are simple and other times they become quite complex. Obviously people are usually the focus of these various types of investigations, and at times emotions run rampant. Do you realize, sir," I continued, "that you came into these offices in a state of rage? Imagine if you had entered with a weapon of some kind and possibly assaulted Ms. Wolkowski or me. You could have placed yourself in extreme jeopardy by an overt act of violence. In fact, you might have ended up in the criminal justice system, landing yourself in jail or another detention facility. This could have developed into a very serious situation. In fact, Mr. Whippleton, you **would** have been in trouble if Mr. Flynn had been here."

"Why is that?" He looked perplexed.

"Mr. Flynn would not have sat you down to talk about it. Instead, the Jack Flynn I know would have called the police and you would be off to the pokey, especially because of the way you were conducting yourself to Ms. Wolkowski. I have done you a favor, Mr. Whippleton. I hope you are able to comprehend my comments."

He began to look sheepish, "I'm beginning to understand what you mean. I want to apologize to Ms. Wolkowski and to you, Mr. Black. I appreciate you taking time to explain it to me. I want you to know that I love my Jessica and I have to blame myself for the trouble I'm going through."

I couldn't help but feel a little sorry for this hulk of a man, who I now realized was intelligent and who seemed sincere at this point.

"What I would like you to do, sir, is go out there and apologize to Ms. Wolkowski. And, Mr. Whippleton, I never want to see you enter the offices of Flynn Investigations as you did a few minutes ago. Do I make myself quite clear on this point?"

"You make yourself very clear, Mr. Black." He hung his head in shame as he extended his hand. We shook hands. He then proceeded to Ruby's office to apologize.

Ruby and I watched as Mr. Whippleton made his way to the door to leave the office. I nodded over to her, grateful that the situation had been resolved peacefully.

"Jason, I'm so glad you were here. Mr. Whippleton sure was in a rage, and you never know what could have happened. We've never had any altercations here in the office, although there was one in the parking lot last year. That time it was a woman who had been photographed during a divorce investigation." She shuddered as she remembered the unpleasant incident.

"Ruby, that's why I don't like handling divorce cases," I asserted emphatically.

"I know exactly what you mean, Jason."

I was relieved that common sense had prevailed. It could have become a serious situation. I had restrained myself. It had been a good thing I had.

Ruby then made us some fresh coffee. Next she called to have the pizza shop prepare and deliver two meatball sandwiches to the office by Sam, the Pizza Man. Sam Trioci was one of the tenants and owned the business three stores down from the office. She introduced us when he made the delivery. He was an amiable fellow and seemed to have a positive attitude.

"Ruby, thanks for the order. How is Jack doing?" Sam asked, showing genuine concern.

"Sam, he's doing well. In another week or so he'll be going to a nursing home for rehab, and then you'll get to see him back here shortly, I bet," she responded.

"Viola and I sent him some flowers from all of us at the pizza shop."

"I know you did, Sam. They are beautiful and Jack appreciated them very much."

Sam tapped me on the shoulder on his way out the door, saying, "Nice to meet you, Jason."

"It was nice to meet you, Sam. Your sandwiches look great."

"Jason, we make them from scratch. We use lean beef for our meatballs and we make our own rolls. It's time-consuming, but worth it. We want our customers happy and we want them to come back. Stop by sometime, Jason. Ruby tells me that you love Italian cuisine, and our pizza shop serves the best," he said proudly.

I could tell Sam was proud of his business and appreciated all his customers. He and Ruby were good friends, she told me. She went on to say that twice a year the owners played host to the tenants and their families, once for a picnic in White Tank Mountains Park and once for a sit-down dinner at an area restaurant. "Jason," she explained, "our yearly picnic and dinner makes for a good relationship. Jack, Jay, and I feel that this gesture is in the best interest of all concerned. Our monthly rents are always on time, if not early. And many times the tenants, instead of calling our two maintenance men, will take care of minor problems that may develop, such as small water leaks or electrical service repairs. We have a team concept going on here at the plaza. It ignites advertising by word of mouth that the small shopping center on 99th Avenue is the place to do business. Usually on weekends there are lines of people waiting to get into Sam, the Pizza Man's Restaurant. All the businesses we rent space to seem satisfied with their customer base. The monies taken in from the plaza go toward our retirement fund, as you already know."

As we finished our sandwiches, I reaffirmed to Ruby my opinion that the purchase of the plaza by the three of them had been a good business venture.

After our lunch, Ruby suggested that we go to the hospital to visit Jack. She had to make a couple of telephone calls before we could leave the office. When we went outside to get into the car, Sam, the Pizza Man in his van tooted his horn at us as he left the parking area to deliver some pizzas. We waved back. I opened the passenger door of the Camaro and helped Ruby into the car.

Traffic was heavy on 99th Avenue with the last of the lunch-hour people rushing back to work. We headed south toward I-10. As we accessed the entrance ramp, a semi-trailer truck was creeping up it. Black smoke from his stacks permeated the already polluted air. We were fortunate to have our windows rolled up and the air conditioning in operation. Ruby and I discussed the need for a strict law to protect the public from the smoking diesel-burning rigs that never change their filters. We talked about the fact that people could develop breathing problems or even lung cancer from this exposure for long periods of time. We concluded that it does keep the undertaking businesses profitable. Neither one of us had ever smoked cigarettes. I told her with a grim smile that we had just passed one of the reasons I prefer the fresh mountain air of the Adirondack Mountains. She agreed sadly that the pollution in Maricopa County is an issue that strongly needed to be addressed.

The parking lot at the Maryvale Medical Center was a busy

place. Nurses going off duty were hurrying to their cars after concluding their shifts of caring for patients. I pulled into a parking space nearest the entrance.

We got out of the car and went inside the hospital directly to the elevators. Our elevator was full to the capacity. The ride to the 6th floor progressed in silence. I looked around the small space at the sad expressions on some of the faces. Each person seemed to be carrying their own load of grief and the anticipation of what they would find when they reached their family member or friend. One elderly gentleman was holding a magazine close to his thick eyeglasses. He dropped his car keys in the crowd and had to wait until several of the people got out of the elevator on the fourth floor before he could retrieve them. Each of these individuals possessed their own thoughts during the stillness inside the metal cage. Soon Ruby and I were exiting at Jack's floor.

We were happy and surprised to see Jack sitting in a wheelchair. He was peering out the window looking down at the vast parking areas. His back was toward us. We did not want to alarm him. Ruby went forward and said softly, "Hi, Jack. Look who's here today to see you."

Jack turned. "Hello, Ruby. And Jason, it's so good to see you! I was beginning to worry, but Ruby has kept me informed of your progress in the case."

"No, buddy, I'm still kicking. Progress has been slow. I do have a few feelers out, and hopefully we'll receive some feedback we can use concerning the Huntley girl," I said, reassuringly.

"You're looking good, Jack," Ruby interjected.

"I feel a lot better, now that the infection has cleared up. Next week, I'll be going to the Sunrise Nursing facility for rehab. I'll be so damned glad to return to work. By the way, Ruby, how is Bill Reidy doing?" Clearly he was eager for news of the office.

"He's great," Ruby said with a smile. "He should be returning today from Flagstaff. He went there to follow up on a telephone call lead. I don't know the results of his trip. I should have some information tomorrow."

"Jason, have you been staying in touch with Huntley? He is so concerned over his missing daughter."

"I will be contacting him again in a few days. In fact, I'll stop by the ranch again to see him personally. I believe the police unfortunately have removed the bug from his telephone. They have some other cases they are using that equipment on."

"Yeah, they're busy with people coming through that area with drugs, contraband, and illegals. It's a shame that our society is becoming infested with the druggies and undesirables. Whatever happened to the so-called good old days, Jason?"

"Jack, I believe that when you were in history class in high school you read about the fall of the Roman Empire. What else can I say? We are the audience watching the show on a big stage. The sad part is that we can't do much at all about it. Authorities have all they can do just to keep their head above water. So, you go along to get along."

"Jason, what are you? Some kind of a philosopher! I know you and I have batted that around for years. In the meantime, we tighten our belts and move on to other things."

I could see that Jack was improving and he was more like his old self with that well known challenging trait he possessed. I would be glad when he was back to work; hopefully we would come to some kind of a conclusion on the Huntley case, either locating Christine alive, or confirming she had come to a tragic end. I sincerely hoped we'd find her alive, maybe with her old boyfriend or some place yet to be revealed. Time would tell. No matter what the conclusion, Patty and I were looking forward to returning to the mountains we loved, our work in New York State, and our soon-to-be-expanded family life.

Ruby went down to the cafeteria to have a cup of coffee, while Jack and I talked about our days in the marines. There had been one incident that we would never forget. Jack and I had gone to the San Diego Zoo. We had never been there before. As we were observing a lion, a seemingly intoxicated person strolled up to us, unsteady on his feet. He shouted out, "I can take on any two marines there is." The man was about six feet tall and weighed approximately two hundred and fifty pounds. All of a sudden he charged into Jack without any provocation, putting his arms around him and squeezing him tightly. Jack's arms were straight down at his sides. I turned toward the man, approached him from the back, and attempted to pull his left arm from Jack's left side. The man straight-armed me and pushed me, causing me to lose my balance. I hit the ground. The drunk continued to squeeze Jack. I got up, approached the man from the rear, and hit him hard in the kidney area of his large frame. The blow was sufficient enough to make the man release his arms from around Jack's chest, though he started cussing us. Someone in the gathering crowd must have called security, for two uniformed men came running toward us. A bit breathlessly, we explained the situation to them. They informed us that they had had problems with the intoxicated man in the past. In a few minutes they took him to their office. Pulling ourselves together, Jack and I continued to enjoy the sights of the zoo.

Jack and I chuckled now over that day we had visited the zoo. We never did learn what had happened to the huge man who had attacked Jack with no provocation. Some mysteries remain unsolved. But today, while Ruby was enjoying her coffee in the hospital cafeteria, Jack and I went over the Huntley case.

"Jason, she may never be located, but we must remain hopeful that she will turn up. Huntley continues to want us to conduct an investigation separate from the police investigation. Hopefully you'll be able to develop some further information." We discussed details again to make certain the facts were clear.

"As I indicated to you, Jack, I'm going back to the ranch to see Huntley. I'll also re-interview my waitress contact at the Cactus Chuck Wagon Restaurant. I still think that there's a good chance we might be able to come up with a clue or two from her. I know it's a shot in the dark. But we both know that you can't rush an investigation. The facts have to unfold. If she is alive and if she is actually with a former boyfriend, why haven't they been spotted? Of course, they could have left the area, maybe gone out-of-state or even out of the country. Her father feels that Christine may have been abducted against her will, due to the fact that she loves the ranch and him and never strays too far away. Furthermore, both he and her friend Maria have emphasized that she is focused on obtaining an academic degree in journalism."

Jack became pensive, "Do the best that you can, Jason. I know that you are relentless when it comes to working on cases. I'm counting on you. I'd be right there with you if I could. Damn, but I hope they get the bastard that shot me." Jack appeared to be a little riled, and I could understand why.

Ruby came into the room, and the three of us talked about other matters. I could tell that she and Jack enjoyed a solid business relationship and that they respected each other.

After another hour with Jack, Ruby and I left the hospital and drove back to the office. We remarked to each other how good he looked and how much more he was like his old self. When we parked next to Ruby's car, I turned the ignition off, got out, went around to the passenger side, and opened the door for her. I followed her into the office where I tried to call Patty at the resort, but there was no answer except the answering machine. I left a message: "Hi, honey. I'll be home in about an hour or so."

"Ruby, I'd better be on my way. Patty must still be in craft class, but I'm sure she'll be back in the motor home soon."

"I wish you good luck in Casa Grande tomorrow. Jason, if anything should develop, I'll call you on the cell. I'll be stopping at the hospital tonight after dinner to check on Jack again. I know he was glad to see you."

"You tell him that he looks great and remind him that when he's all healed and back to work, we'll take him up on that belated Christmas dinner at the Biltmore, the four of us. You know, Ruby, neither Patty nor I were able to do any Christmas shopping out here, but we did manage to get each other a gift. We'll celebrate our Christmas when we return home." As Ruby nodded with a knowing smile, I rose to leave. "Tell Jack that I was happy to see him this afternoon. Take care, Ruby, and be safe."

"Goodbye, Jason. You be safe, too." She turned to open a cabinet to file a report as I left the office. Ruby is an efficient worker.

The flow of traffic on 99th Avenue was heavy at this time of the day, so I made a right-hand turn onto Camelback and headed west. When I reached Litchfield Road, I hung a left to Van Buren and went west onto N. Citrus Road.

I thought of Christine Huntley and wondered if she had run away from her father's ranch. I kept going over in my mind: *did she elope with Bradley Carter, the rich boy from Colorado, or was she in harm's way? Did Bradley assault her?* Many questions kept popping off like firecrackers in my mind. I glanced at my watch; it was 5:15 as I pulled into the resort. I stopped at the office, picked up our mail, and proceeded to the coach. I parked next to it and got out of the car. I noticed that my neighbors were out and there was a note attached to their doorknob.

I was just getting ready to unlock the door when it opened. Standing in the doorway was my precious wife, greeting me with a warm smile. She was wearing a bright red apron dotted with daisies. When I entered, we embraced and our lips met. My arms were around her still slender waist. "I missed you, darling. How are you feeling?"

"Don't worry, I'm feeling just great, and I missed you too, sweetheart."

I wanted this moment to last forever, but from the aroma swirling throughout the coach I sensed that fried chicken was on the dinner menu.

"Honey, honey, don't squeeze me too tight. I've got to finish preparing dinner," she said, gently pushing me away.

"I love your apron, Patty. Is that a new one?" I assumed that she had made it.

"This was one of my projects at crafts. It turned out well," she said proudly.

"It's lovely. You are a talented woman, sweetheart, and I love you."

In a few minutes we were at the dinner table. The platter of southern-fried chicken sat in the center of the table, with sides of mashed potatoes, candied yams, and sweetened cabbage salad. I had to thank Jack Flynn for having a deep-fat fryer in the coach. The chicken was delicious. So was everything else. Patty had first learned to cook from her late mother at their Kentucky home. She had been a good student. The candied yams were especially outstanding, as was evidenced by my second helpings.

"Sweetheart, thank you for that wonderful dinner. By the way, I had called you from the office. Did you get my message?

"Yes, I got your call. That's why I started dinner," she answered.

"Oh, did I tell you Ruby and I went to see Jack this afternoon. In a few days he'll be entering a nursing home for rehab. He sends his regards to you."

"I've been keeping Jack in my prayers, honey."

"I know you have, and I have, too. We're just about the only family he actually has, along with Ruby and Jay Silverstein."

"That's true, dear."

I helped Patty clear the table, I then told her to go into the living room and relax while I did the dishes and tidied up the kitchen and dining area. Again I mentioned that Jack's coach was a palace, but it couldn't replace our Adirondack log home. She agreed. We weren't accustomed to this lifestyle, but as a temporary home while assisting Jack, it certainly was sufficing. He had been more than generous to have us use the coach, and I knew that we both felt secure here in the resort.

The adage of the "Wild West" lives on in Arizona. Shootings and killings occur often in Maricopa County in all neighborhoods, from the poorer areas to the upscale ones. Many of the business places display iron-barred windows and doors, and burglar alarm systems are ever present in residential areas as well, providing the property owner can afford them. Gated communities are alive and well, springing up in many developments throughout the state. Small town newspapers devote sections listing countless individuals who have been introduced into the criminal justice system by being arrested for various violations of the law, from homicide to passing a bad check.

Local crime isn't the only activity. The illegal aliens, often referred to as wetbacks by the locals, pour into the area in a continuous stream across the desert or by being smuggled into the state by the coyote gangs as human cargo for a price. Not having any work to sustain themselves, they often become involved in criminal activity in order to survive. It becomes a vicious circle, especially through the criminal justice system. Sometimes they are deported back to their country of origin, only to return again in the future to repeat their criminal activity.

Jack had used good judgment by having us stay in his coach, knowing that Patty would be alone at times. Ruby had hinted that when Patty and I left after the conclusion of the case, Jack was contemplating a move from his condo into the coach. This possibility was purely speculative at this time, but he was seriously mulling it over. One good reason was that in the event Jack had to travel to another area of the state, he'd have the convenience of his already prepared coach on any given investigation he might become involved in. It would be like having a satellite office on wheels.

I soon had the kitchen and dining area cleaned and looking neat as a pin. Patty had put on one of Andy Williams' discs. "Moon River" was playing. We both love his signature song. We planned to visit Branson, Missouri, sometime in the future to attend Andy's show.

Patty suggested that we take a stroll before retiring for the evening. We slipped on our jackets for a walk around the resort. As we made our way on the paved roadway, we waved at several people sitting outside and at other walkers. The resort is one of the few in the area that allow pets, accounting for the large number of dogs that were being led to the designated pet-walking space. Labrador retrievers seem to be especially popular, but there were assorted breeds, shapes, and sizes, including a German shepherd. He reminded us of Ruben, whom we missed so very much.

We returned to the coach after about an hour's walk. The brilliant sun was sinking quickly on the western horizon, making the sprinkled puffy clouds look like the touches of an artist's brush. Before entering our temporary castle, I held Patty close to my side as we viewed Mother Nature's art on display and we were humbled by the colorful view caused by the setting sun.

I checked the doors on the car to make certain they were locked before I entered the coach. Patty turned on the stereo system again and we listened to some more music until it was time to get ready for bed. I poured myself a glass of red wine and gave Patty a glass of cranberry juice. We sipped our drinks slowly. How fortunate we were to have found each other! We retired early and joyfully expressed our love for one another.

CHAPTER TEN

I was paddling my old canoe down the Colorado River when we struck a rock. I woke up with a fearful feeling that Patty was thrown overboard from the impact before I realized it was a dream. Soon my near-panic left me, however, as the smell of ham cooking tantalizingly entered my nostrils. I threw the covers back, got out of bed, and headed to the bathroom. The water that I splashed onto my face wasn't the Adirondack water that I was accustomed to. I still couldn't get used to this Arizona water that carried a strong scent of chlorine and made my eyes smart for a moment or two. I put on my bathrobe and went to the dining area. Patty was just pouring my green tea and warming the plates in the microwave. I went over to her and embraced her after she had placed the teakettle back on the stove.

"What are you going to do today?" I asked. "Would you like to take a drive with me?"

"I'd love, to honey, but I already promised the girls that I'd join them for lunch," she answered somewhat sheepishly. "I had no idea you would want me to ride along with you today. Do you mind?"

"No, I understand," I replied, somewhat disappointed. "I'll just miss you, sweetheart."

"Honey, sit down before your eggs get cold," she reminded me.

143

I seated myself as Patty followed me closely with my plate of two sunny-side eggs, hash browns, and a succulent slice of ham. She served two slices of sourdough toast on a small plate, then filled my cup with boiling hot water over my green-tea bag.

Patty had scrambled one egg for herself and prepared one slice of toast.

"Honey, is that going to be enough for you to eat?" I asked.

"That's all I'm having, honey. I'm not hungry this morning for some reason," she said, curling her lips into a slight smile. "You know in my present condition I want to avoid any morning sickness."

"Are you going to ride with someone when you go to lunch today?" I inquired, worrying about her in the heavy traffic.

"Yes, Marilyn is going to take six of us in her car. We'll have a three-or-four-car caravan. Don't worry, honey. We'll be careful." She looked at me reassuringly, knowing how much I worry all the time.

"I'm not picking on Arizona, for it's a lovely state, but some of the characters behind the steering wheels do not use the good sense that they should have. You know how strict we are in New York State. Remind Marilyn to drive carefully. Someone told me that they had twelve deaths in one season at this resort a few years ago. So you can understand why I'm concerned."

"We'll be extra careful, Jason."

"Good." I pushed my chair back. "Honey, your breakfast was super, as always. And it gave me an idea: maybe we could have French toast some time this week."

"I know it's one of your favorites. Would you like some, honey? We'll plan on it. Remind me to pick up some more maple syrup when we go to the grocery store."

"I will," I replied.

"It makes me wonder how much longer we'll be here, Jason. I wish you good luck on the Huntley case. I can't help but wonder where the missing girl could be. She could be dead, Jason, or she could be held someplace against her will. Look what I went through with the two escaped killers from Ohio. I still have dreams sometimes of being under their control and wondering if they were going to rape or otherwise assault me. I still shudder at the thought of those two animals that represented the evil elements of our society. My heart goes out to the Huntley girl. I hope she's located soon," Patty said, sounding upset.

"Honey, honey, try not to think about the experience you went through with Norris and Clovis. They're both dead and they'll never bother you again, my dear." I noticed the tears forming in my beloved wife's eyes. How vividly I recalled how Clovis had been flung through the windshield, and how Lieutenant Jack Doyle had been forced to shoot Norris in St. Regis Falls when the blackguard turned toward him, aiming a shotgun at him and another investigator. Jack had drawn in fear of being shot and had fired one fatal bullet with his Smith and Wesson semi-automatic that had struck Norris between the eyes. The criminal career of Norris ended that dark night.

"I think you would have been next, Jason. Thank God that Lieutenant Doyle took the action he did, or he himself could have become another victim."

"Patty, the passing of time will help you forget more and more those terrifying days you went through as their captive and the time you spent in the Saranac Lake Hospital in that coma. I worried about you so much, my sweet."

"I realize that you did, Jason." I kissed away her tears.

While Patty cleaned up the kitchen and dining area, I went into the bathroom and shaved, showered, and dressed before calling Ruby at the office. She told me that she had no additional information concerning Christine at this time. She informed me that Jack had been in a good mood at the hospital when she had stopped by the night before, joking with her and two of his attending nurses. I was glad to hear this and knew in my own mind that my friend Flynn was surely on the road to recovery. I told Ruby that I would be in the Casa Grande area for the day and that I would check with her in the morning. She indicated that she would contact Captain Jay Silverstein of the

Phoenix PD to see if any of their informants had developed any news of the missing coed. I thanked Ruby and hung up.

When I went to retrieve my briefcase from the closet, I spied a new shirt hanging on a hanger. It was in the western style, with snaps instead of buttons. I didn't say anything to Patty, for I guessed that the shirt was meant to be a surprise for me. I took the briefcase and closed the door quietly. On the way out to the car I gave Patty a warm kiss goodbye, which she promptly returned. We are so fortunate to have such a close relationship.

After another hug, I opened the coach door and proceeded to the car. I noticed that moisture covered the windshield and the rear window. Patty was looking out from the coach, waving goodbye. I started the car to warm it up.

I proceeded to I-10, then headed west to Route 85 and south toward Gila Bend. The two-lane macadam highway didn't have many cars or trucks on it this morning, so I opened the Camaro up for a short distance to clean out the carburetor. I enjoyed driving this car. It was a going machine, just the type of vehicle for undercover surveillance, especially on domestic and insurance fraud cases. Gila Bend was a quiet place as I turned onto Route 8 heading toward Casa Grande just off I-10. The sun was brightly shining through the windshield, but the extended sun visor blocked the light from interfering with my vision, although with the intense Arizona sun, I always wear my sunglasses for protection. I met three cars traveling eastbound. I had an open road all the way to I-10.

I had gleaned from my first interview with Jerome Huntley that he would be willing to post a reward for any information that might lead to his daughter, Christine. To date, no such announcement had been placed in the local paper in Casa Grande. I proceeded into the city and into the business district. In my last interview with Huntley he had granted me permission to do so. Therefore, I made my way to the office of the *Desert Journal.* I glanced at my watch, which indicated it was 10:30 a.m. I had made good time. I wondered how long it would have taken if I had been riding a horse, the way they traveled in the past. I estimated it probably would have taken three or four days to make such a trip.

As I drove into the parking lot I noticed that some of the spaces were marked by small signs: Managing Editor, Dick Case; Senior Editor, Kevin Marlin; et al. I pulled in beside the gray Blazer which was in Dick Case's parking spot. After I turned the Camaro off and removed the key from the ignition switch, I reached over the rear seat and grabbed my briefcase. A little twinge developed in my neck as I turned. I rubbed my neck to relax the muscle spasm. "Old age is approaching," I said aloud ruefully. I exited the car and locked it.

There didn't seem to be a great deal of activity as I made my way to the entrance. The front of the building appeared to be well-groomed. Small cactus plants dotted the edge of the fine-stone-covered flowerbed. I noticed some decorative rock formations and a small water fountain surrounded by slabs of granite. It made an impressive flowerbed. A wooden sign hung from the front of the building, displaying the newspaper's name, *Desert Journal*. I entered through the western-style front door. It was thick and heavy, but it opened easily. I found myself in the reception room. An attractive woman, who appeared to be in her forties, was seated at a desk working at a computer screen in front of her. I could see that she was occupied, so I decided to take a seat in one of the four leather chairs while waiting.

I opened my briefcase. As I was about to remove the Huntley case folder, the auburn-haired receptionist turned from her computer.

"May I be of assistance, sir?" she asked in a very business-like voice.

I glanced at her name, Sylvia Grayson, which was engraved on a triangular wooden plaque on her desk. I rose from my comfortable chair and approached her desk.

"Would it be possible to speak with the managing editor, Ms. Grayson? My name is Jason Black. I would like to speak with him concerning a confidential matter."

"I'll buzz him. Just a moment, please." She turned and

spoke softly on the phone, then smiled at me. "Mr. Case will see you now. It is the third door on the right. Just knock before you enter," she informed me.

I proceeded down the hallway. I noticed many plaques hanging on both sides of the walls. I came to the door marked in English lettering, "Richard Case, Managing Editor." I tapped on the wood, which appeared to be solid cherry. "Come in," A muffled voice called.

I entered the office. Mr. Case came from around his desk— also solid cherry—and said, "How can I be of service, Mr. Black?" He was a handsome, medium-built man with distinguished features. He wore steel-rimmed glasses and had a twinkle in his blue eyes. I could tell immediately that he was a professional newspaperman. He reached over and we shook hands.

"There is a matter I would like to discuss with you," I informed him.

"Certainly. Have a seat. Would you care for a cup of coffee or tea?" he asked politely.

"No, thanks. I had a late breakfast," I responded.

"How may I help you?" He looked me directly in the eye.

"Mr. Case, I'm a private investigator with Flynn Investigations working on a missing-person case."

"Do you mean Christine Huntley? I know her dad, Jerome. He is on several boards in the region—the school board, the bank board, and several others."

He seemed well versed on the subject, another sign of a good newspaperman.

"Yes, that's the young lady. Her father has asked my firm to take on the case aside from the routine regular police investigation. He has asked our firm to keep our interest confidential at this time. To date, the leads haven't been too plentiful. I'll be seeing him later today, but in my last interview with him he indicated that he thought a notice should be placed in the local paper: anyone with any information should contact the local police or, if they wish to remain anonymous, they can write to one of your P.O. boxes. It's just a shot in the dark. An extensive investigation has already been accomplished by several law-enforcement agencies, and to my knowledge no useful leads have been developed." I looked over at him for any reaction.

"I'm listening, Mr. Black. Please continue."

"Mr. Huntley has authorized me to offer a reward of five thousand dollars for any substantial information that would lead to the whereabouts of Christine. The way the ranch Jeep was left near the intersection of I-10 and Route 8 with the keys in the ignition is strange. A mechanic checked the Jeep and there was nothing wrong with it. I know the Casa Grande police had it impounded and processed it for evidence. I don't actually know what was found in the Jeep, if anything." I again waited for any response.

"Go ahead, Mr. Black." Mr. Case listened intently.

"I would appreciate it if you could run a notice in your publication concerning Ms. Huntley. It will state the amount of the reward as well as the telephone number of the local police and your P.O. number."

"I'll do that for you, Mr. Black. In addition, I will include a special telephone number here at the *Desert Journal*. As you probably know from your experience, people sometimes feel more comfortable calling the newspaper than a police organization or a private detective agency. In no way am I being critical, but I want to afford you another alternative to receive leads. Hopefully, we may get a response. By the way, I have been approached by law enforcement relative to Ms. Huntley's disappearance. In fact, the Huntley family have been friends of mine for several years. Christine was an intern here at the paper on a part-time basis for two years. She is a very bright young lady with plenty of smarts. She has a promising career ahead of her as a journalist. Her goal in life is to be both a syndicated columnist and part of the horse business on her dad's ranch. Believe me, she has what it takes to fulfill that dream. We here at the paper are very concerned. And as we speak, our sources of information are listening for any information that would shed light on her mysterious disappearance. In all honesty, Mr. Black, Jerome called me a couple days ago and told me that you might be in touch with us. I am pleased that you stopped by." He was candid in his remarks.

"Do you mind if I call you Dick?" I queried.

"I don't mind at all. I'll call you Jason, if that's alright with you." Dick displayed a slight smile that flashed across his face. I could tell he was a sincere gentleman and that he seemed genuinely concerned about Christine.

I presented my card to Dick along with the telephone numbers of my cell, the coach, and the 800 line for Flynn Investigations.

"Dick, I want to thank you for your cooperation in this matter."

"Jason, you're welcome. Say, do you have a minute? I'd like to show you around our newspaper office."

I could tell that Dick was proud of his operation. "I'd love to see it." In all my experiences as a member of the state police, I had always had a great deal of respect for the media.

For the next half hour Dick Case guided me through several offices of the *Desert Journal*, including the newsroom, advertising, photo lab, and the circulation department. He introduced me to several associates on his staff who seemed quite amiable. Some of them had worked with Christine, and they especially wished me good luck on the case and assured me that they would advise the managing editor if they were able to develop any useful information.

We stopped in the employee lounge and sat down for a few minutes while enjoying a cold drink. I looked around the room. There were several comfortable-looking chairs and two large tables. There were dispensers for coffee and hot-chocolate. Dick told me that his staff consisted of approximately thirty-five people, with three satellite offices in Pinal County. He shared with me that he enjoyed living in Arizona. I learned that he was an avid amateur photographer. When I had been in his office I had noticed framed photos on the wall and several different makes of cameras on the top shelf of his bookcase.

We concluded our business and I thanked him again for his assistance. He invited me to come back any time I was in the area and again assured me that he would contact me if anything should develop in the Christine Huntley case.

I stopped by Sylvia Grayson's desk on the way out and thanked her for her courtesy. She was a good representative of the *Desert Journal*.

"Mr. Black, you have a good afternoon," she said.

"Ms. Grayson, it was indeed a pleasure to meet you. Goodbye for now."

I went to the Camaro, unlocked the driver's side door, and got in. I placed my notebook back in my briefcase and set it on the rear seat. I decided to go to the Huntley ranch before I stopped at the Cactus Chuck Wagon Restaurant for a late lunch.

When I turned into the long drive of the ranch, I noticed a large horse trailer being pulled along the right side of the road by a cream-colored pickup truck. It appeared to be loaded. A man wearing a black cowboy hat sat behind the wheel. He waved at me as I passed. I continued on down the drive and parked in the area near the front of the ranch house. Jerome Huntley, standing on the porch, turned his head to watch me arrive. I shut the ignition off and exited the car.

"Good afternoon, Jason. I had a feeling you were going to stop by today. I wish I had some news for you, but I haven't heard a word." I couldn't help but notice the even darker circles under his eyes. His handsome face was drawn tight with worry over Christine. My heart went out to him. I again remembered what I had gone through during Patty's ordeal.

"Jerome, I'm sorry. I would have been here sooner, but I stopped by the *Desert Journal* and met with the editor, Dick Case. He's a fine gentleman. He sends you his regards. I left him the notice to post the five-thousand-dollar reward for information, per our previous discussion."

"I think it's a good idea. Maybe we'll get a call or a lead. I'm so very worried, Jason. It has been too long. Something should have come to light long before this. I'm having to begin

to think seriously she may even be dead." Tears shown in
Jerome's eyes. My heart ached for this man, who loved his
daughter so very much. I reached over and placed my arm
around his shoulder to console him.

"Jerome, I know, I know. It isn't easy, especially when
there's no news. But you can't give up. Remember we haven't
heard anything, except that Marie saw her in the restaurant
with Bradley Carter. You can't give up. Jerome, Dick Case
told me that Christine has a promising future as a journalist, so
you've got to keep your spirits up. She'd want you to. You
know that!" I tried to buck him up as much as I could.

"You're right, Jason. I know it's true. Christine would
stand tall if it was me that was missing." A determined look
began to appear on his face.

"I've never met your daughter, but you and your family are
so very well thought of here. You were a stranger to me until
our first meeting, but I hear well, and what I hear is that you're
a good man and always have worked hard to get where you are
today. Jerome, I'll do everything I can to find your daughter,
one way or another."

"I know you will, Jason. The local police here in Casa
Grande, as well as the feds, have no new developments.

I listened carefully, then replied, "If you hear anything at
all, please call me right away on my cell phone. If Christine is
with Carter, they may be moving from one area to another. If
they are using cash rather than credit cards to purchase
gasoline for his car or a motel or hotel room, it will be difficult
to trace their movements. And we don't know what state of
mind that Carter is in." I kept to myself, for Jerome's sake, my
thought that Carter might have a weapon with him and,
depending on the circumstances, could be holding Christine by
threatening her with bodily harm.

"Jason, I know Christine would call home if she could.
This is a big part of my concern. She is a smart girl. I was
aware of her and Carter's unfortunate romance. It didn't last
long, because Carter was so jealous of anyone else who was
giving Christine any attention. But I never stepped in nor

interfered with their relationship. My daughter wisely wouldn't put up with his jealousy, and they parted. There was some concern at the time, but Luther Watson, my ranch foreman, talked with Carter one evening while he was checking on some of the horses. He came across Christine and Carter while they were having an argument. Carter was just about to slap Christine when Luther stepped in. I was at a board meeting in the city and wasn't here at the time."

"During our initial interview, you didn't mention this." I was concerned. This could be important.

"No, I didn't, because I had heard he had gone back to Colorado and the information just came to me yesterday. Luther has been in the east for at least a week delivering some horses to our customers. It was on his return that I talked with him, and then he told me about this incident. He also told me that he ushered Carter off the property and warned him not to come back. Luther has always been close to Christine, like an uncle. I wish he had mentioned it to me sooner, and so does he. But right after it he left on the eastern trip."

"Do you mind if I interview Luther?" I asked.

"No, not at all. I'll get him for you. Wait here. I'll be right back."

In a few minutes Jerome returned with a ruggedly handsome middle-aged man, probably in his mid to late thirties. He was about six-foot six-inches tall. Jerome spoke first.

"Luther, I'd like to introduce you to Jason Black, a private investigator," Jerome said.

"Luther, it's a pleasure to meet you." I extended my hand to shake his.

"It's a pleasure to meet you, Jason. How can I help you?" he responded.

Jerome excused himself and went into the ranch house to take a phone call.

"I'd like to talk with you a few minutes about the argument that you saw take place between Christine and Bradley Carter. Mr. Huntley told me some of the incident, and I somewhat have a picture of what occurred. Luther, do you have anything else you could add?" I asked, sizing him up.

"Mr. Black, maybe I shouldn't have interfered, but this Carter character was about to strike Christine, and that isn't proper. I talked pretty sharply to Carter and told him to leave the property immediately and not to come back," he answered emphatically.

"Do you have any idea what they were arguing about?" I listened closely for his response.

"Not actually. Christine did tell me after he left the property that Carter had a jealous streak, and was becoming too possessive. She was happy that I had intervened. I do remember he muttered something under his breath."

"Do you remember what he said?"

"I believe it was something like, 'You're going to be sorry, bitch'."

"Was he referring to you or Christine?" I probed.

"Oh, I'm pretty sure he was directing that remark to Christine."

This was important. "Luther, is there anything else that you can think of that would help me in this investigation?"

"I can't think of anything else at this time. I ushered him off the property. I didn't touch him—although I had the urge to teach him a lesson."

"I can appreciate how you must have felt. Are you from Arizona, Luther?"

"Not originally, sir. I'm from Nebraska. I spent a hitch in the U. S. Navy and then settled here in Casa Grande after I answered an ad for a ranch hand. I've been here ever since."

"Are your parents still living?" I was always curious about a person's origin, especially here in Arizona where so many people are from somewhere else.

"Yes, they have a small house near Omaha. Dad won't leave Nebraska."

"Well, Luther, your parents probably prefer their familiar environment. It gets pretty warm here in the summertime. I want to thank you. Can I feel free to call on you if I have any more questions?" I thought a moment. "There is one more question I would like to ask you. This concerns Bradley Carter. Is it your sense that the relationship with Christine was very serious?"

"I really don't know. I'm not one that makes it a point to stick my nose in someone else's business. I do know that he did spend some time here about a year or so ago, but when he dropped out of college I understood he returned to Colorado. I learned from Christine that Carter is from a family with lots of dollars, and according to what she said he'd never have to work if he didn't want to. He acts like a spoiled rich kid. That's about all I know. I personally didn't think he was the type of fellow for Christine, but as I said that was none of my business. It was a pleasure to meet you, sir. And, yes, feel free to call me any time." He reached out to shake my hand.

"Just call me, Jason. It was my pleasure." We shook hands, and Luther went back to his work.

"A nice young man," I said aloud to myself as I watched him walk off toward the stables. I wondered if Luther Watson had feelings for Christine other than just as an employee and the "big brother"; undoubtedly that was the cop in me. He disappeared into the stable area. I turned and was walking toward the ranch house as Jerome Huntley came out and descended the front steps toward me.

"Jason, was Luther able to assist you in any way?" he asked.

"I'm not certain. He seems like a fine man. How long has he been in your employ?" I asked.

"He's been with me for about ten years. I can give you the exact date, if you would like," he offered.

"No, that won't be necessary. I just wondered. What are his duties here on the ranch?" I added.

"As foreman he supervises six people. There's a lot of care when you raise horses. We also train some of the horses here. And we have several studs for breeding purposes. We enjoy a good rating here in Arizona and, of course, a big portion of our business is from out of state."

"I'm impressed, Jerome. I didn't realize just how complex the horse business can be."

"There are a great many horse lovers in our country, and as long as the economy is good, we'll have good horse sales. And the breeding is very lucrative." I could see that Huntley knew the business.

"Jerome, if you receive any more hang-up calls or informative ones that pertain to Christine, please call me right away." I studied Jerome. His missing daughter was beginning to age him prematurely. Again tears formed in his eyes.

"I will, Jason. I have all your numbers."

We bid each other goodbye. He turned and walked toward the stables. I glanced at my wristwatch. It was going on two—a little late for lunch. I got into the Camaro, backed out of the parking space, and headed to the main road. I noticed that the horse trailer and pickup had left. I drove into town and to the restaurant. There were only three cars and a truck full of hay in the parking lot. I sat in the car for a few minutes to gather my thoughts and finish jotting down Luther's comments to me about his incident with Bradley Carter. I got out of the car, locked it, and walked toward the entrance. A tall, burly individual had just come out of the restaurant and was walking toward me. I assumed he was associated with the hay truck. He was chewing on a toothpick. He had on a checkered shirt and blue jeans, with an old western-style straw hat sitting on the top of his head. As he approached me on the walkway, he said, "Afternoon, partner," in a gruff voice.

"Good afternoon," I replied, and added, "Are you the hay truck driver?"

He swung around and said, "Yeah, so what, man?"

"I just wondered. When I was a younger fellow just out of high school my dad bought me a ton-and-a-half Ford truck, and I worked for a hay dealer hauling baled hay from the farmer's lot to the railroad siding where we loaded boxcars. Sometimes the temperatures reached 100 degrees."

The big man's broad face broke out into a smile, and he replied, "That's just how I started, mister. My daddy gave me a two-and-a-half-ton truck at graduation, and I've been in the business ever since. By the way, what's your name?" He had lost his cockiness and now seemed friendly.

"Jason. Just call me Jason," I responded.

"I'm Joe Morris. I hail originally from Douglas, Arizona. Never married and moved here with my parents about ten years ago. We live just outside of Casa Grande. We love it here."

I didn't tell Joe where I was from. I asked him, "Joe, do you by chance know Jerome Huntley?"

"I shore do, Jason. I've delivered many a load of baled hay to those folks. There isn't anyone around these parts that doesn't like Jerome. He's a sharp businessman and one hell of a horse dealer. Why do you ask?" He looked at me rather perplexed.

"Oh, I just wondered. You must know Christine, too?" I probed him further.

"She's come up missing, mister. Why do you ask? Are you a cop or something?" He looked at me with suspicion.

"Not really. I'm a writer looking for a human interest story." I tried to reassure him, thinking he might possibly contribute somehow to the case.

"Oh! Really, mister, I wasn't trying to be nosy." He hung his head for a moment with a blank stare.

"I know you weren't. But you might know something of interest. Tell me, Joe, if you do hear anything, would you call me if I give you my phone number?"

"Shore I will, Jason. I've talked with Christine several times over the years when I was delivering hay to the ranch. She's a lovely young lady. I guess she's going to be a newspaper woman someday and also help her daddy with the ranch. Everybody is feeling sad about her disappearance. Some say she's probably dead, in the desert and others say that she's probably been kidnapped, and others have mentioned that maybe she eloped. It's shore a mystery with her being missing. The local cops already talked with me because of my association with the ranch."

"Thanks for talking with me, Joe." I pulled out my pad,

wrote my phone number—the coach and the cell number—and handed him the slip of paper. "Here's my number. I'd appreciate anything that you may think would be of interest to me."

"I'll be glad to, Jason. Say, hope you won't hold it against me that I sounded so gruff to ya just a minute ago on the walkway. I'm really a caring sort of person. I never had a brother or sister, so I've always been kind of a loner. When I see strangers I always try to sound a little macho," he said apologetically.

"Don't worry, Joe. I didn't take any offense at that. Well, I've got to go inside. I'm getting hungry. I hope they have at least one barbecue left from the noon lunch trade," I said jokingly.

"Oh, they've always got plenty. It's a pleasure to meet ya."

The big guy extended his hand. I shook it. I could hear my bones crack. What a powerful grip! We turned and went in opposite directions. I continued to the door and went inside. The place was almost empty. I spotted Marie Martin in the further dining area. She was wiping off a table after stacking some plates on a tray. I walked up to her as she looked up.

"Hello, Jason. This is a pleasant surprise. You're a little late for lunch."

"I know I am. Do you have any of those great barbecues left?" I asked.

"Yes, we do. What would you like, beef or pork?" She stood holding her pad and pencil in hand, waiting for my response.

"I'll try a beef barbecue, with coleslaw and a large glass of lemonade." I seated myself near the window facing the front door.

"Thank you. I'll be right back with your lemonade."

The aroma of barbecued beef teased my nostrils. I was getting hungrier by the second. While sitting there waiting for my meal, I tried to place all the pieces of the mystery together into a sensible pattern. I asked myself the same questions over and over. Was Christine abducted and by whom? Was she still alive or dead? Was she being held against her will? What happened when she drove the Jeep to town on the day she disappeared? What were Bradley Carter's intentions?

Marie returned shortly with my order. I noticed there were two large beef barbecues on a small platter, with a mound of coleslaw in the center. She brought along a bottle of barbecue sauce and set it down near the platter. I could tell that the barbecue was hot, as steam lifted from the edge of the homemade rolls.

"I only ordered one barbecue, Marie." I was actually pleased to have the two.

"That's what it reads on the order slip, but the cook told me to tell you that you are the lucky one. You're the last order of the day, and the kitchen staff is in a hurry to clean the kitchen. Do you want me to take it back?" she joked.

"Oh, no! I'll take it. Thank the cook for me, whoever he is." I appreciated this generosity.

"She's a woman. Her name is Elena Hernandez. She is the mother of nine children and has to work to supplement her husband's weekly paycheck."

As I took my first bite of the delicious lunch, with coleslaw piled on top of the beef between the homemade rolls, my dream of perfect barbecue had been answered.

"Marie, this is some of the finest I have ever tasted. Umm, yum! Be certain to tell Elena what I said." I continued to enjoy my lunch.

"I certainly will."

"Before you go, Marie, tell me: have you heard anything at all about Christine?"

She seemed somewhat startled by my question, and paused. There was a moment of silence. "Yes, I do have something that may be of interest to you. You finish eating, and I'll be back shortly. I have something I have to do in the kitchen. Is that all right?"

I sensed that she was anxious to talk. "Fine, I'll be here, enjoying my food."

As I was finishing, Marie returned. Apparently she was off

duty, as she had changed from her waitress uniform into a pair of tight blue jeans and a blue denim shirt decorated with a bucking bronco over the left pocket. She pulled out a chair from the table and seated herself before I could rise to seat her.

"Jason, I was going to call you, but I misplaced your phone number and I've been so busy I didn't have a chance to tell you about this. It's uncanny that you picked today to stop by. Yesterday I was working the dining room, as I have been today. Two of the local officers had lunch here. I waited on them. I have known them for a while. They're very nice fellows. I had just served them and started to clean off the table next to theirs. I do not make it a habit to listen in on conversations, but the name Bradley Carter came up. I slowed down my cleaning process and listened. From the conversation I was under the impression that Bradley had been spotted by one of their night patrols. Apparently the patrol had recognized him and intended to stop him for a routine check. Well, Jason, a pursuit started, and the night patrol was unable to pull him over. The officers were actually chuckling about it. Seems the sports car outran the patrol car, and they lost him. "What do you think of that, Mr. Detective?" she said rather smugly.

"Are you serious? So, he must be back in the area, huh?" I found this information very significant.

"Jason, I think there's a good chance that Christine could be with Carter and they could be staying someplace around here. But if so it's troubling that she hasn't tried to contact anyone at all. From what I gathered from the officers, they were only interested in him because of a speeding violation. I don't know if they knew it was him for sure, or if they just recognized his car from past violations."

"I think that Flynn Investigations could use a sharp operative like you," I said, complimenting her.

"I didn't let on to the officers that I heard them. I remembered that you're looking at the case from a different angle, so I made a mental note of it and, surprisingly, here you are today. You know, I think I would like to try my hand as a private detective or investigator."

"It's interesting work. Believe me, a lot of it is being in the right spot at the right time. It calls for a lot of footwork and following all kinds of tips, which sometimes lead you to a dead end. Marie, I want to thank you for this information. It could be very important."

"If I learn anything else, I'll contact you right away. I promise."

"Listen, I appreciate it. Here's another card with my numbers. If I should be out, leave word on my answering machine or a message with my wife, Patty. Marie, the confidential nature of my investigation is important. I believe you already understand that," I stressed again.

"Yes, I do. Christine is my friend, and I wouldn't jeopardize her safety in any way."

"I know you wouldn't. I believe in you, too. By the way, do you know Luther Grayson, the ranch foreman at Huntley's?"

"Yes. In fact, he comes in here frequently. He's really a nice guy. He loves his position at the ranch, and I think Mr. Huntley looks upon him as the son he never had. He's a trustworthy man. And he really cares for Christine like a family member. Why do you ask, Jason?" She looked at me quizzically.

"I figured as much. This is a small city in an area where people meet people all day long. It reminds me a lot of many of the places where I have worked in New York. As you know, Marie, it really is a small world. We have many, many good folks, and then we have a few lemons that can keep us all on edge. Today we have so many pressures placed on all of us. Not only do we have to meet our needs for food, shelter, and clothing, but we have to be alert for the criminal types within our everyday existence."

"You're so right, Jason. I bet you've seen a lot in your lifetime."

"Yes, I have." I nodded in agreement.

I thanked Marie for the information, paid my bill, and left the restaurant. I drove onto I-10 and proceeded to Route 8. The traffic was light this time of the day. I gassed up in Gila Bend before I got onto Route 85 north. I was reminded of the days in my youth when gasoline was fifty cents per gallon. Now it was way over a dollar. The boys in the boardrooms of the large oil syndicates should be happy with their big profits, while the working stiff with a family struggles, holding down sometimes two or more jobs, in order to pay for the commodity they need to go back and forth to their places of employment.

Although the two-lane Route 85 is heavily traveled and dangerous, for me it was a better choice than going through Phoenix to head south toward Casa Grande. When I pulled into Buckeye I stopped for the red light. Two street people were standing at the intersection displaying cardboard signs that read, "Will Work for Food." They were shabbily dressed. It seemed to me I had seen the same individuals in Goodyear at another intersection several days before, displaying the same signs. At any given time in this area you are apt to see poorly dressed street people at busy intersections soliciting funds from the drivers passing.

In approximately fifteen minutes I pulled into the resort and my parking space next to the coach. I was tired and looking forward to seeing my wonderful wife, Patty. I didn't have to wait long, for the door of the coach opened and there she was, colorfully dressed in a yellow blouse and beige skirt. Her long blond hair flowed down onto her shoulders. Her eyes sparkled as she greeted me.

"Jason, sweetheart, I'm so glad you're home. I've missed you so much." She threw up her arms waiting for my embrace. I rushed to her, placed my arms around her slender body and drew her close to me. Our lips met, warmly.

"Patty, I've missed you, too, my darling." We went inside and embraced again. "I wish you could be with me more. Did you happen to pick up the mail, sweetheart? Oh, I just realized I was so anxious to see you that I drove right by the office without stopping."

"Yes, dear, I did. I put it on our dresser."

I went into the bedroom while Patty finished preparing dinner. I hoped I would be able to do justice to her dinner after my late lunch, but it was now after six. The mail was neatly stacked. I looked through the letters, mostly our routine bills and our statement telling us the amount of property tax due. I opened that one right away and learned that it was going up, again. There was also a letter from a civic organization asking for a donation. It seemed to me that everyone was always looking for a handout. I placed the letters back in the pile and picked up the morning newspaper to read in the living room of the coach.

"I meant to ask you, how was your luncheon today?" I queried.

"It was very nice," she replied. "We went to this new place, "Mimi's Café! It was so colorfully decorated and the food was great. We'll have to go there sometime."

"I'm happy you had an enjoyable time, hon." I noticed the aroma wafting through the coach. "Something smells good, Patty. What's on the menu for tonight?" I wasn't able to identify the aroma.

"We're having stuffed peppers, green salad, and a fresh loaf of Italian bread, sweetheart. I hope you'll like it." She glanced at me waiting for my approval.

"I love your stuffed peppers, sweetheart, and everything else you prepare for us."

"I'm using the oven, which is why it seems a little uncomfortable in here," she explained.

"I thought it seemed a little warmer than usual. But I'm sure the meal will be worth it."

"That's the reason, dear."

I assisted Patty with setting the table, poured two glasses of ice water, and returned to the living room. I took my notebook out of the briefcase and jotted down some additional notes of my day in Casa Grande.

Patty appeared to tell me that supper was just about ready. I got up from the comfortable leather chair and went to the kitchen to help her place the steaming stuffed peppers on the table, along with the salad and bread. I seated Patty and then sat down across from my beautiful wife. After saying the blessing, she lit two candles. While the candles flickered I reached for her plate and placed a large stuffed pepper on it, then took care of mine. She served our salads in separate bowls. Fortunately she had removed the butter from the refrigerator so it spread easily on the freshly sliced bread.

Patty's eyes sparkled in the candlelight. A pleasant smile came across her face as I complimented her on the delicious dinner she had prepared.

"Honey, may I ask you a question?" I asked flirtatiously.

"Certainly you may, my dear." She waited in anticipation.

"I believe that I taste a hint of wine in your sauce. Did you use the Burgundy?"

"Yes, I did," she pretended to admit.

"I thought so. It truly adds to the taste."

"One of the girls in craft class gave me the recipe. I thought I'd surprise you."

"The taste is perfect in the stuffed peppers. I look forward to having it again soon," I continued.

After dinner I helped Patty clear the table and I washed the dishes. Again I noted that the coach, for all purposes, could be compared to a small apartment. Everything was accessible, with adequate storage area. I knew that this lifestyle was catching on with many age groups. It used to be retired people who purchased recreational vehicles, but I had noticed here at the resort there were people from their twenties to their eighties now driving these units. I could understand why my friend Jack had invested in his coach. He would be able to use it for business as well as pleasure.

After we squared away the kitchen and dining area, we donned our jackets and took a walk around the resort. As the aroma wafting throughout the resort attested, a few of the residents were grilling their dinners at their individual spaces. Although it was just temporary for Patty and myself, I could understand the appeal of this unique place.

As we walked, Patty and I discussed Christine Huntley and her father, Jerome, suffering from his daughter's disappearance. I had no idea when and if this investigation would be solved. I was becoming a little frustrated with the lack of progress. Only time would tell. I told her I would be going to Flynn's office in the morning and meet with Ruby or Bill Reidy to discuss the results of my day at Casa Grande. There was a possibility that a lead could be developed from the notice that had been placed in the *Desert Journal* at Casa Grande. It was still a wait-and-see scenario.

As we finished our tour around the resort, Art and Marilyn approached. We asked them to join us outside our coach. The four of us sat down on lawn chairs and talked until almost nine. It was a pleasant evening chatting with our neighbors. Art was a champion storyteller and he had us in stitches. We all laughed and laughed. One of his stories entailed his encounter with a New York trooper. Seems that Art had once owned an old Model A Ford coupe which he kept in excellent condition. He sometimes took his prize possession out for a late afternoon drive on the south side of Syracuse. It was on one of those occasions that he had driven it into the hamlet of Nedrow and stopped at a store. He had turned off the engine and gone inside for a few minutes. When he came out, the car was nowhere in sight. It had taken him a while to regain his composure. He distinctly remembered removing the keys before entering the store. Dumbfounded at the disappearance of his Model A, he had called the local troopers' barracks. In a few minutes, a trooper had joined Art in front of the grocery store and was listening to his description of what had transpired.

The trooper suggested that Art join him in his troop car and they would look around the neighborhood. Art climbed in and off they went. The duo took a ride by the Nedrow airport, and Art was relieved to spot a glimpse of a chrome headlight sticking out from behind the main hangar. The trooper pulled over to investigate, and they quietly exited. To their surprise they found the Model A in mint condition. There was no damage to the vehicle. It just sat there in some high grass next to the hangar. Art was so pleased to recover one of the gems in his life, his beloved Model A Ford. To this day the disappearance of Art's Model A from in front of the grocery store remains a mystery.

We ended the visit with vanilla-flavored decaf and some delicious brownies that Marilyn had so graciously baked earlier in the day. This desert hit the spot.

About 10:00 p.m. Patty and I retired to the bedroom. We turned on the radio and listened to some music of the sixties. We drifted off to dreamland curled up in each other's arms.

CHAPTER ELEVEN

After breakfast the next morning I gave Patty a big hug and left for Flynn Investigations to meet Ruby Wolkowski.

Traffic on 99th Avenue was heavy at 8:45, and then a slowdown occurred because of a rear-end accident that had taken place. All vehicles were brought to a complete standstill. As I rolled the window down on the car, I could hear the wail of sirens approaching. Fortunately the shoulders along 99th Avenue were wide enough for emergency vehicles to pass, and the Goodyear ambulance sped by on my right, followed by a police cruiser and a tow truck with a flatbed en route to the scene of the accident.

In about a half hour, northbound traffic began slowly moving again. I apparently didn't move as fast as someone thought I should, for the operator of the car directly behind me laid on his horn. I rolled up my window and slowed down to a creep. The staccato of the horn died out to silence about half a mile further when the car made a right-hand turn onto a side street, squealing his tires as he roared eastbound toward Phoenix. I thought, "That fellow was sure in a hurry." I kept my cool and proceeded on to Flynn's.

I parked next to Ruby's car, got out of the Camaro and, after locking it, went inside the building. I smelled the aroma of freshly made coffee and noticed some fresh pastries on a tray close by. Ruby appeared from her office and seemed a little startled to see me. Evidently she hadn't seen me walk in.

"Jason, good morning. This is a pleasant surprise," she said with a warm grin on her face.

"Good morning, Ruby. How are you, and how's Jack doing? When did you say he would be going into rehab?"

"He was doing so well, his doctor decided to transfer him to the Sunny Side nursing facility late yesterday. He's doing great. It looks as though he'll be getting out of the nursing home sooner than he expected. He's going to live at my house for a few days. A day nurse will stop by to check on him, and I'll be there at night. He asked for you, Jason, and of course wondered how you were coming with the Huntley case. I told him that you are diligently working on it."

"I'm glad that he's in rehab. He'll breeze through that, now that the infection has cleared up. Let's face it, Ruby: none of us enjoys being in a hospital."

"I know, Jason. It can be hell." She nodded her head in agreement.

"It is. I've been there and done that."

I went into Ruby's office. She followed me with a tray carrying two cups of coffee and a paper plate with some assorted pastries. She set it down on the table next to her desk and seated herself, looking thoroughly professional in her gray business suit complemented by a blue silk blouse. I sat within arm's reach of the coffee and the fresh apple fritters. Placing a napkin on the table, I took one of the small paper plates and picked up a fritter. We were relatively quiet as we enjoyed our coffee and donuts. I realized the taste of the fritter could be addictive.

I picked up my napkin and wiped my mouth. My first apple fritter tasted like I should have another one, but I exerted control over myself. I do try to be weight-conscious. Ruby refilled our cups.

"Jason, what were the results of your visit to Case Grande yesterday?" she inquired.

"It was an interesting day. I stopped by the *Desert Journal* office and met the managing editor, Dick Case. He was most receptive and knows the Huntley family quite well. In fact, Christine interned at the newspaper for two summers. He indicated that she had performed her duties very well and seemed to possess a strong desire to enter the field of journalism as a syndicated writer while still maintaining her position on her father's ranch. Dick is well-versed about the Casa Grande region and knows many people from all walks of life. I enjoyed my visit with him. He will be initiating the $5,000 reward notice for any useful information that may lead to some information on Christine's disappearance. This may stimulate some calls to the paper. He has furnished a telephone number and a P.O. Box at the paper for those who want to remain anonymous. Of course, people still have the option to contact the local authorities, if they wish." I hoped I wasn't leaving out any of the details that we had discussed.

"Good idea. Did you see the father, Jerome?" she asked.

"Yes, I went to the ranch and saw him again. I met the foreman, Luther Watson, for the first time. He's about forty years of age and has been with Huntley for several years. Turns out he had an encounter with Bradley Carter, who had been dating Christine. In fact, Watson escorted him off the ranch. Carter made implied threats to Christine at the time," I continued.

"Carter sounds like he could be a person of interest. Funny that his name has just surfaced," she responded with a perplexed expression on her face. Ruby knew too well what rough treatment was like, as she had been the victim of verbal and physical abuse by her former husband.

"That could be. Keep in mind that the waitress from the restaurant admitted she was the one who had called the Huntley ranch with the information that Christine and Bradley were seen together on the day she disappeared," I reminded her.

"That's true. I remember you telling me so." She made some notes on a pad.

"To sum it up, we're in a waiting mode, Ruby. The notice appears in the paper today. Dick Case advised me during my interview with him that he'll call me as soon as possible if any information is received by him from any source. Posters have been distributed to various places where people gather around Arizona, California, New Mexico, and Nevada. Periodically, announcements are still being aired, both radio and television. Christine's been missing for some time, though, and that isn't a good sign. If it is Carter, he could have harmed her or is holding her against her will, or perhaps they've eloped, which I doubt very much. My reason for that belief is the fact that she was so driven to obtain her degree in journalism. She had her aims in life planned with all intentions of reaching her dual goals of writing and being involved in the administration of the Huntley ranch. From my investigation I would conclude that Christine is a very strong-willed individual, and if she has been abducted, she will try to escape from her captor."

"That's most interesting, Jason." She poured herself another cup of coffee while I eyed the remaining apple fritters, but held off reaching for one. "For your information I've stayed in touch with Jay Silverstein of the Phoenix PD. No new information has been developed, he was sorry to say."

"Ruby, there is one additional bit of information that could be important. A night patrol in Casa Grande pursued a 1986 Mazda sport car one night recently and lost it. It was believed to be Carter at the wheel, but there was no mention of a passenger with him. The Mazda outran the cruiser. My informant at the restaurant overheard two policemen talking about it while they were having lunch."

"That information puts Carter in the general location."

"Yes, it's a slight lead that could be helpful. I'll call Colorado—either the police or his family—to see if I can find out his whereabouts."

"Good idea. Let me know what you find out."

"Ruby, how's Bill Reidy? It seems I always miss him when I come to the office."

"He's at a downtown hotel this morning, attending a bank security meeting. They're discussing identity theft, a real problem today."

"I understand there are many issues concerning stolen identities. I've worked on several of those cases. The dilemmas that are created are astronomical," I offered.

"They're time-consuming investigations involving multiple crimes. By the time you have the case ready to present to the grand jury, the perpetrator has flown the coop to the Caribbean to enjoy the proceeds from his criminal career. Of course, that is out of our hands. We have the initial contact with the check maker, and if it turns out to be a larceny it will end up in the hands of law enforcement. I don't know about New York, but here in Arizona we have many people who come to spend a few days in Phoenix and leave town with stolen money derived from cashing bad or forged checks."

"I know exactly what you mean, having been involved with the investigations of transactional crimes for years," I said in agreement. "In the meantime, I will, as I promised Jack, see the Huntley case to some kind of a conclusion, hopefully successful." I set my jaw, determined.

"Speaking of Jack, I will be seeing him this evening at the nursing home. Are there any messages you would like me to deliver to him?" Ruby was very loyal to her boss and friend.

"Just tell him that he is in our thoughts and prayers and that I will get to see him soon."

"I'll do that, Jason." Ruby looked at her watch. "I've got to run to the bank and the post office. Would you mind sitting at my desk until I get back? I'll be about an hour," she advised.

"I'll be glad to. Ruby, do you mind if I make a few out of town calls?"

"Listen, you big lug, as long as you're here in Arizona we consider you an operative of Flynn Investigations. You can make all the calls you want. There's more coffee in the pot and fritters on the plate. You make yourself at home, I'll be back soon."

Ruby left the office with a container full of mail and a deposit bag for the bank. Since Jack's hospitalization the financial responsibilities of collecting rents from their tenants rested completely on her shoulders. Captain Jay Silverstein, being a silent partner of Jack's and Ruby's, was seldom seen at the office because of his demanding responsibilities at the Phoenix PD.

I decided to make my initial call to Denver in an attempt to locate Bradley Carter. At the Carter home, however, I was only able to reach the housekeeper, who said I had to call back to speak to the family. I then contacted the Denver police, explaining the reason for my inquiry, and they advised they would do a follow-up and get back to me. I gave them my phone numbers, and thanked them for their cooperation.

I pulled from my pocket my book containing important telephone numbers. I dialed Dave Wachtel in Saugerties, New York. We had both been with the BCI (Bureau of Criminal Investigation) for several years. Although we had been assigned to different regions, miles apart, we always stayed in touch. Dave, like myself, is a private investigator, but in the Hudson Valley region. His telephone rang.

"Wachtel here. May I help you?" Dave's voice was sharp and crisp.

"David, Jason Black calling. How are you?" I inquired.

"Jason Black, how have you been? I haven't heard from you in a long time. Good to hear your voice, stranger." His own voice warmed.

"David, I'm helping out my friend Jack Flynn in Arizona with a missing person case. Jack was shot by a member of a coyote gang, while en route to Casa Grande. He was southbound on I-10 and came upon two rival coyote gangs trading shots with each other. As he slowed his car down, a bullet came through his windshield and hit him in the shoulder area. He was taken to a hospital, where they removed the slug. Now he's in a nursing home doing his rehab. It's a slow process. Infection set in, so the medics had to work on that. He's going to be alright, though."

"He's lucky he didn't get killed. God bless him. Tell me, Jason, how have you been?"

"Good. I just called to say a quick hello and hope that we can get together sometime during the summer. Do you think there's a chance that you and your wife could plan to come up to the mountains this July or August? I'd like you to see the troopers' display that they have at the Town of Webb Historical Center. It's really quite impressive."

"Is that so? Yeah, I'd definitely like to get up there then. I've been very busy working on some domestic cases. It doesn't seem that anyone wants to stay married too long these days. As you know, Jason, those cases are not my favorite to work on."

"Yes, I understand. They can be dangerous, depending on the individuals involved, especially when alcohol or drugs are a factor," I said in agreement. "At least when we were in the troop we had good backup, but when you're in the world of the PI's, there are times you are working alone and you have to depend on your own good judgment and common sense."

"Jason, I know exactly what you mean."

"You take care of yourself and say hello to your wife."

"I will, Jason. Take care and thanks for checking in with me. Goodbye for now."

"So long, Dave. Stay in touch."

I hung up and then dialed Wayne Beyea in Plattsburgh. Wayne answered in his usual efficient voice.

"Good morning from Phoenix, Arizona," I greeted him.

"Hello," he answered. "It's good hearing from you," he replied.

"Jason here, Wayne. How are you doing? I'm at Flynn Investigations holding the desk down for a while and thought this would be a good time to call you. Is there anything I should know about in the Old Forge area?" I was curious.

"It seems to be rather quiet in your region. I did receive a few checks from the Mountain Bank for collection purposes. Also, I had an inquiry as to the fee you'd charge for surveillance work of a furniture warehouse. I submitted a memo to your address with the pertinent information. The domestic case I have been entailed with is complex. They don't seem to know whether they will divorce or not. To give you an example, one night last week I set up my surveillance near the

Quincy Motel outside of Watertown. It was 10:00 p.m. Two cars pulled into the rear parking area. One car was occupied by the husband I was tailing and the other his girlfriend. I had my telescopic camera ready to take a couple of photos, when all of a sudden the wife of the man I'm tailing comes rolling into the parking lot with their second car. The wife got out of the car and started screaming at her husband and the girlfriend. I never heard such a combination of foul language in all my life," he said, filling me in on the sordid details.

"It sounds as though you were watching a B film. What happened next? You've got me interested."

"Jason, you wouldn't believe it. The wife attacked the girlfriend and knocked her down. Now the wife's on top of the girlfriend. She's pulling the girlfriend's long brown hair and the shrill screams can be heard for half a mile. I took several photos of the melee. The girlfriend was able to push the wife off her and get up and run like heck for her car. The girlfriend left the parking area laying down rubber. Then, Jason, the wife started to throw her fists at her husband. I heard him say, "Now settle down, Irene. Sophia doesn't mean anything to me. It's you that I love, baby." The fracas must have disturbed other guests at the motel, as they were looking out of their windows trying to see what was going on. Believe me, Jason, I got out of there in a hurry."

"That must have been something to see," I said with a chuckle.

"I called Irene the next morning and told her that I quit. I advised her to think about it before she employs another private investigator to follow her husband around. Well, she apologized and told me that she couldn't control her emotions. The girlfriend was her best friend. Case closed, as far as I'm concerned."

"That's some caper, Wayne. Listen, I appreciate very much you keeping an eye on my area while I'm away."

"How is that missing coed case progressing?" he queried.

"I'm still working on it. We've got plenty of feelers out for information, but so far, very little feedback. We are hopeful that something will develop soon. Patty and I are getting homesick."

"How's Jack Flynn progressing?"

"He's in a nursing home doing his rehab. He had to fight off some infection, but he is on the mend. I haven't seen him as much as I would like, but his secretary and assistant keeps in touch with him daily."

"I'm glad he's healing. Those bullet wounds are painful. Have they arrested the shooter?"

"I don't know exactly. I've heard several stories. I believe the feds are involved with the investigation. Several people were killed. It happened on I-10 near Casa Grande. The two gangs had a raging gun battle going on when Jack caught a slug in the shoulder. If the bullet had been a few inches the other way, Jack would have taken a heart shot. He was lucky, Wayne."

"Boy! I guess so! Well, have to get going, Jason. I've got an appointment with a dentist. When you get older the teeth need a little repair," he said jokingly.

"You're correct. Too many chocolates are not good for you, buddy."

Wayne laughed. "Take care, Jason. I'll contact you soon.

We hung up. He had gone out of his way to watch over my territory for me. He was a loyal friend. He and Dave Wachtel had in the past worked on many interesting cases together down along the Hudson Valley area. They both could tell stories that would make anyone's hair stand on end.

When Ruby returned to the office I told her that I had not received any incoming telephone calls. I left, informing her that I'd keep in touch, and headed for the resort. I ran the car through a car wash and topped the tank with gasoline while I was there.

I called Patty on the cell phone, asked her how she had spent her day, and if there was anything I could pick up at the store. She indicated that she and our neighbors had spent the afternoon at the pool reading and relaxing, then advised me not to bother stopping because the next day she'd like to grocery shop.

"Honey, do you mind if we have salmon tonight for supper?" she asked.

"That'll be fine, sweetheart. Do you have enough cabbage to make some of your delicious coleslaw to go with it?"

"I do, honey. Are you on your way home?"

"I'll be there in a while," I said.

"See you at the coach soon, lover," she answered in her usual upbeat tone.

Traffic in this area of the west valley is heavy, especially during the time of day I was driving. Thousands of commuters are headed to their homes located in the Estrella Mountain area, a very popular community. Litchfield Park is another area that contributes to the heavy traffic flow. The high accident rate in the west valley and other urban sections is mainly attributed to the heavy traffic volume in the early morning and late afternoon. A portion of the accidents are considered fender-benders; however, fast-moving vehicular traffic through intersections is sometimes deadly when those intersection crossings exceed fifty miles per hour. Fatalities occur every day of the week. Soon, I hoped to return to the quiet roads of the Adirondacks to enjoy the less traveled Routes 28 and 30.

I reached the resort and stopped at the office to check for mail, that day only the *Boonville Herald* and the *Adirondack Express*. Patty and I enjoy reading these publications, and they are newsworthy. During our stay in Arizona they kept us abreast of all the events in the area while we were away.

I parked and went inside. Patty was waiting and she rushed over to greet me with open arms. Our embrace was warm and loving. Our lips met in a warm kiss of love and appreciation for each other.

"I see that you stopped for the mail, dear. I checked earlier, but it hadn't been sorted at the time."

"The only mail today is the newspapers from home, honey. Were there any calls for me?" I asked.

"No, there weren't, sweetheart. But you might check the answering machine. I was at the pool and the clubhouse for a while today. The activity director is having an artist come in for a painting class. I thought I'd sign up as I knew you wouldn't mind," she said, waiting for my response.

"Patty, why would I mind? I think it's a wonderful idea and a great opportunity for you to hone your artistic ability. You know I admire the few oils you've painted at home. I would assume that here they would be doing some southwestern landscapes. It would seem appropriate. I've noticed that the desert offers a multitude of plant life for an artist to paint. The cactus and flowers are especially beautiful."

Patty's eyes lit up in her anticipation of the painting class. "I knew you'd be happy about it, honey, but I wanted to check with you first, just in case you might have other plans. I know I haven't been riding along with you as planned, but I have enjoyed the activities here. I hope you understand."

"No problem. Right now—besides you and our child-to-be, of course—the main thing on my mind is trying to locate Christine. It's almost like looking for a needle in a haystack. Her father, and many other people—including her college friends and the general public in Casa Grande—are all praying that she is still alive and well. I'm not going to be able to sleep soundly until we know one way or the other." I could not conceal my frustration.

"I know, dear, it must be difficult for you. You have seen so much during your state police career and now as a private investigator. Look what I went through, Jason, with those two Ohio escaped killers. I'm lucky to be alive, and I thank God every day that they didn't rape me. But they played mind games with me, Jason." Tears formed in her eyes as she couldn't help once again reliving her ordeal.

I went to her and held her close to my chest.

"Try to put it out of your mind, my dear. Neither one of them will ever bother you or anyone else ever again."

"Jason, I'll always be indebted to you. I miss Old Forge so very much." Patty's eyes overran with tears that streamed down her cheeks.

"Oh, honey, I know that what you went through was

traumatic, but I'll do everything in my power to make sure you won't ever have to endure anything like that again."

She slowly regained her composure, and dried her tears with a tissue. "Well, I had better get back to my wifely duties," she said with a forced smile.

Patty and I went into the living room area; I read the papers from home while Patty busied herself with her knitting. I must have dozed off. When I awoke, I went to the kitchen. The table had been set, and I knew Patty took comfort in the creative work of preparing our salmon for dinner. She already had the coleslaw chilling in the refrigerator. She enjoyed telling me that she had made some vanilla pudding for dessert.

"Honey, what are we having with the salmon?" I asked.

"I have oven-fried potatoes ready."

"I thought I had picked up that wafting aroma. Sounds great, sweetheart." I love Patty's cooking. She's a true culinary artist.

In a few minutes I was helping to place the hot food on the table. I seated my bride and then I sat down. After saying the blessing, I served Patty and myself. The salmon was perfect, augmented with a tartar sauce of diced hard-boiled eggs and pickle relish, with a bit of lemon juice blended in. Spread over the salmon filet, it teased my taste buds. I told Patty as we ate how much I was enjoying the dinner she had made.

We had just finished cleaning the kitchen when the telephone rang. Patty answered it and handed me the phone, as the caller wanted to speak with me.

"Hello, may I help you?" I asked.

"Jason, this is Dick Case from the *Desert Journal*. Sorry to bother you, but I think you should know that we had a response from the notice you had me put in the paper. The party that called is a male. He didn't want to give me his name over the telephone; however, he's agreed to come to my office tomorrow. I thought you might like to be there when he arrives. I expect him at about 10:00 a.m."

"Would I! Thank you for calling, Dick. I will be there. Have you mentioned this to anyone else?" I asked.

"No, I haven't. The caller seemed hesitant to tell me very much on the telephone. It just may be someone that is attracted to the five-thousand-dollar reward. We'll have to see. That's why I'd rather have you there at the office when he comes," he emphasized.

"Dick, again, thank you for notifying me. I'll see you in the morning." Perhaps this was the lead we had been waiting for.

We spoke for a few minutes longer and then hung up. I would see him at his office in the morning. Hopefully the caller would be able to shed some light on this mystery of the missing Christine. It was as though she had disappeared off the face of the earth. Hundreds of law enforcement officers were keeping their eye peeled for her and possibly one, Bradley Carter. Were the pieces of this puzzle finally coming together? Tomorrow morning we might know or it might be just another dead end. Instinct, though, gave me a sense of confidence in Dick's telephone call.

I missed Jack Flynn. How I wished the smiling complex, Irishman was back at his desk already and enjoying what he loved beyond anything else imaginable, the art of investigation. It was as though the word *inquiry* was tattooed on his heart. I'm a dedicated individual myself, but Jack has always gone the extra mile on all of his cases. He had been one of the lead detectives on the Phoenix Police Department, for the city which is the crossroads of the southwest where tourists, urban citizens, and the incorrigible criminal types blend in with the rest of humanity, resulting in a tug of war, good versus evil.

Jack had been somewhat of a legend at the Phoenix PD. He had usually been the first detective to respond to the grizzly homicides. He worshiped the uniformed members of his department, who would already be at the scene pursuing the preliminary investigation, and sometimes the collection of important evidence. When Jack arrived, with or without a partner, the first individuals he would see were the uniformed people who are the first to respond to the scene. Jack was a good listener—a stickler for detail—and seldom did he miss a clue. He was relentless in pursuing the homicide perpetrator or perpetrators.

There were many attributes that my friend possessed, and one was his charitable side. During holiday seasons he would cook at rescue missions and donate soap, toothpaste, washcloths, and towels to the homeless children of Phoenix as well as the adult castaways.

Captain Jay Silverstein, head of the detective bureau, had told me he had been extremely impressed with Jack's performance. He could always count on Jack, not only as his supervisor, but as his closest friend. They would fish Lake Powell together in Jay's fishing boat. As a result of their close relationship, which remained intact even after Jack's retirement, the captain, Ruby, and Jack had created their business venture that they still maintain today.

I had suspected and hoped that Ruby and Jack would someday become an item; however, it appeared to be only a business arrangement. Jack had always appreciated his secretary and assistant, and there was nothing that he wouldn't do for her, but matrimony between the two of them didn't seem to be a part of their future plans at this time.

As I ruminated, Patty worked on her knitting of a sweater for me, which I would gladly wear when we returned to Old Forge. I sat at the dining area table and removed some papers from my briefcase. I reviewed the material concerning Christine Huntley and Bradley Carter. I looked at two photos. One was of Christine standing by the horse stable entrance on the Huntley ranch, and the other photo was that of Bradley Carter and Christine taken next to Carter's Mazda RX-7. That particular photo was taken near the same horse-stable entrance as the first photo. I reread my notes of the interview with Jerome Huntley and Luther Watson, the ranch foreman.

I checked the photos closely to further acquaint myself with both young people's physical features. It was apparent that they had made a handsome couple. Depending on what the mystery call to Dick Case revealed, I would have the photos with me to show to the caller if it seemed appropriate. After reviewing the complete case file I glanced at my watch. It was

8:45 p.m.

Patty had just placed her yarn and sweater-in-progress in a plastic bag along with her knitting needles and set it aside next to the leather lounge chair. I went over to her as she got up from her chair. We embraced and our lips met in a warm kiss. We decided to retire to the bedroom early because of my appointment with Dick Case in Casa Grande. It was a lovely hour before we drifted off into a deep sleep.

CHAPTER TWELVE

I awoke to the aroma of sizzling bacon and the wafting scent of perked coffee. I pushed the covers back, got out of bed, splashed cold water on my face, and washed my hands. With my robe on I went into the dining area of the coach Jack called his castle on wheels. I went over and gave Patty a lingering kiss on her forehead. Breakfast was ready. While Patty placed the lightly fried eggs, bacon, and home fries on my plate, I sat down and reached for the waiting glass of cold cranberry juice. I put the glass to my lips and slowly drank the juice, which had a snappy, refreshing taste.

The breakfast was delicious, and I concluded my meal with a toasted slice of rye bread generously covered with sugar-free blackberry jelly. The last swallow of coffee made my meal complete. Patty was still eating when I excused myself and got up from the table. She told me that she had hung a freshly ironed shirt in the bedroom closet. Unbeknownst to me, Patty had ironed the shirt upon arising prior to starting breakfast. She takes meticulous care of my needs, and I only hope I do the same for her.

"Thanks, honey. That was wonderful of you to iron my shirt this morning." I always do my best to acknowledge my appreciation of all her efforts.

"I'm going to wash and iron today, Jason, while you're in Casa Grande," she informed me.

"You're welcome to ride with me today, Patty. Would you like to?" I asked.

"I'd better stay home today, Jason. Marilyn and I planned to go grocery shopping and after that I'll work on your sweater. I'm anxious to finish it."

"That's okay, sweetheart. I just want you to know you're welcome to join me. I miss you when you're not with me."

"I know you do, hon, and I'd like to go along, but it is a long, tedious drive, and I do get a little tired sitting in the car. Don't feel bad," she said, apologetically.

"Don't worry, I understand."

I went into the bathroom to shave and shower. When I finished I noticed that Patty had made the bed and had my underwear laid out for me. I dressed and went into the bathroom to comb my hair. When I opened the medicine cabinet I noticed a new bottle of shaving lotion, which I opened, with pleasant curiosity. I put some on my hand, and splashed it onto my face. The new scent delighted and refreshed me. As I turned to leave the bathroom, Patty was standing in the doorway wearing a devilish smile.

"I see you found my little surprise for you," she said. "Hope you like it. I hope I selected a milder scent. "

"It's great, darling. I love it."

She smiled in appreciation. We embraced before I picked up my briefcase and left. The sun was just beginning to climb in the sky over Arizona. It was bright and penetrating. I looked up at the side window of the coach as I entered the car. Patty's face was centered in the window like a portrait in a frame. She smiled and waved. I waved back. Condensation covered the windshield. I started the car and turned on the windshield-wiper blades. Soon the condensation had disappeared.

I let the car warm up before I left the parking area. The engine was fine-tuned and I could feel the energy surge beneath the hood. At fifty-one years of age I still had the urge to "push the pedal to the metal," but refrained from doing so. I could imagine how embarrassing it would be to have an Arizona Highway Patrolman issue me a citation. Jack Flynn wouldn't appreciate it either, especially with me driving a company car. But it wasn't difficult for me to understand why so many of our young people enjoy racing on the go-cart tracks. Many of these small tracks exist throughout the United States because of the popularity of the sport, and it's not uncommon to see a youngster behind the wheel of a go-cart under the watchful eye of his or her parent.

I took 1-10 westerly to Route 85. As I exited, I came upon a personal-injury automobile accident involving a car and a pickup towing a camping trailer. I slowed down and proceeded with caution as the Arizona Highway Patrolman directed westbound traffic to exit at the Route 85 ramp. It appeared that the car had been too closely passing the camper, which then apparently lost control, striking the car. The pickup and camper were both tipped up on their right side in the median. A young man was lying beside the camper, and ambulance personnel were in attendance. A woman was standing nearby dabbing her eyes with a handkerchief. Evidently the accident was pretty serious—yet more evidence of why they call this highway dangerous.

I continued to follow the slowly exiting traffic onto Route 85, south to Buckeye and on to Gila Bend. The traffic on Route 8 toward Casa Grande was light and, as I proceeded eastbound, I could count the westbound vehicles on one hand. I arrived at the *Desert Journal* around 9:50. Luckily I had left the resort early.

I parked in the visitor space nearest the entrance, exited the car, and proceeded to the front door. Several other vehicles were parked in the lot. When I entered, the receptionist recognized me.

"Mr. Black, you can go right in to Mr. Case's office. He's expecting you," she said cordially.

I thanked her and proceeded down the hall to the managing editor's office. I entered after knocking.

Dick Case, sitting behind his desk, looked up at me over his steel-rimmed glasses.

"Good morning, Jason. You're right on time. We could use

a prompt person like you here at the paper," he said, jesting.

"Good morning, Dick. It's going to be another beautiful Arizona day. I didn't run into any traffic on Route 8. However, there was a serious accident on Route 85. It was a good thing I happened to start out as early as I did this morning."

"Route 85, Jason, is unpredictable. It is notorious for the number of accidents. And on Interstate 8, one has to put up with the high winds in the mountain areas. Several times I have almost been swept off the highway."

"I experienced that a few years ago while driving a coach to Chula Vista. Evidently a flatbed tractor-and-trailer outfit loaded with baled hay had been hit by a severe gust of wind, and the driver lost his complete load of hay. I heard him call for assistance over my CB radio. You could hear the fear in his voice. I finally pulled off the highway myself into a rest area. But the wind still fiercely rocked the motor coach. It was unbelievable. Well, that's enough about weather. Have you heard anything else yet?" I was getting anxious.

"Not yet. I don't know who this mystery person is, Jason, but if he shows, maybe we'll learn something in a few minutes." He glanced at his watch.

"We were lucky to receive a call, Dick, and so soon. Often, as you know, people might have knowledge of an event, but avoid getting involved."

"That's certainly true," he agreed.

Just then, Dick's receptionist buzzed him on the intercom with the message that a gentleman was here to see him. He advised the receptionist to escort the man to his office.

There was a light tap on the door. Dick responded, "Come in."

The door opened and a middle-aged man entered the office. Dick motioned politely for him to have a seat next to the desk.

"And what is your name, sir?" Dick asked after introducing himself as the managing editor of the *Desert Journal*.

"My name is Ronald Jamison. Just call me Ron," the man replied nervously.

"Thank you for contacting us, Ron. Now I'd like you to

meet Jason Black, a private detective who is associated with Flynn Investigations of Phoenix. His agency was hired by Christine Huntley's father to conduct a separate inquiry into her disappearance entirely apart from that of the local police. They are not aware of his involvement at this time. Mr. Black is going to sit in with us during our interview. Do you have any objections?" he inquired.

Jamison rather hesitantly extended his hand to me for a shake. I took it as I nodded a greeting.

"No, I have no objections, Mr. Case." He appeared uneasy as he sat on the edge of his chair.

"What type of information do you have concerning the missing Huntley girl?" Dick asked.

"I read your notice in the paper," Jamison began slowly, "and have seen the signs that have been posted at various places concerning Christine Huntley. Then I heard a rumor—I don't know where, maybe on one of the talk shows—that she had dated a Bradley Carter at one time. Well, it was like a light switch going on. About two months ago, you see, I rented one of my properties—a small house and a storage building—to Carter. He paid me in cash for one year's rent. I told him that it wasn't necessary to pay the full amount—that he could pay me every month—but he insisted, giving the reason that he travels frequently and by taking care of the full year there wouldn't be any chance of making a late payment. I took his money and gave him a rent-paid receipt for one year." Even though he had spoken haltingly, his statement seemed believable.

"Where is your rental property located?" Dick asked. He was keeping his tone neutral.

"It's located at the intersection of Irvington Road and Alverton Way in south Tucson. Near the David Monthan Air Force Base. The house is a furnished story-and-a-half, constructed of wood and concrete blocks. There's no number on it, but it's painted green." Jamison talked rapidly now, as though relieved to have delivered his information. I pegged him as in his mid-forties. He had a nervous twitch on the right side of his face, probably due to the stress from the interview.

"Jason, is there anything you'd like to ask Ron?" Dick looked over at me.

"Ron, at the time he rented your property, was he alone or with some one?" I queried.

"He was alone. I remember he was driving a 1986 Mazda sports car with Colorado registration plates. Carter is tall, about twenty-five years of age, and quite sure of himself. He told me he had attended the University of Arizona, but was taking a year off."

"Have you seen him lately, Ron?" I asked, pressing him further. I was getting excited, but also keeping my voice noncommittal.

"No, I haven't. I have the rent for the entire year, and unless he calls me to repair something, I have no need to go there."

"So, let's see if I have this straight. About two months ago, a Bradley Carter from Colorado rented one of your properties for a year and paid you the full year's rent in advance. You state that you've only seen him alone and with no one else. Is that correct?" I wanted to be sure of all the facts.

"Yes, that's correct." he answered, nodding his head. He seemed to be relaxing a little.

"When you saw the notice in the paper, did you go over to your property to see if anyone was there?"

"No, I didn't." His eyes looked a little doubtful, as though wondering if he should have. "I just called the paper here and talked with Mr. Case. I thought it might be important."

"Yes, it is very important. We are both pleased that you called in. However, we mustn't jump to conclusions, nor do we want uniformed police rushing into the neighborhood with sirens wailing. Mr. Jamison, would you happen to have an extra key for the house with you?" I asked hopefully.

"Yes, Jason, as a matter of fact, I do. I own eleven rental properties and always carry extra keys in the event I get a call about leaks in the water systems or other problems that arise when you rent properties." I understood what he meant. "Why? Would you like me to lend you a key?" I could see him gazing at me as if to see if I were trustworthy.

"Yes, I would, if you're willing to. I promise you (and can prove) that I am a fully credentialed private detective. Ron, this could be very serious. Do you trust me with your key, first of all?" I tried to be as up-front as possible.

He dug into his pocket and extricated a heavily laden keychain from his trousers. "Yes, I do. I realize that this could be serious." Jamison handed me the key for his Irvington Road property.

"I will be responsible for returning the key to you. And, I would like your telephone number in the event I have to call you," I added.

"Jason, here's my business card. My office, home, and cell numbers are listed on it."

"Thanks. I see your DBA is Green Valley Rentals of Green Valley, Arizona." I waited for his reply.

"Yes, I reside in Green Valley. My wife, Isabella, is from Green Valley, and we met when I was stationed there at the air force base. I'm originally from Geraldine, Montana. My wife and I own the rental business," he went on to explain.

"Dick, I've taken down all the information. Ron, I want to thank you again for contacting Mr. Case. This is a confidential meeting. We don't really know if Christine is with Carter at the present time or if something tragic has happened to her. I stress the confidentiality of this matter. It is crucial for the time being that it still remains so. I'll contact Jerome Huntley, Christine's father. I may take him along with me when I take a close look at your property, Mr. Jamison. Although it is presently rented and under Carter's control, I will take a chance and check it out. Will you provide me with a short statement giving me permission to enter the house as an electrical inspector to check out the wiring?" I asked, thinking I had better cover myself.

"I certainly will. In the event Carter should be there, it will allow you entrance to the house." Jamison removed a notebook from inside his jacket pocket and scribbled his permission for one Jason Black to check out the wiring at the Irvington Road property. He smiled when he handed me the permission slip.

"Jason, if that was my daughter who was missing, I'd do anything to find out where she was and if she was still alive. I'll back you all the way," he said emphatically.

Dick and I were so pleased that we were getting Ronald Jamison's complete cooperation. It had been a shot in the dark, but I felt fairly confident after meeting Mr. Jamison and hearing what he had told us. I mentioned to Jamison that he would certainly be considered for the reward, depending, of course, on the outcome of the validity of the information that he had contributed to the case. He told Dick and me that it wasn't so much the reward that had stimulated him to make the call as it was the fact of his being a parent himself. Though of course the money would be helpful, he said, his perception of the concern of a parent over the disappearance of their child had motivated him to contact the paper.

Dick Case ordered hot coffee and some fresh donuts as we concluded our meeting. We discussed the parental issues of a modern-day society and the push-and-pull making up the dynamics of childhood development. We learned that Jamison and his wife Isabella were the parents of six daughters. I knew then what Jamison meant when he indicated that he would back me up all the way in the event this case should end up in a court setting. I thanked him personally and expressed my gratitude to Dick Case for allowing us to have the meeting in his office. Dick and I decided that the notice of the missing Huntley girl would continue to run in the paper. Jamison and me left the office together after saying our goodbyes.

I called Jerome Huntley on my cell phone from the parking lot. He answered the telephone himself on the second ring.

"Hello, Jerome, this is Jason Black. Can you take a ride with me?" I asked.

"Good morning, Jason. What's up?" he asked excitedly.

"I'd like you to check something out with me. I can be there in about 15 minutes," I told him.

"Certainly. I'll meet you in front of the ranch house," he answered.

"Keep this confidential for the time being, Jerome," I

cautioned.

"I will, Jason. I'll see you in a little while."

"Oh! Jerome, if you have a couple of pairs of coveralls and a tool box, please bring them along with you. I'll tell you why I need them when I see you." Jerome and I would both be checking the wiring at Jamison's rental property.

"Yes, I have these items in our supply room off the office that is located in the stables. They'll be ready." Jerome didn't ask any questions. He was a smart man.

I had to stop at a signal light behind three pickups. I dialed the coach number, just in case Patty was home. She answered on the third ring.

"Hello," Patty answered cheerfully.

"Hi, sweetheart. Is everything okay?" I asked.

"Yes, it is, except for one thing: you're not here. I miss you," she replied with feigned sadness in her voice.

"Honey, I may be coming home a little late tonight. It appears that something may be developing on the Huntley case. I just wanted to let you know. Be sure to lock up tonight. I have the extra key for the coach entrance door. I miss you, too, my dear."

"Thanks for calling, sweetheart. Talk with you when you get home. Be careful, Jason. I love you."

"I love you, too, dearest. Take care." I clicked the cell off.

The traffic to the Huntley ranch was heavy. When I reached the entrance I had to wait for a pickup pulling a horse trailer to leave the Huntley property. The trailer appeared to be fully loaded. I continued on toward the ranch house.

Jerome was waiting on the porch, and when he saw me approach he immediately walked to the parking area. I pulled in and stopped the car. Jerome came around to the passenger side of the car and opened the door.

"Good afternoon, Jason. Good to see you. What's going on?" he asked with anticipation.

"Some information has come to our attention. We had a response from the reward notice in the paper. I just finished meeting with Dick Case, and a Ronald Jamison. We were able to establish the fact that Carter has rented a house from him."

Jerome listened intently. "He did. Oh, my God! Do you feel that the information is legitimate?" he asked inquisitively.

"We know that Christine was seen with Bradley Carter on the day she disappeared, so this could possibly be a very good lead. Nothing's certain, though." I didn't want to give him any false hope.

"Jason, do you mind if my ranch foreman, Luther Watson, goes along? He's very concerned, too."

"No, not at all. I'd be glad to have him go with us. We have no idea what we're getting into at this point. I have written permission from the owner to enter the house. And if it's locked I have the key that he gave me. He's the man we met with today, and he'd be in line for the reward in the event we strike pay dirt."

"Jason, I'd double the reward if we could find Christine. I'll run and get Luther. We just shipped a trailer load of horses to the San Francisco area."

"Yes, I met them pulling out. You're a busy man."

"That's for sure. We're fortunate, but it's hard work keeping those fillies in line. I'll be right back, Jason," he shot back as he left the vehicle.

Jerome walked over to the stables and went inside. Five minutes later Luther trailed Jerome out of the stables while slipping on a blue denim jacket. I noted again how tall and ruggedly handsome he was. And I remembered that Jerome had said he was an outstanding foreman. Several other ranches had wanted to employ Luther for the abilities he possessed in raising horses, but he was loyal to the Huntleys. I noticed that Jerome was carrying the coveralls and a tool box.

The two men entered the car. Jerome handed the coveralls and tool box to Luther as he took the rear seat while Jerome slid in next to me. We quickly exchanged greetings and headed toward Tucson on I-10. A silence fell over the group. You could hear a pin drop. No one said anything until I turned toward the Davis-Monthan Air Force Base.

Luther finally broke the silence. "Where are we heading,

Mr. Black? If you don't mind my asking."

"We're going to the intersection of Alverton Way and Irvington Road. We're looking for a wooden-framed house with a concrete block front. The house is green in color."

"Thanks. I just wondered," he replied.

Jerome was quiet and deep in thought. When we reached the intersection he noticed the house first. I drove by slowly. There didn't appear to be anyone around or any sign of activity. There was no garage, either attached or free-standing. I told them that I would prefer not to park near the house. The venetian blinds were tightly closed. The house stood alone with the closest neighbor about a half a mile away.

I spotted a storage building a few yards from the house. There was an old D-8 bulldozer next to it. I pulled the car in behind the building so it wouldn't be spotted from the highway. I suggested that we put on the oyster-colored coveralls. After we suited up, I recommended my plan. I would proceed to the house, check the outside property, and then knock on the door or ring the bell, if there was one. I would use the key to enter only if I had no response. Then when I had gained entry, they should follow me into the house through the front door, which I would leave open for them.

I took the toolbox and headed toward the house. Jerome and Luther stood on the driver's side of the Camaro and watched me as I crossed the highway in a diagonal direction. I observed that the rental property appeared to be well maintained and in excellent condition. There were various plants in front of the home and some large cacti in the rear of the property. I circled the entire house, noticing the blinds were tightly closed on all the windows. I didn't hear any noise or movement from inside the building. I then approached the front door and rang the bell. No response. I tried again. After waiting a few more minutes I inserted the key into the deadbolt lock. I turned the key, gently and slowly opened the door, and entered quietly. Soon Jerome and Luther joined me inside. Luther closed the door quietly. There didn't appear to be anyone at home.

We decided to check each room together. The interior of the house was neatly appointed with what appeared to be an excellent grade of cherry furniture. The well-kept kitchen was large for the size of the home and was fully equipped with a refrigerator, electric stove, and dishwasher. There was a formal dining room off the living room. The small den had a beautiful CD player with a stack of diskettes next to it. Throughout the house a distinct odor lingered.

"Marijuana?" I asked, turning to Jerome and Luther. There was no doubt about it in my mind.

"It sure smells like it," Luther answered while Jerome nodded his head in agreement.

Our search continued upstairs into the two bedrooms. The closets contained expensive brand-name men's clothing with jackets, trousers, and golf shirts. The beds were made. We felt uncomfortable going through the house. I could tell that Jerome was nervous and worried. I assured them that legally we had permission from the owner to look through the house in order to check the wiring where applicable. Nothing within the house appeared to be out of the ordinary, except for the smell of pot.

When we went down into the cellar we were surprised to see marijuana plants growing in wooden boxes. It was a full basement with a concrete floor, subdivided into four rooms. One of the rooms was locked with a deadbolt that appeared to have been recently installed, as there were wood shavings on the floor near the bottom of the door. I tried the knob, without results. That's when I heard a soft tapping sound. Luther and Jerome heard it, too, and came to my side.

"What is it, Jason?" Jerome asked.

"I haven't the slightest idea," I said with a frown

"Let's knock the door down and find out what's going on here!" Luther urged.

"I agree, fellows. We've got to open it up. However, it isn't going to be necessary to force the door. I just happen to have my lock picks." They looked at each other perplexed as I reached in my pocket and brought out the small black case containing the picks. I went to work on the deadbolt mechanism. I placed the pick in the keyhole, and in about three minutes I was able to unlock the door.

I opened the door slowly. A musty odor filled my nostrils. The room was pitch-black. Luther ran his hand along the inner wall, found the light switch, and turned it on. We were aghast as our eyes focused on an army cot near the far wall. Suddenly Jerome rushed forward and knelt by the cot.

"Oh my God! It's Christine!" he shouted out.

Christine's ankles and hands were fastened together with duct tape. A handkerchief hung partially out of her mouth. Luther removed the handkerchief then took out a jackknife and carefully cut her bonds. Pale and drawn, with eyes still half-closed, she started to cry.

"Is that you, daddy?" Her voice was so weak it was barely audible.

"Yes, honey, it is. Oh, my God. We'll have you out of here in a moment, sweetheart. You're alive! I've been going crazy worrying about you." With his own tears falling, he sat before her gently stroking her hair.

"Daddy, I—think—maybe you had better take me to a hospital. Bradley beat me. He's been hitting me and forcing me to take cocaine. I've had hardly any food. I feel terrible. I'm so very weak."

Jerome continued to caress her head, trying to soothe her. He dried her eyes with his handkerchief as Luther stood ready to help her up. I looked around the room and noticed a candlestick, a spoon, and the makings for a fix on a small end table.

Christine spoke again. "Luther, is that you?"

"Yes, Chris, it's me. Where's Carter? Do you have any idea?" Luther was working hard to keep his voice gentle.

"I don't know. He's been gone awhile again. I think he's dealing in drugs." She noticed me now.

Jerome introduced me to Christine. As I moved closer I could see bruises on her face, and her hair appeared to have been chopped off raggedly.

"Honey, has he been giving you **anything** to eat?" Jerome asked with great worry. "And what about water?"

"I haven't had very much. I don't really know...," she added in her barely audible voice.

"We're going to take you to the hospital right now and have you checked over head to toe. I want a doctor to give you a complete examination. And we need to know, sweetheart: did he molest you sexually?" her father asked. He waited in apprehension for her reply.

She welled up with more tears, nodded her head, and said, weakly, "Yes. He took full advantage. And he called me terrible names and slapped me around. He's acting like a crazy man. I don't understand what happened to him. It must be the drugs...."

"Jason, did you hear what Christine just said?" Jerome asked, turning to me.

"I heard her." I said grimly. "Carter is going to have to pay for this, Jerome. We'll notify the authorities as soon as we can."

"Let's get Christine to the hospital and call the authorities from there." His expression became complex as loving concern for his daughter began to transform to fierce anger against Carter.

"Good. The sooner the better," Luther added with cold fury.

"Luther, here are the keys to the car." I said. "Bring it to the driveway. We've got to hurry before he returns. We have to get her to the hospital."

Luther took the keys and went upstairs, but within seconds came rushing back down.

"Jason, the bastard's here! He just pulled in. It's the Mazda and Carter's got his trunk lid open. We've got to do something fast." His usual calm countenance had vanished.

"Oh, no," Christine whimpered.

"Quickly! Cover up Christine with the blanket so he won't see that she's no longer bound. Then stand next to me on each side of the door," I directed Jerome and Luther. I rushed to turn the light off.

We could hear the upstairs door, which I had relocked, being opened as Carter entered the house. Cabinet doors opened and closed as he apparently put items on the shelves. Then we heard another door close. Footsteps sounded as he ascended to the upper level. There was a brief silence, and then Carter apparently flushed the upstairs toilet, as water could be heard swishing through the sewer pipe.

I whispered to Jerome and Luther, "We don't know if he has a weapon or not. You fellows grab hold of his arms when he comes through the door. We've got to surprise him."

"Remember, he's strong as an ox," Luther informed us in a hushed tone.

"I'm going to hit him hard. We can't take a chance, not knowing if he's armed," I warned them.

We waited in our positions, Luther on one side of the closed door and Jerome on the other. We had reset the deadbolt in a locked position, so Carter would have to use his key. Tensely we stood there as he moved around some more upstairs. Finally we heard his footsteps on the cellar stairway.

The moment had arrived. I heard the key go into the lock and the click of the deadbolt sliding into the unlocked position. As the door opened, I was standing directly in front of the tall man who entered. My fist slammed into his muscular stomach as I threw my punch backed up by my 220 pounds. He bellowed. I tried to measure the blow to make sure it had rendered him unable to use physical force against us. He was slumped forward with Luther and Jerome breaking his fall as they grabbed him by the arms. My knuckles stung painfully from partially striking Carter's belt buckle. I quickly switched the lights back on.

"You—you rotten bastards!" Carter breathlessly tried to holler as he sucked air back into his lungs. "You bastards!" he repeated furiously.

"Watch your mouth, my friend!" I was right in his face. "You're in deep trouble, Carter. The law is looking for you and that includes the Casa Grande Police Department and the feds.

Look what you've done to this young lady, you punk. You've kidnapped her, you've abused her, forced drugs on her, held her against her will. That's just for a start, Carter."

The young man snarled, "Who the hell are you?"

"I'm a private investigator. My name is Jason Black. At this time you do not have to speak to me. But, I'm making a citizen's arrest and I'm going to turn you over to the Casa Grande authorities. But I'm going to ask you just one question. Do you have any weapons on you?" I asked in my firmest voice.

Perhaps the gravity of the situation was beginning to sink in. "No, not on me. But I do have one in the glove compartment of my car," he answered with less bravado.

"Thank you," I replied, to see if he was being truthful with me, still leery of his reply.

I turned to Jerome who had returned to his still covered daughter's side while Luther kept a sharp eye on the now rather subdued Bradley Carter. "While you take care of your daughter, I'm going to call the Casa Grande Police and the Tucson Police Departments."

I called them both on my cell and was advised that they would send their detectives to the house immediately, if possible.

After duct-taping his wrists behind his back I took Carter upstairs, while Jerome and Luther prepared to get Christine ready for her trip to the hospital. We thought it best to leave Christine downstairs away from Carter until the police arrived. I had Carter sit down. Evidently his bravado returned, as he began to rant and rave, vowing that he'd get even with me.

"Carter, I suggest that you refrain from any further conversation with me. The police detectives are en route, and when they arrive I will turn you over to them, at which time you certainly will have an opportunity to talk with them. At the moment, sir, you are under my control and I strongly urge you to remain mute. It is very apparent from the condition of Christine, and the drug paraphernalia on the table next to the cot, that something was amiss. Nothing will be disturbed. The police will investigate when they arrive. Carter, you have a lot of explaining to do. Law enforcement officials have been looking for Christine for over a month. I will only say to you that you are very fortunate that I'm not her father." My threat was veiled but I was sure he read my meaning—especially in the flexing of my still rather painful fist.

"You maybe from a family of privilege, Carter; however, the injustice of abducting and abusing Christine Huntley was unconscionable. You, sir, will have your day in court."

Luther Watson came up from the cellar and rather eagerly asked, "Mr. Black, do you need any assistance with Carter?"

I realized that Luther was waiting for Carter to make a false move. With him there beside me, trying to control the rage that he felt toward Carter, I calmly replied "Luther, everything is under control." I did not want any undue violence. I glanced over at Carter, now dejectedly sitting with his head hanging as he stared down at the floor.

Luther returned downstairs to wait with Jerome and Christine for the anticipated arrival of the police.

Within the hour, two unmarked detective cruisers pulled into the driveway. The officers pulled in quietly without flashing lights or blaring sirens. I was sure that as they approached the front door they had their weapons ready, not knowing what they would be facing. They knocked on the door and identified themselves. I let them in. Two of the detectives were from the Tucson PD and the other two were from the Casa Grande PD. The four men appeared to be in their mid-thirties to early forties. Detectives Walter Sloan and Paul Richter from Tucson and Detectives Charles Perez and Ray Keller from Casa Grande joined me as I walked toward Carter, who continued to stare down at the floor.

"Stand up, Mr. Carter," I instructed him. He rose reluctantly. I continued, "At this time, Bradley Carter, I, Jason Black, after making a citizen's arrest, am turning you over to the custody of these police detectives." I was relieved to hear the officers advise Carter of his constitutional rights as prescribed by law and reading him his Miranda rights. My part in the capture was officially over.

While Detective Richter kept an eye on Carter, I took the other three men down to the cellar to speak with Christine Huntley as she sat on the cot being comforted by her father. After the formal introductions, the detectives held a short interview with Christine. Jerome, Luther, and I stood on the other side of the room during the questioning. Detective Perez advised us that they would be glad to summon an ambulance, but Jerome informed him that we would be taking her to the hospital ourselves for the examination.

I remembered an important detail. "Detective Perez, Carter indicated to me that he is carrying a weapon in the glove compartment of his Mazda. I didn't check it out myself." The detective thanked me and informed me they would be impounding the vehicle, after which it would be towed to Casa Grande for processing.

The lead detectives from each department, Richter and Perez, held an interview with Jerome Huntley, Luther Watson, and me. Huntley explained to the detectives my participation in the case. They requested that we submit sworn statements to both departments as soon as we could. We agreed to do so. However, our first concern was transporting Christine to St. Joseph's Hospital, 350 N. Wilmont Road in Tucson.

I assured the detectives that after we took Christine to the hospital, we would meet them at the Tucson PD to submit our sworn statements concerning the citizen's arrest of Bradley Carter.

Jerome and Luther assisted Christine into the car. We were leaving the driveway just as the evidence technicians arrived in a police van. We proceeded on to St. Joseph's. Upon our arrival we parked near the emergency room entrance. The police detectives must have called ahead, as the emergency room staff were waiting for us. Christine, although weak from her horrible ordeal, was able to compose herself enough to respond to the medical team's inquiries. A doctor and two nurses took Christine to an examining room. Luther, Jerome, and I sat anxiously in the waiting room; we had no idea of the extent of her physical distress. While we were waiting, I took a minute to call Patty on my cell. She must have gone shopping with Marilyn as there was no answer. I left a message, told her not to worry; I would be tied up on the case, and did not know what time I would be home. I then called Ruby to give her an update, but she was out of the office. I left a brief message and told her I would get in touch with her later.

In about an hour the examining physician came to the entrance of the waiting room and asked us to join him in the hallway. Dr. Harvey Blackson spoke directly to Jerome, advising him that it was crucial to admit Christine to the hospital for further tests and to rebuild her strength. The physician indicated, to our relief, that although Christine was suffering from malnutrition and mental distress, he felt that she would be okay with some proper counseling. Jerome left with the doctor to the admitting office to fill out the paperwork. I returned to the waiting room and sat down next to Luther.

"How does it look for Christine, Jason?" he asked with sincere concern, rubbing his forehead in his stress.

"The doctor believes that she's going to be all right after a full rest and some proper counseling. It's clear that she went through a great deal with that bum."

"Jason, I had all I could do to restrain myself from taking Carter out behind the house and teaching him a lesson that might have been the last in his life." Luther tried to control the anger that was still filling him.

"I know how you feel, Luther, but he isn't worth it. Hopefully the criminal justice system will administer the proper punishment to him for his crimes." I tried to assuage the bitterness building within him.

"I don't know about that. This guy is from a well-to-do family with a lot of connections. Jason, you probably know about that better than I."

"Yes, I do, Luther, sorry to say. There is definitely a double standard of justice in our society. We just hope and pray that proper justice will prevail here. I have observed several injustices in my career as a law enforcement official."

"What do you mean, Jason?" he asked with interest.

"I'll give you an example. Years ago I worked on a case where an unoccupied house was burglarized several times by the same people. I was fortunate when a nearby neighbor was able to make out a Pennsylvania plate number. The witness also told me that the two suspects appeared to be in their twenties. I took a chance and checked with the city traffic ticket bureau, where I struck pay dirt, which led me to the university section of a central New York city. The plate number had appeared on several "John Doe" traffic warrants, and the address appeared on several of the tickets. I proceeded to the area and there was the car, parked next to the curb in a no parking zone. It didn't take long to locate the two young men, who shared an apartment. They were students, and both were from the good state of Pennsylvania, I learned that when I knocked on their door and they let me in. Antique doorknobs, stolen from the house were sitting on their kitchen table, as well as other items that I was able to identify from a list given to me. After meeting them, I called the local police, who impounded the car and arrested both of the young men after they orally admitted their participation in three criminal acts of burglary. The property was recovered. But the case never made it beyond a preliminary hearing. Why, you may ask? They were the sons of two affluent families. Now, at about the same time, a young man from a poor family stole an inexpensive radio from a cow barn and ended up in Attica State Prison for a three-year period. Luther, this is why you see officers with premature gray hair: the unfairness within the justice system."

"Jason, I get the drift." He shook his head in dismay.

Jerome Huntley returned to the waiting room.

"Talk about paperwork. I had to fill out about seven different forms." Luther and I both sympathized. We then went to Christine's hospital room. Luther and I waited in the hallway while Jerome entered the room and kissed his daughter on the forehead. She was sound asleep.

When Jerome rejoined us, he said wearily, "Fellas, while we're here in Tucson, if you don't mind, I think we had better go to the PD and give our statements." Jerome looked exhausted with continued worry. He added, "That bastard violated my daughter."

I didn't know what to say, but I did my best. "I'm sorry to hear of this, Jerome. Let's hope that scoundrel thoroughly pays for his actions."

"She's a pure person and I love her with all my heart. When her mom passed away, it was tough on her, too. We were a very close family. And now this vermin had to come along and hurt us. According to what the doctor told me, Christine told him Carter forced himself upon her." Tears filled in Jerome's eyes.

"She'll rally, Jerome. Just wait and see. She's strong. And she's under good care here." I tried to console him as he wept uncontrollably, his hands covering his face.

Luther turned away not wanting us to see the tears streaming down his cheeks.

Christine had gone through a difficult ordeal with Bradley Carter. With her admitted to St. Joseph's hospital for further tests and observation, Jerome, Luther, and I proceeded down to the Tucson PD to meet with the detectives.

When we arrived at the department, we were taken to the detective division. All four men who had been at the Carter residence were sitting there waiting for us. In three rooms we were each interviewed separately prior to submitting our sworn statements. According to Richter, the feds had been notified that Christine Huntley had been located and that her alleged abductor, Bradley Carter, was indeed in custody.

Detective Charles Perez took my statement, a total of four pages. We remained at the PD for several hours. After our statements were submitted we thanked the detectives involved in the investigation for their courtesy. Detectives Perez and Keller advised Jerome that they would come to the ranch for a further interview with Christine when she was feeling better. They didn't want to disturb her while she was in the hospital recuperating.

Jerome called his ranch and requested that one of his cars

be driven to the hospital for his use. We left the PD and returned to St. Joseph's. En route, we discussed the case, concluding that we were very fortunate to have located Christine before Carter went even further in his abuse. He had been giving her cocaine against her will, and there was no telling what he had in store for her. Jerome speculated that Carter could not stand to be rejected and that when Luther escorted him off the ranch property without Christine objecting, he became enraged. Surely it was at that juncture that Carter had begun to plot his plan for her abduction.

When we reached the hospital, we proceeded to Christine's private room and found her still asleep. I could readily understand why she was receiving liquids intravenously, but I was troubled to see her also hooked up to a heart-monitor unit. My pity went out to her. In my state police career I had seen so many men and women lying in hospital beds because they were the innocent victims of accidents, shootings, assaults, and other violent crimes. I always felt for their pain, but I had also learned, for my own survival, to harden myself against the images in my memory bank that could otherwise overwhelm me and keep me from doing my job to help prevent such violence.

After bidding Jerome farewell and before leaving the hospital, Luther and I stopped for a cup of coffee in the cafeteria.

"Jason, I don't know how to thank you for all your efforts in locating Christine," he said gratefully.

"Luther, it was my pleasure. We sure lucked out. Carter could have hurt us, but we took him by surprise. We can be thankful that he didn't have his gun with him. Someone could have been shot, even killed." I shuddered at the thought, and my mind jumped to my friend Jack Flynn.

"It came as a complete shock to him when you gave him the welcome punch," he said, remembering the incident with satisfaction.

"I didn't want to do it, but it saved us a lot of grief," I acknowledged.

"That's for sure. I'm so glad I've gotten to know you, Jason. I hope we'll meet again. I've heard so much about your area of the country. If I ever get to visit the Adirondacks, may I look you up?" he asked with sincerity.

"Luther, Patty and I would be happy to see you. And that goes for Christine and her father, too," I added.

"Jason, by the way, how is Jack Flynn doing since he got shot by those smugglers? I was lucky that day, you know. I had just passed that location with a trailer-load of horses when the gun battle took place."

"It's good of you to ask. Well, Jack is presently in rehab at a nursing home. He should be able to leave there in about a week. He's going to be very happy to know that Christine has been located. Jack and I have always been close, Luther. We were in the Marines together. He's a good man—and damned lucky to be alive."

"I met him just once, I believe. I know some policemen in Phoenix who had worked with him when he was on the force. They certainly speak well of Flynn."

I was glad to have that few minutes with Luther Watson. He's a squared away man, about twelve years my junior. It's clear he likes his position on the Huntley ranch. And I won't be surprised if he does come to visit the great Adirondacks sometime in the future.

We went back up to Christine's room. She was still asleep. I conversed with Jerome for a while. He thanked me again for our efforts and mentioned that he would await his service bill from Flynn Investigations. I gave him another business card with Flynn's Investigations' telephone number on it, as well as one of my cards from the Adirondacks.

"Jason, why don't you and your wife come down to the ranch before you head back to New York? We would love to have you. We always have had an annual barbecue, but certainly with Christine's disappearance, that was the furthest thing from my mind. If Christine is up to it, we'll make it a barbecue for all our friends and all the people involved in the case. I appreciated all your efforts. We were lucky to locate her alive, Jason. We'll try to make it at the end of next week." The relief of having found Christine had begun to erase the tension of anxiety that had so lined his face. "By the way, I'd like to include Ruby and Jack. Maybe they could ride down with you and your wife," he added.

"Yes, sir, we sure were lucky. I'll talk it over with my wife and I'll give you a call concerning Ruby and Jack one way or the other," I informed him. I hoped Patty could meet Christine, because of their similar ordeals.

"You do that, Jason. We'd love to have you as our guest."

I thanked Luther again and looked over at Christine, who was in a deep sleep. Seeing her in the large white bed brought back memories of when Patty lay so long at the Saranac Lake Hospital in a coma. I clenched my teeth just thinking about the two late killers who had abducted her when she stopped to help them near Old Forge. Both of them had paid the price for their life of crime. I recalled again how one was shot to death at St. Regis Falls and how the other crashed through a windshield, bouncing off the hood of the vehicle he was riding in, violently striking a hardwood tree near Indian Lake. Both their deaths were proof of the phrase, "crime doesn't pay."

Jerome, Luther, and I shook hands. I thanked them both and left the hospital. When I entered the car and turned the ignition switch on, I knew immediately that I had to stop for gas. The fuel tank indicator was floating between empty and one quarter. I left the parking lot and headed to I-10. Before I entered the ramp I pulled into a station and filled the tank. I almost did a flip when I saw the price. The sign read well over a dollar per gallon. The words *highway robbery* came to mind. I could only imagine how the men in the boardroom were smiling as the money poured in from the high fuel prices. I hated to think it was greed, but what else could it possibly be.

I looked at my watch: 8:25. I called Patty again, but there was still no answer. I was a little concerned after having missed her twice but hoped she was out for a walk. I left a message on the machine telling her I would be home shortly. I aimed the vehicle north on I-10, went to Route 8, then continued on westerly toward Route 85 at Gila Bend. Route 8 was completely void of other traffic. I kept the needle on the speedometer right on the speed limit. It was a lonely road, especially in the black of night. About four miles east of Gila Bend I observed a set of headlights bearing down on me from behind. The car was approaching at a fast clip. When it passed me I could feel the vacuum from the speed. It was an Arizona Highway Patrolman, probably headed to a serious accident scene. He wasn't displaying his flashing lights. As I kept the car at the speed limit, I could tell that he was preparing to make a right-hand turn onto Route 85. His taillights came on with two or three blips, and then he was out of sight.

It didn't take very long to find out why the police car had sped by me. Approximately six miles north of Gila Bend on Route 85 was a head-on collision. A body was lying on the smashed hood of one car while two more people were being attended to by some volunteer firefighters. The patrolman's cruiser was pulled off the highway and he was in the process of putting flares out along the road. It was a gruesome sight, of which I had seen many during my career as a trooper. No matter how long a person has been on the job and exposed to accident scenes involving vehicles, he or she never forgets those images. I well remember hearing the moans from the victims so seriously injured, some who never survived. It's those images that pull at a person's heart and nervous system, so difficult to forget.

I slowed down with the intention to stop and lend a hand, but a large man with a large flashlight rushed onto the highway and hollered out, "Keep moving, bud." I shifted into second and kept on going. They seemed to have the scene under control.

When I pulled into the resort I stopped at the security building and displayed my tag that assured me entrance to this peaceful place in the west valley. I was deeply tired. I made a right, then a left at the clubhouse, and finally pulled in beside Jack Flynn's big coach. I was so happy to see Patty as she opened the entrance door. We fell into each other's arms.

"Honey, I'm so glad you're home. I've missed you so very, very much," she said softly as she held me. "What a day you have had!"

"Sweetheart, I've missed you, too. I tried to call, but there was no answer. Did you get my message?" I asked, wondering where she could have been.

"I was at Marilyn's next door. It just came over the news that the authorities have located the missing coed. And they've made an arrest. Were you involved?" she asked excitedly.

"Yes, Patty. I was involved with locating Christine. We had a lucky break from the reward notice that was placed in the newspaper. It all went down so fast. He hadn't treated her very kindly." I deliberately soft pedaled what I told her as I didn't want to bring back Patty's own memories of her ordeal in the Adirondacks, especially with her being pregnant. "I'll fill you in on the details later. Fortunately no one was hurt during the apprehension. I made a citizen's arrest on her abductor, whom she had stopped seeing, and turned him over to law enforcement. That's it."

"I understand, darling. You must be exhausted. And are you hungry? I know it's rather late to eat," she said, glancing up at the clock.

"You know, sweetie, I'm so tired I don't think I could handle a meal. But I could use a cup of hot chocolate and some cinnamon toast." I realized for the first time that I hadn't taken the time to eat all day.

"Okay, we'll both have some." She took the hot chocolate from the cabinet and placed four slices of whole wheat bread into the toaster. While Patty prepared the hot drink I went into the bathroom and washed my hands. As I glanced into the mirror I saw the weariness in my face. I needed at least eight hours of good sleep. It had been a trying day.

"Jason, I almost forgot to tell you. Ruby called after I heard it on the news and told me to have you call her or stop at the office in the morning. She sounded pretty anxious. Maybe you'd better give her a quick call."

"Thanks, honey, I will. And I'll also go to the office in the morning and fill her in on all the details. By the way, did she happen to mention how Jack is doing?" I continue to worry about my good friend.

"Yes, she did. You'll be happy to know Jack is out of rehab and staying at Ruby's home. He has already been doing some walking outside. He may even be able to return to the office next week," she added.

"That's great news!" I was relieved to learn that Jack was doing so well. Then I chuckled to myself, because being a former tough marine, why wouldn't he? I should have known he'd recover just fine. I picked up the phone and gave Ruby a brief explanation of what had transpired, told her I would see her in the morning to give her all the details. I asked to speak to Jack, but he had already fallen off to sleep. I then told her to wish Jack my best.

I joined Patty at the table and we sat down to two cups of steaming hot chocolate and a plate of warm cinnamon toast. I filled her in on more of the events. She was so happy that Christine had been found alive and reunited with her father. When we finished our late-night treat we placed the cups and small plates on the counter, then prepared for bed.

It felt good to finally lie horizontal on a comfortable mattress. I rolled over to embrace my wife and our lips met in a warm, passionate kiss. We fell off to sleep in each other's arms.

CHAPTER THIRTEEN

The radio alarm went off at 7:00 a.m. sharp. The news broadcast consisted of overnight activities that had occurred in the Phoenix region. There were the usual reports of shootings, with three deaths and presently being investigated by the Phoenix PD detectives under the direction of Captain Jay Silverstein, leader of the homicide division. It was music to my ears to hear that the perps had been apprehended and were presently in custody. The next news item was the apprehension of Bradley Carter, who was being charged with the abduction of Christine Huntley, age 21, of Casa Grande. The announcer went on to say that more details would be released later. The ongoing investigation was being continued by detectives of the Casa Grande Police Department. The lead detective, Charles Perez, had indicated that the recipient of the five-thousand-dollar reward had not as yet been determined.

I was relieved my name was not mentioned, but I hoped that credit would be given to Flynn Investigations, which would please Jack Flynn and give free advertising that would reflect favorably on the detective agency. Jack not only had a good background in the field of law enforcement, but was confident that he would prevail with his own agency. And, with that mix plus the true grit he possessed, the agency was now well established. I knew I was welcome to become a permanent member of it, working for Jack. The prospect sounded great, but I also knew the hot summers in Arizona would be disastrous, as Patty and I—true mountain dwellers—would be unable to survive the intense heat.

After a hearty breakfast, a shave, and a hot shower, I dressed and prepared to go to the office. Patty said not to concern myself about her, and advised me that she would again be spending the day at the clubhouse with her friends working on a project. When I was ready to depart I gave her a hug and a goodbye kiss.

"What time will you be home, honey?" she asked.

"I'll call you, sweetheart, and let you know. Maybe we'll go out for dinner to celebrate. See you later, babe."

As I went outside, I was surprised to see my neighbor, Art, placing his outdoor furniture into his large storage compartments. I walked over to see what was going on. I had thought he was going to stay at the resort for another month.

"Good morning, Art. How are you?" I asked, somewhat perplexed.

"Jason, hello. You've been a busy fellow. I've hardly seen you recently. You seem to be gone most of the time." He looked up, happy to see me.

"I've been busier than I wanted to be," I said carefully. "Say, Art! What's going on? Are you packing up?"

"We were to stay another month, but our son will be attending a conference in Tucson. It was kind of a last-minute deal. Someone wasn't able to make it. Fortunately, he was able to get accommodations for the family to go along with him, and we made arrangements at a resort there, so we'll be seeing him, his wife, and the children. Didn't Patty tell you?" he asked, looking puzzled.

"It must have slipped her mind. I got home rather late. Yes, I know what you mean, Art. Life goes by too rapidly. The next thing you realize, the kids are adults and, go out on their own to make their own way or spend time attending a university or college. I don't disagree with you and Marilyn. Enjoy your family and your grandkids." I walked over to shake Art's hand.

"I enjoyed meeting you, Jason," Art said.

I nodded at Art and headed toward the car. I unlocked the door and climbed in. The Arizona morning was cool, probably no higher than forty degrees as usual. I started the car and warmed it up. I backed the Camaro around and headed out the exit road. I tooted at Art, who was closing the storage bin on his motor home.

Route I-10 was bumper to bumper with early morning traffic. I exited onto 99th Avenue and headed north toward the shopping plaza and the home of Flynn's office. When I arrived there I wheeled in next to Ruby's car and turned the Camaro off. I reached into the back seat, grabbed my briefcase containing all my notes and memos on the Huntley case, and walked toward the entrance. I noticed two cars parked nearby with their visors turned down, indicating that they were members of the press. When I entered the office, I could see that Ruby was in deep conversation with two men whom I assumed to be newspaper reporters. Ruby, as always, was a fine representative of the agency, handling the situation at her best. As I walked by the reception area, I heard by the conversation that they were discussing the Huntley abduction. Not wanting to interrupt, I continued on and entered Ruby's office. I made my way to an empty table, where I removed my notes from my briefcase, placed them in chronological order, and discarded some of the duplicates. I promised myself that before I left Flynn's office that day, my Huntley report would be completed and submitted to Ruby and Bill Reidy.

When Ruby completed her press interview she came into the office with a big smile across her face. "Good morning, Mr. Black, the super sleuth. Congratulations on breaking the Huntley case," she said joyfully.

"What's this 'Mr. Black' stuff? You're so formal," I joked. "But thanks for the congratulations, even though actually it was a hunch on my part. The notice we placed in the *Desert Journal* acted like a fishing line, and sure enough we had the right response when Ronald Jamison contacted the paper, as you already know. Dick Case, the managing editor, Ron Jamison, and I had a meeting. Jamison just about floored us when he told us that Bradley Carter was a tenant on one of his rental properties. After I left the paper I went to the ranch and picked up Jerome Huntley and Luther Watson and headed to the Tucson area. I had Jamison give me a written permission note to enter the house to cover myself. By the way, to cover the agency and us for our entry, I will submit the permission slip as an enclosure to my report on the case."

"Good thinking, Jason. We certainly don't want an illegal entry charge against us," Ruby nodded in agreement.

I continued, "We searched the home, and when we went down to the cellar we found marijuana plants being grown, and a locked door with a tapping sound coming from within. Luckily I had my lock picks with me, enabling me to open the door. We found Christine bound and gagged on an old army cot. There were drugs and drug paraphernalia lying on a table near the cot. Ruby, I'm sorry to have to tell you that Christine looked pale and her face was bruised from being hammered by Carter. As you know, they've admitted her to St. Joseph's Hospital in Tucson, where she'll be for a few days."

I caught my breath and continued while I had the details so fresh in my mind. "The lead Detective Charles Perez, in charge of the investigation, will be the one you would contact if any questions arise. I've submitted a lengthy sworn statement of my participation in the case. Detective Perez will be in contact with the federal authorities. They may want to adopt a kidnapping case. Before I leave the office today, I will type up the Huntley case concerning my participation in it."

"I'd appreciate that," Ruby said, clearly pleased with the successful outcome.

"For your information, Mr. Huntley has invited Patty and me to his ranch before we head back to New York." I felt she would like to know. "He hopes you and Jack will come, too."

"That's great, Jason. I've only heard wonderful things about him. He must have been under a tremendous strain with his concern over Christine's disappearance."

"He was, but he tried to remain calm and cool. He's a man who doesn't like to show his emotions, but I just know that he was churning inside. His love for his daughter is immense. The loss of Mrs. Huntley took a toll on him, and now Christine and his ranch are what he's living for."

"Yes, sometimes when one of the spouses passes away it leaves a terrible void that is difficult to replace," Ruby agreed.

"Tell me, Ruby, how is Jack doing? Now that my part in this case is done, I've got to get over to see him."

"He's doing fine. A little antsy, but that's the sign he's getting better. Before you and Patty leave, we'll all have that dinner together. Plan on it," she reminded me.

"We'd love to. And for now, will I be able to use the empty office on the end to write up the Huntley case?" I asked, gathering up my material.

"Certainly. You can use anything you want. We have a new copying machine in the second office down the hall. You'll find a computer set up and paper in the bottom desk drawer. Jason, if there is anything else you need, just call me on the intercom." Her offer was genuine.

"Is Bill Reidy in today?" I asked, looking out into the office.

"Guess you won't be able to see him today. He had to fly to Denver yesterday. He's testifying on an automobile accident case where there was negligence on the part of one of the operators. There was a death, and we were engaged to conduct a separate inquiry into the case. Bill was able to come up with some important information for our client," she explained.

"I remember several court cases like that. The proceedings can go on for days before a verdict can be reached. Litigation, as you know, can become exhausting." I could still hear the judge's gavel when the arguments reached a certain point of frustration. I excused myself as I picked up my briefcase and my notes and went to the office at the far end of the hallway.

The pressures on Ruby and her responsibilities were tremendous, especially with Jack's hospitalization. Running the shopping plaza, an entity separate from Flynn Investigations, meant complying with the entire city, county, and state requirements, which amounted to mounds of paperwork. Then there were the inspectors from various departments to contend with.

The office was a spare one that was used not only for interviews but for report preparation and report writing by some of Jack's out-of-town operatives. I laid my briefcase on top of the desk and placed all my notes in some semblance of order. Before I sat down to enter my report on the computer, I decided to go down to the coffee room and pour myself a cup. I added a half-a-spoon of sugar and some half-and-half. I picked up a glazed donut and returned to the office.

The report flowed well. Having my notes and memos laid out on the desk in front me was most helpful when it came to transposing the written word to the computer. After about an hour and a half of typing, the report took form. All the details had been accounted for, including the fact that Christine Huntley was fortunate to have survived the ordeal. My final notation indicated that the case had been successfully closed. While I was at the desk, the phone in the office rang. Somewhat surprised, I answered it.

"Jason, Ruby here. There is a gentleman on the phone who would like to speak with you." I heard a slight tease in her voice.

"I'll take it, Ruby," I said, and pushed down the lit-up button.

"Hello, Jason Black here. May I help you?" I asked, curious as to who would be calling.

"Jason, this is Jack. How come I haven't heard from you? I've been waiting anxiously to hear how you made out on the Huntley case." I thought I detected a slight chuckle in Jack's tone. "Don't worry. Ruby told me, but I had to pull your leg a little. Can't you tell I'm getting back to my old self? I read in the paper that an operative from an investigation agency had something to do with locating the missing coed."

"How are you feeling, buddy?" I asked, happy to hear his voice so cheerful.

"A lot better, now that I have you on the other end of the telephone. I was only kidding you, Jason. You did one hell of a job finding Christine Huntley. I bet her dad is happy he'll have his daughter back on the ranch. I read that the lead detective from Casa Grande was Charles Perez. I know him, and he's a hardworking cop. I'm proud of your performance, Jason. Remember, buddy, you can feel free to come aboard Flynn Investigations any time you want to. We'd love to have you here in Arizona." I realized Jack would never cease attempts to have me join the agency.

"Listen, marine, I was honored that you asked me to come to Arizona to assist you under the circumstances. But as far as a permanent move here, it's still definitely out of the question," I answered emphatically.

"I know, I know, but you can be sure I'll keep trying to hire you." Jack chuckled again.

"All kidding aside, how are you feeling, buddy?" I asked.

"I'm beginning to feel like my old self. I've been exercising a little. Ruby, as you know, has me staying at her house for the time being. I believe I'll be able to return to my place by next week. When will you and Patty be returning to New York?" he inquired.

"We're going to try to take a few days to see some sights before we leave. I'm going to check on available flights tomorrow and make reservations for about a week from now. By the way, Jerome Huntley would like us all to be his guests at the ranch for a barbecue the end of next week. He'd like both you and Ruby to attend—if you feel up to it, of course," I continued.

"Well, maybe we could. I'll have to check with Ruby. I do have a doctor's appointment in the middle of next week. If he releases me, I'll definitely be there. That's very gracious of Huntley. He's a well respected man in that Casa Grande region and has contributed a lot of time and effort for his community, and that's not all. You may have already learned how very well known he is in the horse business throughout the southwest."

"One question: seeing that my duties are completed here, would you like Patty and me to make arrangements to get a motel for the remainder of our stay in Arizona?" I thought it only fair to inquire, in the event he was in need of his motor home.

"No way! Jason, you, Patty, and Ruby are all the family I have. Feel free to stay in the coach. How are you both enjoying the experience?" I could tell he was sincere in wanting to know.

"We love it. It's a beautiful coach and the resort is an excellent place to park it," I assured him. "I'd thought I might have to take the coach out of the park and use it on the investigation, but it wasn't necessary to do so."

"Listen, Jason, feel free to take it out of the resort. It's available for you to use in any sightseeing jaunts you would like to take," he offered graciously.

"I appreciate the offer, Jack, but it is a large unit and I haven't had that much operating experience driving a coach of this size. Maybe sometime in the future, but not now." I would never be able to forgive myself if something happened to the coach while I was driving. "Besides," I added slyly, "I enjoy driving the Camaro."

"I understand. Well, buddy, I'd better get going. I want to surprise Ruby tonight. I'm having a dinner catered here for us. She has been doing triple duty at the office with me on sick leave. It's a surprise, so don't say anything to her about my plans," he cautioned.

"I promise I won't. Take care, Jack. We'll be in touch."

"You did a great job locating Christine Huntley. Take care, buddy."

I heard the click of his receiver, and put mine down.

I appreciated Jack's telephone call. He normally was a man of few words, but he had made clear to me that it meant a lot to him for Patty and me to come to Arizona. I read my report over and checked it for any errors. All in all, the report was factual and accurate. I took the report and made several copies of it for the agency, plus one for my New York files at home, which I tucked into my briefcase. In the event I would have to appear in court to testify, I'd have my own copy to review. I returned to the office at the end of the hall and secured it, leaving it the way I found it, neat and squared away.

I returned to Ruby's office and knocked on the open door.

"Come in, Jason, and have a seat," she offered, beckoning.

I entered and sat down in the comfortable leather chair next to her desk.

"Gosh, Ruby, this chair is so comfortable I could fall asleep."

"Jason, are you kidding? I didn't think you ever slept. Patty told me that you pace the floors at night sometimes."

"Oh, she did, did she?" Startled, I wondered to myself what other secrets she might have divulged.

Ruby broke out in a warm smile and said, "Just kidding, Detective Black." She laughed, probably catching the worried look that had crossed my face.

Ruby poured me a cup of coffee from the almost empty pot. We sat while sipping our coffee in the office talking about various cases that Jack had worked on. We talked about the Marine Corps days that Jack Flynn and Jason Black had shared. Some of the tales that Ruby chuckled about were stories that were now only a faint memory to me. I quickly induced from the conversation that Jack had been relating some of those military adventures to Ruby during his convalescence to explain our strong bond. As we concluded our visit, Ruby asked me to present a voucher for my time and services to Flynn Investigations, so that she could properly bill Mr. Huntley. She would then issue me an agency paycheck before I departed for the northeast.

When I got up to leave, she extended her hand and grabbed mine. "Thank you, Jason. You are a lifesaver. I don't know what we would have done without you." Tears welled up in her eyes.

"I'm only happy that I could help a little." I reached over and gave her a hug as I got up to leave. "Tell Jack that I'll be in touch with him about the barbecue and thank him for his generosity with the use of his coach. By the way, did Jack mention to you that Patty and I may try to take in some sights as long as we have next week free?"

"Yes, Jason. He did," she acknowledged.

I then left the office with my briefcase, walked to the Camaro, unlocked the door, and climbed in. Before long I was in the middle of bumper to bumper traffic headed south on 99th Avenue, homebound to my wonderful Patty.

The traffic on I-10, both westbound and eastbound, was heavy. The semi-trailer rigs were all in the passing lane, and I was stuck behind an old-model stake-rack truck carrying a partial load of baled hay. The left rear dual wheels wobbled and smoke poured out of the exhaust pipe. Undoubtedly, the owner of this antique was trying to keep his vehicle until the wheels fell off. Under my breath, I muttered, "What a hazard!" I checked my rearview mirror to see if I could safely move to the passing lane. All was clear. When I was abreast of the slow-moving hay truck, I took a quick glance at the operator. His long white beard matched the snow-white hair that hung from under his straw hat. His glasses were perched on the end of his nose as he hunched over, gripping the steering wheel with both hands. I mused to myself, with a glimpse at my own future how difficult it must be to give up one's driving privilege when old age becomes a factor. When a large diesel truck blasted me with its air horn, I accelerated and pulled over into the right lane as quickly as I could so as not to impede the flow of traffic.

When I turned off at exit 124, my thoughts drifted back to the bearded man hanging on to his steering wheel with his load of baled hay, perhaps for a couple of horses he owned. Too bad he couldn't have had it delivered, but that expense was probably beyond him. I made my way to Van Buren Road and west to Citrus Road, contented with the thought that I had successfully completed the Huntley case and submitted the report. I was eager to return to the Adirondacks, where spring would soon be in the offing in a few months. The Arizona desert has its own beauty, with an abundance of cacti and flowers nestled throughout their mountain ranges, my heart and soul belongs to the Adirondack region and our chain of lakes nestled among the tree-covered rolling mountains.

As I drove into the resort, three large coaches pulling SUV's were in line to be checked into the campground. The operators were walking toward the entrance of the office to sign in. I knew that sometimes rigs would stay a night only to depart for their intended destination in the morning. These three operators appeared to be in their mid-to-late forties. I had already observed that many young people were beginning to adopt the recreational-vehicle-lifestyle. I wondered, though, where these folks got their money to purchase these expensive diesel coaches that cost well into six figures. That was a mystery to me. I could only hope they acquired the funds through honest means.

I pulled next to Jack Flynn's coach and turned off the engine. I missed seeing the Panighetti's coach that had been parked next to us. They were probably already situated in a resort in Tucson. We would certainly miss our good neighbors. I got out of the car as Patty opened the door on our coach.

"Welcome to our home away from home," she called as she held up a cup of tea to toast me. "Here, have a sip."

"Hi, sweetheart! Gosh, you look beautiful standing there in the doorway. I missed you," I said, giving her a big hug. "Hey, I'm famished. I didn't have any lunch, but I grabbed a couple of donuts at the office. It took me almost all day. Something smells good. Is it Southern fried chicken?" I asked.

"You're so perceptive when it comes to food."

"Honey, you know how I love your fried chicken and your coleslaw," I replied.

"That's the menu. Everything will be ready shortly."

After giving Patty a kiss on the cheek, I placed my briefcase in the closet off the dining area. She had already set the table, there was a platter of hot fried chicken sitting on top of the counter next to a pan of cornbread that she must have baked. I hurried into the bathroom and washed my hands before dinner.

"How did it go today, Jason?" she asked with interest.

"Good, honey. I talked with Ruby and managed to get my report on the case typed."

"You had two telephone calls this afternoon, probably after you left the office. One was from a Dick Case in Casa Grande and one from Jerome Huntley. They would like you to call them in the morning after nine," she stated.

"I'll do that," I responded, sorry I had missed their calls.

"Okay, honey. Everything is ready. Have a seat."

I pulled her chair out from the table and seated her. The aroma of the chicken teased my taste buds. I passed the platter to Patty and she took a golden-brown breast. I took the other breast and a drumstick, along with some coleslaw. Patty sliced us each a generous piece of cornbread. It was still warm as I spread the sweet butter on top of it. The yams were perfectly seasoned with brown sugar mixed with some sweet butter—delicious! We enjoyed the southern entrée she had so skillfully prepared. Patty beamed when I told her that she had outdone herself this time and it truly was the best Southern fried chicken that I had ever tasted.

"Honey, do I have a surprise for you! One of your favorites. Can you guess?" she asked, prettily wrinkling her nose.

Surmising it was dessert she was referring to, I ventured "Is it ice cream?"

"You're way off, Jason. I'll tell you. It starts with an *m* and the second word begins with a *p*," she said as she broke into a smile.

"Is it mincemeat pie?" I guessed with joy.

"You're right, honey. I thought I'd surprise you. I know how much you love it. They had some jars left from Christmas, and luckily I spotted them on one of my shopping trips with Marilyn." She was clearly delighted with her find.

"Some of these kids today have never heard of mincemeat pie," I replied.

"As we've discussed many times, Jason, today the fast food chains have changed so many people's eating patterns, especially young people. It's probably one of the reasons we see so many overweight problems. Jason, if you're not careful, you could easily go to 250 pounds. That's why I try to make us plenty of salads and vegetables, and fixed grilled chicken when we can. But once in a while, I have to spoil you. And you certainly deserve it after what you've just done for Flynn Investigations."

Patty warmed two small pieces of mincemeat pie and poured us two cups of decaf. She had a point about food. I rather regretfully remembered the donut I had eaten while doing my report. When she served the warmed pie and decaf, I caught the look on her face warning me to not to ask for a second piece.

After we finished our decaf, I helped Patty clear the table, informing her that I'd do the dishes and clean up the kitchen. She came over to me, placed her arms around my neck, held me close, looked up into my eyes, and said, "I love you, Jason Black. How could I have been so lucky to have met you on my life's journey? And now we're going to have a baby together." She began to tear up.

I told her, "I am the lucky one, my darling. I feel that I've known you all my life." I took out my handkerchief and patted her tear-filled eyes. She'd been having more emotional moments lately that I attributed to her pregnancy, with her body experiencing hormonal changes, but I still knew her words and feelings were sincere. I walked her over to the leather davenport and sat her down. "Honey, I want you to rest while I do the dishes and square away the kitchen."

"Jason, you're so good to me. Maybe I'm getting a little homesick for Old Forge, our place in the mountains, and our good friends. I miss going to work at John's Diner. I hope I'll have my job when we get back!" she exclaimed.

"Patty, you worry too much. Everything will work out for us. I really didn't want to come out here to Arizona, but I couldn't let Jack down. He could have assigned someone else to handle the Huntley matter, but I know how Jack is. When we were in the marines we promised each other that in the event one of us needed the other, we'd drop everything. That is the reason we're here. Jack's improving, and as soon as we can we'll go home. I know you have your doctor's appointment coming up." I tried to reassure her.

I handed Patty a magazine to look at as I returned to the kitchen to finish my chores.

We went to bed early. Patty turned the radio on and we listened to a talk show until we both drifted off to sleep in each other's arms.

CHAPTER FOURTEEN

When I opened my eyes I looked over to Patty's side of the bed. She wasn't there. Then I heard the shower running and realized that she was in the bathroom. I pushed the covers back and got out of bed. I missed Ruben's tugging at the bedspread. I sure would look forward to seeing him again. I went into the kitchen, switched on the coffeepot, washed my hands, and then set the table to surprise Patty. I returned to the bedroom to dress, planning to call Dick Case and Jerome Huntley after breakfast.

Patty came out of the bathroom and joined me in the bedroom. She was wearing her oyster-colored robe, with her freshly washed hair wrapped in a towel turban-style. I walked over and gave her a peck on the cheek and a quick hug.

"Do I smell the coffee brewing, my dear?"

"Yes, I turned it on while you were showering, sweetheart. I thought you'd like a fresh cup. I know how you love your morning coffee." Patty was always up first, making breakfast preparations. With her present condition, I determined that I should do more, helping her as much as possible.

"What would you like for breakfast?" she asked.

"Let's see. How about if we have some French toast this morning with that sourdough bread?" We both enjoyed it made with sourdough bread.

"That's a good idea. Would you like some crisp bacon with

it?"

"Sounds good to me," I eagerly agreed.

She opened the breadbox. In less than thirty minutes we were both sitting at the table enjoying the golden brown French toast. The sourdough bread gave it a special taste. The crisp bacon and the warm maple syrup complemented the flavor. I refilled our cups. We reminisced about Old Forge, how much we missed our friends, and our loyal dog, Ruben. Patty had placed a picture of him in the bedroom of the coach. The big K-9 was always in our thoughts. We both knew that he missed us, too. I assured Patty that I would call Wilt this afternoon to find out what, if anything, had been going on in our Adirondack region. Wilt would know the entire latest scoop around the area. The diner was an excellent source of information with customers' morning coffee. After our breakfast I helped clean off the table and put things away. I offered to do the dishes, but Patty said she'd gladly take care of them, if I would run the vacuum cleaner.

"Honey, after I finish running the cleaner, I'll take out the trash." Four dumpsters were strategically placed around the park for the campers' convenience.

"I'd appreciate it."

The coach's interior was well laid out with several closets and storage areas. Considered a basement model, it offered large storage compartments accessible only from the outside of the coach. It was a home on wheels. I was frankly pleased that I didn't have to drive, because of the constant heavy flow of traffic in Maricopa County. If we had taken it out for a run and been involved in an accident, I would have been heartbroken, although Jack would have forgiven me.

I called Dick Case at the paper in Casa Grande around 9:15. The receptionist buzzed his line and he answered.

I returned his greeting. "Good morning, Dick."

"How are you this morning, Jason? Thank you for calling. I tried to reach you on your cell phone, but couldn't get it to ring. I wanted to let you know that Jerome Huntley and I met with Ronald Jamison at my office and presented him with a bank check for $5000. Jamison deserved the reward. That was good information. And, Jason, you deserve a lot of credit for following up on that lead," he said.

"Dick, I'm glad that it came out the way it did. Hopefully Christine will do fine. It was a terrible experience for her to go through, but luckily Carter is now behind bars and will be punished for the crimes he's being charged with if the justice system works the way it's supposed to. I have to commend Detective Perez, his partner, and the detectives from the Tucson PD for all the work they put forth."

"Yes, Jason, we do have dedicated people on our police forces. I'm hoping the judicial system will do their job as well. It certainly was my pleasure to meet you."

"I was indeed glad to have met you, too, sir."

"Have you been in touch with Jerome Huntley?" he asked.

"I'm going to call him next. Why do you ask?"

"When he was here at my office he indicated that he will be putting on a beef barbecue at the ranch for everyone who was involved in the case. He mentioned that he was going to ask some of the staff from Flynn Investigations, including you and your wife."

"He has already mentioned it to me," I replied. "That's very nice of him."

"Yes, Jerome's that kind of a guy, totally unselfish." His voice was warm with admiration.

"When I interviewed Mr. Huntley I sensed that he was a charitable person," I offered.

"Yes, and Christine is just like her dad."

"I want to thank you, Dick. Hopefully, I'll see you at the ranch. So long for now."

"Take care, Jason Black."

I hung up the telephone and dialed Jerome Huntley, who picked it up on the third ring.

"The Huntley ranch," he answered.

"Hello, Jerome. Jason Black here," I responded.

"Just the man I want to talk with. How are you?" His tone had become almost jovial since Christine's return.

"Good, sir. How is Christine feeling?" I asked with genuine concern, knowing what she had been through.

"Jason, she is remarkable. She's had some good rest and continues to progress daily. Her spirits are good, Jason, considering what she has endured. I want to thank you for all your efforts in finding her. If there is ever anything I can do to assist you in this region, do not hesitate to let me know. Christine is the most important part of my life," he said emphatically.

"It all came together better than I had expected, sir. Thank God for Jamison."

"How's Jack Flynn? Is he home yet?" he inquired.

"He's doing okay. His rehab has been completed and he's currently walking and exercising. You can't keep a former marine down."

"I'm so pleased to hear this. I'm glad you called. I just wanted to remind you of the beef barbecue here at the ranch next week Saturday. We'd love to have you and your wife. Also, I've spoken to Jack Flynn, and his secretary, Ruby. Could you arrange to bring the two of them along with you if he's able to make it?" he asked.

"I'll see what I can do about that. What time would you like us there?"

"Come early, Jason. Anytime after 11:00," he replied.

"We'll be there, and thank you for inviting us."

"You're always welcome here," he said with sincerity ringing in his voice.

"We'll see you then, sir," I replied.

"Goodbye for now, Jason."

"So long, sir."

I returned to the kitchen, where I found Patty drinking a glass of ice water. "Would you like a cup of coffee or green tea, honey?" she asked, looking up.

"No, I think I've had enough this morning. Maybe later on, love."

"Jason, I'm going out for a walk with some of the girls. Do you mind?"

"Not at all. I thought we'd make some calls to our friends at home, but first I want to wash the car and give it a wax job."

"Do you want me to help you?" she offered.

"No, it's not necessary. Walking is good for you. How are you feeling?"

"Great, honey. I've been fortunate. Hardly any morning sickness lately."

"You know how I worry about you, dearest, especially now that you're pregnant. Be careful walking, especially over those speed bumps. I don't want you falling," I cautioned.

"I'll be careful, Jason. I promise. I've got good sturdy shoes. See you later. I see the girls coming this way to pick me up," Patty said. She slipped on a lightweight jacket, gave me an embrace and a kiss, and headed out the door. I returned her friends' waves and closed the door. I watched the group go around the corner of our street, feeling happy that Patty had someone to walk and talk with.

I prepared to wash the car and put a coat of wax on it. I wanted it in the same condition that I had I found it in when Patty and I had arrived. I proceeded to fill a bucket with water and add some liquid soap. In one of the larger storage compartments I found a long-handled brush for the job. Then I began my project. The soapsuds slid down the windows and sides of the dust-laden Camaro. After washing and rinsing the car, I dried it with an old towel that had been stored next to the brush.

The next step was to apply the wax, first to the top of the car, I waited until it dried, then took another soft towel and brought it to a glossy finish. The liquid wax was easy to apply. I followed through with the rest of the vehicle. With the chore completed, I placed the wax and cloths back in the storage area. I examined my project, pleased with the results, then opened the door to enter the coach.

I called Ruby to remind her of the invitation to the Huntley ranch the following Saturday. She informed me that Jack had gone for a short walk but would return shortly.

"Jason, as it stands now, we'll meet you at the resort about nine. If Jack for some reason doesn't feel up to par, I'll have him give you a call, but as it stands now we'll be seeing you and Patty on Saturday."

"How is Jack feeling, Ruby?" I asked.

"He's more like his old self. Jack wants to get back to work and, like I've told you before, he seems fidgety."

"Well, try to talk him into going. It will do him good to have a change of pace."

"I'll do my best. If you don't hear from us beforehand, we'll be at the resort around 9:00. How's Patty feeling, Jason?" she asked, changing the subject.

"She's feeling great. At the moment she's out walking with some of the ladies from the resort."

"That's good for her. A little exercise will do her good. Tell her to be careful."

"Thanks for your interest, Ruby. Patty's a precious person. She's been through a lot, as you know."

"I realize that. We look forward to seeing you both on Saturday."

"Right. You and Jack take care driving over here. We'll leave your car parked here, and I'll drive the Camaro. I just finished washing and waxing it."

"You didn't have to do that," she scolded.

"I know, but I wanted to. Anyway, it's good exercise."

"See you, Jason."

I heard the click as Ruby hung up her receiver. I then dialed Wilt Chambers in Boonville and soon heard that familiar voice.

"Chambers' Logging, Wilt speaking."

"What's this Chambers' Logging? Wilt, Jason here." I chuckled to myself.

"By gosh, Jason, where in the heck have you been? I haven't heard from you in a while. How are you and Patty, and when are you coming home? Everybody misses you," he fired out quickly.

"We're both doing fine. I doubt whether everyone misses us. How are you, Wilt?" I asked.

"Well, the ones that count do, Jason. I've been good."

"Is Ruben being a good dog for you?"

"He certainly is. He's sitting right in front of me with his ears sticking straight up. That dog is smart. I think he knows you're on the other end of this telephone. Here, I'll put the receiver up to his ear."

I spoke clearly and slowly. "I'll be home soon, Ruben. Good dog." I heard an answering bark.

"Did you catch that, Jason? Yep, he knows his master's voice alright."

I laughed appreciatively, then inquired, "Have you had a lot of snow?"

"We've had a couple of good storms. The snowmobiles have had a good run for the past few days."

"How's the gang at the diner in Old Forge?"

"Very good, Jason. As I said, everyone asks about you and Patty. And we sure do miss Patty at the diner. She's one of the best waitresses in the North Country. There isn't too much activity going on. I've been going through some of my equipment. I did purchase a very good used log skidder from a fellow up in Tupper Lake. And in my spare time I've got two carved black bears almost completed."

"I'd say you've been busy, Wilt." I know he'll be keeping busy every minute of his waking life.

"I hate to tell you this, Jason, but Charlie Perkins was involved in a bad accident over in Vermont. It wasn't his fault. He had a load of hardwood on coming down a steep mountain road, when all of a sudden an old pickup backed out of a driveway without looking. Charlie had to make a split-second decision either to run the pickup down or go off the highway. You know Charlie: he wouldn't hurt anyone or anything. He found a clearing and aimed the Peterbilt for it with that heavy load of hardwood." He paused.

"Well, what happened?" I asked anxiously. "Was he hurt?"

"What happened, Jason, was that Charlie collided with a two-story chicken house and went clean through it. It did a job on the Peterbilt, but luckily Charlie was wearing his seatbelt and just got badly shook up. The wood and the trailer were hardly touched. By Charlie's account, the old codger in the pickup backs out of that driveway about every morning at the same time, according to the Vermont troopers that investigated it. Over the years Charlie had traveled that particular highway several times and had seen the old truck backing down the driveway, but this once the timing was unfortunate. The fellow operating that truck was lucky."

"You can say that again. What a story! Well, it's been great talking with you, Wilt. I'd better be going now."

"I understand. Oh! I want you to know that I've got a couple of two-man saws for your collection. When you get home I'll bring them over with Ruben. Give Patty my love, and we'll be glad when you're home. Goodbye."

"Take care, Wilt. We'll be seeing you in the very near future. It looks like the case I came out to work on has been pretty well wrapped up. I'll fill you in on all the details when I see you. My friend Jack is out of the hospital, and it looks like we'll be leaving in about a week. I'll let you know as soon as I make our reservations. Tell Ruben we'll be seeing him soon."

Wilt seemed pleased with the news. "Jason! Great news! Ruben and I will both be glad to see you and Patty. Let me know when, and I'll be at the airport."

We exchanged our goodbyes and I placed the next call to Wayne, who answered on the second ring.

"Beyea Investigations. May I help you?" he answered in his usual business-like manner.

"Wayne, you certainly sound official on the telephone."

"Jason Black. Is that you? I'm glad that you called. How's Patty?"

"She's fine. And how are you and Kathy? Surviving the winter?"

"Yes, we are. Fortunately, we're in good shape. Jason, the domestic case I worked on for you turned out very well, unfortunately it ended up in a divorce. The wife has remarried a fellow fifteen years her junior, and they've taken off for Bermuda. I'm glad the case is completed. The attorney for the husband had some photos that would make your eye sockets pop out."

"Wayne, as I may have mentioned to you before, the domestic cases are not to my liking. But I will say that in present-day society there are so many pressures put on everyone, especially in the lower socioeconomic classes." I tried to explain to Wayne my observations of years of talking to the spouses who had gone through this painful ordeal. "I've had several cases where I've told the potential client to go home and think about what they're doing. Some do. A few seek marriage counseling and many times they start anew, which benefits the family, especially where children are concerned. So many family internal issues could be negotiated if they would only take time to discuss their dilemmas and put the cards on the table."

"Jason, I share the same advice with my clients: try to avoid the pains of divorce, but if all else fails, I'll regretfully work on their cases. Yes, we agree on that approach," he responded.

"How did you make out on the other case you mentioned during our last telephone conversation?"

"Jason, that case is still in the early stages of the investigation. Also, I've had some check cases from some of the banks, and I'm still trying to define this check-21 concept," he informed me.

"I'll notify you on our return to Old Forge next week or so. I appreciate your assistance on that marital case. Oh! By the way, I have been in touch with Dave Wachtel in the Hudson Valley Region. He's been busy over the winter."

"Dave is an excellent investigator. He—I'm sorry, I have another call coming in. We'll stay in touch, Jason.

"Thanks, Wayne. I wish you and your family the very best."

We hung up and I dialed Dale Rush's telephone number in Old Forge.

"Hello," he answered with a raspy voice.

"Jason Black calling. Do you have a cold? You sound

hoarse," I said with concern.

"Just getting over one. 'Tis the season. What's up, Jason? We miss you. When are you two coming home?"

"We plan to leave in a week or two. We're anxious to get home. Patty's quite homesick and she has a doctor's appointment she doesn't want to miss."

"How's she feeling, Jason?"

"She's been good, except for a little morning sickness."

"I'm glad to hear that she's okay. Evelyn and I both have had colds. Mine's breaking up; you can tell by my voice. I met Wilt, Charlie, and Jack at John's Diner last Saturday for breakfast. Many of the town people have gone to Florida for a few weeks. We were planning to go down, but Jim Jenny was alone at the marina. I've been helping him with some snowmobile repairs, and we both have been checking over my Stinson. We couldn't leave Jim alone with the volume of business that is coming into the shop," he added.

"Jim has a very good mechanical background. Evelyn is fortunate to have him on her staff. He's a good pilot, too."

"Yes, he is. I did hear that he's flown under a couple of bridges."

"I heard that rumor. I don't believe it. But he is an excellent pilot. How's Robert Moore, the supervisor? I imagine he's busy this time of year?"

"Jason, Bob is an excellent supervisor, and he's in his office before eight every working day. He has a full schedule of meetings and various functions in the township. He's got my support."

"I feel the same way about Bob. He takes good care of his job and is accessible to the citizens of our community. That means a great deal to the taxpayers."

"Not to change the subject, how is your buddy Jack Flynn doing? I heard he was shot on I-10 by that coyote gang. I was checking the news on the computer in the Phoenix newspaper and came across the details of the shootout. That region of Arizona seems to be a dangerous place, from what I read," he commented.

"You're right there. Jack has just finished his rehab and will be returning to work next week. I haven't had much of a chance to visit with him. But we've all been invited to a barbecue to be held at a ranch just outside of Casa Grande next Saturday. Patty and I are planning on taking Jack and his secretary, Ruby, to the affair," I informed him.

"That should be fun, Jason. You know you take life too darn serious at times. Relax a little and enjoy some play time."

"Yeah, I suppose you're right. I've been to the ranch. The gentleman who owns it is a horse dealer. It's a beautiful place with mountains in the background. I'll tell you all about it when I see you in person." I didn't want to go into too many details on the phone about the Huntley case.

"Jason, Evelyn and I have been doing some ice-fishing this winter. She's never ice-fished before, and she loves it."

"I enjoy it, too, but I haven't ice-fished in several years."

"I usually go with Jack Falsey, but he and his wife have gone to Florida."

"Dale, I just wanted to check in with you. We're looking forward to seeing you and Evelyn on our return. And I'm waiting patiently to hear the word from you about a wedding sometime this year."

"Evelyn and I are thinking seriously about it. We're going to have the ceremony in the air above the Fulton chain of lakes. Of course, the reception will take place at one of the local establishments. Keep it between you and Patty, Jason," he cautioned.

"My lips are sealed. Patty and I certainly wish you both the very best."

"Don't worry, you two are going to be at the head of the guest list. Take care, buddy."

"Take care of yourself, and you and Evelyn get over those colds. Be careful on the icy highways."

I hung up the phone. I had wanted to call Jack Falsey, but I didn't have his telephone number in Florida.

While Patty was out walking with her friends, I decided to run the vacuum. Even though the coach was airtight, dust seemed to enter the interior. Wind often sent the sand swirling across the flat desert surface. The resort had a cement-block wall around the perimeter, but even with this well-constructed protection, the blowing sand and dust somehow found its way into the coaches and trailers. After running the cleaner I decided to wash the windows.

Patty returned from her hike. She shared some of the resort gossip with me, consisting of bits and pieces of who went to lunch with whom, and who was asked to join the group. She prepared a light lunch of a green salad and tuna fish sandwiches, with a pitcher of lemonade made from the lemons on our lot. We looked forward to the barbecue at the Bar H Ranch the next Saturday. In the meantime we would take a few day trips to enjoy the Arizona desert and surrounding mountains.

The next day we each packed a small bag in the event we decided to stay overnight as we traveled. After a light breakfast we called Ruby and told her we were setting out to visit some of the Arizona sites. Ruby thought our plan was fantastic. She urged us to take the Camaro instead of renting a car. After thanking her, I informed Ruby that our planned Biltmore dinner would have to be postponed until a future trip to the area because we were anxious to return east. Ruby understood and indicated she would inform Jack. We said goodbye, secured the coach, and hit the road. We were both looking forward to this adventure in the Wild West State of Arizona. We left the resort and drove to Goodyear to gas up the Camaro. Before we left the gas station, Patty and I checked the Arizona road map and decided to head to the red-rock area of Sedona.

I-10 was bumper to bumper as we drove toward I-17. Thousands of vehicles travel I-10 daily; there were people going to work, people returning from work, large trucks, and numerous tourists. It took us approximately forty-five minutes to reach I-17. We scooted north, passing several shopping areas with northbound traffic zooming off the exit ramps and more traffic coming onto I-17 from the entrance ramps. It was a checker game on the highway as these fearless drivers pulled directly into each other's lanes, narrowly avoiding a collision by only a few inches. My usual nerves of steel were definitely being challenged by the numerous assorted personalities gripping their steering wheels. Patty and I were amateurs, but the Camaro held its own as we surged ahead northbound to Sedona, the famous red-rock area, where we had heard that many famous people were building their large villas on the sides of the mountains. We swung off I-17 at the Sedona exit and stopped at a tourist center for information. We learned that Sedona had many offerings for the inquisitive sightseer. Sedona is located among the red-hued rocks of the Oak Creek Canyon. Overlooking Oak Creek, an observer could be overwhelmed by the beauty of the buttes and the existing contrast of the surrounding forest and various types of fauna. We were awestruck by what we saw. We soon learned that Sedona is widely recognized as a center for the traditional arts and is becoming an upscale retirement and tourism location.

We stopped and went through some of the unique gift shops. The price ranges for their wares were definitely on the high side, so our purchases were limited to a decorative letter opener and a small Mexican vase displaying miniature sombreros painted on the outside. Patty was charmed by the vase, and I was tired of opening my mail without a letter opener. So we were both satisfied with our purchases.

We learned that Oak Creek Canyon Drive, actually SR 89A, had started out as a cattle trail across the canyon's east wall and had subsequently been changed into a rough wagon road by one James Munds, as he used it for a shortcut into Flagstaff. We were now on this historic old cattle trail, which had become a two-lane macadam highway. The drive from the vista point on the Mogollon Rim to Sedona offered us a display of changing natural beauty. We found it breathtaking to view the changes in vegetation as the altitude increased along our drive.

We visited the Chapel of the Holy Cross located on Chapel Road, just off SR 179. This Catholic shrine is constructed on the area's noted red-rock. Built in 1956, it is situated between

two red sandstone peaks, with a ramp leading to the entrance.
A ninety-foot cross dominates the structure. No matter what
faith one follows, this chapel is awesome. We were both
panting a bit after we had climbed the roadway to the ramp. I
asked Patty if she cared to rest before completing the ascent,
but she indicated she was fine. We both expressed our hope to
return to Sedona someday and spend more time there
absorbing all the region had to offer while we were equipped
with our paints and easels. In the meantime we would have to
settle for photos from our one-time-use camera that we had
purchased. The potential for prize-winning landscape scenes
was plentiful. Although Patty and I are only novices, we
recognized the reason that so many artists are drawn to the
area.

Just as the sun was receding over the mountains we pulled
into Prescott and checked into the Comfort Inn, located on
Montezuma Street near the intersection of White Spar Road. I
pulled under the canopy directly in front of the entrance to the
motel. Patty and I exited the car and went inside. The desk
clerk, a very polite middle-aged gentleman, greeted us
cordially. "Good evening, folks. Can I be of assistance?" I
signed in. We were fortunate to be given a first-floor room
with two queen-sized beds. After thanking the clerk, we went
to the car, removed our bags, parked the Camaro in a nearby
space, and reentered the motel. Room 101 was just down the
hall. I placed the card key into the slot, and as the green light
came on, we entered. The room was a large one, with a
refrigerator, an iron and ironing board, and a coffee maker,
along with attractive furnishings. Patty and I decided that we'd
stay in Prescott for three or four days and take our day trips
from the motel, returning each evening.

We agreed that our first night in Prescott should be a time
for a little celebration, so we opted to go to Ciliberto
Agostino's Italian Cucina, which had been highly
recommended by the clerk. We arrived at the restaurant about
8:00. The hostess led us to a large booth and seated us. The
interior of this upscale establishment displayed elaborate

Italian art, with soft violin music playing in the background. After looking at the wine list, I decided on a small bottle of Chianti, while Patty selected a caffeine-free coke. The menu offered numerous choices of Italian cuisine. We both decided on the veal parmesan with spaghetti and extra sauce. The male waiter was very polite and courteous. He lit two long candles and placed them on our table. They flickered and helped to set the mood for us.

While Patty and I waited for our dinner to be served, we sipped our drinks. The lighting in the restaurant was low, and it created a very romantic atmosphere with the violins and the candles. Our eyes were focused on each other and I gently held Patty's hand. The romantic trance we enjoyed was broken only when the waiter appeared at our booth with a large serving tray. He placed a heaping plate in front of Patty. She unfolded her linen napkin and placed it on her lap. Then he placed my plate of wonderful food in front of me. Patty and I bowed our heads for a moment while I quietly said grace.

We enjoyed our cuisine at Agostino's. The veal was tender and the sauce was seasoned to perfection. Neither one of us had had such delicious garlic bread before. The blend of the garlic and butter was so perfect that we had to order more. We enjoyed every moment.

It was well after ten when Patty and I went to bed. We were both relaxed from the atmosphere and food, and we were feeling very romantic. We embraced fully and warmly expressed our love for one another. Midnight arrived before we finally drifted off to sleep.

CHAPTER FIFTEEN

The three nights planned for the Comfort Inn in Prescott turned into four memorable days. One day we journeyed to Jerome to visit the copper-mining area, with its museum containing all the related artifacts from years ago. The town, years before when the mines were flourishing, had constructed homes on the side of the mountain. Today they are still standing, but give the appearance of potentially sliding down the slopes. To our surprise, many of these homes are presently occupied. Once a ghost town, the area has become a tourist attraction with numerous shops, galleries, and studios that appeal to the many visitors.

Another day found us at the south rim of the Grand Canyon taking in the beauty of its various rock formations. This wonder of the world is 277 miles long and averages 10 miles in width from rim to rim. We ventured into Grand Canyon Village to take in the sights and were amazed at the large structures that had been built there.

The next day we spent in Flagstaff, browsing through the many shops and tourist attractions. We took a self-guided tour around its historic downtown, following a map we had picked up at the visitors center. We saw the Lowell Observatory with its nine telescopes, which include the 24-inch Clark refracting telescope. One of the main features, the Pluto Walk, delighted us with its model of the planets in their order of sequence.

We then took a drive around the campus of Northern Arizona University and visited the Museum of Northern Arizona. We were amazed by the displays of archeology, biology, ethnology, geology, anthropology, and the fine arts of northern Arizona. We easily could have spent a week at the museum alone and still would not have been able to cover all that was there.

We had wanted to spend our last day of our mini-vacation touring Fort Apache, but it would not be open to the public until after Memorial Day, so we decided that we'd finish our tour in the Cordes Junction region near the Bradshaw Mountains. There we found several deserted mining camps and several ghost towns, although we didn't actually see or observe any ghosts. It was again amazing to us two Adirondackers to experience the vastness of the northern Arizona region, but in our minds even this great beauty could never take the place of our beloved Adirondack Park in northern New York.

We made one final stop before we headed back to our Goodyear resort. At Rock Springs, just off I-17 about 35 miles north of Phoenix, we pulled into the parking lot of the Rock Springs Café. It was crowded with cars, campers, and pickups. We had heard through the grapevine at our resort about their famous Jack Daniels pecan pie. This delicacy would top off our trip. We entered and were fortunate to find a small table in the far corner in one of their two dining rooms. The rustic interior featured unmatched tables and chairs that had to be at least fifty years old. Finally, a busy waitress noticed us sitting there.

"Can I get you something to drink, folks?" she asked.

"I understand you serve a Jack Daniels pecan pie here," I said.

"We certainly do. Would you each like a piece?" she asked.

We each ordered a slice of pie along with a cup of decaf. The waitress wrote down the order and scurried off to the kitchen. We couldn't help but notice that she was wearing very tight blue jeans.

"Jason, I wonder how she breathes in those," Patty

remarked quietly.

"Yeah! They do appear to be a bit snug," I replied in agreement.

In a few minutes the waitress appeared with two sizable pieces of pecan pie and two cups of steaming decaf. Again our taste buds experienced a first. The pie was delicious, with the flavor of Jack Daniels mostly not apparent but seeming to counteract the normally oversweet taste of the syrup. The rumor we had heard at the Roadrunner Resort had paid off. The Rock Springs Café turned out be one of our most enjoyable stops, one we hope to make again.

We concluded our four-day journey as we pulled into the resort and parked the Camaro next to Jack's large coach. Time had gone by rapidly. After our interesting travels, we decided to buy a few groceries and take a day to rest around the pool at our resort.

Before leaving the coach, I decided I had better call the airport and make a reservation for our return flight home shortly after the Huntley gathering. We had enjoyed our stay, but we were anxious to return. Luckily there was a flight open on the Monday after the party. With the arrangements completed, I then called Ruby to inform her of our flight plans and to verify if she would be available to take us to the airport. Patty and I left for the pool. We found two lounge chairs unoccupied and decided to relax in the desert sun. We talked about the forthcoming party at the Huntley ranch.

"Honey, I thought I'd wear my blue jeans and a denim shirt, the one with the New York bluebird over the pocket. Do you think that would be appropriate, Jason?" She looked over at me, and waited for my response.

"Sweetheart, I think that'll be just fine. Blue jeans are very popular in this region. I thought I'd wear mine with my short-sleeve denim shirt. You know, honey, I should have bought you a pair of western boots to match mine."

"No, dear, I wouldn't be able to wear them if you did. They're too pointed at the toe. I'll wear my sandals. They're plenty comfortable," she asserted.

"That'll be fine, dear. We should have a great time. I imagine that Jerome is an excellent host. I hope you'll have an opportunity to talk with Christine. From what I understand, she certainly seems like a fine young lady with definite sights on her future. I hope this ordeal hasn't impacted her too badly."

"I'm looking forward to being there, Jason. It'll be our first barbecue on a western ranch. Do you think Ruby and Jack will be able to join us?"

"I'm certain they will. Jack and Ruby have resided in Arizona for a long time, and they're very familiar with the Wild West, the ranches, the fabulous scenery, and all that makes up the western theme. I don't know about Ruby, but I do know that Jack will never leave this beautiful country, except maybe for a short visit to other areas. It's the same with us, sweetheart. We'll never leave our mountains on a permanent basis."

"You're right, honey. I'll be honest: I do miss Kentucky and my brothers, but they have their own life to lead and I have mine."

"I know you do. Maybe someday after the baby's birth, we could take a trip to Kentucky, see the horse farms, the Kentucky blue grass, and of course, visit your brothers." I knew Patty was feeling sentimental thinking about her childhood.

"I'm so lucky to be married to you, Jason." She reached over and squeezed my hand.

"We're very fortunate to have met each other on this life's journey. I appreciate all that you do for us, working in John's Diner and standing on your feet all day. You know, now with the baby coming I might have to find another part-time job. You and the baby are the most important part of my life."

She gave my hand another squeeze in appreciation. Then she grinned. "And, of course, we can't forget Ruben."

I smiled as I thought of our loyal dog.

Patty continued more seriously, "I know, honey, I'll have to stay at home for a while until the baby is old enough to go to day care." Her face became troubled as she thought ahead of the changes we would soon be facing.

"Well, we'll see what happens," I replied. "Well, I hate to leave the pool, but we'd better think about getting back to the coach. Didn't you say you wanted to do a load of wash?" I asked.

"You're right," Patty agreed.

We quickly gathered up our things and returned to our coach, I helped Patty carry the wash to the laundry. Although the coach provided a suitable washer and dryer, we had found it easier to use the resort laundry room which provided an ample number of washers and dryers, allowing us to do more than one load at a time. While Patty was at the laundry, I cleaned through the coach, and then went through my briefcase to organize it.

I reread the Huntley case report to see if I had made any errors. In addition, I placed in the briefcase notes from my conversation with Wayne Beyea. Communicating with other investigators throughout the state and across the nation was advantageous in the event that I was required to seek information in other geographical locations. In today's world, hi-tech information was only minutes away, either by telephone, e-mail, internet, or fax.

I placed my briefcase in the closet, went into the living room, and lay down on the comfortable leather davenport. I must have drifted off to sleep for a few minutes, because I heard a knocking in the distance. I came to with a start and heard Patty's voice.

"Honey, open the door for me, please?" she asked.

I got up and opened the door. I took the basket of freshly washed and dried laundry from her and set it down in the hallway.

"Honey, I don't want you lifting. You should have come to get me and I would have carried it for you. You've got to be careful in your condition, sweetheart." I found myself almost admonishing her in my concern.

"I promise that the next time I do the washing I'll come and get you, precious," she said, lightly brushing off my worry.

"We pregnant women can be stronger than people suppose."

"I don't know how precious I am, but I'm concerned for your welfare, my dear," I answered firmly.

The balance of the day was spent ironing, putting the clothes away, jointly preparing a light dinner, and watching television. We retired early in order to be ready at nine for Ruby's and Jack's arrival.

CHAPTER SIXTEEN

The brightness of the rising sun blinded me for a moment as I pulled open the drapes in the front of the Prevost. It was 7:00 a.m. Ruby and Jack would be arriving at approximately 9:00. Patty was already in the shower, and as soon as she was finished, I would take mine. I turned the coffeepot on and set the table, then flicked on the radio for the early morning news.

Patty emerged from the bathroom wearing her robe. "Jason, while you shower I'll dress and be out of your way. Thanks for starting the coffee. Any news on the radio?" she asked.

"There were some overnight accidents, and a couple of drive-by shootings," I said grimly as I went into the bathroom.

I shaved first. The lather felt good on my face. The water was very hot, which made for a clean shave. I pulled the shiny stainless-steel straight razor down on each side of my face. When I went to shave under my nose I felt a sting. Blood appeared in the form of a small droplet. I opened the medicine chest, quickly removed the styptic pencil, and drew it across the tiny laceration. I finished shaving and followed it with a hot shower. There's nothing like a good hot shower to start the day off right. When I turned on the ice cold water to rinse, I couldn't help but think of my military service days at Camp Pendleton, where I showered in cold water most of the time. I turned the water off, grabbed the large towel from the rack, and dried myself off. I put my robe on and went into the bedroom

247

to dress.

Patty called from the kitchen, "Are you about ready for breakfast, Jason?"

"I will be in about five minutes, sweetheart. All I have to do is dress. I won't be long."

I took my pressed blue jeans, denim shirt, and western boots out of the closet. I slipped on the jeans and then put the boots on. They were narrow and still placed some pressure on my toes. I wore them only on special occasions, and the Bar H Ranch barbecue was to be a special event. I didn't put on the denim shirt yet, but went into the dining area. Patty was already seated waiting for me. I sat down in front of my plate of scrambled eggs and one slice of whole-wheat toast.

"Honey, would you care for a glass of orange juice?" Patty asked.

"I don't think so, thanks," I replied.

When we were done eating, Patty went to the bedroom to finish getting ready. I cleared the table and washed the few dishes we had used. I had just finished putting them away in the cupboard, and had returned to the bedroom to slip on my shirt when there was a knock at the door.

I went to the door and opened it. Ruby and Jack were standing by the step.

"Good morning, Jason," Ruby said.

"Hello, Jason," chimed in Jack.

"Good morning, you two. You're right on the button. Come on in. Patty is getting ready. She'll be right out."

"Jason, I'll wait for her in the living room leaving you and Jack to talk," Ruby said, grabbing the paper from the rack.

"How do you like the Prevost, Jason?" Jack asked, looking around proudly and waiting for my response.

"We love the coach, Jack. You are a fortunate fellow to own such a fine vehicle as this."

"I was able to get it at a good price, so I took it. It was a once-in-a-lifetime chance and, as you know, they don't come by every day."

"She's a beauty. And the Roadrunner Resort is an excellent

place to stay. It has a great deal to offer."

"I did some investigative work for the former owner about two years ago. It was through that contact that I found out about this place. The former owner's brother worked for a motor home dealership and when this one came in he called me. I fell in love with it at first sight. There was some difficulty with the electrical system, but that was easily remedied. Jason, did I tell you I was planning a trip to Alaska when the Huntley case came to my attention? Shucks, I'd be in Anchorage right now, if this case had developed a week later." He shook his head in disappointment.

"Jack, you were lucky you didn't get killed when that bullet came through the windshield."

"Yes, I could have been killed very easily. You and I both know the laws aren't strict enough. Gangs just like that one are springing up all over the place. Every day or so the police get word of another drop house. You wouldn't believe some of the upscale neighborhoods they've found them in, with as many as fifty or more living on the premises. During some of the raids they've had, the police have come across dozens of people hiding from the authorities. I cannot understand how the neighbors are unaware. I don't know what they are doing about it. But I do know one thing; I'll be ready for them the next time. No one should be shot in their car or any other place." He set his jaw, unable to conceal his anger.

"That's true, Jack," I felt my own anger rise, as I thought of how he might not have survived.

"Well, let's turn to more pleasant truths. I'm glad you enjoyed your stay here, Jason. Wish you were here all the time. By the way, did you and Patty have a good time on your trip?"

"We certainly did! What a beautiful state with a lot to offer. But, Jack, but that's impossible to think of moving out here. I was glad we could break away to assist you during your hospitalization. You're fortunate to have a guy like Bill Reidy managing the office during your absence."

"Yes, Bill is okay. He handles all our cases in Tucson. A fine gentleman," he agreed.

"We'd better get the girls together and prepare to leave for the ranch," I suggested, not knowing what the traffic would be like.

The three others gathered in front of the coach as I went over to lock the door. I asked Jack if he'd mind if I drove the Camaro. He thought it would be a good idea. I circled the perimeter of the coach before we left to make certain that everything was in order. I placed the two lawn chairs in the storage compartment. We then entered the car. Jack sat in front with me and the two girls sat in the back seat. It was great to see Jack feeling more like his old self.

As we drove out we had to wait for two large motor homes towing vehicles that were parked at the main entrance waiting for Citrus Road traffic to pass. The odor of the exhaust from their diesel fuel seeped into the vehicle. Jack removed a handkerchief from his pocket and held it up to his nose.

"Gosh, Jason! That diesel smell is hard to take." Jack coughed.

"You can say that again," I agreed. "Sometimes the filters need changing. The rig ahead of us is filling the air with pollution."

Soon the traffic cleared and we made our way on to the road and on our way to the interstate in a westerly direction toward Route 85. I used extreme caution on that section of two-lane macadam highway notorious for fatalities. Too often, impatient drivers pull out from behind large trucks and cause head-on collisions.

Jack expressed how happy he was to be out of the hospital. The nurses and the staff had been good to him, but it had been difficult for him to get his proper rest, as too often staff members would come into his room during all times of day or night for reasons not totally clear. He informed us that when he had moved into the nursing home for his rehab, he had been better able to achieve a good night's sleep. And now at Ruby's, of course, he was enjoying his uninterrupted eight hours.

Route 8 to Casa Grande had very little traffic on it. The girls were talking in the back seat. I overheard Patty telling

Ruby that soon after we returned to Old Forge she would have to purchase some maternity clothes. Then I heard Ruby say, "Patty, you're not yet showing your pregnancy. You have a long way to go before you'll need them."

"Jack, aren't you amazed at the vast land acreage here in Arizona that is still uninhabited?"

"No, not really, Jason. We still have some range land, but generally the rest is desert. You can go for miles without seeing a structure of any kind. Let's face it, Jason, this is still the Wild West, and don't ever forget it." Jack knows the state of Arizona very well and loves it as much as I love the Adirondacks in New York.

We arrived at the Bar H Ranch around ten-thirty. Two horse trailers were pulling away from the entrance; one of the trailers appeared empty, while the other was loaded. The drivers gave us a wave. I tooted the horn in response. The drive to the ranch house was a short one. I pulled the car into the parking area. Luther was just opening the stable door. He looked our way and waved, but continued to enter the large building. Several horses in a holding area all watched us. As we exited the car, Christine Huntley came out of the side door of the ranch house and walked toward us. She was wearing a blue denim shirt and beige riding britches. Moving with strength and grace, she looked so different from the day we had found her in the house in Tucson.

"Good morning!" she said warmly. There was a welcoming smile on her face. "I'm so glad you could come today, Jason."

"Christine, I'd like to introduce you to Ruby, Jack, and my wife, Patty."

"Welcome to the Bar-H Ranch, folks. It's a pleasure to have you here for our annual barbecue. Dad will be here in a few minutes. He's on the telephone." She turned to me. "Now I'm able to thank you for rescuing me from that madman, Bradley Carter. He's a very dangerous person." Her eyes began to well with tears. I could still see the shadows of bruises on her face.

"How are you feeling, Christine?" Ruby asked, while Jack

looked on.

"I'm feeling better."

I could see that she was getting the color back in her cheeks. She had been so pale on the day that we had located her. "You look great," I told her honestly.

"Mr. Flynn, you also had quite an ordeal, according to what my father told me. That shootout was just up the road. I hope you're feeling better, sir."

"Yes, I was headed here to interview your dad about you when it happened. Thank you for asking. I've completed my rehab and will be returning to my office next week. I'm glad you and I are able to meet, young lady."

"You are well known in the state, Mr. Flynn," she said.

"Oh! Is that so?" Jack's face could not disguise how pleased he was by her remark.

"I understand, Jason, that you and your lovely wife are from upstate New York. I hope you have gotten to enjoy some of your visit to our state."

"Yes, we have, Christine. Jack and I have been friends for years. I came down as soon as I heard he needed me," I informed her.

"I certainly appreciate what you both have done on my case. Dad is so pleased with Flynn Investigations."

"Thank you for your compliment, Christine," Jack said, giving me a significant nod. "I'm just glad we were able to come to your aid."

Jerome Huntley joined us, immediately walked over to Jack, and shook his hand. "Mr. Flynn, how are you feeling after your ordeal?"

"I'm fortunate, Jerome. If that bullet had been two inches to the right I wouldn't be here today. As you know, I was en route to interview you here at the ranch when I came across the two gangs exchanging gunfire. Can you imagine such a thing happening in broad daylight?" The outrage again crossed his face.

"It was horrible, Jack. I don't know what's going to happen to our society if that activity continues. I wanted to visit you at the hospital, but I was unable to leave the ranch as I awaited any news about Christine," he apologized.

"I wouldn't expect you to. I wasn't able to have visitors for several days anyway. The doctors wanted me to keep still. I wasn't able to be interviewed by the authorities for a period of time," he went on to explain.

"I'm pleased that you were able to join us today." Jerome spoke with genuine sincerity. Just then, I noticed Christine turned to walk away. I stopped her to inform her that my wife, Patty, would so very much like to speak to her because she had experienced a similar ordeal. I called Patty over, and Christine, Ruby, and Patty walked away to have an uninterrupted exchange. I walked back to rejoin Jack and Jerome.

I heard some vehicles approaching the ranch house. Luther, along with two ranch hands, was busy at the large barbecue pit in the rear yard of the ranch house.

The cars that were arriving parked in a large area. As the new arrivals were getting out of their vehicles, I recognized Dick Case, the managing editor of the *Desert Journal*; Detective Charles Perez, of the Casa Grande Police Department; Ronald Jamison, the owner of the property where Christine had been found; and to my surprise, Marie, the waitress from the Cactus Chuck Wagon Restaurant. I became involved in a lengthy conversation with Dick regarding how fortunate we had been to have Jamison contact his office. As we all gathered around Jerome, Christine, Patty, and Ruby rejoined the group and introductions were made. Jerome suggested that we go to the ranch house for coffee. As we approached the house, Patty and Ruby joined Jack and me as we followed the other guests. Marie walked up to the four of us.

"Jason Black, it is so good to see you," she said as she neared.

"Marie, I'd like you to meet my friend, Jack Flynn and his associate, Ruby Wolkowski. You remember Patty. She was with me at the restaurant," I reminded her.

"Oh, yes, I do. It is nice to meet you folks," Marie

acknowledged, walking just ahead of Jack.

We all entered the large ranch house as Jerome led the way. We followed him into a large family room where plenty of chairs had been arranged. As we took our seats, Dick Case walked over to Jack and me. I made the introduction.

"Jack, how are you doing?" Dick asked with concern.

"I'm feeling much better, although I find that I tire easily. Thank you for asking."

"I feel as though I know you, Jack. I've got some extra newspapers in the car I'll give you before you leave today. One of our reporters followed the events of the gang shootings. He wrote the incident up well. You were fortunate. We're all glad you could make it today," Dick said with a sense of pride for the paper's reporter who had written the articles.

"Thank you, Dick, for your comments. I'm just glad to be alive."

"Have you heard when the court proceedings will take place? They are keeping a tight lid on the information about the shootings," Dick asked as an interested newspaperman.

"I really don't know, Dick. If I hear anything at all, I'll give you a call."

"Usually we receive the information early on, but this gang killing spree has been kept really quiet." He shook his head, perplexed.

Dick chatted with us for a few minutes before returning to his group. We were subsequently joined by Detective Perez, who had walked over to say hello to Jack.

"You're looking good, Jack," he said embracing him. It was apparent to me that Perez knew Jack very well.

"Charlie, you've already met Jason and Ruby. I'd like to introduce you to Patty, Jason's wife. I was best man at their wedding," Jack said proudly, giving Patty a quick hug.

"It's a pleasure to meet you, Mrs. Black," the seasoned detective said. "Patty, you should have seen Jason in action the other day when we located Christine. I never saw a pugilist throw a punch any faster than Jason. Bradley Carter will remember that for a long, long time."

"Come on, Charlie, you're telling tales," I said.

"I'm just ribbing you a little. Bradley Carter could have been a tough person to subdue. The other detectives and I appreciated what you did for us."

"I suppose it could have gone the other way. Our mission was to locate Christine, and that was accomplished," I acknowledged.

Detective Perez informed us that our locating Christine had taken a lot of pressure off law enforcement throughout the state. He added, "I've heard through the grapevine that Flynn Investigations may be receiving a letter of commendation."

"I have to give all the credit to Jason on this case," Jack affirmed.

Charles Perez left to visit Christine, who was talking to Ronald Jamison. Jerome instructed his maid, Anita Cullen, to make certain that there was plenty of coffee and to keep the tray of pastries replenished. I observed her as she unobtrusively passed her tray of pastries and poured refills as needed.

After our coffee and pastries, Jerome asked the group if they would be interested in seeing a film that he used to show prospective customers that were interested in the breeding and raising of horses at the Bar H Ranch.

Everyone indicated that they would like to see his presentation. Jerome went to a small wall cabinet and opened the cherry wood door which had concealed a large television. He then slid a video cassette into the slot.

The film lasted about thirty minutes. It was of historical significance, showing the ranch house and buildings, including the modern facilities where the horses were stabled, along with a large equipment shed, an indoor training track, and horses being trained and ridden by the employees. I believe everyone in the room enjoyed it.

Next Detective Perez gave an update concerning Bradley Carter, who was presently at the Pinal County Jail to await action of the grand jury. Bail had been set at $250,000. Perez told us that he had heard there was a possibility that he could be bailed out today.

I looked over at Christine, who was sitting by her father to see her reaction. I saw her dry her eyes with a tissue. Jerome placed his arm around his daughter's shoulders to comfort her.

Detective Perez concluded his comments by thanking Jack Flynn, the Flynn Investigation Agency, and myself for developing the lead that had led to locating Christine in Tucson. He emphasized that it was this lead that had brought the case to a successful conclusion with the arrest of Bradley Carter.

Jerome stood up and thanked Detective Perez for his participation in the case, and directed the same appreciation to Jack Flynn and me.

Jerome told us that it was now time to enjoy some good southwestern barbecue. At his direction we all followed him outside to the rear of the ranch house, where a large tent had been erected. Tables and chairs had been arranged to accommodate the large group evidently neighbors, friends, associates, and the group that were involved in locating her. Luther was under the tent, accompanied by three young men all dressed as cowboys in western style garb. They were standing behind a large table laden with two large pans of beef barbecue, beans, potato salad, coleslaw, warmed Kaiser rolls, and assorted dishes of pickles and corn relish ready to serve the guests.

The guests stood back to allow Christine and her father to begin. The rest of us lined up behind them. The barbecued beef was piping hot. Luther was actively supervising the three cowboys as they served each of the guests individually. Patty and I were just behind Dick Case. The line moved quickly. We proceeded to our table, which we shared with Dick, Ruby, and Jack. The tables filled quickly and soon all the guests were seated.

We had just begun to eat the excellent fare when I heard the sound of an electric guitar playing behind me. I turned and saw that two of the three cowboys who had been serving were now playing their guitar and banjo for the guests. Luther joined them on his harmonica. The trio sounded very good, and several of us stopped eating for a moment to enjoy the music. They entertained us all, playing western music while we all enjoyed the food.

"Darling, these fellows really know how to play," Patty whispered in my ear. I could see by the expression on her face that she was enthralled with the event.

The cowboy left behind the serving line continued to give seconds to those who were interested. I didn't return to the line, as I had gotten plenty the first time. I even found myself loosening my belt.

Jerome went around all the tables asking if everything were alright. Several late arrivals drifted in and proceeded through the line. I didn't recognize any of them. One, however, appeared to be a police detective, as he was wearing a shoulder holster under his jacket that I could tell contained a semi-automatic. I thought, "The cops sure know where the good food is." This fellow appeared to be well over six feet tall with a muscular build. He was wearing a gold earring in his left earlobe. I surmised that he probably was an undercover officer. When he passed through the line, the detective sat down at a table by himself. I observed Detective Perez walk over and converse with him quietly.

"Honey, the barbecue is just about the best I've ever tasted," Patty remarked.

"The sauce has just the right amount of zest," I agreed. "We'll sure miss our barbecues when we return north."

"Yes, we will." She sighed in slight disappointment. "It's so wonderful of Mr. Huntley to have us here today. He certainly has a beautiful ranch. Ruby and I walked over to where the horses were in the holding area. Did you see them, Jason?"

"Yes, honey, I did. I believe they are going to be shipped out to the east soon. It's too bad that we don't have enough room at home, or we might dream about buying a couple. Of course," I added with a chuckle, "we wouldn't have enough money to even buy the feed."

"True, Jason. But today we can enjoy looking at them. It

appears that Mr. Huntley has a good handle on the horse business." She looked around in admiration.

"Yes, he does. He certainly knows what he's doing. There's a great deal of hard work in having a spread like this and tremendous responsibility that goes along with it."

"That is true, Jason. Oh, honey. I'll just be glad to return to our little home. It feels like we've been away for a long time."

"We're going home shortly. Our flight leaves on Monday, remember. I know that Ruben will be glad to see us."

"You don't have to worry, Jason. Wilt's taking good care of him until we get home."

"I know he is, honey," I replied. There was no doubt in my mind about that.

I glanced over at Jerome and Christine just as Jerome stood up and tapped a spoon on his water glass.

"May I have your attention for a moment, folks?" he asked. A hush fell over the group.

"Christine and I are so pleased that you were able join us today. Did you enjoy the barbecue?"

A large affirmative response resounded from the crowd.

Jerome continued, "The purpose in having you here at the ranch was to thank you all for your participation and prayers for the return of my beloved daughter, Christine. I want to thank my personal friend, Detective Charles Perez, and all the other law-enforcement people for the efforts in the search and the many days they expended, some on their off-duty time, in looking for my daughter. I'm indebted to all of you." He paused, looked out at his audience, lifted his glass of water, sipping it, and continued,

"I employed Flynn Investigations of Phoenix to look into the case to see it from a different perspective. Fortunately, we decided to post a notice in the *Desert Journal* offering a reward for any information leading to Christine's location. As most of you know by now, important information came to our attention. We learned that Bradley Carter, a former acquaintance of Christine's, had rented a house near the air force base at Tucson. Jason Black a private investigator, working for Flynn's, accompanied by my ranch foreman and myself, went to Carter's rented property and found Christine in the cellar, where he was apprehended by us. The ordeal was traumatic for Christine. We were all concerned for her personal safety. Fortunately, she is home and will return to her studies and pursue her goals to become a nationally syndicated writer for newspapers, as well as sharing some responsibility in running the Bar H Ranch." He looked over lovingly at his daughter.

I looked over at Christine to see how she was reacting to her father's remarks. I was pleased to see she was smiling and nodding in approval.

He went on, "Again, I wanted to gather you all here to thank you for helping in saving Christine's life. Jason Black and Jack Flynn, I want everyone here to know that as the result of your actions my daughter is sitting beside me at this gathering. Jack Flynn, thank you, especially for making Jason Black available to us during your hospitalization. I would be remiss if I didn't also thank the gentleman who made the call to Dick Case at the *Desert Journal*. Ronald Jamison, please stand up. Thank you, sir, for making that important call. And lastly, all of you who were involved in the case are welcome to return to the Bar H Ranch whenever you pass this way." The audience, who had been quiet during his speech, suddenly broke their silence. Jerome's words were met with a round of applause.

"Jason, Mr. Huntley truly loves his daughter," Patty whispered to me.

"Patty, yes, he certainly does."

Patty and Ruby got up from the table and walked over to Christine and her father to thank them for the delightful afternoon and the delicious barbecue. They were soon joined by others who wished to extend their wishes to their hosts.

As the crowd dispersed, Jack and I walked over to Jerome to thank him for his generous remarks. He extended his gratitude to us and turned to Jack. "If I ever need to call upon a private investigator, you can rest assured it will be Flynn's

Investigations. Jack, I'm glad that you're feeling better and I thank you again for assigning Jason Black to the case.

"Jerome, thank you. Call on us anytime," Jack replied.

"I will, Jack," Jerome assured him.

Patty walked toward me accompanied by Marie, the waitress from the Cactus Chuck Wagon Barbecue.

"Jason Black, it was a pleasure to meet you. I just mentioned to your wife that if you folks are ever in the area, be sure to stop at the restaurant to see us," Marie said with sincerity.

"It was our pleasure to meet you, Marie. You're a lovely young lady and a great waitress. Thank you for the information regarding Christine and Carter. That was an important observation you made. It gave me a clue that Carter could undoubtedly be involved in Christine's disappearance. Everything worked out. And, yes, if Patty and I pass this way, we'll be certain to stop by to see you." Marie gave us each a warm embrace.

While Patty talked to Marie, I excused myself and went over to a group of people who were still gathered under the tent. I wanted to meet the fellow who was wearing the shoulder holster, but apparently he had already left. I asked Detective Perez if the man was with his department.

"Jason, I'm sorry you missed him. His name is George Murray. He came to our department from the air force. He works narcotic investigations and is a member of a task force. He's a good friend of Jerome's. George used to board his two Arabian horses here on the ranch. He was stationed at Davis-Monthan when he was discharged," he said.

I thanked Charlie for the information and gave him one of my upstate New York business cards. I told him that if he ever made it up to the Adirondack Mountains he should be sure to look us up. He thanked me and walked over to where a group was milling around Jerome.

I returned to our table just as Patty, Ruby, and Jack made their way back.

"Jason, did you have enough to eat?" Jack chided me,

knowing my love of food.

"I've had plenty. How about you, pal?" I responded.

"I'm good. What a feast!" he remarked.

We decided to walk off some of the barbecue. As we neared the parking area, suddenly I heard a loud roar. For a moment I thought it was a plane, but then I observed a cloud of dust rising from the entrance road to the ranch. As the dust settled, I spied a black SUV speeding toward the ranch house.

"What the heck is this?" I shouted loudly. I noticed several people running toward the ranch house. I turned to Ruby and Patty and told them to return to the ranch until we found out what was going on. The SUV kept racing toward us. It suddenly went into a skid as the operator tried to negotiate a sharp left-hand turn, then finally stopped. Charlie Perez came running over.

"What's going on with that SUV, fellows?" Charlie asked in alarm.

The operator remained in the vehicle. We were unable to distinguish who was driving, as the dark tinted windows did not allow us to see inside, but a shadowy form could be seen moving around. It seemed an eternity, but in reality, probably only a matter of minutes, we were joined by Jerome and Luther, both wondering who or what was causing the disturbance. Although it was only five, the sun had already set, and darkness was beginning to fall.

Finally the driver's door opened. A tall man emerged, dressed in black and wearing dark sunglasses, in a hooded sweatshirt which covered the upper portion of his face. He had what appeared to be a weapon in his hands, possibly a rifle or shotgun and stood behind his vehicle as if using it for protection. We were stunned!

Detective Perez quickly removed a weapon from his ankle holster and, to my surprise, reached inside his sports jacket and removed another handgun.

"Charlie, I'm glad to see you came equipped," I said, admiringly.

While waiting for the hooded intruder to make his next

move, Perez explained, "Jason, in Arizona many of us carry
our weapons on duty or off duty. We're still in the Wild West,
with plenty of mindsets that think in terms of shoot to kill or be
shot, which went on in days gone by. Believe me, Jason, it
hasn't changed much according to my historical readings and
observations of the present time period," he whispered quietly
as we waited for the next move. We dared not approach as we
had no way of knowing if he was serious about using his
weapon.

Finally, Charlie shouted out. "Who are you? And what do
you want?" Charlie challenged.

Silence. He stood approximately one hundred feet from us.
I looked closely to try to identify the object that appeared to be
a weapon, but he must have placed it on the hood of the vehicle
or next to him. I was relieved that the girls had gone into the
ranch house. I looked around for Luther, but he had
disappeared. I had a gut feeling that maybe he and his three
associates were discussing a plan of their own.

Charlie attempted again to engage the individual in
conversation. No response. I could see that Jerome was
worried. He walked over to us and spoke quietly to Charlie. He
then called someone on his cell phone. By his conversation, I
realized he was talking to Luther, his ranch foreman. After he
hung up, he turned to me.

"Jason, Luther believes that the man by the SUV is Bradley
Carter and that he appears armed. Luther called the Pinal
County Jail and was advised by a friend of his that works there
that Carter was bailed out today. I know that Carter is from a
well-to-do family in Denver, and apparently his father called
an attorney in Casa Grande and subsequently the attorney was
wired the money for the bail."

Jerome continued. "If Charlie calls in a swat team or
backup, somebody could get hurt or possibly killed. This is my
land and I'll determine who comes and goes. Charlie told me to
try my own plan, and here it is. As we speak, Luther and three
of our cowboys are watching him through a pair of night
binoculars that luckily I had in the shed. Two of the fellows are

going to ride their horses across the lot near the car and create
a diversion. While this is taking place, Luther and the other
cowboy are going to approach Carter from the rear. See that
hedge that runs along the edge of the lawn? In ten minutes,
you'll see the two horsemen sprint across the lot whooping it
up. Carter will notice and be momentarily off guard—at least,
we hope so. Charlie is getting into position to approach Carter
and snap the cuffs on him. He is trespassing on my property.
He's also in possession of a weapon. Now, we know Carter is
strong as an ox and will be hard to take down, but we've got to
take action against him. Luther's friend also told him that
Carter's attorney at the time of his release had to tell Carter
more than once to keep his mouth shut. Carter made statements
that he was going to get even with someone for putting him
through this indignity. Someone was going to pay for this."
Jerome set his jaw as his face hardened; displaying a side of
him I had never seen before. This was a man who could be
ruthless when necessary.

"Jerome, it sounds like a good plan. I hope that Luther will
try to get rid of the weapon. Jack, I want you to go to the ranch
house and advise the folks not to leave. I don't want you to
become involved in any physical confrontation or take a
chance of getting shot again."

"I'll head to the ranch right now, Jason. If I hadn't just got
out of the hospital, I'd run up there and punch that sucker in
the nose. You fellows be careful," Jack said reluctantly as he
headed toward the ranch house.

Jerome checked his watch. Suddenly, the hooded person
made his move. He picked up the weapon, wildly fired a single
shot into the air, and screamed out in a loud voice, "I want to
talk with Christine right now or there's going to be trouble. Do
you hear me? Do you?" He sounded disturbed and irrational. It
was definitely Bradley Carter.

Charlie took up a position behind some bales of hay.
Bradley, this is Detective Perez of the Casa Grande Police
Department. Put your gun down and walk away from the
vehicle with your hands up in the air. You don't need any more

trouble than you're already involved in," he advised in a calm voice, not wanting to antagonize the young man further.

"I want to talk to Christine, right now!" Carter shouted. Then he fired another shot into the air. The weapon's report sounded like a high-powered rifle.

"Bradley, please think about it. You can talk to Christine, but you'll have to drop your weapon first and put your hands up. Do you hear me?" Charlie still crouched behind the bales of hay with his revolver drawn.

Bradley Carter did not reply, as his attention had been diverted by the sounds of the hooves of the two galloping quarter horses bearing down on him. The riders were hollering and whooping it up. Jerome's plan had been set in motion. The two cowboys began to circle the confused Carter and his vehicle as seen in the western movies of the days when the Indians circled the settlers in their wagon trains. They continued to shout and holler, keeping Carter's attention drawn to them.

The moon had risen and I was better able to focus my eyes. I could just make out the silhouettes of three men crouched down and running toward Carter along the high hedgerow. One, I was sure, was Luther. Bradley Carter appeared to be focusing on the two cowboys rather than being aware of any other activity. Charlie continued to take shelter behind the baled hay. Jerome and I were safely shielded by two large trees, but we had a view of the scenario that was transpiring.

The distance from the end of the hedgerow to the SUV was approximately fifty yards. The trio stood at the edge of the hedgerow. Carter, still gripping his weapon, stood in confusion as the two horsemen circled him. Luther raised his arm to signal the two men behind him, and then they ran, staying low to the ground, directly toward Carter. At this moment, Charlie, in order to distract him, called out to Carter.

"Bradley! Bradley! Let's discuss this situation before someone gets hurt!"

Carter turned to look at Perez, but was unable to respond, as Luther and one of his men dealt him a hard blow while the other grabbed the weapon from his hands, immediately unloaded it, and cast it aside. Charlie, Jerome, and I ran to their assistance. Enraged, Carter grabbed one of the men and threw him to the ground, then dealt a punch to Luther's face. Fists and arms flailed in the combat.

Charlie holstered his weapon as we entered the melee of wild fisticuffs. Luther continued to fight as his nose bled. Carter was a one-man fighting machine. My memory quickly returned to a similar case that I had been involved in, when on two separate occasions it took ten strong men to restrain two men, when their adrenaline glands had been unleashed. The two horsemen arrived, dismounted and joined the fracas. One of them managed to wrap a lasso around Carter's kicking legs. Finally, Carter slumped and lay on the ground. Charlie slapped handcuffs on his wrists, pulled tightly behind his back.

Carter swore mightily with words that I hadn't heard in a long time. He glared at me with wild eyes. "You're the son of a bitch that punched me in the stomach." He started up another tirade, this time directed at me.

I cut him off sharply. "Carter, I don't know you and you don't know me, but you'd better keep your mouth shut before I remove your cuffs and show you a few tricks. You tortured Christine, abused a defenseless person. And yet you managed to be bailed out of jail." I shook my head in disgust.

Charlie read Carter his Miranda rights. Two Casa Grande PD cruisers arrived and he turned a still defiant Carter over to them.

Arrangements were made to impound the SUV which had been stolen. No one yet knew how Carter had acquired the .308 caliber rifle, which Charlie secured as evidence. Soon we were joined by the people who had sought shelter in the ranch house who had been waiting for permission to leave. Christine rushed to Luther with a first aid kit, cleaning and bandaging a bite on his arm. Fortunately his nose had stopped bleeding. There were no other injuries. Thankfully no one had been shot or otherwise seriously hurt.

Jerome spoke loudly to get everyone's attention. "Folks, I

want to apologize for the uninvited guest that disrupted the festivities. It was, indeed, Bradley Carter. He is now en route to police headquarters. Hopefully this time he will be held without bail. He should have never been released in the first place. Christine and I want to thank you all for coming today. Luther, I want to thank you and our staff here at the ranch for aiding in the capture of Carter. Hopefully he won't ever again try to come back here." He paused. "I believe Christine has something she would like to say."

An obviously shaken Christine rose and stood in front of the group, took a deep breath, and spoke. "I want to thank everyone here that had anything to do with my rescue. As you can see, Bradley is in desperate need of help. How I wish I had never met him! I am sorry that this joyous day was interrupted by his actions. Believe me, I had no idea he was like this. He was able to hide this side of his personality from me." She began to weep, and returned to her father's side who immediately put his arm around her lovingly.

Jerome returned to the podium and announced they had planned to have entertainment for anyone who wished to stay. He realized the incident had interrupted the festivities, but we would hate it if the celebration for Christine were ruined. He urged us all to stay, if we could.

I could see that Jack had been bothered by the ordeal and the potential danger that Carter put us all in.

"Come on, Jack, forget Carter. I feel the same way as you, but it's over with, and Carter will pay for his shenanigans. Detective Perez will take further criminal action and Mr. Carter will be a guest of the state of Arizona, unless his father pulls more political strings. Hopefully he'll let his son do the time. Apparently Jerome knows people that know the father and he intends to have them talk with him. But, Jack, do you feel you'd be up to staying?" I asked with concern.

"I'm a little tired, but we'll leave it up to Ruby and Patty," he responded.

While Jack and I exchanged comments, Ruby and Patty were in deep conversation. I interrupted them to ask if they'd be interested in staying. They both expressed their desire to stay if Jack felt up to it. A few of the guests had left, but the majority remained.

Jerome again returned to the podium. "We have a surprise tonight. When a dear friend of Christine's, whom she met at a poetry reading in Tucson, heard of Christine's abduction, she contacted me to see if she could be of any assistance. She happens to be staying locally for a writing conference. Not only is she a writing professor and a poet, but also a teacher of the art of belly dancing. We are fortunate tonight that she has graciously agreed to perform for us." Taped Arabic music suddenly filled the air with drumming and instrumentation. He turned as a middle aged woman with brown hair approached the makeshift stage. "I would like you to meet Zajal."

Lights had been erected under the large tent. About fifty chairs were arranged in a semicircle around the elevated stage. We all took seats as the dancer in fuchsia, turquoise, and silver smiled and turned.

She moved with freedom, joy, and grace to the Middle Eastern rhythms. Her bright costume and movements brought out the deep spirit of life offered by the dance. Zajal's artistic ability in belly dancing held and carried us, and we all applauded and rose to our feet at the conclusion of her performance. Christine called out in delight, and the audience requested an encore. Zajal again reached out to us with graceful motion as the rhythm reached out to our hearts where we sat under the tent. Attractive Zajal brought us strength and joy. We all applauded enthusiastically, rising to our feet, and cheered as Zajal bowed in appreciation. Christine returned to the stage and stood by her poet friend, as a line of people formed to meet the talented lady. The four of us waited our turn to introduce ourselves. We individually congratulated the lovely Zajal for her splendid performance. She smiled warmly and thanked us for the compliments, saying how much it meant to her to be able to dance in celebration of Christine.

Jack and I located Jerome Huntley, while Ruby and Patty continued their conversation with Zajal and Christine.

"Jerome, it has been a pleasure to spend time with you. If you ever come to the Adirondacks, please look us up. We don't have a ranch, but we have a modest home on the lakes among the animal life that reside within the park. Again, it was a pleasure, sir, and my wife and I are so glad that your daughter is home, safe and sound," I said.

"Jason Black, you and Patty are always welcome here at the Bar H Ranch. I can tell that Jack Flynn indeed has a true friend in you. In today's climate of the general population, a true friend is a valuable commodity," Jerome said, patting me on the shoulder.

While Jack spoke with Jerome, I returned to meet Patty and Ruby as they continued their conversation with Zajal and Christine. As I went over to Christine, to my surprise she came toward me and embraced me.

"Jason, thank you for being there for me. Your actions saved my life. I do hope the justice system will deal with Bradley. He needs a lot of help. I was sure I would die when he brutalized me, and I'll probably remember that horrible experience for the rest of my life." Tears glistened in her eyes. I felt so sorry for her.

"You're a strong young lady, Christine. I know that you'll be alright. My wife and I wish you every success in your future, and someday I expect to read a syndicated column by you."

"You're so kind, Jason. Remember you and Patty are always welcome here at the ranch."

"I told your dad that you both are welcome to visit us in the Adirondacks."

"I've heard it's a beautiful place," she replied. "I'd like to go there."

"Yes, it is still one of Mother Nature's best-kept secrets. Well, take care of yourself, and good luck."

"Good-bye, Jason."

I walked over to Patty and Ruby, who were still talking to Zajal. Christine had just joined them. I again commended Zajal on her performance, and she smiled and thanked us, adding that after talking with Patty she hoped she **would** begin to study belly dance back in the North Country maybe with the Watertown dancer named Marta. We proceeded over to where Jack and Jerome were deep in conversation. Luther had joined them. I thanked Luther for his assistance in Carter's return and recapture. We shook hands, and again I noticed he had a firm grip. Jack completed his conversation and we all said our good-byes. We went to the car and got in. As other vehicles also left the ranch at about nine-thirty, we found ourselves in a line to enter the main highway.

The drive back to the Roadrunner was a joyous one. Everybody had their comments to offer, but the general consensus was that the festivities to celebrate Christine's safe return to her father were a success. Although marred by the dangerous recapture of Bradley Carter, the barbecue at the ranch, with the captivating performance by Zajal, had been wonderful. We were all impressed.

Route 8 to Route 85 was pitch-black except for the headlights on the Camaro. Just before we reached Gila Bend, two small coyotes darted across the highway in front of us. Luckily, we didn't hit them. They looked shaggy in the bright lights of the car.

North of Buckeye we came across a serious automobile accident. The Arizona Highway Patrol seemed to have the situation under control. An ambulance driver had just closed the rear door of her vehicle and returned to the driver's seat. The flashing lights at the scene were eerie in the dark of night. Both cars involved appeared totally damaged. We were held up for about twenty minutes before the officer gave his hand signal for us to proceed.

The rest of the trip to the Roadrunner Resort went without incident. I looked over at Jack sitting next to me, who had fallen off to sleep. This had been a long day for him. When I pulled into the resort, the security guard motioned me to proceed through the entrance gate. We continued on the road to the coach and pulled into the parking space. Because of the late hour, Jack and Ruby did not come in, but confirmed that we'd see each other Monday morning at the office. They went to Ruby's car and waved goodbye. She backed out of the parking space and drove toward the exit gate.

With our plane leaving on Monday afternoon, we would use Sunday to pack our bags, tidy the coach and say our goodbyes to some of the resort residents. We decided it was time to go to bed. I would call Wilt in the morning and give him the flight arrival time in Syracuse.

Because of all the excitement at the ranch and our pending departure, we rolled and tossed most the night. Somehow at some point, though, we each managed to drift off to sleep.

We arose Sunday morning, Patty prepared scrambled eggs, toast, and decaf for breakfast. We busied ourselves doing the dishes, cleaning the coach, and packing our luggage. The rest of the day was spent leisurely resting up before our flight home. We decided to eat our next two meals at the coach to use up the food we had in our refrigerator. We set the alarm and retired early in anticipation of the long day ahead of us.

CHAPTER SEVENTEEN

It seemed like only seconds before the radio alarm went off. Patty took her shower first, while I lathered up and sharpened the straight razor. The water was very hot, and the downward draw of the razor removed my whiskers, but when I moved the blade across my chin I felt the sting of a small laceration, and realized it might be time for me to select a different type of razor. Or maybe shaving this early in the morning wasn't a good thing for me to do, especially when I hadn't slept well. The styptic pencil was close by and I pushed it against the tiny wound. Patty finished her shower and dressed. I took her place under the spray. This definitely wasn't the Adirondack water to which I would soon be returning. The soap wouldn't suds up.

By 7:45 we had finished packing a few left over items, placed my call to Wilt to give him our flight number and estimated time of arrival, and said good-bye to some of the residents and the office staff. We locked the coach for the final time and headed to Flynn's Investigations on 99th Avenue. The resort experience had been a good one. We had especially enjoyed the fruit trees with their abundance of lemons, oranges, and grapefruit. We would always remember the Roadrunner Resort, 25 miles west of Phoenix. We made our way to I-10 and joined other eastbound traffic. The bumper to bumper congestion again tested my driving skills, for a wrong move on this fast-traveled highway with a posted speed limit of 75 mph could take a person to the hospital or the funeral home. I proceeded with caution. The needle on the speedometer was on 75. The palms of my hands were perspiring.

When we reached the plaza I pulled the car into the parking space next to Ruby's four-door sedan. Our baggage was in the rear seat and our carry-ons were in the trunk. We got out of the car and went into the office.

Inside we found Ruby with the telephone to her ear. Evidently from the conversation she was talking with Sky Harbor Airport, probably checking on our flight to see if there was a delay. She gave us a hurried greeting when she hung up as she looked at her watch.

"You and Patty do not have any time to waste. It is 9:15 and your flight departs 11:15 a.m. It's best to get there an hour ahead of time in the event there is a problem," Ruby said, with her usual efficiency.

"Where's Jack, Ruby?" I inquired.

"He wasn't feeling quite up to par this morning. He's sleeping in. He would like you to call him when you arrive home in New York, but wants you to know he definitely felt badly that he couldn't be here. He gave me this envelope for you and he told me to tell you not to open it until you're home—and he stressed that that was an **order**," Ruby explained.

I took the envelope and put it into my pocket. "Thanks, Ruby, for the envelope and confirming the information on the flight. Would you rather we ordered a cab?" I offered.

"Certainly not! I'm taking you to the airport. You're not going to rent a cab. If we leave now, maybe we'll even be able to have a cup of coffee together when we get there."

While the girls used the wash room, I went outside and moved our luggage and carry-ons to the trunk of Ruby's sedan. I had just closed the trunk lid and taken the Camaro keys into the office, when they told me they were ready to leave.

We went outside. Ruby placed a card on the door which indicated that the office would be closed until 1:00 p.m. We entered the sedan. Ruby drove. I took the back seat, while Patty sat in front with Ruby. Traffic was heavy on 99th Avenue, and when we reached I-10 the eastbound traffic was almost at a complete standstill. Ruby opted to turn around, go back to McDowell, and turn to the east toward downtown Phoenix. At 35th Avenue, Ruby turned right and we entered I-10. Traffic was fairly light from that point on to Sky Harbor International Airport. We theorized that an accident must have taken place on I-10 west of 35th Avenue.

After we parked the car and removed the baggage, we went into the terminal building to sign in and check our baggage through. According to the schedule, flight number 234 would be departing on time.

Ruby joined Patty and me for a cup of coffee at the airport restaurant. We talked about our visit of less than a month to the area, and Ruby assured us that we would always be welcome to stay with her if we returned to Phoenix. We invited Ruby and Jack to the Adirondacks. It was a sad parting for us. My friend Jack and I had had too little time to spend together because of his hospitalization. Patty had made friendly connections at the resort through the craft class and had gotten to like Ruby very much. We hoped we would all get together again in the not-too-distant future. After our coffee and conversation we bid farewell to Ruby. We parted, dear friends forever.

Flight number 234 was on time. We went through a security check and on to the waiting area. We had been there only about five minutes when we began to board. I had been able to call Wilt Chambers from the restaurant to confirm that our flight was leaving on time. We'd have an hour layover in Pittsburgh, then fly on to our home state. Wilt was overjoyed and indicated that he would pick us up at the Syracuse Airport.

"Don't worry, Jason. I'll be there, and if you're a little late, I'll wait for you and Patty. Give Patty my love, Jason," Wilt had said.

"I will, Wilt. See you a little later," I had replied.

Once on board the plane, we learned it was an Airbus 320 with a seating capacity of 100 to 150, three seats on each side, and three flight attendants on board. Patty took the inside seat ahead of the wing on the port side of the airplane while I slid into the aisle seat, with an unoccupied seat between us. We had to wait for twenty minutes before the pilot was cleared for takeoff. The flight attendants were busy in the first class section. They came by reminding everyone to make certain their seatbelts were on.

The plane moved up the line and into position for takeoff. Soon the two engines lifted us into the bright sky. We felt the thrust of the powerful jets as they pressed us back against our seats. We passed through some upper wind currents that gave the fuselage a slight vibration. Eventually we leveled off at 32,000 feet heading northeast. The pilot came on the intercom and advised us that the weather ahead looked good.

I reached over to Patty and held her hand for a few minutes. Her hand was warm and her smile was contagious.

"Honey, I'm so glad to be headed home," I said.

"So am I, Jason," she replied happily.

"We do have to touchdown at Pittsburgh, remember, for about an hour, but then we'll be on our way again. Isn't life amazing? You know, Patty, Jack is a lucky fellow. He could so easily have been killed when that bullet came through the windshield." I shuddered at the thought.

"He is very lucky, hon. And the Huntleys are wonderful people. Christine is such a lovely young lady. She certainly has a bright future. I hope we see them again someday, Jason."

"Yes, Jerome is a caring father. With the loss of his wife, Christine is about all the family he has left. And how did you like the ranch foreman, Luther?" I asked.

"He seems like a fine gentleman. Ruby and I watched him handle a couple of spirited studs in the holding area. He gave each of the horses a sugar cube and patted their long necks. By the time he left the corral, the two horses were at his boot heels."

"Yes, he can handle himself very well. And I know for certain that Luther truly cares for Christine. I wouldn't be surprised if there's some romance in the future between the two of them."

"Bradley Carter's actions certainly must have come as a shock for Christine. It just goes to show that sometimes you really never know someone. I never dreamed that my former husband could have changed the way he did. Alcohol and drugs do terrible things to people."

"I understand only too well what you're saying. How many times on the job did I see a father under the influence perform violent acts on their wives and families totally out of character. Patty, look at that situation that occurred at the ranch, it could have resulted in death or serious injuries to many of us there. I would say from my observations that Carter needs serious treatment with a mental health professional. He was way off base!" I became upset just remembering the events.

The flight attendant stopped by to take our drink order. We each ordered a caffeine-free cola. In a few minutes she returned and handed me the two drinks. She asked if we were comfortable and I informed her that we were fine.

About half an hour from Pittsburgh we experienced a downdraft and felt more vibrations. The captain came on the intercom and informed us that the turbulence we had experienced was only momentary. The remaining flight to Pittsburgh was smooth. As we descended into the airport we looked out at the field below us. The landing was perfect. Our layover was of short duration, and soon we were again winging our way to Syracuse and Hancock Field.

Our longing for the splendor of the Adirondack region was building in both of us. How much longer before many more large homes would be built in the woods. We had seen how the once productive cotton fields of Goodyear had changed into crowded tracts with houses only about fifteen feet from each other. We feared this change could take place in our region of the Adirondack Mountains, where elements of our society greedily sought to change the pristine area to large apartment complexes and businesses that could change the ambiance forever.

Historically, in the 1920's the Adirondack region was the

playground for the rich and famous, and then other places attracted their attention. The once famous Great Camps were deserted, and many were left to decay. By the 1980's some of them had been refurbished, and they stand today in their original beauty. Patty and I both appreciate this restoration.

The captain announced over the intercom that we were in the descent and would be landing shortly. Patty and I were glad when the wheels touched down on the tarmac. Our flights from Phoenix and then Pittsburgh had brought us to Syracuse, safe and sound. We deplaned and made our way to the baggage claim area. As we walked down the corridor with the other passengers we caught sight of Wilt Chambers before picking it up. Our friend eagerly made his way toward us. He embraced Patty and then turned toward me to shake my hand. "Welcome home, you two! I've really missed you."

"We've missed you, too, Wilt," I said sincerely.

Patty's eyes welled up with tears. "Wilt, I'm so happy to see you."

"Before I came down to pick you up, I took Ruben to your place and put him in the house. He had plenty of food and water. And I thought it would be a good idea to turn your thermostat up so you and Patty will find the house warm. We've had some cold temperatures and we do have lots of snow on the ground," he said.

"I know, Wilt. That's why we're wearing our warmer clothes," I responded.

"Wilt, you look as though you've lost more weight. You're looking good," Patty injected.

"Yeah! I've tried to cut my portions down even a little more. And I've been splitting wood and piling it for next season. The exercise works as long as you cut the flour and sugar out. By the way, Patty, how are you feeling? You haven't had any problems, have you?" he asked with his usual concern. Because Wilt thought of Patty as though she were his daughter, he was concerned about her pregnancy.

"I've been feeling very well, thanks. I've only had a couple days of morning sickness," Patty replied.

"She got involved in the craft class at the resort, Wilt, and made some new friends. How's Ruben? Are you sure he was a good dog?" I asked.

"He's been moping around the house for the last couple days. I would say that Ruben has been a little depressed. He continually looks out the window, probably hoping you'll drive in," Wilt replied.

He accompanied us to the baggage area and I removed our bags from the moving conveyor.

When I started to carry them, Wilt took them both from me and said, "I need the exercise."

As we made our way to the big Dodge pickup the cold air stung our faces. What a difference without the desert sun. Wilt placed our bags in the rear. In a few minutes we were on the New York State thruway headed to Old Forge. Wilt filled us in with all the news. He mentioned that several snowmobiles had gone through the ice on Fourth Lake during the January thaw, and told us that the operators of the machines had been rescued and were lucky to be alive.

"Wilt, how is everything at John's Diner?" Patty asked. "I've called once or twice, but I can always tell when Lila's busy. I do hate to disturb her."

"I stopped in before I headed to the airport. Lila is anxious to see you. Everything has been good at the diner. Jack Falsey, Dale, Jim Jenny, Charlie Perkins, and me all had breakfast together just before Jack left for Florida. More folks came up to me and asked when you two were returning. You know me, I didn't want to give out too much information. I did tell them that I had been in touch with you both."

"Well, we're glad to be home. My friend Jack Flynn is back to work and my mission was accomplished, so here we are."

"Jason, did you find that college coed that was missing?" Wilt asked.

I briefly summarized it for him. "Yes, we did. She's from a ranch family near Casa Grande, Arizona and an old boyfriend abducted her. Yes, Wilt, she's back home with her father, and the boyfriend is in jail. There are some serious charges pending against him. He's from a wealthy family in Colorado, and was going to school in Tucson until he dropped out because of his illegal drug usage. He was casually dating the coed, and when she rejected him, he kidnapped her."

"That sounds like an interesting case," Wilt replied.

"It was, Wilt," I agreed. "But the best part of it all was finding her alive."

As we drove north from Utica, I noticed the snow banks got higher. When we pulled into Old Forge, many snowmobiles were parked at the motels and restaurants. It appeared just as busy as it does in the heart of summer. Patty was delighted to see the crowded parking lot at John's diner.

It had taken about two hours before we pulled into our driveway. Patty and I were happy to be home. Even though we had taken ourselves away from where we loved in order to assist Jack in Arizona, we both felt that it had been the right thing to do. But we knew we could never stay in Arizona, even with its natural beauty and its popularity for thousands of people migrating to avoid the harsh winters of the North. Patty and I love our great Adirondacks where we live and work. And now we were looking forward to the birth of our son or daughter.

Wilt pulled up close to the side door of our log home and turned the ignition off. Evidently Wilt had someone plow the driveway and had shoveled the paths leading to the house. As I went to the door to unlock it, loud barks emanated from within. I unlocked the door then Patty and I rushed over to our faithful Ruben. His ears were straight up. He went nuts, barking and leaping upon us. He jumped up on me and his large mouth opened, showing his sharp teeth. I stroked his head and he finally settled down. I didn't want him to jump up on Patty in her condition. She came over and gave Ruben a big hug and patted him. Wilt stood by happily looking on.

"Ruben certainly missed you two," he said, rubbing his hands together.

"He certainly did, Wilt. Thanks for taking care of him. I'll carry the bags in."

"No, you won't. I'll carry them in," Wilt said, as he went out to his truck and brought in two large bags from the rear of his pickup.

I held the door open for Wilt as he brought the bags in and set them down in the kitchen. I noticed that Wilt had brushed both our vehicles off.

"By the way, Jason, I started up both the Bronco and Patty's Jeep. I had to take both batteries down to Doc Norton's and have them charged, but they're fully charged now."

"That was wonderful of you, Wilt," Patty remarked.

"Glad to do it for you and Jason," Wilt responded.

I looked around the log house and found everything in good shape. Our loyal friend had everything operational. When I opened the refrigerator door, I was amazed to see that Wilt had also grocery-shopped for us.

"Wilt, what did you do? It looks as though you bought us enough groceries for a month."

"I felt that you two wouldn't want to have to go out shopping as soon as you arrived home. So I picked up a few staples—milk, butter, eggs, bacon, bread. Just a few things, Jason," he said.

Both Patty and I were well aware of Wilt's generosity and how he cared about his friends and neighbors. That's Wilt.

Before Wilt left, we all sat down to a cup of hot green tea while Ruben went out for a run. We let him back into the house and he lay down on his air mattress. With his head placed between his paws, he looked up, his eyes focused on the three of us.

Wilt got up to leave in about half an hour, and we told him that we'd see him again soon. Before he left I slipped him some money to cover his gasoline and the groceries. He didn't want to accept it, but I managed to convince him that it was the right thing to do. I can be stubborn, too.

I helped Patty unpack the bags and put things in their proper places. She had washed clothes in Arizona, so we had only a minimal amount to add to the already filled laundry basket which we were unable to do before our hurried departure. With all respect to my close friend, Jack Flynn, it sure felt good to be in our own home surrounded by the pristine beauty of the Adirondack Mountains. We were looking forward to a good night of sleep in our own bed, getting over our jet lag. Before we retired for the night we reset our wristwatches. We soon drifted off to dreamland.

CHAPTER EIGHTEEN

Ruben was holding a black bear at bay. The large bear roared and made advances toward the dog. I then heard the alarm clock as it buzzed in my ear. I woke up with a start. Ruben was at the foot of the bed pulling on the bedspread. I looked over at Patty. Her back in a familiar flannel nightgown was toward me and she appeared to be in a deep sleep. I love my wife dearly. We both were praying that her pregnancy would be without problems. I was committed to her and our unborn child.

I pushed my covers back and quietly got out of bed. I would let Patty sleep as long as she wanted to. I let Ruben outside. He hesitated on the porch to see if I were following. "Go ahead, boy, go ahead," I told him. Ruben bounced off the steps and headed to the woods. I closed the door, then filled the teakettle with water and placed it over the lit burner. When I looked outside I found that Ruben had returned to his dog run.

The cold water of the Adirondacks felt good on my face. It was much different than the treated water of Goodyear, Arizona. We had left the warmth of the southwest to return to our harsh northeast winter. Spring was still a couple months away. I gazed out the bathroom window to see our evergreens laden with snow. What a picture! I dried my face and got dressed.

I then went to the kitchen to prepare the coffee. When it

was ready, I poured myself a cup. As I sipped it, Patty came out of the bedroom rubbing her eyes. I got up and went over to her. I held her gently against me and kissed her warmly.

"What would you like for breakfast, honey? I'm the chef this morning," I said.

"Okay, chef, I'd like scrambled eggs, toast, and coffee," she replied.

"Alright, dear, you go get dressed. I'm going to make a couple of slices of French toast. Are you certain you wouldn't like to change your mind?"

"No, honey, I'll stick with the scrambled eggs, sweetheart."

Patty went in to dress. She soon returned to the kitchen. Her long blond hair was pulled back in a bun, and she was wearing a beige blouse and brown slacks. She looked refreshed and alluring. I had the table set. I seated her.

I warmed her plate before I placed on it the scrambled eggs along with two slices of lightly buttered toast that I had cut diagonally. I then poured her coffee. My French toast was ready. I buttered it and placed it on my warm plate, then removed the warmed maple syrup and poured it into a small pitcher. After I joined Patty at the table, we talked about our plans for the day. She planned to see Lila and tell her that she'd report to work on Monday, if that was okay. That would give us several days to get reoriented from the time we had been away from our mountain home.

After breakfast I cleared the table and did the dishes. I then ran the cleaner and tidied up the house, while Patty went to the bedroom and made the bed. She had mentioned to me that she'd like to go to the store. I advised her to drive her Jeep and take care of any errands she had in town, as I had to make several telephone calls. We agreed to meet at John's Diner around one for some lunch.

"Patty, I'll go to the post office and pick up the mail and do a few chores. Just be careful if the highways are slippery. You know how I worry about you and the little one, sweetheart," I cautioned.

"Don't worry, dear. I'll be careful," she reassured me.

I went outside and prepared the Jeep for Patty. It started right up. Wilt had done a good job in having our batteries charged. The engine sounded good. I drove it up near the side door and turned it around so it was headed out toward Route 28.

While I was outside I decided to start the Bronco and bring it closer to the house. I noticed that I had neglected to close the gate on the dog run, so I ran over to take care of it. Ruben, evidently thinking I was coming to get him, rushed over to me. I patted him on his big head. Offended, he headed into his doghouse and put his back toward me. After I turned the Bronco off, I was just getting ready to go inside the house when Patty came out wearing her heavy winter jacket, a scarf around her shoulders, and her wool cap on her head. She was smart to dress warmly after our return from the sunny climate.

"I see you're all ready to go downtown," I said.

"Yes, honey. I'll see you at John's around one as we planned," she said as she kissed me on the cheek.

I watched Patty get into her Jeep. She drove toward Route 28. I heard her toot the horn good-bye. I waved at her, then turned and went inside.

My office was unbelievably neat, considering our hasty departure to Arizona. I checked my work calendar. As I sat there I felt a little chill, so I went out to the kitchen to turn up the thermostat. Evidently my body had become accustomed to the warmer temperatures of the southwest.

I returned to the office, opened the envelope Ruby had given me on my departure, and was stunned to see the amount of the check, and then immediately placed a call to Flynn Investigations. Ruby answered.

"Ruby, Jason here, in snowy New York. I just wanted to let you and Jack know that we returned home safe and sound. Listen, young lady, I just opened the envelope that Jack gave me. In it I found his note, your note, and a check which seems to be excessive. I'll cash it and send you a check for half the amount," I told her in my sternest voice.

"No, you will not, Jason Black. You have no idea what it

meant to Jack that you dropped everything and flew out here when he needed you. We are indebted to you, Jason," she said firmly.

"I won't argue the point, but I do believe that it's too much for the work I did. Jack furnished us a place to stay and a car to drive," I argued.

"I don't want to hear any more of this nonsense, Jason. That's an order from Jack Flynn himself."

"Is he there?" I asked, wanting to speak to him.

"No, he flew to San Francisco this morning on business. He will not be returning for a week. It's so good to see him feeling more like his old self! I did hear from Jerome Huntley. He was so grateful for your help in locating his daughter. Another thing, Jason: remember the lovely belly dancer, Zajal? I talked with her quite a bit at the ranch. She is coming to Phoenix next month to perform for a woman's business organization that I belong to. Isn't that wonderful?" she inquired.

"Wonderful! She is a very talented lady."

"She certainly is. And I may even be taking a class in belly dancing myself."

"I imagine you will do well. I'm certain it is good exercise, too," I said.

"I'll keep you and Patty posted on how I make out," she replied. "Maybe Patty and I will get to compare notes, if she signs up for a class near you."

We talked for a few more minutes and then I bade Ruby farewell, promising to stay in touch and to let her know how Patty was progressing in her pregnancy.

I then called Wayne Beyea in Plattsburgh. He answered on the second ring.

"Hello, Jason, is that you?"

"Yes. How are you, Wayne? Just calling to let you know that I am back in the territory and to thank you for making yourself available. I'll certainly return the favor in the event you ever have to go out of town," I offered.

"I was glad to be of service. Except for those cases we discussed on the phone, it was quiet. I've sent you the case papers and the expenses that I incurred. The price of gasoline is ridiculous. Between OPEC and the oil companies, they are really squeezing the hell out of our pocketbooks."

"You can say that again. You can't get ahead nowadays," I said.

"True. You don't really think the big boys care, do you?"

"I know exactly how you feel."

Wayne promised that we would get together later in the year and maybe do some bass fishing.

My next call was to Dave Wachtel in Saugerties. His answering machine came on and I left him a message. I had just closed a file drawer when the telephone rang.

"Hello," I answered.

"Jason, is that you?" Dale asked.

"Yes, it's me. We just got back. How are you, Dale?" I inquired happily.

"Good, Jason. Jim Jenny and I just got back from Toronto. I didn't want to, but we put skis on the Stinson. We had to fly up there for some parts from one of the snowmobile factories. We just got in a few minutes ago."

"How's Jim Jenny doing?"

"He's a darn good worker. Not only that, he's an excellent pilot. I let him fly the Stinson back from Toronto. He knows his business."

"How's Evelyn?"

"Wonderful! I'm in love, Jason," he offered.

"Patty and I are very happy for you two. Any idea when the wedding will take place?"

"We're looking forward to an autumn wedding when the foliage is in full color. Then we'll tie the knot. How's Patty feeling?"

"She's great. She went to town to do some shopping. Don't forget to put me on the guest list," I reminded him.

"As I keep telling you, you're on top of the list, my friend," Dale said with a chuckle.

"We're looking forward to it."

"Listen, Jason, I called to let you know that there is going

to be a party at the Hard Times Café, Wednesday night at 7:00.
I believe the last party we planned was at Drew's, so we opted
for Lisa's place this time," he explained.

"What's the occasion?" I asked.

"Never mind the reason or what it's for. Can you two make
it?" he asked.

"Sure, we love parties. What's the dress code?"

"Just come casual."

"We'll be there," I assured him.

Dale and I talked for a few minutes longer and I told him
that we'd look forward to seeing him at the Hard Times on
Wednesday. After we hung up I decided to take our soiled
laundry to the laundromat for Patty.

I removed the sheets from the bed along with the
pillowcases. I remade the bed with clean linen. I packed the
laundry basket and placed a large towel over the top. I had just
time enough to get the wash completed by the time I was to
meet Patty at the diner. I placed the bleach and soap on top of
the basket and carried it out to the Bronco. I went back to the
house and locked up. Ruben was sitting in front of his
doghouse with his ears straight up, watching my every move.

"See you later, big boy," I said as I climbed into the car.

The Bronco fired up on the first engagement of the starter. I
drove out of our driveway onto Route 28. There was
considerable snow in the woods; the roadway, however, was
bare except for spots of sand that had been put there by the
sand trucks. When I arrived at the laundromat I noticed that
there was only one car in the front by the door. I parked the
Bronco, got out, and removed the laundry basket from the rear
seat.

When I entered the building I placed the basket on the floor
by one of the washing machines. I placed the bedding in one of
the machines, whites in another, and colored in the third
machine. I then put soap in each and bleach in the whites. I
placed four quarters in each of the coin holders and punched
the buttons for the appropriate wash. The three machines
hummed quietly. With a half-hour to spare, I placed our empty

basket under the folding table and went outside to the Bronco.

I drove to the post office and pulled in next to the postmaster's car in the rear of the parking lot. When I went inside to open my mailbox I removed the contents, which consisted of a letter, magazines, newspapers, and a few advertisements. I threw the junk mail into a recycling bin located near the door. I was so happy to see the *Boonville Herald* and a copy of the *Griff* in the mail. I closed the box and went inside to the customer desk. The postmaster and staff were busy. We exchanged greetings and I left the office for the laundromat. I checked my watch and was surprised that the time had gone by so rapidly. In forty-five minutes I had to meet Patty at John's Diner.

As I left the post office I met the retired Chief of Police, Robert Crofut. I stopped and chatted with him. I noticed that he had a new dog that was watching us from his truck. It appeared to be a Chihuahua. The retired chief told me that her name was Cheech and that he was looking after the pooch for a friend.

"That's very nice of you, Chief. How have you been?" I asked.

"I've been good, Jason. I heard you were working on a case in Arizona," he said.

"Yes, Bob, I went out to assist my good friend, Jack Flynn. He accidentally took a bullet in his shoulder and ended up in an Arizona hospital."

"That's too bad. How'd it happen?" the chief asked, curiously.

"You probably heard of the coyote gangs that smuggle humans across the Mexican border into the U.S. Well, two of these rival gangs had a gun battle on I-10 near Casa Grande in broad daylight. Unluckily, one of the bullets found its way through Jack's windshield and into his shoulder. If it had been a couple inches closer, it would have struck his heart. He was one lucky fellow. He's out of the hospital now and is back to work at his detective agency," I said.

"Whew! He certainly **was** lucky. I read something in the paper about that shooting. Some of the people were killed, I believe."

"Yes, I believe there were four or five deaths as a result of that confrontation. Bob, that Arizona is still the Wild West, no other words to describe it. Yet people are moving there by the thousands, and new housing units are being erected as we speak. There are many fine people migrating there, but you do have the criminal element. Meth labs are predominant around Maricopa County, and an assortment of incorrigibles have been migrating into the state from California and other states. Law enforcement officials are busy in an attempt to curb the lawlessness," I went on.

"I imagine the burglar-alarm providers do a landslide business."

"They certainly do. Well, Bob, it's great to see you, but I have to run now. I'm doing the laundry and I have to meet Patty at John's Diner at one for lunch." I wanted to chat with Bob longer, but time was getting short.

"See you later, Jason. Welcome back, and take care of yourself. By the way, except for a few snowmobile mishaps, it has been quiet since you've been away. Say hello to Patty for me."

"I will. Say hello to your wife and family. I haven't seen Casey yet."

"He's busy all the time."

"I know he is. He has a good group of people keeping the roads clear. In fact, Bob, we're fortunate here at Old Forge. All the departments do a fine job. Well, I've got to run."

"See you, Jason."

When I arrived at the laundromat I transferred the washed clothes to three dryers. I placed three quarters in each dryer, then I checked my wristwatch. I had just enough time to finish the laundry. After selecting a magazine from the rack, I sat down near the dryers. In about thirty-five minutes I checked the dryers and removed all the laundry except for three pairs of white socks. I left the socks in the dryer and restarted it. I then folded the dried laundry and placed it in the clothes-basket. In five minutes I rechecked the dryer and removed the socks. I was surprised that I was still the only one in the laundromat. I took the basket outside and placed it in the rear of the Bronco.

It was 1:05 p.m. when I headed to John's Diner and parked in the far end of the lot. I noticed Patty's Jeep next to Lila's pickup.

When I entered the diner, several people nodded a greeting. Patty was sitting at a table with her back to me. I waved at Lila as I passed the kitchen. She smiled back and returned my wave.

. "Hello, sweetheart," I said as I took the chair across from my wife.

"I thought sure you'd be here waiting for me. Did something happen?" she asked. "I was beginning to worry."

"No, honey. I finished tidying up the house, changed the sheets, and then took the wash to the laundromat. I have the clean laundry in the Bronco."

"Aren't you a precious dear," she remarked, pleased.

"How was your morning, Patty?"

"I was going to wait for my regular appointment with the doctor next week, but I took a chance and stopped by his office. I'm glad I did. He found my blood pressure a little elevated," she replied.

"Patty, what did the doctor say?" I asked, concerned.

"He thought it could have been the excitement in Casa Grande. I told him about the incident that had occurred at the ranch. He wants me to stop at the medical building on Monday of next week and have it rechecked. Otherwise, everything else seems okay. He said my weight gain is progressing just as it should."

The waitress came to our table and we each ordered an egg salad sandwich and hot tea. Patty introduced me to the waitress who had been hired temporarily to fill in during her absence. She was very polite and efficient.

"Just before you arrived, Lila came over and asked me if I definitely wanted to resume next week. I told her that I was looking forward to it. Is that okay, Jason?" she asked, crinkling her nose.

"No, honey. I'd rather have you home during your pregnancy, but it's up to you. If you feel good and want to keep busy, I have no problem with that. I just don't want you to get over-tired, that's all."

"Here's what I'll do. I'll work for a while, but if I have problems with my pregnancy, I'll stay home. Is that okay with you?"

"That'll be fine, honey," I responded, reaching over to touch her hand. I only wish I had enough income so Patty would be able to stay at home.

Teresa came to our table with two large egg-salad sandwiches on whole wheat bread. The two cups of tea were steaming hot. She asked us if there were anything else we would like. I thanked her and told her that everything was fine. She returned to the kitchen.

Patty and I finished our lunch, paid the check, and left the diner. I knew she was looking forward to reporting for work soon.

Patty told me that she had to stop at the grocery store to pick up a few odds and ends.

"I'll see you at home, sweetheart." I reached over and gave her a kiss on the cheek.

"I'll see you there, Jason."

I drove straight home. Ruben was at the gate of the dog run when I turned the Bronco off. I let him out and he made a beeline for the woods. He returned in a few minutes and we went inside. Ruben settled on his air mattress and I went back out to the car to retrieve the laundry before going into my office to check my files. After I finished, I took the check out of the envelope from Jack for me. I still felt that I wanted to send some of it back to him. I greatly appreciated his generosity. There had been an element of danger for me in the Huntley case, and apparently Jack wanted to compensate me for flying to Arizona on such short notice to assist him. There was no doubt that we could use the money, especially with the baby on the way and the unexpected increase in our property taxes. Jack's kindness meant a great deal to me. I mulled over the idea of taking a part-time job. I would seriously consider it, if it became necessary to pay the bills. Time would tell.

When Patty drove in, I went out to meet her and carried the groceries in for her. She confessed she was a little tired. I helped her put them away and then went back into the office.

CHAPTER NINETEEN

Wednesday night arrived, and Patty and I left the house around 6:45 p.m. to drive to The Hard Times Café. We were surprised by the number of cars and pickup trucks in the parking lot. We found the last space near the rear and went inside. The bar and the adjacent room were empty. I glanced at Patty. Then we heard, "Welcome back!!" We were momentarily startled to see a room full of smiling people. Without saying a word I realized that Patty and I had walked into a surprise party. Everyone was there, including Tom Huston from the Breakshire Lodge at Lake Placid, Sergeant Joe Kelly of the RCMP, Wilt Chambers, Charlie Perkins, Dale Rush and his wife-to-be Evelyn O'Brien, Penny and Sharon Younger and the Rhythm Riders, Charlie Perkins, John and Lila from John's diner, Bob and Gertie from Long Lake, and several more of our friends, including Chief of Police Todd Wilson and some of his staff members.

Several of the women surrounded Patty and asked how she was feeling. I overheard one of the women ask Patty when the baby was expected. Patty and I were completely taken off our feet as the Rhythm Riders began playing. I noticed Lisa, owner of the Hard Times, and her staff readying a most impressive-looking buffet. Mike Drew was there carrying a large cake to a nearby table. I just assumed that Lisa and Mike had joined forces in putting on this gala event. I walked over to Wilt.

"Wilt, what's this all about?" I asked.

The big man took a deep breath and replied, "Jason, we all missed you and Patty, and with the new baby on the way, several of us decided that this was the time to celebrate your homecoming and to let Patty know how much we care about her. After all, in a few months you and Patty will be parents. We just thought it was the right thing to do. You both have been kind to so many people in this community, and we just appreciate having you around. The customers at John's missed seeing Patty, and they are happy you're both back."

"We're happy to be home, Wilt. We have missed you all."

"Jason, with spring approaching, we'd better start building that addition onto your log home. I've got a crew ready to go as soon as you say the word," Wilt volunteered.

"Yes, Wilt, I've been thinking about it. Are you certain that you want to tackle that job?" I asked, knowing the addition would be quite an undertaking.

"We're ready. Just say the word. Penny Younger told me the other day that he's got about ten carpenters that are ready to assist my group. All you've got to do is buy the material and supply some good food, and we'll take care of the rest."

"That's wonderful of you and your friends, Wilt, but I've got some money put aside for the room, which will give us some much needed additional living space. You let me know what you need and I'll order it and have it delivered."

Wilt and I finished our conversation and joined our friends. His mention of Penny Younger reminded me of this unique individual who loved people and, through his WBRV Western Jamboree show, touched many lives and loyal listeners. He always had kind words for people who might be going through a period of sickness or sadness in their families. He was truly a people person, with more contacts among the general population than anyone I have ever known—and I know a great many people myself.

Again, it isn't the riches that make a person. Although they may bring material goods in life, there are many more things that are more valuable, such as a kind word here and there or a good deed in helping out a friend or neighbor. There are many kind people like Penny Younger in the North Country, and the good deeds rendered by these people will never be forgotten.

Patty was busy talking to some of her long-time customers. I looked over at her from across the room and could readily see how popular she was with the folks gathered here at the Hard Times Café. It was understandable why I had chosen to live in this Adirondack Mountain town. This joyous evening provided plenty of food, entertainment, good cheer, and just a nice time. I noticed my good friend, Wilt, mingling among the crowd. I wondered if he were taking orders for carved bears or locating wood lots for harvest. Whatever it was, he was popular with this group of people. As I moved about speaking with the folks, I overheard Wilt asking Sergeant Kelly about their load limitations when hauling logs over the Canadian highway system. I never did hear the response because the musicians had started playing.

It was almost midnight before the crowd dispersed. Everyone thanked Lisa and Mike for the appetizing buffet they had prepared. I was certain that this special get-together had been arranged by Wilt and a few others. It was another memorable evening in the great Adirondacks.

Not only were Patty and I again surrounded by the pristine beauty of these old mountains, which brought us a sense of peace, but tonight at this time and place we had met with many of our fellow Americans who took time out of their busy lives to share with us their warm friendship and to show us that, when in need, the Adirondackers are always there.

The past, present, and future of these precious mountains inside the Blue Line have in various ways touched many people, whether they be the permanent residents of the Adirondacks or the millions of people who come here to visit.

Patty and I went to bed that night looking forward to the blessed event of our child being born. With the new addition to our log home there would be sufficient room for the nursery. We knew we are most fortunate to have good friends volunteering to become involved in the building project. The money I had set aside would cover the expenses of the materials as well as the labor cost. Construction of the added room would take place as soon as warmer temperatures prevailed.

In a few months our lives would change when the baby arrived. Again, we knew only time would tell what lay ahead of us. The challenges would be many, but I knew in my heart that this baby would be wanted and loved. What better place to raise a child than here in the Adirondacks surrounded by good friends?

Born in Theresa, New York he moved to Syracuse during the late 1930's, then in Throopsville, New York, where he graduated from Port Byron Central School in 1948.

He served three years and three months with the 27th Infantry Division until 1950, when he entered the U.S.Air Force during the Korean War, serving in Keflavik, Iceland. In 1953 he became a member of the New York State Police where he served in Troop "D" and Troop "B" first in uniform and then as a member of the Bureau of Criminal Investigation. After retiring he served in the banking sector for seven years. A life-long learner, after high school, he attended Central Radio and Television School in Kansas City, Auburn Business School and received his B.S. Degree from the State University of New York. He resides in the Adirondack Park of New York State. He is a published poet and the writer of short stories.

Adirondack Detective Jason Black is back and better than ever. This time readers get treated not only to the Adirondacks, but also to Arizona, as Jason answers a friend's long distance call for help. This is a must read for all those dedicated Jason Black fans. Written by retired New York State Police BCI investigator John Briant, who has "been there and done that" during his long and distinguished career in law enforcement. This is Jason Black at his best and this time out West.

— Joe Kelly, publisher of the
Boonville Herald and *Adirondack Tourist*, and
host of the weekly Utica television show that bears his name.

"Trouble finds Jason Black far from his beloved Adirondack Mountains. Author John Briant shows he can handle a starkly different Arizona desert landscape, mostly because his protagonist, the retired NYS Trooper Jason Black is the same man no matter what the climate. He comes to the aid of a friend wounded in a coyote shootout, and what follows is the quality story we've come to expect from this author."

Ed Dee
Author of *The Con Man's Daughter*

In Adirondack Detective Goes West, Author John Briant cleverly continues the saga of Private Detective (retired State Police officer) Jason Black, who in trying to live an idyllic life in retirement somehow manages to get tangled into resolving criminal activity at various places in the United States.

Folksy, Private Detective Jason Black is the sort of American folk hero all honest, law abiding Americans can relate to and, wish their local enforcement officers would be. This fourth book in the series Adirondack Detective is a magnificent read and Author John Briant deserves praise for a job well done. Already looking forward to another Jason Black mystery.

Wayne E. Beyea
http://webpages.charter.net/web2108/